D1245210

TO THOSE WHO
KILLED ME

A NeWest
MYSTERY

Library and Archives Canada Cataloguing in Publication

Title: To those who killed me / J.T. Siemens.
Names: Siemens, J. T., author.
Description: Series statement: Sloane Donovan mysteries ; 1
Identifiers: Canadiana (print) 20210212659 | Canadiana (ebook) 20210212780
    | ISBN 9781774390436 (softcover) | ISBN 9781774390443 (ebook)
Subjects: LCGFT: Novels.
Classification: LCC PS8637.I27 T6 2022 | DDC C813/.6—dc23

Editor for the Press: Matt Bowes
Cover and interior design: Michel Vrana
Interior image: Liezle Moreland
Author photo: Tamea Burd Photography

NeWest Press wishes to acknowledge that the land on which we operate is Treaty 6 territory and a traditional meeting ground and home for many Indigenous Peoples, including Cree, Saulteaux, Niitsitapi (Blackfoot), Métis, and Nakota Sioux.

 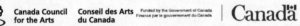   

NeWest Press acknowledges the Canada Council for the Arts, the Alberta Foundation for the Arts, and the Edmonton Arts Council for support of our publishing program. We acknowledge the financial support of the Government of Canada through the Canada Book Fund for our publishing activities.

NeWest Press
#201, 8540-109 Street
Edmonton, Alberta T6G 1E6
www.newestpress.com

No bison were harmed in the making of this book.

Printed and bound in Canada
22 23 24 25 5 4 3 2 1

For Wendy

A
SLOANE
DONOVAN
MYSTERY

TO
THOSE
WHO
KILLED
ME

J.T. SIEMENS

NeWest Press

CHAPTER 1

Thursday, October 10, 2019

THE BRUNETTE IN THE SILVER AUDI CONVERT-ible was dead. Even from thirty feet away, I knew from the stillness and the angle of her slumped head, down and to the right. I had seen that angle before. As I approached the rear of the vehicle, blood slammed through my neck and temples, my body still buzzing with endorphins from my twelve-mile run up and down the hills of West Vancouver. As I came closer I saw the small woven dream catcher hanging from the rear-view mirror. My throat made a strangled sound as I stopped breathing.

It was my friend Geri's car, and she was in the driver's seat.

Geri, oh my God.

I sprinted to the convertible, shouting her name as I reached in and shook her shoulders. Her head lolled further down and her skin was pale where normally it was olive. I pushed my fingers through her thick hair to check for a pulse that wasn't there.

Bringing my face near hers, I couldn't feel any breath, though the smell of wine was strong. An open S'well bottle sat in the centre console.

The car's digital clock read: 4:24 PM.

An unsealed white envelope and an iPhone sat on her lap. On the floor mat of the passenger side was an open bottle of prescription pills, some of which had spilled out. Zolpidem. Sleeping pills.

I pulled out my phone and called 911. "My name is Sloane Donovan. I found a woman in her car who seems to have OD'ed on sleeping pills. No vitals. Hillside Country Club. 930 Crosscreek Road, West Vancouver. End of the south service road."

Yanking open the driver's door, I got my hands under her armpits and dragged her onto the road. Her phone clattered onto the gravel nearby. As I knelt to begin CPR, everything around me constricted, swirled, and blurred: the trees, the car, my friend on the road. A second later, reality came roaring back. Impossible. I'd spoken to her only a few days earlier. This was wrong, a waking nightmare, a sick joke. Interlacing my fists together, I pumped her sternum.

After thirty compressions, I tilted her head back, pinched her nose, lowered my lips to hers, and gave two breaths. Following three more cycles of CPR, I thought I saw her facial muscles twitch. Another cycle. One of her brown eyes was partially open.

Five cycles.

No response.

Another cycle.

Nothing.

In the polished chrome rim of the rear wheel, I caught a distorted reflection of myself, eyes wild, red ponytail bobbing up and down. In the branches of a hemlock above, a crow mocked me and flew off.

Give up, it seemed to say.

No.

A drop of sweat from my face splashed onto Geri's blue lips, rolled down her cheek before getting lost in the twisted gulley of her ear. After countless rounds of CPR, I got dizzy and had to stop and breathe and shake out my hands. Only then did I take in the tight red and black silk cocktail dress she wore, its pattern like angry Japanese characters. Her fingernails were painted the same red as her dress. Her wedding ring was off. So was one of her black leather pumps, probably still in the car.

Twenty feet in front of us sat a rusty blue shipping container. Beside it were several stacks of old tires and a pile of discarded lumber. Country club junkyard.

I continued CPR.

Blink. My sister, Stephanie, her nails bitten to the quick. Blink. Little Charlie, blond hair neatly parted, purple Barney dinosaur beside him. Blink. Blue-faced baby Emma, snuggled into Steph's cold bosom. Blink. Steph's head cocked down at that same final angle Geri's had just been.

The phone buzzed on the gravel nearby. As I pumped her chest, I glanced over. The display read: PAYPHONE 604-615-6761.

From habit, I quickly recited the number under my breath before going back to mouth-to-mouth, running the digits through my head a few times so they stuck.

Sirens howled beyond the trees. I saw the envelope a few feet away.

The sirens grew louder. I remembered finding Steph's note on the bedside table and reading the words that would haunt me forever. I'd made the mistake of showing the note to my mother, thinking she needed to know. She didn't.

I grabbed the envelope and shoved it into the waistband of my tights, pulling my shirt over it just before a fire engine crested the rise. The truck rumbled to a halt twenty feet away. Four firefighters jumped out. A burly middle-aged man and a younger guy carrying EMT kits rushed to Geri's body as I moved back. They checked her vitals. "How long ago did you find her?" the young guy asked.

"Five minutes. She was unresponsive to CPR."

He knelt down and started CPR again while the older firefighter prepped the defibrillator. A third came in with a syringe of Narcan, inserted the end into Geri's right nostril and pressed the plunger. I've seen OD victims go from dead and blue to babbling and animated only seconds after being dosed with Narcan. Geri didn't even twitch. The fourth firefighter looked inside the car and took notes.

A police cruiser pulled up nearly the same time as an ambulance. Two paramedics—a male and a female—hustled over bearing a stretcher and cardiac support pump. Suddenly the area was abuzz with professionals trying against hope to raise the dead. The female medic radioed ahead to the ER doc.

The two cops got out and stood on the periphery. The driver was a tall guy in his early twenties with newbie eyes. His partner was a shaven-head, body-builder Persian, maybe mid-thirties. He squinted an assessment of the scene: Geri's body, me, his watch.

Constable Ghorbani, his nameplate read. The newbie's name was Hershaw.

"This how you found her?" Ghorbani said.

"She was in the driver's seat," I said, my voice cracking. "Her name is Geri Harp. She's my friend."

Hershaw jotted my name and the details of what I saw when I arrived on the scene. Ghorbani took photos. As he leaned into the car, he sniffed the open S'well bottle and raised his thick brows.

"Someone called her from a payphone a few minutes before you arrived," I said.

Ghorbani straightened and studied me. "So?"

"Something's not right about this. I spoke to Geri just a few days ago, and she seemed normal. I don't think—"

"I remember your picture in the paper," he said. "You used to be a cop."

Hershaw cocked an eyebrow. A couple of the firefighters glanced over.

"That's right," I said.

Ghorbani's eyes narrowed as he nodded again, accessing my file in the database somewhere in his stubbly head. I looked over at Geri being worked on by the EMTs. With forced calm, I asked for his card.

"We've got your information," he said. "We'll contact you if we need more."

"All the same," I said.

Ghorbani gave me a hard stare as he unsnapped a pocket on his utility belt, right behind his Glock. He handed me a card.

Constable Cyrus Ghorbani.

An olive-green Lincoln Navigator crunched up to the left of the cruiser and a man got out. Of course it had to be big, bad, bald Steve Bolger. I'd have recognized his basketball-sized head a mile off. The coroner had been around forever and we had worked downtown at the same time. He had voiced strong public approval regarding my termination. During his thirty-plus years on the job, he'd also voiced strong *private* disapproval of women on the force.

I had nothing to say to him, so I turned and started up the hill.

"Donovan!" Bolger called out. "You call this in?"

I turned back and looked at him, still walking backwards. Even from twenty feet away Bolger had the kind of face that made you want to lance him like a boil.

"Yeah," I said.

He offered a crooked smirk and raised an eyebrow.

I turned again and climbed the steep, curving drive, past the groundskeeper's sheds. Two crows bickered atop a light post. The post was twenty feet high, and perched three-quarters of the way up was a security camera. I looked at the camera, then down the hill where the coroner and the two cops stood watching me. Murmurs floated up the hill and I assumed that Bolger was filling them in on my less-than-graceful exit from law enforcement.

Bolger pulled on latex gloves and caught up to Geri's body just before she was lifted into the ambulance. He checked her vitals along with the time, then narrated into his smartphone. The doors slammed shut, followed by three perfect seconds of silence. Then came faint *thocks* and grunts, club members commencing a late afternoon tennis match, oblivious that just down the hill, one of their own had died amid the junk that no one wanted to see.

CHAPTER 2

THE QUICKEST ACCESS TO THE CLUB WAS through the Zamboni garage. I cut past the ice rink viewing gallery, where a bevy of blonde trophy wives sipped wine and gossiped while watching their kids' hockey practice. Passing a window, I saw two hefty Hillside security guards hustling down the hill toward the junkyard.

I paused at the entrance to the women's spa, the exact spot where I'd spoken with Geri on Monday. Three days ago. She had seemed her typical effervescent self that day. What had happened since?

She had been smiling, decked out in tennis whites. We'd hugged and Geri kissed my cheek. Now that I thought about it, maybe the smile had been a bit sad, forced. It was the kind of smile I often saw in the mirror.

"Sloane," she said, "I've been meaning to call you."

"Me too," I said. "I have no good excuse. How's the tennis?"

"Turns out my *coach* cancelled today. Again."

"Why don't you do a workout with me? I have an opening."

"Thanks, but no thanks. I'd like to be able to walk tomorrow." She paused. "But I could use your advice about something."

"What is it?"

"Too much to get into right now. Do you still finish early on Fridays?"

"This week I do. How about lunch at The Flying Pig, say, around one?"

"Perfect. It'll give me something to look forward to."

"Me too. Hey, I heard that New Ways expanded recently."

"Big time. You wouldn't even recognize the place from before."

"That's great."

"Doesn't keep the women from dying and disappearing." She paused again, face turning serious. "Continue this on Friday?"

"For sure."

We hugged and went our separate ways. That was the last time I saw her alive. Tomorrow was supposed to be our lunch date, and now my wrists ached from doing hundreds of chest compressions on her corpse. I stood stunned in that same hall, replaying that conversation over again, trying to find deeper meaning in her words.

Doesn't keep the women from dying and disappearing.

Someone slapped my ass. That could only be one person: Karin, fellow trainer and my one true friend. A few inches shorter and a few years younger than me, Karin had dirty blonde hair and slightly thick brows over wide-set eyes that missed nothing. Back before the market meltdown in '08, she and her family had been club members. Now she worked here, but she still had the West Van gene, which gave her an "in" that I would never possess. It also meant that she knew a lot of people, and more importantly, she had the dirt on many of those same people.

Her smile faded the instant she saw my face. "Sloane, what's wrong?"

"Geri's dead," I said, almost choking on the words. "I found her."

"*What?* What do mean you found her? How did—are you sure?"

"She's gone."

"*How?*"

"Overdose. I tried CPR, but it was too late. She was gone."

"That's why all the crazy shit was going on behind the club," she said. "Fire trucks and cop cars."

I nodded.

She hugged me. "Jesus Christ. I'm so sorry, Sloane."

Glancing down over her shoulder, I spied the corner of her laptop peeking from her gym bag. A red USB drive stuck out from a side pocket.

I plucked it out. "I need to borrow this, Kare."

"Right *now?* Your friend practically dies in your arms—"

"I'll explain later," I said, turning and jogging down the hall.

Several years ago, Hillside was security camera-free. Despite having a squad of troll-like guards shambling the grounds, theft was rampant. Late-night drug deals were common in the lower parking lot and the service road. As a deterrent, the club installed twenty-five cameras to cover every entrance, inside and out.

The door to the security office was locked, so I snuck into the janitor's closet and lifted a ring of keys from a tack on a bulletin board. I walked back to the security office, unlocked the door and slipped in.

Three computer monitors sat on the desk, each screen divided into a tic-tac-toe pattern, each square showing a view from a different camera. On the right-hand monitor, I located the service road camera. The fire truck and ambulance were already gone, but Bolger and the cops remained. The resolution on the pan-tilt-zoom camera was crystal, so much so that when I used the mouse to zoom in, even in black-and-white, I managed to spot a suspicious mole on Bolger's neck. Maybe someday I'd recommend a good dermatologist. He made a few notes on a clipboard. The notes would go into a file that would end up in a cabinet with many such files that would sit and never be looked at again.

Inserting Karin's USB into the computer, I downloaded the last twenty-four hours of footage from every camera in the club. Then I removed the stick and deleted the entire day from the hard drive. I erased the entire file history as well, and left the cameras off so they wouldn't pick me up exiting the security room.

As I climbed into my Jeep in the lower parking lot, first thing I saw was the small purple dream catcher hanging from the rear-view, identical to the one in Geri's car.

Driving out of the parking lot, I saw the police cruiser up ahead, turning left from the service road, followed by Bolger's Navigator.

Meanwhile, Geri was headed for a slab.

The Harp family had no idea of the bomb about to be detonated, one that would rip apart hearts and souls, leaving scars that would never fully heal. Ghorbani and Hershaw would likely be sent to notify Grady of his wife's death. I didn't know Grady well. Tall, handsome, and imposing, his serious manner contrasted sharply with his wife's exuberance. The way Geri had always spoken of him gave the impression he was one of those absentee husbands, frequently away on business.

I thought of her in the convertible, dressed up but missing her wedding ring. Had something happened between her and Grady? Is that what she wanted to discuss over lunch?

I blinked, pulling myself back to the present. I hoped Darci would not be the one to answer that doorbell or that call. She would be around twenty now, and it had been several years since I'd seen her. I'd worked out with her a few times in the gym, but it hadn't been her thing. Not long after, she'd cancelled her Hillside membership, claiming she couldn't stand belonging to a "clique of ostentatious elitists."

Darci was a good kid. I liked her. She didn't deserve this.

It wasn't my place, but I thought of calling her before either of the two cops had a chance to bungle the job. My real fear was that Bolger would be the one to draw that straw. His bedside manner made Donald Trump look like Mother Teresa. Guy like that probably relished the thought of being the bearer of the worst tidings possible.

Geri's scent was still on my hands, and when I blinked I saw her dead face.

I hung back, gripping the wheel tight, breathing in for four, out for four, repeat, repeat. I followed the cops onto the Upper Levels Highway. They took the Taylor Way exit and I kept going, to North Vancouver. I stopped at the Westview Liquor Store for a bottle of Sauvignon Blanc. I thought about the S'well bottle in Geri's car. Tomorrow we were supposed to be clinking our wine glasses together in our favourite restaurant.

We would never do that again.

My friend was about to be tagged and put in a drawer until she had a turn on the slab. If I'd only run a little faster—

I pulled into my stall in the underground garage of my Seymour Heights condo. Tears spilled down my cheeks and my whole body shook. Why did I have to run that route today?

Like I was meant to.

After taking several deep breaths, I whispered, "What happened to you, Geri?"

Then I remembered the envelope.

CHAPTER 3

TO THOSE WHO KILLED ME,
You murdered me before I even wrote
this. I should hate you both. I
wish I could hate you, but I'm not
evil like you both are.
My only question is WHY?
Why did you push me to this?
Once you figure it out—
LIVE WITH IT.
Because I won't have to

I READ AND RE-READ THE LETTER. WITH THE caps and the dramatic language, it felt stagey to me. "You both," she had written. Without mentioning names, she'd been hurt and betrayed by two people. Who had she wanted to find that note, the "you" she referred to? And who had called from the payphone?

burnthis

Once inside my condo I flicked on all the lights and the gas fireplace. I set the letter on my rectangular black oak table, bare except for my MacBook Air and my lucky blue coffee cup. The coffee cup was the oldest thing I owned; I'd nicked it from a coffee shop in Tofino when I was thirteen. In truth, it hadn't made me very lucky. Maybe I just liked the colour.

The slate-grey walls were bare except for a large painting of a blood-red sunset reflected on a lake. The painting was titled "Heaven Burning," and in the lower right-hand corner were the initials S.D. It had been a birthday gift from my sister.

Eclipse, my giant black cat, sprang onto the table. He sniffed the letter. I knuckled him under his chin and he tried to fang my wrist. "Bastard," I said.

I glanced out the window at the dark patio. The two Adirondack chairs were covered in red leaves from the Japanese maple above. I'd done nothing with the flowerbed except toss in some pumpkins. The barbecue had sat unused all summer. I'd thought of putting out some tiki torches or Chinese lanterns and having co-workers over for steaks and corn-on-the-cob, but it never happened.

The pumpkins made me think of Sam. My ex was a big pumpkin carving kind of guy. He had special tools to create award-winning gourd art that would scare tiny trick-or-treaters. I never got into his carving thing, even though he tried to teach me. I never got into a lot of things. At that moment, for all I knew, he could be carving a pumpkin with his new wife, who, I'd heard, was not only gorgeous, but a successful architect—and pregnant to boot.

In my past life, before shit went seriously south, Sam had invested a significant chunk of his nest egg in barely legal cannabis stocks. When I lost my job and had to go away for a spell, those stocks went from pennies to dollars, and unbeknownst to me, Sam had used the windfall to pay off the mortgage on our condo. He waited until I was out of psych to break up with me. Some might call that a dick move, but put me in his shoes and I'd have left me long before. And I certainly wouldn't have left me with a condo, mortgage paid in full.

Sam did.

He's a great guy. I hope he's very happy, I really do.

So I guess I got the damn pumpkins to torture myself. If I had a shotgun I would've blasted their slimy orange guts all over the courtyard.

In the bathroom, I opened the cabinet and reached for the lithium. I shook a round blue pill into my palm and was about to slap it into my mouth when I looked in the mirror. I smiled with my mouth but couldn't get my eyes to follow suit. I've been told I have a nice mouth. Good teeth, and despite an angular face, my lips were full. My grade five teacher once described my nose as aquiline, and my eyes look grey or blue depending on my mood or someone else's perspective. If you looked deep enough to see my soul, you could see the cracks in it.

Blink. In the mirror I saw Geri's face, now cyanotic blue around the lips, nostrils, and eyes.

The pill clinked down the drain.

In the kitchen I poured myself a tumbler of wine and took a gulp. I knew I should eat, but I wasn't hungry. One of the warning signs I tend to ignore.

Flattening the note beside the computer, I read it again and thought of my friend. Thought of her in that dress, head slumped. The typed note.

She had wanted someone to find her.

She hadn't intended on that someone being me.

Drinking more wine, I closed my eyes and rewound the tape seven years, to the first time I met Geri. Back then, New Ways Women's Shelter was located in a blighted area of the Downtown Eastside that consisted of chicken packing plants, abandoned warehouses, and boarded-up storefronts layered with several generations of ghetto graffiti.

* * *

When my partner, Quin, and I had entered the New Ways clinic, my eyes immediately centred on the dark-haired woman hovering over a cot, tending to a semi-conscious teenage girl. When she turned to face us, my first thought was, *this woman is pissed.* She marched over, her ensemble at the time consisting not of a cocktail dress, but a loose sweat-shirt, jeans, and old sneakers. Her hair was pulled back in a loose bun, and she wore glasses and no makeup.

"Three times I called," she said, "complaining of a pimp targeting girls here. And three times, you've done sweet fuck all."

"Take it easy," Quin said. "We're here to—"

"You're here to take a victim statement, I know," she said. "Crystal's too doped up to even speak. The last girl he did this to almost died."

"Any witnesses see him give her drugs?" he asked.

"Someone reported seeing her on the Stroll," she said. "When I went down there I found her with a trick on a mat-tress behind a dumpster—in her present state. She's fourteen, by the way."

I looked at the girl on the cot. She appeared little more than a child wearing a miniskirt and too much makeup. Her dull, nickel-sized pupils were focused on nothing.

"What happened to the trick?" I asked.

She gestured to a Louisville Slugger leaning near the doorway. "A little gentle persuasion," she said. "He's lucky I didn't take his head off."

I smiled.

"You should've called us," Quin said. "People take matters in their own hands, it usually spins back on them." He glanced at his watch, then handed her his card.

"You're kidding, right? If I waited for you to show up, Crystal might be dead now."

"We respond to every call in due course," he said. "It's a zoo out there today; we're getting twice the calls. That's Welfare Wednesday for ya. Now, since Crystal is unconscious, and in the absence of witnesses, someone will return when she's awake. When do you think that'll be?"

"I don't know," she said acidly. "Why don't you go down to the Stroll, have Yuri spike you up, then see how long it takes for whatever shit-mix is in there to leave your body."

"You said Yuri?" I asked. "Big bald guy?"

"And ugly as sin," she said. "You know him?"

"Only by reputation," I replied. I didn't mention that during the six months I spent posing as a hooker for john stings, whispers of the name Yuri Vashilov evoked twitchy-eyed fear from even the hardest of street pimps. He was bad news. He dealt the hardest of drugs and pimped the youngest of girls, some of whom disappeared. It was rumoured they ended up in shipping containers bound for Eastern Europe where they were likely to spend the rest of their short lives as sex slaves.

Before leaving the shelter, I handed Geri my card as well. In that moment we'd held each other's gaze, and there was an unspoken sense we were on the same page.

I hadn't expected her to phone an hour later, just as we were heading back to the station to sign off our shift.

"He's here," she said.

"Where?"

"I'm watching from an upstairs window. He's in the alley behind the shelter, with his girl Neko, who'd lured Crystal to him in the first place. She was pointing at New Ways. I think she was telling him where Crys is. Crystal had some cash on her when I found her. He's probably looking to collect."

"We'll be right there," I said.

"If not, I'm going out there with the Slugger."

"Don't do that. We'll be there in less than five."

"Jesus Christ," Quin said, from behind the wheel. "I got Canucks tickets tonight. Let's keep this simple, order the Russian off our streets, and be on our way."

Yuri looked up as our cruiser turned the corner into the alley, said something to his waifish redhead companion who spun around, and booked it the other direction as fast as her black pleather pants would let her.

"That would be the lovely Neko," I said.

"What do you want to bet she's holding his stash," Quin said, aiming the nose of the cruiser toward Yuri's kneecaps. At the last second, he braked hard, putting the bumper a few yards from crippling the man. Yuri didn't flinch, merely gave a small smile.

"I'll get the girl," I said.

"Better you than me," Quin said.

I moved past Yuri and began running down the squalid alley, dodging potholes and picking up speed until I was going full out. No easy task doing a 200-yard sprint in a police uniform. The utility belt threw off my stride, but nevertheless, I caught the hooker trying to climb a rickety fence leading into a scrap metal yard. She kicked as I brought her down. A clear plastic baggie of foil pellets spilled onto the street.

"Shit ain't mine," Neko said.

"In that case," I said, "you won't care if we just leave the happy rocks here for the pigeons. You're under arrest." I twisted one arm behind her back, cuffed the wrist, then did the same to the other, before pulling her upright.

"Yuri's not gonna like it," she said.

"That's Yuri's problem."

Over her shoulder, I saw what looked to be an angry red welt above her left breast. A burn. As she struggled, her bra strap slid sideways, revealing the full extent of the damage: six inches long with a small pus-swollen pitchfork shape at the end. A pimp's brand.

"Yuri do this?" I asked.

"What you gonna to do about it?" she accused. "Fuckin' nothing."

Back at the cruiser, Quin sat playing chess on his phone. Yuri was gone.

"Where is he?" I asked, guiding Neko into the back seat.

"He moved on quite amicably," he said, not glancing up from his game. "I told him to keep away from the area. We got nothing to hold him on."

When I looked up, I could see the back of the Russian's bald head thirty feet away, turning the corner. "Like hell we don't," I said, shutting the door on Neko and jogging after Yuri. Behind me, Quin cursed.

"Yo, Yuri," I called out. "Hold up."

The pimp stopped and slowly turned, gold incisors flashing as he smiled. Yuri held an easy two-twenty on six-three. He flexed his massive hands, each finger adorned with several gold rings.

"You're under arrest."

Yuri looked at my nameplate, then at the expandable steel baton in my hand. "Constable Donovan," he said, "you're a scared little girl."

"Turn around, get on your knees, and put your hands behind your head."

He shrugged with his palms outstretched. "Your partner say I could go."

"He didn't see what you did to that girl. Now turn around."

He turned and began calmly walking away. His chuckle sounded like stones grating together.

"I'm going to ask you one more—"

He plunged his hand into his jacket pocket.

Snapping the baton to its full length, I stepped up and swung low, smashing him behind his right knee. His leg buckled, but he didn't go down. He whirled and backhanded me hard on the side of the head. I stumbled dizzily. Warmth ran down my cheek. He turned and I cracked him in the face with the baton. Red shot from his splintered nose. He staggered back, touching his face.

"Down! Now!" I shouted.

He came at me again. I brought the weapon down hard, shattering his collarbone, then looped it around and caught him behind the knees.

He dropped. From behind came the flash of lights and the burst of a siren. Quin braked hard. I kicked Yuri face down on the pavement, and with all my strength, wrenched one arm behind his back. He bucked and cursed, nearly knocking me off. Applying pressure at the wrist, I pulled his arm higher. My mind flashed to the pitchfork seared into Neko's skin, and I got a solid grip on Yuri's wrist with both hands. A sharp upward torque, and his shoulder popped as tendons separated from bone. He screamed and collapsed back down.

"Why the fuck didn't you wait?" Quin said.

"Cuz you're too damn slow."

"You're hurt."

"I am hurt!" Yuri barked. "Fucking bitch tore my rotator."

Quin nudged me aside, taking over. *Shut the fuck up!*

Everything suddenly went greasy and dim. My partner eyed me while he finished cuffing the Russian.

The world spun, and I fell.

Feet slapped on pavement. Geri Harp now crouched by my side. A few other women from the shelter had followed her out; a blonde teenager with serious eyes studied me from over Geri's shoulder, and even with foggy vision I could see a resemblance. As Quin shouted into his radio that a cop was down, I retched and Geri turned me on my side, cupping my skull as I puked on the pavement.

* * *

I plugged in the USB drive, got out a yellow legal pad, and went to work. First the junkyard footage. The time stamp in the top-left corner of the image showed Geri driving her Audi to her final spot at 4:03, only twenty-one minutes before I arrived. I jotted down the timeline. The camera showed her fixing her hair in the rear-view mirror and taking a sip from the S'well bottle. She went for the pills and took what could've been one or ten, swallowing them down with more wine. Then she read her own letter and put it back in the envelope. Her head lolled suddenly like she was nodding off. 4:15. *Very* fast acting pills, wine or no. Then she shook herself awake. Following three minutes of fumbling with her phone, she made a call. 4:18.

Mid-call, her arm fell and her head slumped forward. Her head jerked several times and drooped further. She didn't move again.

I played the scene over and over, imagining her heart stopping, blood becoming lazy mud in the tributaries of her limbs, brain fading to black. Before all that, she had fixed her hair, something the average pre-suicide victim—unless they are exceptionally vain—isn't terribly concerned with. The Geri I knew wasn't vain. The Geri I knew wore sweatpants to work and drove a Prius.

It occurred to me that maybe I didn't know Geri as well as I thought.

My wine disappeared. At 10:49 I laced up and jogged up the road to the liquor mart. I bought a bottle of Portuguese white and went back outside. The fog was so thick I almost didn't see the payphone by the Safeway. I walked over, plunked in a quarter, and from memory dialed the number that had appeared on Geri's phone, even though you can't call payphones back anymore. Drug dealers wrecked that for everyone. I let it ring thirty times anyhow.

After a bottle and a half of wine, a normal person's brain becomes dopey. I was not a normal person; when in one of my "productive" phases, moderate-to-high alcohol consumption served to slow my mind down to a manageable rate. I still got hangovers though. I worried about my liver.

Back home, I zoomed in on camera #1's footage of Hillside's stately hedged entrance off Crosscreek Road. I rewound the feed at high speed and watched Benzes, Beemers, Porsches, and Lamborghinis zip in and out. The Hondas and Fords belonged to staff. At 3:51 Geri's Audi pulled through the gates. I checked my notes. Geri didn't end up at the dirt road until 4:03. Twelve minutes to drive down a road that normally took thirty seconds.

First I checked the footage from the bar and grill, thinking that maybe she popped in for a quick drink. Half a dozen moneyed barflies sat watching sports on the big screen, none of them Geri Harp. No sign of her going through the main club entrance. Camera #7 showed her Audi parked outside the entrance to the tennis bubble, which housed a collection of courts, along with pro offices and a small reception area. Time stamp: 3:52. Geri got out and walked with quick, purposeful strides into the club. *Sober* strides.

Flicking over to camera #15, I watched her have a three-minute conversation with the young, blonde receptionist. From the angle, I couldn't get a clear bead on Geri's face, but from her fast, snappy hand gestures, she seemed more agitated than distraught. High-strung rather than doped out. The receptionist checked the computer and shook her head. Then Geri walked to the left and pushed open the door of what looked like an office. Three seconds later she emerged and walked back outside. She got in her car and spent the next seven minutes staring out the window. Then she took a gulp from her bottle, started the car, and drove the rest of the way down the hill.

Replaying the footage of her inside the Tennis Centre, I slowed it down when she opened the office door. I could barely make out the nameplate on the frosted glass window to the right of the door. I paused the footage and squinted at the screen.

ANDY PERETTI — TENNIS PRO

Why would anyone about to check out need to see a tennis pro? I thought back to our last conversation.

Turns out my coach *cancelled today. Again.*

I called Karin and asked if she had any dirt on Andy Peretti.

"You mean *Dogger*, the guy who drives the blue Porsche and who's boinked half the married women in West Van? Does this have anything to do with you finding Geri today?"

"Could be," I said. "Other than tennis, were they rumoured to have something going on?"

"He seems to prefer his women on the married side, so maybe. I'll ask around."

"Don't. I wouldn't want to spread anything that could get back to her family. You know how gossipy that place is."

"All too well. How are *you* doing, by the way?"

"I'm okay. I don't think it's fully sunk in yet. But I keep thinking back to Monday, when I spoke to her. She said she needed my advice about something."

"What was it?"

"I don't know. She didn't want to talk at the club, so we had arranged to go for lunch tomorrow."

"And she didn't leave a note behind or anything?"

"No."

"Are you *sure* you're okay?"

"I'm okay. Don't worry, Karin."

"Are you going to fill me in on the reason you needed to steal my USB drive?"

I refilled my wine, and told her she wouldn't approve.

Over the next five hours I watched Geri's final minutes over and over, until the scene was seared into my brain. I dug up an old online directory that listed payphones across the Lower Mainland. Scanning down the list, I found the number registered to a Bell booth on Main Street. I jotted down the address and thought about taking a cab there, but no, it could wait till tomorrow. Instead I paced from my living room to kitchen to bedroom and back again, my cage getting smaller with each lap. Eclipse's yellow eyes followed me. The wine was long gone. I thought of the pills in the cabinet and said no. Every week or so, I flushed the correct number of pills in case my meddling mother visited.

It took every ounce of discipline to go to bed at five a.m. My mind was awhirl and I knew I would look like shit at work. I tried to meditate for a bit and Eclipse leapt up beside me, nestling into the crook of my elbow. His purring was hypnotic. For a moment or two I managed to focus on nothing; eternal blackness, what it must be like to be dead.

It seemed like only several seconds later when I awoke to my shrill alarm. I smacked it off and lay there with my eyes closed and my temples throbbing. Almost each day began the same, with the futility of me looking back at the tragic trajectory of my sister's life, and hearing the last words she ever spoke to me: *Don't worry, Sloane. This will never happen again.*

CHAPTER 4

MY OLDER SISTER STEPHANIE HAD THE LOOKS
of a doomed goddess: tall with long raven hair and flaw-
less pale skin. Even as a child, her unsmiling yet arresting
emerald eyes made her seem older than she was. We were
only two years apart, but I don't recall many fun moments
together. She was a listless child who had zero interest in
toys, or jumping rope, or building living-room forts. I could
never get a rise out of her by stealing her toys or felt-penning
mustaches on her neglected Cabbage Patch Kids.

One thing Steph was good at, however, was sleeping.
She could sleep entire days away. Left to her own devices,
she would hibernate all weekend. My nickname for her was
Steph van Winkle.

Things improved when she was about twelve, because
my mother—a long-time pharmaceutical advocate—took
her to a shrink, who prescribed Prozac. It was like a miracle;
two weeks later Steph was outside throwing a ball to Max,
our Irish setter. She would actually speak in full sentences
at the dinner table. We were dumbstruck when she laughed

watching *Friends*. A few times I even saw her dancing in her room with her Discman on. She started pulling off good grades, making the honour roll in grade eight. She taught herself to play the guitar and was even in a girl band that won first place in the junior high talent show. Stephanie Donovan, future rocker.

What goes up must come down. By grade ten, Steph refused to get out of bed for a week and was diagnosed with severe depression. Prozac didn't work anymore, so she was prescribed the combination of Celexa, Paxil, and Adderall. The drug cocktail got my sister out of bed, but it seemed like she was going through the motions just to avoid future hassle. She said the right words, got average grades, but the music stopped and she began chain-smoking, which we all detested.

Her damaged beauty attracted not just boys, but men. She quickly earned a reputation in Comox as the town slut, which caused my mother to get her on the pill, and resulted in my father's escalating hypertension. He walked around with a perpetually clenched jaw, seeming to wonder what sin he'd committed to deserve such a fucked-up kid. He was a dentist, and had worked on half the mouths in town. He knew how people talked.

All of this proved advantageous to me, allowing my *own* issues to skim beneath the radar. As I began high school I acted out impulses that weren't exactly normal, like break-ing into neighbours' homes while they were away and trying on their clothes, masturbating in their beds, eating their ice cream, and having bubble baths. Then there was my klepto phase, where I stole everything from an auction house's collectible silver spoons to a six-foot boa constrictor from a pet store (which got loose, leading to the decimation of the neighbourhood cat population). I also screwed some older boys, but thankfully Steph's indiscretions made me cautious enough that I only did it with seniors from nearby towns, and I always used a fake name and fibbed about what school I went to. Lying becomes second nature when you have a mental illness but have to pretend to the world that you don't.

Late one night I donned a ski mask and snuck into a neighbour's backyard, with the intention of purloining some garden gnomes. A flashlight beam lit up the tomato patch before me. "Hold it right there!" old Mr. Edelman barked. "I called the cops."

I took off, vaulting his waist-high chain-link fence. The rock he threw glanced off my shoulder, but I kept running. I couldn't very well turn down our driveway, so I booked it across the fields. I amazed myself by running for three hours that night. I didn't want to stop; it was a whole new high.

Running became my personal saviour. The endorphin rush I discovered through logging endless miles likely kept me from getting locked up, or riddled with STDs, or addicted to something far worse. Up till then, I had never been particularly athletic, but the summer I turned sixteen I ran my first marathon and placed third in the junior division. My mother began to get worried when people told her they saw me running ten, twenty, thirty kilometres outside town. I took to sneaking out late at night to run, using a headlamp. I've never needed much sleep; I am the opposite of my sister that way. But, if you push too hard, too long, the body will just up and quit on you, which is why on three occasions people found me unconscious on the side of the road at dawn, the beam from the headlamp cutting a swath across the misty fields of Vancouver Island.

This running habit was deemed more harmful than my sister's chronic lethargy. And to my mother's credit, she did not have me committed to the psych wing, but she did drag me to Dr. Henrikson, Stephanie's original shrink. I was told that if my aberrant and dangerous behaviour continued, he would have no choice but to recommend a period of "observation." Having recently watched *One Flew Over the Cuckoo's Nest*, I was justifiably scared of being locked up. No more running. So I swallowed a pill and became a good little Zoloft-zombie for the duration of the year. At least I got caught up on my sleep. Later, when my mother let her guard down, I began flushing the meds down the toilet. Being artificially modulated was no way to go through life. I *loved* life.

My dad died of a massive stroke when I was seventeen, leaving us with the proceeds of a life insurance policy that were not quite enough to support the family. My mother resumed work as a special-needs teacher. Steph dropped out of high school and found some dubious modeling work (always a good choice for those with mental issues), where she was introduced to cocaine, and subsequently dabbled in anorexia and bulimia. Steph spent her nineteenth birthday in rehab. She busted out after two weeks and shacked up with some winner she had met there. After telling my mom and me to fuck off, she dumped the dude, moved to Vancouver, and jumped onto someone else's failure train.

What saved Steph for a spell in her twenties was painting, which she'd picked up in rehab. She'd always been a talented girl, but like many whose artistic gifts came too easily, she tended to squander them. Occasionally, in the depths of despair, Steph would take to the easel and create something darkly awesome. Over the next year, she produced, in the words of an art critic who attended her first and last gallery show, "a brooding series of neo-Gothic masterpieces." The modest sales of some of her paintings pulled Steph from her funk. I had just graduated when she reunited with our family. I even lived with her that summer, and she showed me around the city. For the first time, we bonded as sisters. I had a fake ID and we would go clubbing together. I had never seen this side of Steph. People were actually drawn to her haunting beauty and nihilistic charisma. I was proud of my older sister.

One night, Steph and I had just come out of The Roxy on Granville Street when we staggered into the aftermath of a gang shooting. A black SUV was wrapped around a telephone pole, and two tatted-up thugs were bleeding out on the street. A female cop had a man in a hoodie face down on the pavement, and more cops were cordoning off the scene and canvassing witnesses. Tough and assured professionals, creating order out of chaos. Something clicked; this appealed to me like nothing else, not even running. This was a way to channel my energy into something positive; give me a sense of purpose, while at the same time satisfying my craving for risky situations.

"I'm going to be a cop," I told Steph.

She laughed, but then told me she could see it, adding, "Mom will shit."

Steph was working at a gallery when she met Bill. My mother approved of Bill, being that he was a med student who convinced Steph to give Wellbutrin a shot, to "pull her out of the shadows a bit more." The antidepressant transformed her back into her teenage slug self, but seemingly overnight she gained forty pounds. She wasn't down, she wasn't up, she just took on kind of a grey persona, and her normally arresting eyes began to droop at the corners, giving her a hangdog look.

Despite that, Steph managed. We stopped worrying. She was heavy, but she was getting up in the morning and working and seemed generally content. And then Bill graduated, became a Botox doctor, and left her for someone slimmer and devoid of mental health issues.

Steph went off her meds, lost a few pounds, and spent the next year hanging out in seamy bars and having sex with strangers. You know that little voice that tells you something is a bad idea? My little voice tends to whisper in a language I can't understand; I'm sure that's the way it was for my sister.

When she met Phil the welder, he was coming out of a divorce, but he had a union job, with benefits, and owned a condo a block off hipster Main Street. She started talking about kids, as though getting knocked up would cure her neurotransmitter fuckedupedness. Phil and Steph were married in the backyard of the family house in Comox that summer, and everyone was actually happy for about five minutes.

CHAPTER 5

Friday, October 11

IT WAS A COOL, CRISP, CLEAR MORNING, FULL of sharp shadows and rustling carpets of red and gold leaves. Standing near the spot where I'd found Geri, there was no sign that a woman had died here less than twenty-four hours earlier.

I imagined her daughter Darci crying, or perhaps numb with shock and disbelief. I thought to call her, but a knot chunked in my throat. Later. Keep it together.

Hillside was quiet as I entered the building. A Filipino cleaner pushed a mop in the foyer as I walked into the administrative wing and into the personnel office. I flicked on the light. There was a camera in the corner, but I acted like I belonged, quickly locating the filing section marked TENNIS DEPT.

Peretti, Andrew. DOB 20/09/85. I took the file to the copy room and three minutes later I had one of my own. I returned his file to its spot, and walking back down the hall,

I passed Floyd, Hillside's Chief of Security, who had just come from the security room.

"Yesterday was an odd one, huh?" he said.

"Sure was."

"You found the body?"

That "body" was my friend, fuckhead. "That's right," I said.

"Must've done a number on you," he said. "You look like you didn't sleep a wink last night."

My first client of the day was Tanis Wettlestrom, who nearly fell off the treadmill when she found out I was the one to discover Geri Harp.

"Oh my God," she said. "She was a friend of yours, wasn't she?"

I nodded, suddenly feeling like if I spoke I would crack open.

"That's horrible," she said. "I am so sorry. She always seemed like such an amazing and caring person."

By mid-morning the news had fanned throughout the Fitness Centre that I was the one to find Geri. The s-word was spoken in hushed tones, like it was something possibly contagious. *Oh, how awful are you sure you're all right maybe you need to talk to someone that poor family oh the family Grady and Darci how will they cope if you want to end the session early, Sloane, I totally understand—*

"Actually, Barb," I responded to client number three, "I'm feeling pretty off. Think I'll take you up on that."

Before leaving, I went into the Personal Training office and used the computer to log onto Bookings Plus, the program we use to bill clients. It's the same system used by the other departments, including tennis. Two mouse clicks and

I had Peretti's tennis lesson schedule for the entire year. I keyed Geri Harp into the search and saw that she was booked for lessons every Monday, Wednesday, and Friday at ten a.m. The lessons had been going on week in, week out, for more or less the entire year. I printed off the list.

I walked up to the Tennis Centre and went inside. Distant grunts and thocks of rackets meeting balls echoed from the courts. A camera was situated just above a trophy case, in which three of the largest belonged to Andy "Dogger" Peretti. On the Wall of Fame was a photo of him, sweaty and wild-eyed as he kissed the massive silver Odlum Brown Cup.

Behind the reception desk sat the same young, blonde receptionist that I had seen on camera talking to Geri. Kaitlin, her nameplate read. Kaitlin looked rattled.

"Hi, Kaitlin," I said. "I'm Sloane; I work in Fitness."

"Oh, yeah, how are you?" she said.

"I was the one who found Geri Harp yesterday."

Her face blanched. "Oh, wow."

"I understand she came in here and spoke with you briefly."

"Yeah, when I found out what happened after, it really messed with my head."

"I get that. How did Geri seem yesterday?"

"She was always super polite and friendly. Yesterday she was, too, but she also seemed a bit, uh, wound up, I guess."

"Upset?"

"A little, maybe."

"What did she say?"

"She was looking for Andy," she said. "I had just gotten on shift, but I told her I hadn't seen him yet, and he didn't have any courts booked. It seemed to put her off a little. She even went and checked his office."

A sweaty-faced middle-aged man wearing glasses and tennis whites stuck his head into the room from one of the courts. "We're out of towels."

"'Kay," she said, getting up. "I'll bring some right away."

"Thanks for your help, Kaitlin," I said, heading for the door. She picked up a stack of towels and disappeared down the hall.

I moved back around the reception desk to the computer. After clicking on the *Court Bookings* icon, I pulled the billings printout from my pocket and checked it against the schedule on the screen, starting in September. According to my printout, Geri was billed for lessons on twelve dates in September. Interestingly, out of all those dates, only on the 8th and the 20th did her name appear on the court schedule. Whatever Dogger had been teaching her, it wasn't tennis.

Something else caught my eye. Grady Harp's name appeared on the schedule, court five on the 4th, 14th, and 23rd of the same month. Instructor: *A. Peretti*. Dogger liked to live dangerously.

I jotted down the dates and times. October had a similar booking pattern. The last session she'd been billed for was Monday the 7th, same day she spoke to me, complaining of a cancelled session. Took a special brand of asshole to pull a no-show for a lesson and charge the client anyway.

Unless it was just for appearances on the monthly billing statement. When things are consistent across the board, few questions are raised at home.

Footsteps came from down the hall. I exited the screen and walked out.

Donning a black ball cap and sunglasses, I drove to Dogger's address on 3rd and Lonsdale, in North Vancouver. The area was a mishmash of old and new, with drab three-storey walk-ups sandwiched between sleek glass condos.

Pensioners buzzed around in motorized carts, scowling through coffee shop windows at their usurpers: bed-headed beardo hipsters who managed to loaf around all day, tapping on their Macs while sipping seven-dollar lattes.

Dogger's place was a mod six-floor blue and white condo development with ornamental trees on the roof. I parked near a Starbucks with a view of his underground parking garage. Almost one p.m. I sipped a coffee and reviewed his file.

Pretty standard. A photo of him, lean-faced, tousled black hair, thick brows, two-day stubble, and a roguish grin. Quintessential bad boy. Address, phone number, social insurance number. Emergency contact: Judy Peretti, his mother, who lived in Calgary. His annual contract showed a salary plus eighty percent of all tennis lesson fees. That and full benefits, as well as an honourary club membership. Not bad.

He'd been at Hillside for seven years, two years longer than I had. Thirty-four years old, he'd won the Odlum Brown in 2013 and a list of other tournaments prior to that.

I got out and stood near the entrance to his parking garage and pretended to fiddle with my phone. Two minutes later, the gate opened. A white BMW drove out and I strolled in. Two levels of parking and not a Porsche in sight. Maybe Dogger had taken a conveniently timed holiday.

The payphone was located on an industrial stretch of Main Street, in an area thick with auto-body shops and tire stores. Northbound traffic was backed up due to never-ending roadwork near Terminal. Semis and delivery vans rumbled past; busses hissed and belched. To make sure it was the right phone, I inserted a quarter and called my own number. My iPhone buzzed and the number on the screen matched what had come up on Geri's phone.

I looked around. To the south, Main Street steepened, and several blocks away, across the street from a condo construction site, peeked the sign for the Mount Pleasant Inn. I headed for it on foot.

Back in my cop days, the Mount Pleasant Inn had a reputation for bedbugs and portable meth lab start-ups. It also accepted pay by the month, day, or hour, and was one of the few remaining motels around that accepted cash over credit card, making it the lodging of choice among crooks, cheating spouses, and people on the lam. Judging from the dilapidated exterior I saw no reason to assume anything had changed for the better.

A few beater sedans and pickup trucks were parked in the front lot. Through an open door of one of the rooms on the first floor, an obese maid in a white tracksuit vacuumed a threadbare carpet, a cigarette hanging on her bottom lip.

Turning the corner, I stopped short. A dirty, blue Porsche Boxster ragtop was parked outside Room 17. A red Mazda Miata beside it. Walking past the room, I saw the curtains were pulled tight, but I could hear faint voices, a man and a woman arguing.

Looping around the building, I exited onto 6th and walked back down the hill to my car. At a nearby gas station, I went inside to pee, then bought a coffee, two bottles of water, salted almonds, and a bag of beef jerky. I drove back to the motel.

A six-foot-high snaggletooth brown fence topped with rusty loops of barbed wire separated the motel from the alley behind. Parking by a dumpster reeking of spoiled meat, I got out and walked to the fence, sidestepping used condoms. The wood was warped and rotted; one of its many cracks provided a partial view of the parking lot.

I couldn't stay crouched and peeping through a fence all day, so I snapped off enough of a wooden slat to get a decent view of Room 17 while seated in my Jeep. Nikon binoculars in my lap, I pulled as close as possible to the fence without being seen from the other side. Sophisticated surveillance.

At 5:28 the door to 17 opened and a brunette walked out wearing a form-fitting tan suede jacket and designer jeans. Spanish or Middle Eastern. She wobbled slightly in tall, white pumps.

"If you're going to keep bullshitting me," she shouted, "then fuck right off!" She climbed into the Miata. Andy "Dogger" Peretti ran out barefoot, skinny-jeaned and shirtless. Nice bod. He leaned in the driver's window. I couldn't hear what he said, but his answer proved unsatisfactory, because the Miata screeched into reverse, nearly crunching his feet.

"Call up one of your other bitches!" she yelled, flipping him off as she peeled out of the parking lot.

He looked sheepish as he returned to the room.

You got a way with the ladies, *Dogger*.

At 6:13, a white Nissan NX pulled up in front of the room. A skinny, morose-looking Asian kid around eighteen climbed out, dressed in a baggy green tracksuit, a black-and-white knit cap pulled low over his eyes. Gangsta. He rapped on 17's door.

Dogger answered the door, now wearing a white T-shirt. Paper cup in hand, he stuck his head outside to look around, then pulled the kid in and shut the door. Thirty seconds later the kid was back out. From his pocket, he took out a device that resembled a walkie-talkie and strolled around the circumference of his car. Only the most cautious of drug dealers sweep for bugs or GPS transmitters. I recorded the

Nissan's licence plate, just before the kid reversed and pulled back onto Main.

I looked up the number for the Inn on my phone. I called the reception desk and got a tired-sounding woman with an Indian accent. "Hi there," I said, "I stayed in Room 17 a few days ago and I think I left my watch by the bed. Is there anyone there now?"

"Room 17 is occupied. Sorry."

"For how long?"

"Until Sunday."

"By the same person?"

"I cannot give you that information, ma'am. But our housekeeper didn't find any watch there or it would surely be in the lost and found."

At 9:02 I was about to pack it in, when the kid in the Nissan returned. Dogger pulled him back inside.

Four minutes later the kid came out, did another bug sweep, and checked his phone as he got behind the wheel. He drove out of the parking lot, and since Dogger didn't appear to be going anywhere, I followed the kid.

The kid looked like a punk, but he didn't drive like one; the most successful dealers have spotless driving records.

A sporadic rain began spitting as we drove north. The Nissan pulled into a McDonald's parking lot on Main and backed into a corner slot. I parked across the street, realizing that my Jeep made a less-than-ideal shadow vehicle. For all I knew, he had already noticed me and was watching me watch him.

Five minutes later the kid drove away, zigzagging through quiet residential areas. I turned off my headlights so as not to get made. He turned left on Commercial Drive. I hung back and once I was in traffic again, flicked my lights back on. I watched him do a drop at an apartment near Hastings before cruising west, into the downtown core. He pulled over on Cordova and went inside the Fairmont Pacific Rim Residences for six minutes, then returned and swept for bugs again. Methodical. Doubling back east, three vehicles separated the Nissan from mine, and I followed him back to Commercial where he headed south. A light changed from yellow to red at Commercial and 1st. The kid squeaked through and I watched his taillights recede and melt into traffic up ahead. By the time it changed to green, he was gone.

Having zero desire to go home to an empty condo, I toyed with the idea of getting a room at the Mount Pleasant Inn. Then I remembered I'd forgotten to feed Eclipse, which meant coming home to a potentially shredded couch.

Glancing at the empty bags of nuts and jerky, I thought of Sam and his pregnant wife. I wondered what they'd had for dinner that night, or if they were out someplace, shining, happy, laughing.

Cruising up Commercial past Broadway, I caught a peripheral flash of white to my left and turned my head to see the Nissan backing into the shadows behind a convenience store. Circling the block, I pulled into an alley across the street and backed in so I was facing the store. I reclined the seat so I could just see over the dash.

The kid shuffled into the store. Through the window I saw him pour a large black coffee and pay for it. He walked outside, leaned on the hood of his car, looked at the ground, and hung his head. The coffee steamed on the hood beside him, but he didn't drink any.

A navy-blue Dodge Ram rolled into the parking lot and backed in beside the Nissan. The thick-necked driver had a goatee and a ponytail the colour of steel wool. The kid picked up the coffee and moved to the driver's side window.

I jotted down the truck's plate. Words were exchanged, and Ponytail handed over a brown paper bag. The kid had him hold his coffee for a moment so he could look inside the bag. Shaking his head, the kid set the bag down on the hood of the truck. He took back the coffee and immediately splashed it in Ponytail's face. I could hear the scream from across the street.

The kid snapped several quick and vicious jabs to Ponytail's steaming face through the window. Ponytail put up his hands, but the kid zipped another punch to the side of his head, before reaching into the man's jacket and grabbing a wallet. The kid pulled out the bills, gave a quick count, put them in the paper bag and said something to Ponytail, who gasped and nodded, gingerly touching his scalded cheek. The kid tossed the wallet through the window of the truck. He picked up the coffee cup where it had fallen on the pavement and deposited it into a nearby garbage can.

Out on the street, a police cruiser glided slowly past and the cop didn't see a thing. The kid saw the cop, though, and slid calmly into his car. He started the engine, then looked up and *right at me*.

His eyes narrowed as though sighting a gun.

We stared at each other for ten seconds before the kid pulled out and drove south onto Commercial, where he was eaten up by the night.

CHAPTER 6

Saturday, October 12

THE FOLLOWING DAY, I WAS GASSING UP AT the Lonsdale Chevron station when my phone buzzed with a number I didn't recognize. "Sloane speaking," I said.

"Hello, Sloane, this is Grady Harp."

"Oh, hello." My voice came out as surprised, even though I shouldn't have been. I had planned on contacting him that day, and here he'd beaten me to it. "I am so sorry, Grady."

"Thank you," he said. "I understand you were the first person to find Geri, and I wanted to thank you for doing your best to help."

"I only wish I'd gotten there a bit sooner."

"At the end of the day," he said, voice thickening, "I don't think it would've mattered."

An ambulance screamed past on the highway nearby, making me wince. "How's Darci?"

"I don't think the reality has sunk in yet," he said. "I was out of town, so the real tragedy is that she had to be the one to identify her mother's body and collect her things."

43

"Darci's strong," I said. God, I suck at this.

"She is that."

"I spoke with Geri this past Monday," I said.

A pause on his end. He cleared his throat. "I hadn't seen her in ten days. My wife had her demons, but I never imagined in a million years…"

"Geri was always there to help me when I needed her," I said, "so, if there's anything—"

"There's really nothing to be done at this stage," he replied, "but thank you."

The afternoon turned cold, rainy, and dark, with heavy, claustrophobic clouds pushing down over the city. Living where I did, in the shadow of Mount Seymour, the rainfall could be of near-biblical proportions. On the way home I stopped for a bottle of Pergolas, getting soaked in the five-second dash between Jeep and store. Once in the store, I grabbed an extra bottle. Just in case.

Feeling twitchy, I geared up and headed out to hit the Old Buck, a trail that runs up to the ski hill parking lot and which is steep enough to create an instant cardio-endorphin rush. The weather meant nothing to me. I run in anything.

Ninety minutes later I arrived home, sopping and thrashed of body, my mind bouncing, jittering, and writhing. I switched on the gas fireplace and put on some Black Keys. When I came out of the shower, "Sinister Kid" was playing, which made me think of the dealer from last night. In my mind I replayed his attack on the guy with the ponytail.

I poured a tumbler full of wine and drank it while standing at the counter. I stared at the rain pelting the window and thought of Geri's face when I'd found her. Wind whistled through the trees outside, and I could hear an echo of her laughter.

My friend.

Gone.

I drained the wine and poured more.

From the vacuum cleaner bag in the closet, I removed the large Ziploc containing Geri's letter. I carried the bottle to the table. Eclipse leapt up and rubbed his whiskers on the corner of the laptop. Flipping to a fresh sheet on a legal pad, I wrote GERI HARP, with an arrow connecting her to DOGGER, and with smaller, shorter arrows connected him to MIATA GIRL and DRUG DEALER, and from him, another branch connecting to PONYTAIL. Why was Dogger hiding out at a no-tell motel across town? He was obviously rattled over Geri's death. Given what I'd seen and heard about him, it was highly probable they'd been doing the deed. I suppose I might stay out of sight for a bit if the married woman I was screwing died suddenly.

I read the letter again. Like many suicide notes, it was designed to instill guilt. But the timeline bothered me. Geri had gone looking for Dogger in the Tennis Centre, driven to the junkyard, popped pills, drank, made a phone call, and died—in just over a half-hour.

It felt wrong.

I needed more.

Sunday, October 13

GERALDINE ANNETTE HARP

GERI LEFT US SUDDENLY ON OCTOBER 10, 2019. BELOVED MOTHER OF DARCI HARP, AND ADORED WIFE OF GRADY HARP, HER LOSS IS MOURNED BY THE MANY PEOPLE WHO LOVED HER AND WERE BLESSED BY HER PRESENCE. SHE IS SURVIVED BY HER FATHER, DOMENIC SOLICINO, AND MOTHER, MARIA SOLICINO.

GERI HAD A GENUINE PASSION FOR LIFE, WHICH
TOUCHED ALL THOSE SHE CAME IN CONTACT WITH. A TRUE
HUMANITARIAN, GERI SPENT MUCH OF HER TIME HELPING
THE MARGINALIZED COMMUNITIES OF THE DOWNTOWN
EASTSIDE, WHERE SHE FOUNDED THE NEW WAYS WOMEN'S
SHELTER, AS WELL AS OUTREACH PROGRAMS FOR CHILDREN
AND TEENS. HER WORK HAS SAVED AND BETTERED THE LIVES
OF MANY PEOPLE, AND SHE WILL BE SORELY MISSED. IN LIEU
OF FLOWERS, DONATIONS MAY BE MADE TO THE NEW WAYS
WOMEN'S SHELTER.

FUNERAL SERVICES ARE TO BE HELD AT ST. PAUL'S
CATHOLIC CHURCH IN BURNABY AT II A.M., ON TUESDAY,
OCTOBER 15, 2019.

I stared at the tiny black-and-white photo of Geri above the
obituary. In the picture she appeared to be at some kind of
party. The camera had caught her mid-laugh, and even in
grainy newspaper print, her eyes were festive.

Something jolted me and I remembered I was in a super-
market. A woman with a grocery cart apologized and moved
on. I tore the obit from the newspaper and left.

Back in my car, I phoned the number for RainCity
Investigators. A recording informed me that the number was
no longer in service. Next I pulled up the Hastings Racetrack
schedule and discovered it was the final race week of the year.

I went home and took down a shoebox from a shelf in
the den closet. Rifling through it, I found a 2x2 photo of
me in my police blues. It was taken when I was bright-eyed
and twenty-two, a recent Academy grad. I took it into the
bedroom and I compared it to my current reflection in the
mirror. Nine years later felt like a hundred, and it showed
mostly in my eyes. Miraculously, despite my thirsty lifestyle,

the rest of me looked more or less the same. At least that's how it appeared to me. What other people saw I had no idea.

CHAPTER 7

THE SUN WAS MAKING A VALIANT YET FAILING
run against the purple clouds that massed from the east as
I drove over the Ironworkers Memorial Bridge and hung a
right on McGill. I turned left on Renfrew and pulled into
the lot at Hastings Park.

Walking up the racetrack stands, I scanned the few
dozen weathered faces in the crowd. Most were men with
rumpled clothes and questionable hygiene who looked one
bad bet away from living in a cardboard box.

Eight horses bearing jockeys trotted down the track to
the starting gate. From the marshy centre oval, a flock of
Canada geese took flight, spooking horse number three into
an unexpected gallop, forcing the jockey to rein in hard.

I walked up the stairs and into the lounge, where Wayne
Capson and I spotted each other at the same time. He sat
in a booth fifty feet away, nursing a beer, sporting a black-
and-white pinstriped fedora and a five-day beard. A white
Budweiser T-shirt stretched across his broad, bear-like chest.

His gut had grown from years of eating too many burgers while watching other men and women cheat on their spouses.

On my way over, I passed an elderly woman perched on a stool. She was heavily made up and wore a big, floppy sunhat, a pearl necklace, and a diamond-encrusted watch. Her gnarled hand shook as she examined a ticket. "Six to win, six to win, six to win..." she said in the soft voice of a much younger woman.

I smiled at her and she grinned, her face a maze of wrinkles. "Boots Gray's my nag," she said.

"Good luck," I replied.

I sat down across from Wayne, and he gave me a once-over. "Sloane Donovan," he announced. I could tell by the lager sheen on his blue eyes he'd been there the entire afternoon. I could also tell by the half-dozen shredded tickets on the table that the ponies had shat on him good.

"Wayne Train," I said. "How're tricks?"

"Never trust anything that can run and crap at the same time."

"Words to live by," I said, gesturing toward the track. "Who do you like for this race?"

"I got a triactor on two, five, and seven. Can't lose this one. The papers are too good."

"Old lady there says six is going to take it."

"Six is a washed-up old whore," he said. "Just like me."

"Why so glum? You're bumming me out already."

Wayne snorted and finished his beer. "Maggie divorced my ass and took the house; I only get to see Theo every other weekend. He tells me my place stinks, because it does, but I can't tell him I have to live in a shitbox because his mother is a fucking twat. Unlike *her*, I don't believe parents should badmouth each other in front of the kid."

"You sound like you could use another drink," I said.

I ordered two beers while Wayne's attention was riveted to the race. He raised his mini-binoculars as the horses rocketed out of the gate and down the stretch, ripping up large clumps of mud in their wake. Five took the lead by several lengths, followed by two and eight. Then seven galloped ahead and eight fell back. Wayne jumped up in his seat. "*C'mon,* c'mon, you fucking nags! I got child support."

His horses were leading by a narrow margin for the first lap, but as they looped around for the final furlong, number five slipped in the mud and nearly went down, the jockey fighting to remain in the saddle. Number six came up from the rear like a dirty white blur to overtake the pack and win by a full length.

"*Woooo-hoooo!*" shouted the old lady.

I grinned back at her and she did an excited little jig. I told Wayne he ought to take gambling tips from her.

He methodically shredded another ticket, looking like he had a foul taste in his mouth. "Don't engage her," he said.

"Why not?" I asked. "She seems like the least depressing person here."

"I've been hired to babysit her."

I laughed. "What? Why aren't you sitting with her then?"

"Because she doesn't know. Old bat is loaded. Her late husband used to own thoroughbreds. Now she's at an age where thousand-dollar wagers can seem like a good idea. She's been losing a bundle down here every race day. Her kids are worried they're not going to see much in the way of an inheritance if it keeps up, so I keep tabs on her. If she starts losing big, I call her daughter and she comes to get her." He sighed. "Since I'm charging hourly, it's not a bad gig."

"Especially since you'd be here anyway."

The old lady raised her winning ticket in the air and announced to everyone in the lounge: "I better go collect before this dump goes bust." She hobbled in the direction of the teller windows.

Wayne rose, just as the beers arrived.

"Where you going?" I asked.

"It's also my job to see no one rolls the old lady for her winnings," he said. "Look at the deadbeats around here. They'd whore out their mothers in exchange for a twenty-dollar win. When I get back you can tell me why you're here."

"Must be your ungodly charm."

Ten minutes later the old lady returned, very carefully balancing a glass of white wine. She took a tiny sip and her eyebrows shot up with glee. Wayne arrived from another direction, setting down a shot of whisky by his beer.

"Where's mine?" I asked.

"As I recall," he said, slamming the shot, "you're not even supposed to drink with your condition."

"You're a doctor now?"

"You on meds?"

"I'm in complete remission."

He shot me a sideways don't-bullshit-a-bullshitter look and clinked his beer against mine. "Well, to your health. You're looking good anyway. What are you doing these days?"

"I'm a personal trainer in West Van."

"No shit."

"Yeah. When was the last time you changed that shirt?"

Wayne gulped his beer and wiped his whiskers with a brick-like wrist. "Gotta look the part. Why're *you* here?"

"I need you to get me backgrounds on six people—three of which I don't have any names, only plates."

Wayne didn't reply. He looked like he'd aged ten years in the previous five. Divorce and crushing debt will do that. He drummed his thick fingers on his racing form. "Don't you have any friends left on the force?"

"Would I be here if I did?"

"Right. Well, normally, I'd charge at least a grand a pop, but because you're a friend, sort of, it'll be eight hundred."

"What do you have in the way of a mid-range background?"

"If I only go back, say three years. Four hundred each."

I slid five one-hundred-dollar bills across the table. "For all six," I said. "I'm on a budget."

He muttered something about me being a cheap-ass as he scooped up the money and waved the waitress for another round. "On you," he said. "What's all this about?"

"A friend of mine died several days ago."

"Sorry to hear. How'd it happen?"

"OD. But I think there was more to it."

After studying me for several moments, he pulled out a pen and pad and handed them to me. Old school. "Write down names, plates, and anything else that might make my job easier. Give me a few days."

"I need one more thing," I said.

Wayne winced as if he had trapped gas. "What might that be?"

I slipped him my photo. "A badge."

His face got even more pained.

CHAPTER 8

Tuesday, October 15

I BACKED MY JEEP INTO A CORNER STALL OF the church parking lot and killed the engine. Watched the long procession of mourners file up the stairs below a gold-plated effigy of the Virgin Mary. A limo rolled up. A minute passed before the tall figure of Grady Harp climbed out wearing a black suit and navy tie. He had a full head of hair, completely silver. His eyes were red and his jaw was set. Stoic.

Grady reached back into the limo to take his daughter's hand. Last time I'd seen Darci she had been a somewhat plump teen. In the past few years, she had transformed into a confident-looking woman who carried her curves well, along with her mother's features. But where Geri had that trade-mark Mediterranean glow, Darci's complexion was milk against her long black dress. Her short blonde hair was done in a funky, choppy cut. She wore sunglasses and her face was puffy from a weekend of tears.

Father and daughter climbed the stairs amid embraces and handshakes. A rodent lodged in my throat. I sipped from a blue S'well bottle filled with Sauvignon Blanc, then put the bottle in my purse. I stepped into a light drizzle and smoothed out my black, long-sleeved dress.

The organ music filled me with doom as I took one of the only remaining seats at the back and as close to the exit as possible. I sipped more wine and scanned the crowd.

Front and centre, directly before the shiny mahogany coffin, sat the Harp family. Beside the coffin was a tripod bearing a jumbo-sized photo of Geri, smiling her hundred-watt smile.

Darci sat between her father on the left and an elderly couple on the right I assumed were Geri's parents. The old lady sobbed and her husband, bald and mustached, slowly shook his head. Darci turned to comfort her grandmother.

I took another sip and looked around. The church was vast; the masonry would outlast everyone here. Amid the sea of chic West Van hairstyles, I recognized a few Hillside members.

It was the shelter ladies who stood out, taking up the last four pews across the aisle. Of the thirty-plus people, a few looked like counsellors or volunteers, while the rest of the sunken-cheeked survivors looked like they'd done hard time on the street. They ranged in age from fifteen to fifty.

A pale and emaciated blonde no older than eighteen sat on the final pew, her vacant eyes fixed on nothing. She wore a black sweater and jeans. Her lank hair hung over half her face, almost masking a badly scarred cheek.

The suit in front of me tapped on his BlackBerry and murmured something to his equine-faced wife. The funeral was probably cutting into his billable hours. My heart raced. I wanted to get in my Jeep and drive far away from everything I had ever known. I closed my eyes for twenty seconds and willed my emotions back into their cage.

Reopening my eyes, the first thing I saw was Darci walking up the aisle. She had removed her sunglasses and a ray of sun slanting through a high stained-glass window illuminated the shimmering tears in her pale blue eyes. People half-turned in their seats as she approached the New Ways' ladies. They all stood as Darci moved up and down the pews. Whispering, she thanked each of them for coming, including the girl with the damaged face. Some of the women sobbed and hugged her. My heart clawed its way up my throat.

Before I lost it completely, I stood and walked out. The organ music followed me.

I stood on the steps outside and took a gulp from the bottle. The organ was driving me nuts. I *was* nuts. I was afraid that if I wasn't careful, I could end up like one of those shelter women, just one step away from eating out of a dumpster.

Another gulp.

My mind pinballed around, bouncing from Geri to Steph to Sam to the drug dealer to Dogger to the time I was thirteen and we'd taken a school field trip to the local police station and I'd lifted a stapler off a cop's desk and put it in my knapsack. Cherry popsicles. Oral sex. Tyrannosaurus Rex. *Shutupshutupshutup.*

I walked across the parking lot and stopped. The white Nissan NX from the other night was parked near the street. Same plates. I hadn't seen the dealer inside, but his presence put him one degree of separation from Geri instead of two.

Climbing back into my Jeep, I drank wine and closed my eyes and did some deep breathing. Therapists recommend it as a method of calming the nervous system, and I want to believe that works, but usually it only takes me back in time, where I try to figure out where it all started to go horribly wrong. Then it becomes another form of self-torture, and I suppose that makes me a mental masochist.

The best years of my life occurred between the ages of nineteen and twenty-six. I got a lot done. I left home with a track scholarship to UBC, where I cleaned up in all the distance events while earning a criminology degree. I did so well my mother stopped checking to see if I was on my meds.

Steph and Phil had been nesting across town. I went over for the occasional barbecue, but truthfully, I couldn't stand him. He'd seemed like a nice enough guy before the wedding, but since then he'd morphed into a belittling bastard, always on Steph's case about something. He'd call her his "little 'tard princess" in front of people and make cracks about all the meds she needed just to function. After I got in his face a few times, Steph leapt to his defense and told me to mind my own business, saying that I had no idea what it was like to have love in my life. At least I got a rise out of her. She didn't talk to me for over a year. It scared me how quickly she had mutated from the hauntingly beautiful up-and-coming artist to a sallow-faced part-time Walmart employee with prematurely greying hair.

Oddly, my mother thought she was doing just fine. She always maintained that in our family, stability was number one. I, on the other hand, caused a monumental stir when she discovered I was attending the Justice Institute. An interviewer had phoned her to inquire about any history of mental illness in the family. Never one to open up to strangers, my mother had responded that the Donovan clan was all of sound mind and body. She must have been sufficiently convincing because he didn't dig deeper. And by then I'd already passed a polygraph. Through years of distance running, I had conditioned my system such that I could manipulate a significant dip or rise in heart rate through simple breathing patterns. This made the so-called lie detector test absurdly easy to fool by going into the test with a slightly erratic heart rate during the irrelevant questions. While this is going on, I also clenched my sphincter, which quickly elevated my blood pressure. Subtlety is key. I didn't want to come in looking like I just completed a marathon while experiencing a bad case of the trots. The trick is timing. When the potentially nerve-inducing questions arrives (have you ever used illegal drugs ... stolen anything ... lied under oath ... been on anti-depressants), I relax my sphincter and deepened my breath. It also didn't hurt to have a mental disorder that enables me to lie with ease.

During the final part of my training, I cut everyone off. I thrived on the discipline, and kept focused enough to ace all the legal and social science exams. I finessed the driving skills training, and felt natural with a 9mm in my hand, and grew quite fond of the power of a 12-gauge. Where I really turned heads was in the mock-ups, where I had to chase down perps on foot. I could run anyone to the ground inside of thirty seconds, even if they had a ten-second lead. And despite my size, my speed was not limited to running; I proved effective at takedowns using finger and arm locks. Supplemental Krav Maga training filled in the gaps, allowing me to hold my own against most men, so long as I followed my instructor Sergei's mantra: Hit first, hit fast, and do not stop until your attacker is down or dead.

Less than a year later, I was working as a beat cop on the mean streets of Vancouver, quickly progressing to under-cover work. Hooker detail, mostly john stings. Coming off the job one morning I made a fluky solo bust of a dangerous pedophile. This arrest earned me good press and took some of the tarnish off the VPD's rep, which was in the toilet at the time after some high-profile corruption cases. It also gave me the jump to detective, rankling more than a few members of the old boys' club—guys who had spent decades humping for promotions that never came.

I hung out with cops, all my friends were cops, but I didn't want to date a cop. At a Christmas party at a local pub, I ended up swooning over the tall, handsome bartender and giving him my number. This was Sam, and a month later we were living together. Sam came from a big, extended Maritime family, and he wanted a whole bunch of things I couldn't see in the cards. Kids. A home in the suburbs. A woman who would wise up, get off the streets, and let her ass broaden behind a desk. He didn't get that it was the juice of imminent danger that kept me from tumbling over the edge into the *true* dark side.

Meanwhile, Steph got pregnant. I didn't know it then, but she'd been fired from Walmart for stealing. My mother moved in with her and Phil for a time, to make sure Steph was taking care of herself. In the end, she couldn't hack the sorry state of their home: sink overflowing with food-encrusted dishes, dirty clothes everywhere, mouse turds in the Corn Flakes, oily engine parts on newspapers in the living room (one of Phil's never-to-be-completed projects).

Most women gain weight when they're pregnant; Steph got skinny again. Being with child, Steph had to stop her meds. Times I'd visit, Phil was sullen. He watched his wife resentfully, like the thing growing in her was a tumour. He kept his mouth shut around me, but I suspected he launched the verbal assaults again the moment they were alone. I could tell she'd been crying, a lot, but when she bottomed out, Steph never opened up to anyone.

When Charlie was born, Sam and I were climbing the Inca Trail to Machu Picchu. Facebook posts showed Steph grinning with her tiny baby boy. I was happy for her. Maybe she *had* finally discovered her purpose in life: to be a mother.

It lasted a year and a half. Steph went back on the meds, gained weight, and promptly got pregnant again. This time when she halted the meds, she took to her bed and refused any visitors. My mother was worried about Charlie and talked to me about getting Child Services involved. Having seen families torn apart by kids being relocated, I quashed the idea. We were Donovan women; we struggled with our issues, but at the end of the day, we survived.

Emma Sloane Pilchek was born early in the spring of 2014. We weren't religious, but Steph got both children baptized at the Methodist church. I was there for the dunking. The kids yowled like scrapping alley cats. My mother saw it as a good sign. I saw it as weird. Steph looked anemic and drawn. My mother asked if she was on her meds. Steph stared at her blankly, then opened her purse and shook it so we could see and hear the clinking of pills. Phil wasn't at the christening.

On May 6 of that year, my partner and I were wrapping up a late-night stakeout when I heard a radio call of a domestic assault at Steph's address. When we got there, Steph was cleaning the blood from her face where Phil'd hit her. The condo was filthy and reeked of cat piss. Charlie and Emma were screaming in the bedroom. Phil was long gone, having fled after a neighbour called the cops.

We grabbed the kids, and I cradled Emma while Steph held Charlie. I looked at the filth and squalor and told her I had to report the situation. She broke down and begged me, actually *pleaded* for me not to. In my whole life I had never seen her so emotional. She said she only wanted to keep the three of them together. "I'm taking them someplace safe soon, I swear," she said.

"What about Phil?" I asked.

"Don't worry, Sloane. This will *never* happen again."

My partner looked around the condo and said that it needed to be written up. Steph began sobbing and pleading anew. "Just this once, Steph," I said. "Get the kids to Mom's."

A week later I was at the station filling out an arrest sheet when I got a text from Steph.

SIS: COME OVER TO CONDO. BRING YOUR PALS. NO RUSH.

I arrived just after nine p.m. with my partner. Two uniforms were already waiting at the door. I knocked and got no reply. A deep dread filled me like ammonia. I knocked again. We woke the building manager and had her open the door. The condo had been completely cleaned, everything put in its place. The tiles shone with fresh wax. It was like someone else had moved in.

The only sound was a steady drip of water from the bathroom. I called out to Steph and got no response. I flicked on the kitchen light and moved through the living room to the hall bathroom, and turned on the light.

Phil was naked and dead in the bathtub, his wrists slit. The faucet dripped into the tub full of dark red water.

I checked for a pulse, found none, and ran down the hall to the bedroom. The other cops tried to keep me from going in, but I forced past. When I saw them all nestled in bed—Charlie and Emma snuggled on either side of Steph—I nearly breathed a sigh of relief. But all their lips were blue, and Steph's head was drooped at that terrible angle. On the bedside table sat a pill bottle and a bottle of Stoli.

And a letter.

CHAPTER 9

VOICES CAME FROM OUTSIDE MY JEEP. MY EYES snapped open and I shook my head to clear the morbid past from my mind. I could've used a coffee, but since that wasn't going to happen, I found my hand reaching for the S'well bottle again. Slow down, I told myself as I took a sip. I set the bottle back. Seconds later, I picked it up and took another slug, troubled by my increasing lack of control. I thought of Geri, drinking alone in her car the previous week and I suddenly felt incomparably sad and isolated from the rest of the world.

A few of the shelter women walked by my passenger window, the blonde with the scarred face among them. Looking toward the entrance of the church, I saw Darci and Grady Harp emerge and climb into the waiting limo. I noticed the white Nissan was gone from its spot, as were half the vehicles from the lot. I took another drink and started the engine.

Howe Sound Lane was choked with Beemers and Escalades, forcing me to park further down, on Water Lane. During the walk in, I used the time to focus on my breath to calm my racing mind. I really wanted to kick off my pumps and run, barefoot, anywhere. But before I knew it, I had arrived at the house.

The driveway circled around a marble fountain that looked transported from Rome, with muscular deities and plump cherubs eating grapes. Casa Harp was a white-walled three-storey Mediterranean-style villa with a red tiled roof. On the left of the house was a guest cottage with an infinity pool.

The massive front door was open and I paused, listening to the murmur of voices inside. To the left of the door was an incongruously homey wooden cutout of a family of happy ducks. Below it read: HOME IS WHERE THE HATE IS.

Blinking, I shook my head.

HOME IS WHERE THE HARPS ARE.

The house swallowed me up. Grady Harp was suddenly shaking my hand, his glacial blue eyes seeming to stare right through me. "Sloane," he said, "thank you for coming."

A couple behind me waited to pay their respects. He turned to them and I walked through the foyer, pausing at the family photos on the wall. Geri and Grady on their wedding day, twenty-five years ago. Darci as an infant, grinning ear to ear. Family shots in front of the Eiffel Tower, Buckingham Palace, the Coliseum, the Great Wall of China.

Following the buzz of voices, I continued down the hall to the kitchen, which was larger than my entire condo, with granite tile floors and stainless-steel appliances. The counters were covered with casseroles, cakes, trays of cheese and crackers, and bowls of olives. A large wooden sideboard was packed with enough wine and spirits to get you where you needed to go.

The sunken living room had a twenty-foot-high ceiling supported by massive blonde wood beams. Multiple white and tan couches and chairs were occupied. Floor-to-ceiling windows offered a panoramic view of Bowen Island and the Georgia Strait. Off to the left of the kitchen, French doors opened onto a balcony. One of the doors was ajar.

Well-heeled men and women hovered in neat circular cliques, sipping wine and conversing in hushed tones. At the bar, I searched past the pinot noir and Scotch until I found some Kiwi white. A healthy pour, and I scanned the crowd.

To those who killed me...

Near the bar, two middle-aged socialites quietly gossiped. I caught snippets against the buzz of the living room: "—yes, I *know*, but I heard she got a little cracked around the time she gave up acting."

The other woman said, "It was the eighties. Who *wasn't* a little cracked back then?"

"She *was* a great actress though, but then she gained all that weight. Maybe it was the meds. I heard she was on five different drugs."

Bitches.

The acting part piqued my curiosity. Geri had never mentioned it.

Geri's parents sat on a sofa, leafing through an old photo album. They looked like at any moment their frail bodies could break into a thousand pieces and blow away like dried leaves.

Taking my wine to the balcony, I found Darci alone, sitting in a chaise lounge. An angry rain had begun. She wore sunglasses and smoked a cigarette while staring out at the wind-whipped ocean caps. Her black pumps had been kicked off next to a nearly empty bottle of Chianti.

"Hi Darci," I said softly. Her head swivelled to me, and she hastily butted her cigarette against the arm of the chaise.

"Sorry," she said, voice raspy. "I don't usually smoke, but it's just—"

She swung her legs up and stood, teetering a bit as wine spilled from her glass and onto the stone balcony. She set her glass down and we hugged. She squeezed me tight. "I'm sorry, Darci," I said.

"You found my mom," she said, her voice barely a whisper.

"I did."

We broke apart and Darci sat back on the chaise and removed her sunglasses. Her eyes were glassy and bloodshot. I pulled over a deck chair.

"Sorry you have to see me like this," she said. "I'm a mess."

"Not at all," I said. "It's really rough."

"It's bizarre, isn't it," she said, "how death can bring people back into each other's spheres? I mean, you and I probably wouldn't be together right now if my mom hadn't died. It all just seems so…"—her voice cracked and her face contorted—"*fucked.*" A fat tear rolled down her face. "I just keep thinking my alarm is going to go off and I'm going to wake up from this."

I reached over and gripped her arm for a moment, then released it. I closed my eyes.

"You guys were supposed to have lunch last week," she said.

I opened my eyes and nodded slowly.

"My mom mentioned it. Said she was looking forward to it. Does that make any sense to you? Does any of this make any fucking sense?"

"No."

She squinted out at the ocean. "You see a lot of dead people when you were with the police?"

"Some."

"Did you get used to it?"

"Never."

Darci finished her wine and poured the remainder of the bottle into her glass. Veins of lightning illuminated the grey horizon, followed by the distant growl of thunder. The wind drove the rain at a hard slant. She shivered. "I don't want to go in there alone," she said. "You ready for a top-up?"

"Sure am."

Back inside, people turned and offered sympathetic faces. Darci responded with a tight smile.

"If I have to endure much more of this I'm going to scream," she mumbled as we moved back to the bar. I told her she was doing fine.

Grady watched us from across the room.

"How's your dad holding up?" I asked.

"My dad, the robot," she said, pouring more wine for the both of us. "In some ways I'm more like him. I wish I wasn't, but—" she sipped her wine and gave a little *c'est la vie* shrug, "we are who we are."

Her eyes traveled over my shoulder. "Look who decided to make an appearance," she said.

I caught a whiff of Scotch mixed with musk and there he was: Andy "Dogger" Peretti, looking like he hadn't showered or shaved in three days. But he wore a black bespoke suit, and his leather wingtips were polished. In his right hand he held a tumbler of Scotch. He hugged Darci. She stiffened and pulled back.

"I'm really sorry, Darce," he said.

She nodded. "So, how was the vacay?"

He glanced away. "Quick getaway."

"Sloane, you know Andy, don't you? Of course you would, seeing as how you both work at the club."

I shook his hand. "I think we've met once, at a Christmas party or something."

He nodded, but it was clear he didn't remember. Nor did I, because it never happened. I never went to Christmas parties.

"You coached Geri?" I asked. "Grady, too?"

"Yeah," he said. From across the room, Grady looked over again.

"Sloane's a runner," Darci said. "She can run, like, a thousand miles at a stretch. She used to be a cop, too, so don't mess with her."

Shit.

From across the room the photo album dropped to the floor. A loud hiccupping sob came from Geri's mother as she buried her face in her hands. Her husband just sat there, frozen, staring at the fallen album, a portal to a better past.

Darci handed me her glass and sped across the room, slipping her arms around her grandmother, whispering into her ear.

"How long had you coached Geri?" I asked Dogger.

"Three years," he answered. "How do you know her?"

"We were friends," I said, looking into his eyes. "I actually spoke to her just a few days before her death. She seemed fairly normal. I keep wondering what could have happened in between."

He stared out the window.

"How did she seem the last time you saw her?" I asked.

A pause. "Normal, I guess."

"Darci said you were on vacation," I said. "Where'd you get off to? Someplace warm, I hope."

"No. Just Seattle for a couple days."

Liar, liar, Dogger on fire.

Leaning close, I whispered, "Do you think there were marital problems?"

"I think marriage itself is a problem," he said.

"Maybe there was someone else in the picture."

His eyes flicked my way.

"Sorry," I said. "These things always make me nervous. I drink too much and then blabber like a fool."

He worked his jaw side to side, then drained his glass. "God, I hate funerals."

"Technically, this is a reception, not a funeral."

He abruptly excused himself and weaved through the crowd, to where Grady stood with a couple of other silver-haired mogul types. I watched Dogger give what I assumed were condolences along with a handshake. Grady nodded, his expression inscrutable.

I finished my wine and the room spun for a second. Picking up a cracker off a tray, I nibbled it as I wandered back down the hall to use the bathroom. The door was locked.

A quick glance around and I headed upstairs. On the landing, I stopped and looked at more photos on the wall. One was a beach shot of Darci when she would have been about five, buried up to her neck in sand, sticking out her tongue. Underwater shots of mother and daughter clowning. Some were only of Geri, mugging cross-eyed for the camera.

Moving down the second-floor hallway, there were two doors on the right, one on the left. Checking each, I found them locked. At the end of the hall a door was ajar, leading into the master bedroom. Remembering the day Geri had given me the tour, I had commented that the honeymoon suite at the Four Seasons had nothing on this. A low king-size bed with a white duvet. Two-person Jacuzzi by the balcony. Gauzy white curtains partway open, offering a peek at the ocean. In the middle of the room was a blue glass fireplace with two reading chairs.

During that tour, Geri had seemed somewhat embarrassed by the opulence of the home; she felt it clashed with the work she did on the streets. While she had been raised around money, Grady had not, hence his lifelong dream to live in relative splendor.

Nearby stood a shelf full of books and photo albums. Amid the novels of Trevanian and Gillian Flynn, several titles jumped out: *Why Pro-Life? Caring for the Unborn and their Mothers* and *Defending Life: A Moral and Legal Case Against Abortion Choice.* I pulled out one of the photo albums. It went back to the pre-digital, pre-Darci eighties. Party shots of Geri with big hair. Back then Grady looked like a blond, tanned Ken doll. There were several pages of Geri on stage in Shakespearean garb. Magazine clippings of her in ads for Pepsi and Dove soap. A racy Miller Lite ad of her dancing in the back of a pickup truck wearing only a white teddy and underwear. Black-and-white headshots with Geri sporting different hairstyles and expressions: joyous, sad, fierce, contemplative. Stamped on the bottom of some of the photos was ATLAS TALENT.

I wondered again why she'd never mentioned a former acting career. Maybe it was one of those things that once you're done with it, you're *done.* No looking back. I considered the conversation I'd heard downstairs, about Geri going a little "cracked" around the time she gave up acting. It had obviously been a huge part of her life. What made her turn her back on it so suddenly?

Footsteps in the hall made me dash into the ensuite bathroom. Big glass cube shower, two toilets demurely facing away from each other, and an old-fashioned clawfoot tub. I sat on the toilet and listened to the murmur of two voices. One of them was Darci, though I couldn't catch her words. I sat there for a full minute.

I stood and flushed, then ran the faucet, using the noise to check the bathroom cabinet. Among the Advil and Tylenol were prescription pill bottles of zolpidem, lorazepam, and the antipsychotic aripiprazole, all drugs I had known intimately at one time or another.

I closed the cabinet and walked back into the bedroom. Geri's mother lay on the bed, one arm over her eyes. She knew someone was there, because she waved her other arm, a message for me to get the hell out.

I did.

Nothing worse than losing a child. I thought of my own mother. Walking back downstairs, I pulled out my phone and texted: **LOVE YOU, MOM!**

On the bottom step, the first person my eyes collided with was the drug dealer from the other night, staring at me from a seat across the room. His head was shaved to the skull and he wore a white Oxford with khakis. At first I didn't recognize the frail Filipina woman sniffling beside him. She wore a black headdress and her eyebrows were missing. It was Rosie, their housekeeper, whom I'd met years ago. At the time she'd been a robust and energetic woman. Now she appeared sick, possibly terminal. The kid handed her a glass of water, while at the same time fixing me with a look that was both sad and hard.

No sign of Darci and Dogger, so I took my wine buzz and split. A wind had whipped up and the rain came down like it was trying to teach me a lesson. At the top of the driveway, I was already drenched, and that seemed about right. I slipped off my heels, liking the sensation of the sharp stones beneath my feet.

Sidestepping puddles, I passed a grey '70s-era Oldsmobile parked between a Bentley and an Escalade. In the driver's seat sat a man in his mid-thirties with a black pompadour, a thick mustache, and a soul patch. On his neck was a large black tattoo of what looked like an almond-shaped eye with an insect symbol in the middle. Beside him sat a woman wearing a dark hoodie and cat-eye sunglasses. Her window was down halfway and I could smell cigarettes, chemicals, and sweat.

Once past, I looked back. In the passenger-side mirror I caught the woman watching me. I felt a twinge of familiarity, like I had seen her before.

CHAPTER 10

BACK HOME IN THE KITCHEN, ECLIPSE DID figure eights around my calves while I heated up some minestrone and opened a beer. Something was eating at me, so I sat down at the computer and Googled "Atlas Talent Agency." I found their website, sat thinking for a few moments, then grabbed my phone.

"Hello, I'm Sandra Donnelly," I said, "a journalist for *The Globe and Mail*. I'm doing a piece on an actress from the eighties who was repped by your agency. Her name was Geri Harp, and she passed away recently. I was wondering if I might be able to have a word with her agent from that time."

The receptionist told me that she would speak with Mr. Temple, who handled most of the actors back them. I thanked her and gave my number. Then I promptly changed my phone's outgoing message to a generic one with no name.

Next morning was chockablock with clients and classes. I attempted to steer people's conversation to Geri, but it was already old news. People were back to talking about whose husbands were schtupping the nannies and what prestigious schools their superhuman progenies would be attending the following year.

At noon I checked my voicemail and there was a message from Kayvon Temple at Atlas Talent, saying that he would speak with me if I would care to make an appointment.

I called and made an appointment for the following morning.

Thursday, October 17

Driving up Roche Point, I saw snow on Mount Seymour that hadn't been there yesterday. My phone buzzed as I turned onto the parkway. At the next set of lights, I checked it.

HI S, IT'S DARCE
WONDERING IF YOU
COULD TRAIN ME?
I FEEL GROSS.
CALL ME

Smile Diner on Pender is a kitschy Chinese/Canadian restaurant that feels like stepping back in time forty years. The wall above the counter on the left bore posters of a young Sylvester Stallone and Michael Jackson, while below, patrons washed down bacon and eggs specials with old-school chocolate shakes—precisely what Wayne Capson was doing from a stool near the back. With his grey knit cap, red mackinaw, and scraggly beard, he fit in with the other breakfasting Gastown hipsters.

He turned to see me coming, appraising my getup. I wore a black, knee-length skirt and matching blouse with a charcoal and blue pinstriped jacket and heels. My hair was down and I wore black-framed glasses.

"Who you trying to be?" he asked.

"Journalist," I replied.

"Too well-groomed."

I took the empty stool to his left and he slid me a slim, yellow folder, just before the waitress came with coffee. I ordered granola and yogurt.

After she left, I peeked into the file and saw police photos of a dead Geri and the scene.

I stared at a photo of my friend's dead face, and the emotions of that day came rushing back. I heard myself ask Wayne about the coroner's report.

"Too early," he said. "But I found who the plates are registered to. The Miata belongs to Nazreen Farooz, a hairdresser who lives in North Van and has no priors. The Nissan is registered to a kid by the name of Kai Abacon, whose mother has been the housekeeper for the Harps for the past twelve years. Kai's been in the country only seven of those, but pretty much the moment he arrived from Manila, he showed a wayward streak. Nineteen years old and he's got a juvie record for hacking, identity theft, *and* assault. And then there's the drug dealing, everything from blow to fentanyl. Kid went through probation two years ago and his record has been clean ever since."

"Yeah, right," I said, thinking back to the drug deals I'd witnessed last Friday. The coffee assault. I asked Wayne about Ponytail.

"Timothy Womack. Thirty-eight. In '06 he got pinched for trucking a load of weed into the States. He did nine years, but since then, just like Kai, he seems to have found the light."

"Tim have an address?"

Wayne shook his head. "He's got an RV listed in his name. Probably lives in it like a nomad. Likely be me in a few years."

"What about Peretti?"

"Clean, except for a charge against him that was later dropped. Since he doesn't officially have a sheet, it'll take some more digging."

"Anything on Grady?"

"Zip. Your friend Geri had some troubles, though. A couple DUIs over the years. She lost her licence and the judge recommended rehab. You didn't know about that?"

"I knew she was fond of her wine, but no." A different picture was beginning to emerge of my friend, one of booze and drugs and infidelity. How could I not have seen the signs earlier?

"Some people are good at hiding the monkeys on their backs," he said, as if he'd heard the question I asked myself. "What's all this to you anyway?"

"You're going to think I'm nuts."

"We crossed that bridge years ago."

I reached into my purse and pulled out Geri's letter.

He read it. "Jesus, Donovan," he said, pinching the bridge of his nose between his thumb and index finger. "I don't care if you're her friend, it's not your place—"

"I believe someone killed Geri and made it look like suicide," I said. Wayne opened his mouth, but I raised my hand. "Just hear me out."

He nodded, and I began with the conversation I'd had with Geri, then cut to last Thursday, when I found her body. The phone call. Tracking the payphone that led me to Dogger's motel. He and Nazreen Farooz's parking lot spat. Kai delivering drugs to Dogger. Tailing Kai, and the coffee attack on Womack. The funeral. Talking to Dogger and the weird vibes he gave off. Seeing Kai there.

"So you think someone, what, OD'ed Geri in her car? Planted the letter? For what motive? Because she was fucking her tennis coach?"

"I know no one planted the letter, because I have the video footage of her death."

"How'd you obtain that?"

"I stole it. Look, all I know is it doesn't feel right."

"Suicides never do," he said. "*Especially* when—"

"Especially when my sister killed herself, right?"

"Absolutely. I think this thing has hit you too close to home."

I picked up my fork, pressing the edge of my finger into the tines until I felt pain. Wayne watched me. I put down the fork. "I know what this looks like, but it's different. Months before Steph did what she did, the signs were there. She'd given up; the spark was gone. I spoke with Geri, face to face—three days before she allegedly killed herself—and she seemed happy. She said she needed my advice on something, and we made lunch plans."

"She *seemed* happy," he said. "Geri was a closet drunk. Who knows what kind of pain she was in? Plus she was an actress. Look, I'm seriously advising you to let this go. In good conscience, I shouldn't even be taking your money."

I held out my hand. "You think I'm crazy, give it back."

He paused.

"It's already gone, isn't it?" I asked.

Wayne looked sheepish.

I smiled. "Okay, where's the other thing I asked for?"

"Patience," he said. "A bogus shield is some felonious shit, and that means more time." He rubbed his fingers together. "And more money."

CHAPTER 11

"SANDRA DONNELLY," I SAID TO THE RECEP-tionist behind the desk at Atlas Talent. "I'm here to see Mr. Temple."

"He'll be with you shortly," she said, gesturing to the leather chairs.

Five minutes later a stocky, middle-aged man with curly salt-and-pepper hair appeared, wearing a black turtleneck and jeans. "Sandra?" he asked. I stood, and we shook hands. "Kayvon Temple, good to meet you."

"You, too."

I followed him down a hall and into his office. Despite the dismal day, it had a sweeping view of the inlet and the North Shore Mountains. The walls were full of photos of him with celebrities: Michael J. Fox, Ryan Reynolds, Seth Rogen. A low shelf behind him held stacks of scripts. On the desk was a faded, pink file folder. The label read SOLECINO, GERI. We took seats on either side of his glass desk, and I took out a notebook and a pen.

Temple asked me if I'd done any acting or modeling.

"I played a tree in grade six," I said. "Does that count?"

His laugh was deep, and like most salesmen, excessively loud. "There's always a demand for slender redheads. Especially for commercials."

"Too self-conscious."

"You said you're doing a piece on Geri. I heard she is doing great things in the Downtown Eastside. How is she?"

"She passed away last week."

Temple's eyes went sad, and his shoulders dropped. "I'm very sorry to hear that. I actually haven't had any contact with Geri in many years. We used to run into each other at the odd fundraiser, but that's about it. How did she die?"

"Overdose."

He shook his head. "Fucking drugs," he said. "Excuse my language. I'm sorry, it's just that I've seen too much of that in this business. So much talent, so much *life*, just flushed away. What a blow that must be to her family. Geri was such a beauty, so natural in front of the camera. But I always worried about her; she was naïve. Emotional. Rejection used to devastate her."

I scribbled down: *naïve, emotional, rejection, devastate.*

"Is that why she gave up acting?" I asked.

He squinted and looked briefly at the ceiling, his mind rewinding a quarter-century. "She had been doing more stage work at the time, so I didn't see her as much. But the last time I did, she told me she just couldn't do any of it anymore. It was so long ago; the exact details elude this old brain, but she had gained some weight and seemed overly stressed. I could tell she'd been crying—" He paused. "What kind of piece is it that you're writing? I wouldn't want to smear Geri's name in any way."

"Of course not," I said. "I actually knew Geri—she was someone I admired. Only after her death did I find out about her acting, which got me intrigued about her early life. It's a spec piece and may not even go into print. I just felt I had to do my part to honour her."

"I understand. Well, I don't know how much more I can tell you, other than give you a list of her acting credits. It's all in this folder, along with headshots and stills. It's not doing any good sitting in my filing cabinet; if you want it, it's yours."

I thanked him and picked up the folder. Temple escorted me to the door, and paused. "One person you might talk to is Ingrid Wright. Ingrid and Geri were inseparable in the eighties. I no longer represent Ingrid, but she still acts on the local stage. I've got her number around here someplace."

Minutes later, I sat in my car as rain drummed on the roof. It felt strange opening my friend's file and leafing through photos and newspaper clippings from a lifetime ago. Her old acting CV revealed that she started out in small theatre productions in the early eighties, and by mid-decade she was doing a lot of bit parts in movies and TV. Shampoo and beer commercials. In '89 she played Stella in the Alliance Theatre's *A Streetcar Named Desire*. Geri would have been twenty then, and every still of her, whether crying, laughing, or screaming, depicted an intensely beautiful woman.

Some of the stills showed her kissing or screaming at a handsome, dark-haired actor who played Stanley in *Streetcar*. The cast sheet told me his name was Henry Bourain. The way they gazed into each other's eyes, acting or no, made me think they either loved each other or wanted to kill each other.

There were more photos with Geri and Henry, at the after-parties, where all the debauched actors were hanging off each other. In one, Geri looked at Henry sidelong. 1989. Where was Grady then?

I called up Darci.

"Sloane! Thanks for calling me back."

I continued to leaf through the photos. "No problem. How are you doing?"

"Pretty shitty," she said. "I've been eating and smoking too much, and since that doesn't seem to be helping, I thought I'd give the healthy route a shot."

"I've got time this afternoon," I said.

"The rest of this week sucks for me. I've got a ton of lawyer stuff to deal with. How's Monday afternoon work for you, say, around four?"

Flipping open my Day-Timer, I crossed out Nancy Wilk's name and wrote Darci above it.

"Done. Where do you want to train now that you're no longer a Hillside member?"

She laughed. It made me happy to hear it. "I categorically hate all gyms. So I was thinking I'd like you to teach me to run fast enough to escape my problems. That works, right?"

"With mixed results," I said.

"I can't tell you how much I appreciate having you in my corner right now, Sloane."

"Anytime, Darci."

After all, your mother was there for me during *my* worst time.

On the night of May 12, 2014, at approximately 6:30 p.m., my sister made a meal of chicken strips and mashed potatoes. She opened a PBR for Phil and fixed herself a Stoli and soda. The kids had apple juice. The mashed potatoes, along with the apple juice and Phil's beer, were heavily laced with Halcion.

After dinner, it is surmised that Phil fell asleep, either on the couch or the bed. The kids conked out, perhaps on the living-room floor. Steph ran a warm bath and carried her son Charlie, two years old and sleeping, into the bathroom, where she took off his clothes and drowned him. Then she towel-dried him and dressed him in blue pyjamas, combed his hair, and put him in her bed. She repeated the process with Emma, dressing the baby in the fleecy pink jumper I'd bought for her shower earlier that year.

She then drained the water and ran a cold bath for Phil. Phil was a small guy, shorter than my sister and slight of build, weighing maybe one hundred and forty pounds. Even so, it would've taken some work for my sister to drag him into the bathroom, strip him naked, and put him in the tub. He wouldn't have felt a thing as she drowned him, and for good measure, slit his wrists.

Steph climbed into bed with her children, where she popped Halcion and sipped Stoli, and drifted away forever.

The whole experience of discovering the bodies thrust me into a waking coma, where I could function on a minimal level, yet retain no memory of the subsequent forty-eight hours. They took me to the station, but couldn't get a statement out of me. It was there that my partner came forward to tell them about the earlier incident, where he'd wanted to make a report, but I'd refused. The brass asked me if this was true, and they claim I nodded and eventually signed the statement.

Sam picked me up and stood by me every step of the way. I'm sure he said all the right things, but I didn't hear a word.

The funeral came and went. A week of catatonia turned into months of numbness. In the middle of this, someone tipped off the press that the police were negligent in saving the lives of two beautiful young children. Charlie and Emma's angelic faces made the front page of the Province, under the headline: **POLICE APATHY BLAMED FOR CHILDREN'S MURDERS.**

It didn't take them long to find me responsible. Sam wanted to hire a lawyer on my behalf, but I turned him down. I *wanted* punishment. My name was stomped on for weeks and I took every blow. Letters to the editor of the local papers showed that the public actually had sympathy for my case. But while Joe Public took pity on me, my brothers and sisters in law enforcement sought only to cover their asses. Especially when a police watchdog group discovered that I'd lied about my psychiatric past to get on the force in the first place.

Put me back on the front page.

Followed by a quiet resignation. An aborted career, ended in disgrace.

Back then, I wouldn't have minded someone putting me out of my misery. Sam couldn't handle me alone, and called my mother for help. At the time, I weighed a hundred pounds and was running the equivalent of three marathons a week. She and Sam had me locked up for two weeks of psychiatric observation that turned into two months.

In the hospital, I met a caring shrink named Dr. Northwood. We discovered that we'd both competed in the Boston Marathon the previous year. She asked me what I wanted to do most when I got out.

"I need to move," I croaked through my lithium fog. "I need fresh air."

"Gain ten pounds and I'll sign your release," she said. "And promise me you're going to stay on your meds."

"Promise," I said.

"You're going to get through this, Sloane. Do you believe me?"

Yeah, sure.

Upon my release several weeks later, my first visitor was Geri Harp.

CHAPTER 12

Friday, October 18

THE CULTCH IS AN AVANT-GARDE PERFORM-
ance space off Commercial Drive, a magnet for bohemians
and lefties. Being that it was close to Halloween, if you came
in costume, you got in half-price. So I donned a Zorro mask
and joined the box office queue of naughty Stormtroopers,
pirates, and zombie couples. I bought a ticket to *The Bitching
Hour,* starring Ingrid Wright, and found a seat near the back
of the theatre.

As I waited for the curtains to rise, something Kayvon
Temple had said about Geri's weight began to niggle at me.

Ingrid took to the stage as a black-haired, martini-
swilling, past-her-prime witch who kept casting spells to
transform her overweight and boorish couch potato husband into a desirable mate. A massive cauldron sat centre
stage, and each time the witch concocted a potion, hunched
Gollum-like figures rose from the floor and danced creep-
ily in the shadows. I sipped wine and watched. It was an
entertaining diversion that went on far too long. Finally, the

potbellied husband disappeared in a puff of smoke and out of the cauldron climbed a chiselled, ebony god with the voice of a neutered goat. The next incarnation was a biker mama who thought her pogo stick was a Harley. Finally, an eight-inch talking penis leapt from the cauldron with a voice like Morgan Freeman. The flying dildo chased Ingrid around the stage as she ran, jumping and shrieking, eventually tossing the dick back into the cauldron, which resulted in a pyrotechnic flash and a billow of smoke.

Looking around at one point, I realized I was alone amid a sea of costumed couples laughing their asses off. Gnawing doom set in, starting in my chest and creeping up my neck, into my skull and down to my limbs. My fingers and toes were losing sensation and my head felt like it was leaving my body. Closing my eyes before full panic set in, I focused on breathing. In for four, out for four. *This will pass. This will pass. It always does.*

When I opened my eyes again, the play was over and the theatre was mostly empty. Roughly half an hour had passed. Several minutes later I was back outside, drinking in the cold night air and feeling my limbs come back to life. I was already halfway up the street when I glanced back at the corner window of the theatre.

Ingrid Wright—now blonde—was having a drink at the concession bar and chatting with theatregoers.

I steeled my resolve and walked back inside. Sidling up to the bar, I ordered a glass of Cab Sauv. Ingrid was working on a Scotch. Rain plinked against the window to the left. Ingrid finished her drink and slipped into her coat.

She was about to leave when I said, "Excuse me, Ms. Wright?" Ingrid turned to me with a weary smile.

"I really enjoyed your performance tonight," I said, pulling out a photo and pen from my handbag. "Especially the part where the dick nearly chased you offstage. May I have your autograph?"

"Of course," she said, laughing. As she took the photo and pen, her smile fell away and she looked up at me. I had handed her an 8x10 of Ingrid, Geri, and Henry Bourain, circa 1989.

"Where did you get this?" she asked.

"I talked to Kayvon Temple yesterday," I said. "He said you and Geri Harp used to be good friends."

She looked down at the photo. "I heard that Geri passed. It broke my heart. God, look at us—when the hell was this taken?"

I gestured to the barstools. "Can I buy you a drink, Ingrid?"

More actors emerged from the dressing rooms down the hall. They called Ingrid to join them.

"I'll meet you there," she said, then turned back to me. "What's this about?"

"My name is Sandra Donnelly, and I'm a freelancer for *The Province*. I'm doing a piece on Geri Harp's life."

She set the photo back on the bar. "It's been a very long time since I've had *anything* to do with her life."

I sipped some wine. "That's the part of the story I'm stuck on," I said. Thirty years ago. Being her best friend, I was hoping you could shed some light—"

"Look, we were never best friends. I don't think I can help you."

I pushed the photo closer to her. "Look at the two of you in that photo. Must have been heady days back then. Why did Geri turn her back on acting so suddenly? I mean, it must have been a huge part of her life, something she loved—could you see yourself doing something like that? Just dropping out?"

"The reality is, this is an unstable business that attracts unstable people," she said. "Some just can't hack it and quit."

"What about her husband? Did Grady pressure her to quit, do you think? He seems like a pretty buttoned-down guy. Maybe he didn't like his wife-to-be getting all hot and heavy with other men on stage. And off."

Ingrid paused, sizing me up. "I wouldn't know. Look, Geri just quit. One day she severed all ties with everything and everyone in the business. She left the city for a while. Her family was loaded; she didn't need to work."

"That must've hurt, to be cut out of her life like that."

"It didn't surprise me. Geri was always tempestuous. It was all or nothing with her. As I recall, Grady was away in Asia doing business for a long time, and when we weren't working we'd be partying our faces off in clubs."

"So she just wanted to clean up and start over?"

"I suppose."

I pointed to Henry Bourain in the photo. "How about Henry here?" I asked. "Was he one of the reasons she left?"

"What do I know? Let's just say Geri needed a lot of *attention* from men."

"And she got that from Henry? You said Grady was out of the picture at the time, so—"

"I really have to go," she said. "Good luck."

Ingrid opened the door and swirled outside. I gulped back my wine, and followed.

"What happened to Henry?" I called after her, squinting against the howling wind and spitting rain.

Ingrid turned back to me with challenging eyes. "Henry's dead."

"How did that happen?"

"Broken heart," she said. "Plus a pint of bourbon and a fast car."

"When?"

Ingrid scoffed and shook her head. She pulled out a cigarette and lit it. "For a journalist, you haven't done much homework. What did you say your name was again?"

"Who broke his heart?" I asked. "Geri?"

"It was another lifetime," she said, turning again.

"She was pregnant with his baby, wasn't she? Grady didn't know. Is that why she left, to carry the baby to term in privacy?"

A Range Rover pulled up to the curb, its headlights illuminating the tautness of Ingrid's facial muscles.

"What happened to the baby, Ingrid?" I asked. She opened the door and climbed in. "Did Grady find out?"

"Have a nice night," Ingrid said coldly, then shut the door.

As I walked through the rain, my phone pinged with a text from Wayne: **Dug up more dirt.**

I texted back: **So did I.**

CHAPTER 13

I SLIPPED MY ZORRO MASK BACK ON JUST before stepping through the door of the No5 Orange. Bass from a Jay-Z song vibrated through the floor and up my legs. The steroidal doorman smiled and raised his eyebrows as I handed him ten for cover. A woman arriving alone at a strip bar can mean only one thing: she digs naked women. Men dig women who dig naked women. Last time I was in "the Five," it was to bust some bikers who were unloading Smith & Wessons out the back door.

As my eyes adjusted to the frenetic purple and red strobe lights in the packed club, I saw a leggy dancer undulating in nothing but red devil horns and white, feathery wings. She flexed the muscles of her coppery bubble butt in time to the music. In gyno row, guys hooted and clinked bottles on the edge of the stage, which bore the traditional brass pole and glassed-in shower area. A clear Lucite ladder ran from the far end of the stage up into a square trap door between two ceiling speakers.

Off to the left, some rednecks shot pool and eyed me up as I passed. Aside from a table of butch women, every seat and booth was filled with males of every stripe, from crusty-crotched letches to businessmen sealing deals by buying each other blow jobs in the "lap dancing" rooms upstairs.

Scanning the shadowy booths on the raised section to the right, I recognized Wayne's brawny forearms and thick torso. A buxom blonde massage girl stood behind him, kneading his traps, her tits resting atop his head. His white T-shirt said *Don't Mess with Texas,* and he wore a John Deere ball cap and tinted glasses that made him look like a perv, but I knew there was a micro camera built into the frame.

"What's up, Wayne?" I asked, sliding into the booth beside him.

He cocked an eyebrow at me. "Lose the mask," he said. "I'm on the job. Don't need the attention."

I obliged. The song ended, and so did the massage. Wayne slipped the girl two twenties, and she kissed him on the cheek. She asked if I wanted a massage, too: "Ladies get two songs for one."

"Another time," I said.

"Later, Dave," she said to Wayne, before swivelling away to hustle the next table.

"Now I see where your leftover track money goes, *Dave,*" I said. A tan messenger bag sat on the floor beside his chair.

Wayne waved over a waitress with purple hair and full-sleeve tats. "Shot o' Jameson and another Canadian, darlin'. What're you drinking, Sandra?"

"What do you have for wine?"

"Bring her a Canadian," he told her, and she headed off. "This look like a place to sip vino?" he said.

"Who's the mark?" I asked. "One of the suits across the room?"

"Guy went upstairs to get his knob polished, like he's done every night this week. He's been up there twenty minutes. Weird thing is, his wife who hired me is hotter than half the broads in here."

The stripper on stage finished her act and climbed the ladder, disappearing to a chorus of whistles and monosyllabic yells. Our drinks arrived. I slipped the waitress twenty on sixteen-fifty, and told her to keep it. She left, and I leaned closer to Wayne.

"I believe Geri got pregnant nearly thirty years ago by an actor named Henry Bourain, who died soon after. At the time, Grady was doing business out of the country for an extended period. I think the pregnancy plus Henry's death drove her give up acting."

"There's no record of her having any other children," he said. "Maybe she had an abortion."

"I don't think so," I said, mentioning the pro-life literature I saw on her bookshelf. "Her agent said she gained weight just before she gave up acting, and her friend Ingrid said she left town for a while. I think she may have carried the baby to term somewhere else."

"What makes you think that?"

"It's what I'd have done if I had means but didn't believe in abortion—and didn't want my family or fiancé knowing. Can we dig deeper?"

"Medical records are tricky to obtain, even through legal channels. And if she did have the baby somewhere else all those years ago? Good luck. Hell, maybe she miscarried, who knows. I suggest you keep things more recent, like her autopsy report. Which I did procure. Say 'thank you, Dave.'"

We toasted. "Thank you, Dave."

Wayne slammed his Jameson and we drank.

"You're welcome," he said. "Geri's blood alcohol level was point oh-nine when she died, and she had Ambien and fentanyl in her system. It was the fentanyl that killed her, and it was in her water bottle."

"Kai deals that shit," I said.

"So does every other dealer these days. Or it sneaks into other street drugs. Geri *did* have a history of alcohol and substance abuse *and* she worked in the Downtown Eastside."

"Okay, then why the Ambien? A relatively mild sleeping pill. And point oh-nine?" I mused, doing mental math. "For her size, that'd be around four or five glasses of wine. That water bottle in her car would hold maybe two glasses."

"Maybe she'd been warming up at home," he offered. "Her daughter reported another empty bottle at home."

"But not with fentanyl in it."

"Right," he said. "I don't imagine a person could drive very straight after dosing up on an opioid a hundred times more potent than heroin. Mixing it with wine is not the pre-ferred choice of addicts, but it would still do the trick for the recreational user, if they were so inclined."

"Okay, but she didn't do that with the Ambien. It's not consistent. Did it raise any suspicions with the police?"

He gave me a knowing glance as he sipped his beer. "In the absence of a suicide note, and given her history, cause of death has been ruled *accidental*."

The waitress passed by. Wayne pointed down at our empty drinks and held up two fingers. A minute later our libations were replenished.

"What else do we have?" I asked.

"Grady's had trouble with Canada Revenue on three occasions regarding undeclared income from his Chinese businesses. Lucky for him his passport's not Chinese or he'd face a firing squad. He has factories over there that make the kind of cheap shit they sell in dollar stores all over North America. Before the market tanked, his net worth sat at ninety million. His pocketbook's taken a beating, but he's still living like a king. I got into the wrong business." He paused to admire a passing pink fishnet-clad dancer. "Another thing," he continued, "other than the house, and a mutual chequing account for day-to-day expenses, Geri and Grady's finances were completely separate. Different lawyers, too. Not uncommon when you're talking about that kind of wealth. Individuals become like corporations. One of them sinks, it doesn't drown the other."

"What was Geri's net worth?"

"Sixty million plus. Old money. You never knew how rich your friend was?"

"I knew her family was wealthy, but she wasn't one to flaunt it."

Wayne's eyes moved to the staircase by the DJ booth. A tall, Black dancer, wearing a sheer white negligee, led a reedy, fifty-ish man down the stairs. She pushed him into a plush sofa and straddled his lap. As she cooed in his ear, his eyes grew dopey.

"Poor bastard," Wayne muttered.

"What about Dogger?" I asked.

"Five years ago, Peretti was accused of raping a tennis player named Yvette Cherlenko. Charges were dropped and Cherlenko retired from the tennis circuit shortly after."

"Charmer," I said.

A pair of neon pink heels descended the ladder, followed by the willowy legs of a blonde in a skin-tight latex jumpsuit that matched the shoes. I wondered where these women would be in five years. Where would *I* be in five years?

"You want a burger or something?" Wayne asked. "You're lookin' a little *frail*."

I drained my beer. "Already ate."

He reached down and handed me the files. "One more thing. Yvette claimed Peretti drugged her before he tied her up and got rough. Her name is Parsons now, lives in the Valley."

Back in my Jeep, I opened the envelope, and a well-worn badge slid into my hand. Sandra Donnelly, Major Crimes. So long as it wasn't scrutinized by other law enforcement types, it would pass muster.

When I got home, Eclipse was bushy-tailed and yowling at a raccoon that was trying to claw through the living-room window. The raccoon stared me down with bandit eyes. I clapped my hands and the animal sauntered away.

CHAPTER 14

Saturday, October 19

YVETTE PARSONS OPENED THE DOWNSTAIRS door of her townhouse before I had a chance to ring. She held an infant in the crook of her arm. Tall and blonde, she had the broad shoulders of a former athlete. Now she'd grown hips to match, but on her frame she carried them well. She wore a yellow Juicy Couture sweatsuit with baby-puke stains on the chest.

"Yvette," I said, "I'm Sandra." She glanced at the badge hanging from the lanyard around my neck. "Thanks for meeting on short notice."

She offered a tense smile and led me inside. I could hear kids playing video games: bullets, bombs, and screams.

"Don't bother taking off your boots," she said, walking upstairs and scissoring her legs over the mesh child barrier. We took seats at the round oak table in the kitchen, which bore the typical mess of an overburdened working-class family. Crayon marks on the walls, a half-folded pile of laundry on the table, Cheerios on the floor. "Excuse the mess," she said.

I smiled. "It's nothing. What's his name?"

"Todd Thomas," she said. "Do you have any?" She walked into the living room and set him into a crib.

"A big black cat," I said. "About all I can handle right now."

"So what's Dogger done?" she asked, fussing about in the kitchen, absently wiping the counter.

"Like I said on the phone, I'm investigating a suspicious death, and he was connected to the deceased. I got your name from another investigator, who told me what Dogger did to you. He said Dogger was arrested, but you later dropped the charges."

"If I could go back, I wouldn't have," she said, her voice cracking. "I was young, dumb, and scared. Tennis had been my entire life from the time I was eight. I trained five hours a day and turned semi-pro when I was fifteen. I'd never had a serious boyfriend. My dad was my coach and he told me I had to stay focused on my career, turn pro, win some big matches, and then the sponsorship money would roll in. My life was all mapped out."

Yvette looked around her townhouse with the resigned eyes of someone who had aimed for much more, of product endorsements and a winter retreat on Maui, maybe. "And then I met *Dogger*," she said, making the name sound like a tumour. "I'd seen him at the tournaments, strutting around like a peacock. He had a wicked reputation, and all the girls loved him. His career was on fire and he'd just turned pro. I was eight years younger and had a *huge* crush on him. He came up to me at an awards dinner and told me he'd been watching my legs all season. The next night he took me out, got me hammered, and brought me back to his place.

I passed out and next thing I knew, I was cuffed to his bed by my wrists and ankles. I told him to stop." She shook her head as though trying to eradicate the memory. "He didn't."

"You told the police he drugged you?"

She closed her eyes for several seconds and opened them again. "All of a sudden it was like I couldn't control my movements or think straight, like I was drifting in and out of consciousness."

"And not just from the booze?"

"I hadn't had much alcohol before that, but I knew it was different than being drunk."

"Did he hurt you?"

"He put a belt around my neck and choked me until I nearly blacked out. I thought I was going to die. I had marks on my wrists and ankles for weeks. The police took photos."

"Did he wear a condom?"

"Yes, he used a condom—to rape me. A true fuckin' gentleman."

"How long did you wait to go to the police?"

She seemed distracted by a hangnail on her left index finger and picked at it. "Two days," she said. "I was confused and ashamed. I didn't want to admit it even happened."

"And in that two days, did he attempt to contact you?"

"No."

"Did that upset you?"

"Did what upset me?"

"That he didn't call."

"It upset me that he drugged and *raped* me."

"Of course. Did your parents know?"

She nodded, face tight, looking down.

"How did they react?"

"My dad was managing me. I was on the verge of signing a contract with Wilson. He told me that if it went to court it would stir up a shit-storm of controversy around my name and no one would touch me. That's when I dropped the charges."

The baby began to mewl. Yvette ignored him and stared out the kitchen window with distant eyes. "Two months later, I tore my ACL so bad I could never play again at that level. And that asshole went on to win more tournaments. I've been in therapy ever since it happened, and I don't think I'll ever get back to normal. He should be in jail. I hope you send him there."

CHAPTER 15

Sunday, October 20

THE FOLLOWING DAY WAS COLD AND OVERCAST when I drove to Capilano Mall and parked in the upper garage. I walked over to Hertz and rented their cheapest car, a grey Chevy Spark, a car that made me feel soulless and invisible as I drove back to Lonsdale.

From Starbucks, I got a coffee and a bottle of water, then drove and parked a half-block from the entrance to Dogger's garage. I got out and stood near the shrubs by the gate. Several minutes later, the gate opened. A Range Rover pulled out and I strolled in. Dogger's Porsche was parked one level down. I walked back out and was just getting into my rental when I spotted the hairdresser, Nazreen Farooz, walking across Lonsdale toward the building's front entrance, wearing a blue ball cap and mirrored aviators. She disappeared inside.

At 11:34 a.m. came the rev of a sports car and the squeal of tires. The gate slid open and the Porsche drove out, Dogger and Nazreen inside. It turned south on Lonsdale and hung a right on 3rd. I started the Nissan and followed.

The Porsche turned right on Chesterfield, then zig-zagged west to Jones, past fields where kids were playing soccer.

I was right behind the Porsche at the lights by Carson Graham High School. The light turned green, and Dogger ripped left on West 23rd, then right on Westview. Once he hit the eastbound entrance to the Upper Levels Highway, he was *gone*, roaring up and passing a semi-trailer and veering into the left lane. By the time I got around the semi, the Porsche had weaved past several SUVs and a Mercedes. The Spark was gutless; when I passed the first SUV, the Porsche was already a distant blue blip.

Taking the next exit, I doubled back to Dogger's building. In my pocket were tools I hadn't used in over six years.

A middle-aged woman walked up the steps to the front of the building. I quickly got out carrying my coffee and pretended to fumble in my pockets for keys. The lady smiled and held the door for me. I smiled and thanked her.

We waited by the elevator and idly discussed how quickly the seasons seem to change now. Out of the corner of my eye, situated above a large, gilded mirror, I spotted an opaque, black bubble housing a security camera. The doors opened and the woman held her key fob to the console where it beeped before she hit the third-floor button. I made a show of trying to adjust my bags to get my keys.

"What floor?" she asked.

"Uh, six please."

She tapped the fob again and hit six. "Water facing?"

"Mountains," I said. "Almost as good."

The woman got off on the third floor and we wished each other a great day. Too easy. That changed when I arrived at

#603. The deadbolt was secure, which didn't pose a major problem. The octagonal green Alarmshield sticker above the peephole also didn't overly concern me, as Dogger didn't strike me as the type to set his alarm every time he left. It was the camera bubble in the corner of the hall—identical to the one in the lobby—that gave me pause. Even though there was a good chance no one was watching the camera monitor in real time, I wasn't about to take the risk of spending the next thirty seconds picking a lock.

I took the stairs down to the lobby and back out to my car.

Nazreen's address proved to be only several minutes away, in the Beaconhill Apartments on West Keith. Beaconhill was a twelve-storey, ill-maintained, thirty-year-old building streaked with green mould on the upper balconies.

Someone was moving out; boxes propped open the front doors leading into a stale-smelling lobby. I stepped aside for two movers carrying an armoire through the doors. Groceries in hand, I found the stairwell and jogged up. The eighth-floor hall smelled no better than the lobby. Suite #806 was at the far end of the corridor. I knocked and listened. Five seconds later, I knocked again.

The lock was a typical 5-pin Dexter, and the deadbolt was not engaged. Not a camera in sight. I set my coffee cup down and pulled on latex gloves. I took out my tools and crouched down. Using my right hand, I inserted the short tension lever into the keyhole. My left hand held the small, silver S-rake that had popped more than a hundred locks in its day. I also had the short hook for backup, but that was merely for insurance. I poked the tip inside the steel slit, confidently flicked all five pins, and *snick,* I was in.

To the right was a small and messy bathroom. Hair and skin products, hair dryers, brushes, nail polish, and a box of tampons took up every inch of counter space. Hair extensions hung behind the door. The brown-encrusted toilet bowl looked like it had never been cleaned.

Opposite the bathroom was the bedroom, with an unmade bed and a view of Grouse Mountain. The room smelled of sex and weed. The small closet was packed to overflowing with jeans, dresses, and tops. Lots of Louis Vuitton and Prada. Hanging neatly in the corner of the closet were two wide-necked bodybuilder sweatshirts. Gold's Gym, XXL. Too big for Dogger.

The kitchen was small with worn linoleum and scorch marks on the green counters. Sink full of dishes. The fridge held five cans of Stella Artois, two pre-made Safeway salads, a carton of egg whites, and a wheel of Gouda. Beside the butter tray were three large vials of testosterone. In the freezer was a bottle of Grey Goose and half a bar of dark chocolate. I took the bar and munched on it as I walked into the living room. It brought back teenage memories of pillaging neighbour's refrigerators during my B&E escapades. Chocolate always tastes better when it belongs to other people.

Several framed photos on the far wall drew my eye. I nibbled another chunk of chocolate and stepped closer. One shot was of a young Naz with an older Persian couple, her parents presumably. Another was of her partying with some girlfriends in the back of a limo. Also, a snap of her smooching with some big, bald guy. I looked closer. It certainly wasn't Andy "Dogger" Peretti, but it *was* the cop from the day I found Geri. Cyrus Ghorbani.

Ghorbani was Naz's juiced-up cop boyfriend.

Dogger was screwing Naz.

Dogger had been screwing Geri.

Dogger liked playing with fire.

To those who killed me.

I sat down on the couch to think about what this could mean. Other than rampant infidelity, there was still nothing tangible tying anything to Geri, who seemed more and more dead as each day went by. Outside the window, gulls and crows wheeled and swooped against the darkening sky.

On a round, glass coffee table sat a laptop. The screen showed Nazreen and Ghorbani, smiling, white-clad, with palm trees and ocean in the background. Beside the laptop was a Visa bill, showing that Naz owed $18,436.89 and had a penchant for Holt Renfrew and Nordstrom. She was late in her payments.

Voices in the hall bounced me to my feet. I ran to the door and peeped out. A young Asian couple walked past to another apartment. Darting back to the kitchen, I slipped a can of Stella into my grocery bag and left, making sure to lock the door on my way out.

CHAPTER 16

Monday, October 21

I PULLED INTO THE HARP DRIVEWAY AND parked by the fountain, same place I had all the times I'd come to visit Geri. I had to pause for a second and remember why I was here. My friend was gone forever, but her daughter wasn't, and she was the one who needed help now.

The moment I climbed out of my Jeep, the silver Audi slid into the driveway and parked. Darci climbed from the driver's seat, wearing a form-fitting orange top and black tights. She held an envelope in her hand.

"God, I need this," she said. "I feel disgusting."

"You look great," I said, giving her a hug. Over her shoulder I got a flash of Geri slumped in the seat, eyes open, face deep blue.

Darci caught me looking at the car. "Must be nearly as weird for you seeing this car as it is for me to drive it."

"Kind of."

She pointed through the window of my Jeep. "I just noticed you have the same dream catcher as my mom."

I nodded. "You remember Crystal, the girl that Yuri was pimping years ago?"

"How could I forget? The day I met you, you took the bastard down hard. Super badass."

"Actually, it nearly got me killed, going after him alone like that. Anyway, after Crystal got clean, her mother came down and gave the dream catchers to your mom and me. They kind of symbolized our friendship. Back then your mom drove a Prius."

"The Prius is still in the garage." Gesturing back toward the Audi, she said, "Dad gave her this car on her last birthday, but she hardly ever drove it, especially not to the shelter."

"How's your dad doing?"

"The same. It's almost like a bad cliché: wife dies and businessman soldiers on, burying himself in his work. If Dad grieves at all, he does it on his own time."

A pre-winter wind arrived like a slap in the face. Darci handed me the envelope. Inside was a crisp stack of hundreds.

"Cash is king," she said. "Two thousand for twenty sessions. That is, *if* you'll take this sad sack on as a regular client."

"That's too much. I can't—"

"Non-negotiable," she said. "You won't win an argument about money with me."

I zipped the envelope into the back pouch of my running jacket. "Okay then."

We walked up the driveway. "How much does Hillside pay you? If you don't mind me asking?"

"The club charges eighty an hour and I get sixty of that, so seventy-five percent. Pretty standard."

"Those assholes could pay a lot more. I was born here, so I'm allowed to say that. You should be pocketing at least a hundred. Collectively they spend more on Botox than the

GDP of some African nations. West Van is such a phony bubble, I can't stand it sometimes. That's why I got a place in Railtown. My dad calls it a rancid hovel, but it's *my* rancid hovel."

I laughed. We jogged down the street, turning right onto Bear Lane. From there, we hung another right on Beacon Lane. I asked her how school was going.

"I got my MBA this year, along with my CA licence. Accounting is boring, but it's important to know where your money's going."

"You don't mess around."

"That's what skipping three grades of high school gets you: fucked up, zero friends, but out into the real world that much *faster*."

"I remember your mother saying she worried about that. She also always said how proud she was of you."

"That must have been a while ago," she said. "She wasn't overly big on praise near the end."

Choosing my words carefully, I said, "The last time she spoke, your mother seemed to have a lot on her mind."

"No doubt."

"New Ways?"

"Probably. It's grown a ton. Of all the non-profits in the Downtown Eastside, none of them come close to providing the services we do. My mom would've called that bragging, but it's true."

Passing the Lighthouse Park sign, we stepped onto the trail and into the shadows of the forest. I decided to switch gears abruptly. "Dogger seemed kind of strange at the reception."

She glanced over.

"You can talk to me about anything, Darci," I said.

"That's part of the reason I contacted you. You were always a good listener. Remember when you used to train me and I would chat your ear off about sex and stuff? You always gave me the straight goods. I could never talk to my mother about stuff like that."

"Why not?"

We started up a light incline, our feet dodging roots and wet rocks.

"I loved my mom, but she was a stress-case. If things didn't go her way, she'd completely lose her shit."

We veered left onto the Valley of the Giants Trail, with its massive stands of old-growth red cedar. Darci proved an aggressive runner, strong thighs gunning her up the steep sections. Going downhill, I suggested she take shorter, quicker strides and land on the balls of her feet to minimize impact. For twenty minutes we picked up the pace and ran silently, fluid and focused, our breath pluming the air before us. As we passed the lighthouse, Darci took the lead and sprinted ahead.

At the Juniper Point cliffs, she stopped, gasping for breath, hands on her knees, her cheeks sporting rose blossoms. I stretched my quads. "You're not even breathing hard," she said. "This is nothing for you, huh?"

"I've been at it a while."

"You used to race, right?"

A harsh north wind strafed through the trees. "Used to."

"Why not anymore?" she asked. Mimicking my stretch, her free hand grasped a weather-stripped arbutus tree clinging tenuously to the cliff edge. I guided her back a few paces, to safety.

I gestured toward the crashing surf below. "Long way down."

She nodded, squinting at the dark grey horizon. "I wonder where she is now."

Her face tightened as she tried to hold herself together. I put my hand on her shoulder.

"Ten days ago she was here and now she's not," she said. "Where do you think she is? Do you think she's out there somewhere?"

"I don't know."

"You've never thought about it?"

"I've thought about it."

"Sorry. My head's in a weird place these days."

"My sister and her kids are the reason I don't race anymore," I said.

Darci looked at me, her mouth partway open like she was about to say something but changed her mind.

"When I was released from psych," I said, "your mom was there for me. She got me back on track, and she's the whole reason I got the job at Hillside. She also encouraged me to race again, but the few times I did, I'd see their faces in the crowd by the finish line. Steph, Charlie, and Emma, just staring at me. A few of my final races, I actually veered off just before the finish. I just kept running. People thought I was nuts."

Darci looked me in the eye. "You know the people I hate the most? The ones who say, 'I know how you feel.' They're fucking liars. But you *do* know, Sloane. You *know* what it is to lose people you love. And I'm really sorry you had to be the one to find my mom."

"They're out there somewhere," I said. "I just know they're not here."

"And they're not coming back."

I shook my head, and in that moment, I came close to telling her everything I'd been doing. Only, my voice didn't work. When she took my hand, I closed my eyes and saw my sister's face.

* * *

Through the windshield, the silver sickle moon appeared ready to fall from the sky and impale the downtown sky-scrapers. I was about to pass the 15th Street exit on the Upper Levels, when impulse guided my wheel to the right.

Two minutes later, I was at Hillside. Beneath a street lamp near the tennis bubbles sat the blue Boxster.

I parked beside it and walked into the tennis depart-ment. A different receptionist from before was on the phone and paid me no heed. I took a seat in the waiting area and picked up a tennis magazine. In a spread for this past year's Wimbledon, under the heading RISING STARS, there was a photo of a tall Valkyrie that made me think of Yvette Parsons.

From the courts came the steady *thock* of balls, the squeak of tennis shoes, grunts, and murmuring voices. Several les-sons wrapped up; coaches and students trickled through the room in tennis whites. I heard a woman's laughter and a man's voice. A moment later, Dogger and a sable-haired Barbie-type walked past me and into his office, where they continued to get their flirt on for a couple more minutes. He kissed her cheek and she batted her eyes and left with a smile on her face, wedding ring winking like a disco ball.

Through the glass, Dogger unselfconsciously yanked off his shorts revealing tight boxers featuring a Mexican skull motif right atop his junk. We made eye contact as he pulled on a black-and-white Adidas tracksuit. He twisted his white ball cap backwards and walked out of the office, cocksure smile on his face as we locked eyes.

"What's up? *Sloane*, right?"

You know damn well it is. I nodded. "I was thinking about booking a tennis lesson, but then I realized I have no interest in the sport."

"Good thing, because I'm booked up."

Sure you are. "How about a drink then?"

CHAPTER 17

AS SOON AS WE ENTERED THE RIVERSIDE PUB, a squalid, blue-collar dive near the Ironworkers Memorial, the first thing the female bartender said was: "Your credit's no good here, Dogger. Cash only."

"Pam, you know how I hate paying for drinks," he said. "That's why I brought this fetching lady along tonight."

Fifteen minutes later, Dogger slammed his second shot of Patrón, while I nursed a rancid-tasting glass of house white. I asked him how long he had been at Hillside.

"Long enough," he said.

"I've been there five years," I said. "And I never even knew your name."

His look was incredulous. *"Really?"*

"Did you know mine?"

He leaned in close enough to bite me. "I saw you around. You always seemed aloof. Thought maybe you played for the other team. Not that I have a problem with that."

"I'm not aloof," I said.

"Maybe intense is a better word. But then you used to be a cop, so—"

"In another lifetime."

"Really? 'Cause you kind of still *seem* like a cop."

"How many cops have you known?"

Seemed like when he didn't want to reply, Dogger's default was to grin. We held each other's gaze until it got tiresome and I turned away.

His eyes flicked to the mirror, where behind us, two amply endowed cougars racked up balls for a game of pool. He was practically salivating, a teenage boy in a man's body, at the mercy of a sex drive he couldn't control. That was my in.

"I was looking at a magazine in the Tennis Centre," I said, "and couldn't help but notice that female tennis players are way more attractive now than they were, say, twenty years ago? Back then, they looked like East German truck drivers. What's up with that?"

He pushed back from the bar and stood. "Hold that thought." At first I thought he was going to go hit on the cougs, but then he walked the other way, past the flashing Keno screen and cigarette vending machines, disappearing through the door marked ME, because some joker had blacked out the N.

The house white was crap, so I drained it and asked Pam if they had a different vintage.

"No."

"A Corona then. And another shot for him."

Dogger returned with a bigger grin and brighter eyes.

"Feel better?" I asked.

"Women are evolving," he said, tilting his head from side to side to stretch his neck.

"Huh?"

Our drinks arrived. Dogger clapped. "Pam, you are a goddess in a slop house." He winked at the bartender. "Who says you only get one shot in life?"

We raised our drinks.

"To Geri," I said, and took a sip.

He paused for a second before knocking back his shot. "To Geri," he said quietly.

"You were about to tell me about the evolution of my kind."

"Your kind is getting better looking with each generation. I mean, your mom is probably a fine-looking woman, maybe even turned some heads in her day. But not like you do."

"Yeah, right."

"It's true, you're just too aloof to notice the attention."

"I thought intense was the better word."

"No. Now that I've thought about it, aloof seems to fit."

"Whatever. I think it's just that standards have changed. Or maybe it's just better makeup and fashion and breast implants."

He shook his head. "Before photographs, there were paintings. During the Renaissance, artists loved to paint fat chicks with homely faces because that's the best they had back then, but the artists were likely gay and would rather have a nude dude in front of them. I'm not judging; these are facts."

He swiped his nose with the back of his hand. "Jumping ahead in time, I think of old black and white photos from my grandparents' era, and guess what?"

"They never smiled or showed cleavage?"

He raised a finger. "Wouldn't matter if they had, because back then, every woman without exception was butt-fucking-ugly. Sorry if that sounds cruel, but I don't even know how guys performed. Viagra wasn't even around."

"I guess it was more about the survival of the line. Families needed eight kids because half died from war and plague."

He was too enraptured by own his talking jag for that to even register. "With the advent of film, women made an aesthetic quantum leap. All of a sudden, out of nowhere we had Marlene Dietrich, Kim Novak, Brigitte Bardot, Raquel Welch, Sophia Loren, Pam Grier, et cetera. Where the hell did all these sirens come from in only a few generations? Jump further forward and along came Kim Basinger, Halle Berry, Charlize Theron, Scarlett Johansson. Now every other woman on the streets of downtown Vancouver is the next Emma Stone. It's like a beauty virus, and it's fucking *rad*. The next generation will be better still."

"The same could be said for men," I said. "Men have gotten better looking."

He shook his head. "Not even close. There've always been handsome men and average men and ugly men. Best any of 'em can do is work out and dress better, but men peaked a long time ago. We'll probably be rendered obsolete at some point, but until then"—he clinked his bottle against mine—"just gotta enjoy the ride, baby."

I looked him in the eye. "To those who killed me."

He nearly choked on his beer. "What?"

"It's a line from an old Sophia Loren movie," I said. "I like her. She's one of those full-figured *real* women, like Geri ... was."

He removed his eyes from mine and tilted back his beer.

"Do you miss her?" I asked.

His eyes darkened. "What's your deal?"

I watched him. "I found her dead in her car on last Thursday. We were supposed to have lunch the following day.

I'm having a tough time getting my head around that. *That's my fucking deal.*"

He said nothing.

I took a deep breath, let out a sigh. "I also went for a run with Darci today. Just before I saw you, actually. She seems to be doing well, considering. She told me her dad's kind of withdrawn into his work. You heard from him?"

He studied the varieties of bourbon on the shelf above the bar. "I think he's out of the country. I don't really know."

"Kind of strange. Your wife just dies and it's business as usual."

"Life goes on."

"How long were you and Geri fucking?"

He drew back like I had slapped him.

"Look," I said, "I've had an affair with a club member, too, and when I saw you at the Harp house that day, it was like I was watching myself."

He swiped his nostrils again. "Anything you *think* you saw was a little something called *grief.* Someone you've known for years suddenly dies, it tends to be upsetting."

I raised my hands. "All right, but you will admit: you've got a certain Lothario reputation around the club."

"Is that why you're buying me drinks, to ask about my *reputation?*"

"We've all got one." I waved the bartender over and told her I was switching to shots like my pal here.

Dogger checked a text on his phone. "How come you gave up the career in law enforcement? You seem so *good* at it."

Our drinks arrived. "Fucked the wrong married staff sergeant when I was on duty. My third such infraction." Pam raised her eyebrows. I leaned closer and nudged Dogger. "I'm what you call a repeat offender."

His leg touched mine. His smile was back, part predatory, part proprietary.

"It's just more fun when they're married," I said. "You must agree."

He raised an eyebrow.

"Next round's on you, stud," I said. "Actually, from here on out, I've decided to make *you* pay."

We toasted and did our shots. The fire spread through my chest and into my limbs.

"So, besides married, what's your type?" I asked.

He laughed. "What do you think?"

"I don't think you have a type, but I think you're a pathological playa. Married women are drawn to your pseudocharm because you give them the attention they aren't getting from their hubbies. You like married women because the perks are sweet and yet they can't tie you down, allowing you to keep the upper hand. Judging by your earlier diatribe on the female form, I'd wager that you're also addicted to sex. How'd I do?"

He chuckled silently, but his eyes turned guarded as he stood. "Gotta get some money for the drinks." He walked toward the ATM in the corner, glancing at the cougars as he passed. The women appraised him by raising their microplucked eyebrows. He withdrew cash, crumpled the receipt, and tossed it toward the garbage can. It bounced off the edge and ended up under a table. He winked at me and headed for the washroom again.

The bar had filled up: construction workers, pinball-playing punks, Keno-addicted pensioners, and representatives of the Squamish Nation.

Dogger returned, and we got down to serious drinking. I matched him shot for shot and beer for beer, and at some indefinable point, crossed the line toward oblivion. He danced off to the washroom every twenty minutes, more or less nullifying his booze consumption. I ordered a burger and fries and ate half, ending up with ketchup on my jacket. I went to the washroom to wash it off and splash cold water on my face.

When I returned to the bar, Dogger was chatting up the cougars and checking a text. He waved me over and introduced me to Rachel and Blue. "They agree with me, that they are, without a doubt, finer specimens than their mamas, and certainly their grandmamas."

Leaning in close, I spoke through the corner of my mouth, "What about their *daughters?*"

"Let's play some pool!" he sang.

We teamed up against the cougs, who, for all their bling, eyeliner, and double-D cannons, were surprisingly shy. Both were recent divorcees and a little uncomfortable being back on the market. I was so shitty at pool that I actually missed the cue ball several times, but I did manage to sink several of the ladies' balls. Dogger's peacocky prowess made up for my lack, as he danced and strutted around the table, cleanly sinking some behind-the-back shots. At one point, mid-game, he engaged Blue in a little grinding dance. I saw two white balls where there was one. Shot. Missed. Fell on the table.

"Fucking fuck," I said.

Dogger spun away from Blue and pressed himself into me from behind, his cheek next to mine. "You're trying too hard," he whispered. "Breathe in, breathe out, focus, shoot. Simple."

I shot. Sunk one of the striped balls, forgetting we were solids. He laughed, and the next thing I knew, the game was over and we were on the dance floor, just us and the cougs, rocking out to Bowie's "Suffragette City." The music went from Bowie to Metallica to Springsteen to Sir Mix-a-Lot. Dogger bought a round of kamikazes for the group. We knocked them back and cheered, just as Cyndi Lauper's "Girls Just Want to Have Fun" came on. The cougs went nuts. Blue and Dogger bounced off to the washroom and left me dancing with Rachel who leaned in and told me I had a great ass. She tried to kiss me, but her breath was sour so I couldn't get into it.

Ten minutes later, Dogger and Blue returned. He had lipstick on his earlobe. He also couldn't take his eyes off me as I rolled out my best dance moves. During a thunderous drum solo on Green Day's "Holiday," I grabbed him and kissed him. One of his hands went to my lower back; the other snaked behind my neck, holding me while he slipped his tongue in my mouth.

I opened my eyes to find the cougs standing jealously off to the side. Neil Young warbled from the speakers. "Let's jet!" Dogger yelled.

"You sure you don't want the cougs?" I asked. "Blue seems to have a thing for you."

"Divorcees give off a sad vibe," he said. "I hate being sad."

We ran out into the freezing night. Dogger beeped his Porsche and actually held the door for me. When we were both inside, he crushed my lips with his, stealing my breath. He kissed my neck. Something buzzed repeatedly, and suddenly he was checking his phone.

"Shit, Sloane, I'm sorry but I have to go."

I tried to peek at his phone, but he put it away. "Who's the chick?"

"I forgot about a prior engagement." He kissed me again. "Another time, yeah?"

I opened the door. "Fuck yourself." Before climbing out of his car I noted the time on the dash was 1:06 a.m. Jesus, what a waste of time.

"I had fun," he said.

I slammed the door. As he drove away, the asshole was texting.

After watching the Porsche squeal west onto Main, I sprinted over to my Jeep and got in, fumbled with the ignition, and backed into the door panel of a Ford pickup parked behind me. Metal screeched on metal.

After moving the Jeep to the far end of the lot, I got out and went back into the bar. I told Pam to call me a cab and ordered another beer to drink while I waited.

I sipped, and looked around the room. The crowd had thinned to a handful of bleary-faced desperado drinkers. A stooped old man pushed a broom under the tables near the ATM. He was just about to sweep up Dogger's bank statement when I walked over and snatched it up. The paper showed a chequing balance of $84.18. No wonder they wouldn't let Dogger run a tab. The booger sugar must be bleeding him dry.

My cab pulled up, and I staggered outside.

Fifteen minutes later, the cabbie poked my shoulder with the back of a pen to wake me up. The fog outside was so thick, I could barely see the sign for the Raven Woods condos. I pulled the envelope from my pocket. The driver didn't like changing a hundred on an eighteen-buck fare, but he did anyway, and I let him keep twelve.

I marched up the concrete stairs to the glass lobby doors. The light above the door was out. My feet crunched on broken glass. In putting the envelope back in my pocket, my keys slipped and fell to the doormat. When I bent down to pick them up, a tall shadow reflected in the glass slipped up from behind. Something tightened around my throat, so suddenly I thought my eyes were going to explode. I smelled chemicals and sweat. I threw an elbow strike, and it glanced off my attacker's head. Raising my legs, I pressed my heels into the stone pillar by the entrance and shoved back. It sent him back a few paces, but he only grunted and tightened his grip.

He licked my cheek and whispered in my ear, "Keep fucking around and next time it's a bullet."

White pain exploded in my head. Then nothing.

CHAPTER 18

Tuesday, October 22

I AWOKE IN A SHALLOW GRAVE. DARK SHAPES
and blurry shadows all around. Panic. I scrambled onto all
fours, gasping, not knowing where I was, or who might be
there. I could hear water flowing in a river or stream nearby.
When I stood, everything went sideways, and I fell back
down and puked. I touched the wound on my left temple,
and my fingers came away sticky with blood.

After several minutes I was able to stand, but was forced
to steady myself against trees as I weaved up a path. Rising
above the trees to my left, I saw the outline of the Raven
Woods. I had been dragged or carried about a hundred yards
down the trail that cut through the forest behind my place.
My pockets had been cleaned out: no keys, no phone, no
envelope of cash, no photo of Geri and friends.

Leaving me no choice but to buzz the building manager.

I pressed the intercom button. "Luis, it's Sloane. I was
out for a run, and fell down and lost my keys. Could you let
me in?"

Luis answered the door in a flannel robe and slippers. His face contorted at the sight of me. *"Madre!"* he said, sniffing my breath. "You drink and go out running in the middle of the night? You crazy?"

I waved off his suggestion to go to the hospital. "Just a bath and a Band-Aid, Luis. Good as new by morning."

At my door, he put the key in, and frowned. "Already unlocked."

Shit. "Guess I forgot."

"That's why I haven't touched a drop in twenty years," he said. "Quit while you still can."

He shuffled away. I pushed open the door, listening for sounds and hearing nothing except water rushing through pipes in the suite above. Moving into the kitchen, I grabbed a Henckel from the knife rack on the counter.

When I shut the door and flicked the lights, I was glad Luis hadn't looked in. The place had been tossed. Kitchen cupboards opened and drawers yanked out, their contents all over the floor. Broken dishes and shards of glass were everywhere, mingling with heaps of oatmeal and protein powder, like a recipe gone horribly wrong.

In the living room, the table and chairs had been flipped on their sides, along with the granite coffee table. Couch cushions had been sliced open, foamy polyurethane innards spilling out. My sister's painting was heaped unceremoniously in the corner, but its frame was intact.

In the den, the contents of the desk drawers carpeted the floor: papers, tax returns, old photos. I picked up one of Steph and I building a sand castle in Parksville. I was three, eager-eyed and grinning; Steph at five, eerily stone-faced. I set the photo on the desk.

I rushed to the closet and checked the vacuum cleaner bag. Whoever had done this was either in a hurry or inexperienced, because the Ziploc containing the letter, files, and notes were still there. Luckily the laptop was still in my car, parked outside the bar.

A gust of cold air ripped in from the open patio door. "Eclipse! Where are you, boy?" He didn't come running. I searched everywhere: bathtub, closets, beneath the sink. Eclipse was gone.

Pulling on a down jacket, I set out with a flashlight. For the next three hours I searched the shrubs and wooded area around Raven Woods.

"Eclipse, come on out, boy."

I happened upon three other cats, a skunk, and a family of raccoons sauntering across the street, but no Eclipse. Coyotes howled in the distance.

Keep fucking around and next time it's a bullet.

Back inside, I locked the door and set the alarm, but left the patio door open enough to let Eclipse squeeze through. I was soaked, and my hands were covered with blood and grime. My reflection in the bathroom mirror was shocking: neck bruised, face streaked with blood, a purple swelling above my right eyebrow.

I turned on the shower, peeled off my clothes, and climbed in. The steaming water turned pink as it trickled down the drain. After ten minutes, I climbed out and dried off. I disinfected the cut and bandaged it.

I put on my robe and went to the kitchen. I picked up the landline and began to dial 911. I stopped. Set the phone down. Imagined the headline.

MENTALLY ILL EX-COP ATTACKED FOR CONDUCTING A HOMICIDE INVESTIGATION

But—

This *proved* that Geri's death was not a suicide.

My inner voice told me I needed sleep to get things done, so I took three Advil and three melatonin and carried the Henckel back to the bedroom.

The clock said 4:02 a.m. I set the alarm for six.

...next time it's a bullet.

"SHITSHITSHIT," I said, one good eye snapping open at 9:59. I'd slept through my alarm and my first two clients.

In the harsh light of day, I looked even worse than the night before. The side of my face had ballooned. My neck was a brutally tender black and blue. My ribs were bruised, along with my ass and left knee, likely from when I'd been thrown down.

I put on shoes to avoid cutting my feet on broken glass. The coffee maker was intact, so I made a pot. While it brewed, I swept up the glass and righted the table and chairs. I poured a cup of coffee and sat down. Just another day. Get on with it.

I left apologetic messages for my missed clients, telling them I had a "bit of an accident" last night, but that I was fine and would call them to re-book.

The next three hours were spent cleaning the mess as best I could. I would need new dishes and glasses, and my couch was toast. But so what? It was only stuff, objects left over from a long-extinct relationship. Things I'd been meaning to replace.

I stood looking out the window at the courtyard, where a tiny brown bird hopped on the brick walkway, pecking at invisible crumbs. I closed my eyes and tried to recall the attacker from last night. I didn't see his face, but he was strong, and his gravel-voiced threat had sounded sincere.

I called Luis to tell him I needed the locks changed. "Hundred dollars," he said.

"Fine."

I found the spare car key and took a cab back to the Riverside. As I opened the car door, a scratching sound from behind made me whirl. I expected a baseball bat to smash my skull, but it was only a leaf skittering across the concrete. I tamped down my paranoia and started the engine, but couldn't keep myself from checking the rear-view mirror every two seconds, all the way home.

CHAPTER 19

AT LUNCHTIME, SMILE DINER WAS PACKED with construction workers, hipsters, and even a few middle-aged women slumming from the 'burbs. Wayne sat at the counter, reading the sports section and looking like a burned-out PI with two-day stubble and a rumpled sports jacket.

I took the stool to his right. The moment he saw my face, he shook his head. "*Whatever* the fuck it is, the answer is a hard no. I told you to drop this shit."

"Because you didn't believe me," I said. "Someone attacked me last night outside my home and threatened to kill me. He also trashed my place."

"This keeps getting better and better. Tell me you went to the cops at least."

I shook my head. The waitress appeared and poured coffee. Wayne ordered an eggs benny.

After the waitress left, Wayne told me to start at the beginning. I opened with the visit to Yvette Parsons and what she told me about Dogger. I went on to describe my "date" with Dogger, leaving out the wet bits. I capped off the story with the attack.

"You say Dogger took off suddenly last night. How much time passed before you got jumped?"

"Half-hour. The guy that got me was too big to be Dogger or Kai."

"What about Grady Harp?"

"Wrong voice. And this guy was rough."

"People mask their voices," he said, "and you were drunk. Look, my advice is that you go to the police. Make a statement. You don't have to tell them anything about what you've been doing, just say you were attacked and robbed."

I looked around, and told him I needed a gun.

"No fucking way."

"C'mon, Wayne, don't make me go to some biker bar in Surrey."

"I get you a gun, and someone's going to wind up dead."

"Least it won't be me."

"Someone got the jump on you last night. You of all people know a gun wouldn't have prevented that."

The waitress arrived with Wayne's benny. He ordered a slice of lemon meringue pie and tossed a thumb at me. "For the Million Dollar Baby here," he said.

When the waitress left, I asked him how much it would cost to put surveillance on Dogger and Kai.

He sponged up hollandaise with a piece of sourdough and slopped it in his gob. "Forget it. I don't like the look in your eyes. No good can come of this."

I waved him off like a foul odour.

"Take stock," he said. "You're fit and young, and when you aren't beat to shit, you're not bad-looking. But you're not thinking clearly, probably because you're not on your meds."

I pushed myself up and was halfway to the door when Wayne called after me, "Where you goin'?"

"To Surrey."

"Sit."

I turned and glared. My pie arrived. I sat back down. We ate in silence. In a booth to the left, a Japanese hipster couple covertly fed a waffle to their pet ferret under the table.

Food finished, Wayne paid and we exited onto Pender Street. He motioned me toward a black Toyota 4Runner with a rusty bumper, and we climbed in. The interior smelled of cigars and fast food. He popped the glovebox and removed what looked like a flashlight with a foot-long black handle. Small, metal prongs jutted around the perimeter of the light source.

"An Enforcer," he said, handing it over. "Basically a stun gun on steroids. Two *million* volts. Take your average Taser to a mean mofo and it'll only piss him off. This *will* put him down, buy you some time."

"Looks like a flashlight."

"That's the point."

"Legal?"

"Since when do you care?"

Karin waited for me on the steps where I had been attacked twelve hours earlier. When I tried to show the good side of my face, she stood and grabbed my chin.

She pulled out her phone. "That's it. I know things haven't been right with you. I promised your mom I'd call her if—"

"I was out for a run, and I slipped and I fell. Big deal. Could've happened to anyone."

"Tell me the truth. I know when you're lying about something."

Over her shoulder, I saw Luis peering through his second-floor window. I motioned Karin inside. Once in my place, she marched into the bathroom, flicked on the light, and rifled through my medicine cabinet. She emerged a few moments later with the lithium and a glass of water.

Fuck.

"Already took it this morning," I said.

"Last time we went through this song and dance, you told me you only took it at night."

She shook a pill into her hand, made me open my mouth like a little kid and dropped the pill on my tongue, then pressed my jaw shut. A few seconds later, she checked my mouth and made me lift my tongue.

"Don't you have a job to go to?" I asked.

"I could ask you the same. Not going to lie; a few of your clients are pissy about you bailing these past few weeks. You can't show up to work looking like that, so I want you to take the next few days off and rest. That means no running, dammit." She paused and looked around. "Where's Eclipse? And why the fuck are your couches disembowelled?"

"Someone broke in."

"*What?* And they attacked you, too? That's why your face is like that."

She shook her head in disbelief. "This all has something to do with Geri Harp, doesn't it?"

"Yes, but it's fine," I said. "Everything's fine. And I can't jeopardize the case—"

"The *case?* What're you, working with the police?"

"Not exactly."

"Did they find the people who did this?"

"Not yet. Look, I'll tell you more as I know more. But everything *is* all right. *I'm* all right. I promise you. I've just been a little stressed."

She frowned at my eviscerated couch. "No shit."

I reached into my pocket and pulled out her flash drive. "Here's your USB back, by the way."

She pocketed it, then asked again about Eclipse. I told her about finding the patio door open.

"Have you put up any posters?"

"I was sort of expecting him to return by now."

Karin tsk-tsked, and sat down with my laptop. Ten minutes later, my printer began spitting out MISSING CAT posters, showing a photo of Eclipse gazing at the camera with a look that some might mistake for loving, but that I recognized as baleful. The knot in my throat reminded me how much I loved the beast.

We went out and tacked posters to every post in a three-block radius. Karin called the SPCA to see if any black cats had been turned in. Of course, none had.

Karin stayed, and we ordered Chinese and watched *The Americans*. Before leaving, she promised to come over the next day. That night, I was in bed by eight, Wayne's Enforcer within arm's reach.

CHAPTER 20

Wednesday, October 23

EXPERTS CLAIM THAT LITHIUM TAKES AT least a week to kick in, but with my hypersensitive chemistry, it always messed me up straightaway. The next day, I stayed in bed till eleven, finally rousting myself enough to shamble aimlessly around the condo with a cup of coffee in my hand.

Suddenly it was 3:12 and I knew I ought to be at work, but my head felt lost in a fog. I sat down and attempted to get my client schedule on track for the remainder of the week.

The coffee wasn't working. I laced up, put on sunglasses, and went out to the woods, passing an elderly couple wearing matching red windbreakers and walking sweater-wearing pugs. I turned and stared. They turned and stared back. Even their dogs stared. I told myself that none of this was real, it's just my perception; things would equalize shortly.

Or not.

I found myself at the shallow dugout near the stream, the spot I had been dumped the other night. Several large boot prints were frozen in the mud. Why bother dragging me all the way out here if he hadn't intended on killing me? To scare me?

Well, it scared me, all right.

But it thrilled me more.

In the days and weeks to come, as the lithium built in my system, my will would become weaker. The thrills would disappear. I thought of my zombie days, and shuddered.

I'd rather be—

Dead.

To clear the lethargy, I broke into a jog, then a run. Several minutes later, I stood at the south end of the trail, above the ever-multiplying condo developments and Indian Arm. Across the water squatted the Chevron refinery, the ugly monstrosity that gave tumours to sea life for miles around.

It was a cold, slate-grey day and my head was full of static. My face throbbed. I sat on a large rock and called my mother. It rang four times. I was about to disconnect when she answered. It felt like I was listening to someone else's conversation.

Dawn Donovan: How are you, my daughter?

Sloane: Just great, Mom. I'm just sitting outside enjoying the day.

D: Aren't you working today?

S: Not today.

D: But everything's good at work? You're doing okay?

S: Of course.

D: Are you sure you're all right? You sound peculiar.

S: Must be the connection. I have a new phone.

D: Have you heard from Sam at all? I saw on Facebook that he's—

S: Mom, I have to go. I love you.
D: I worry about you, Sloane.
S: I know you do. It's starting to rain now.
D: Give Eclipse a hug for me. Has he lost any weight?
S: He's on a diet. Goodbye, Mom.

Just past five, Karin picked me up in her white Kia. We drove over Ironworkers Memorial and grabbed some thin-crust pizza at Nicli on Cordova. The chill in the air felt more like winter than fall. A glass of red wine would've helped, but Karin denied me. To her credit, she wasn't drinking either. But she would break soon.

We went to the International Village to see *Rocketman*. Twenty minutes in, I woke to Karin's elbow in my ribs. "You're snoring," she whispered.

"You made me take the fucking pills," I hissed.

After the movie, I went to the washroom and dumped two packets of Pre-Workout Energizer in my water bottle, shook it up, and chugged it back. "Pre" is the herbal equivalent of speed.

Perked up for the ride home, I told Karin to take a spin through the Downtown Eastside. "Why?"

"This used to be my beat when I first became a cop. I have a fondness for the locale." I looked over at a homeless encampment on the Hastings Street sidewalk. Tarps over shopping carts. Despite the cold, a pair of filthy, bare feet stuck out from under a jumble of soiled sheets.

"Turn left here," I said, "then right on Cordova."

Half a dozen blocks later, on the right side of the street, was a large, red brick building with a blue awning that read: *New Ways Women's Shelter*. I told her to pull over.

She did. "Isn't that Geri Harp's shelter?"

"The new one, yeah. The old one was further down. They tore down that block last year to make room for condos."

"Only goddamn hipsters would think it's cool to buy a place on skid row."

"It's where I first met Geri," I said.

"When you were with the cops?"

"Yeah. There was a pimp down there, a really outstanding human being named Yuri. Me and my partner got the call, and we arrested him, but not before he nearly punched me out."

"How could I *not* have heard this story?"

"It wasn't my finest hour," I said. "See this scar on my scalp? That's from one of his rings. Anyway, Geri and Darci were there when I went down, and they got me into their clinic, and then to the hospital. *And* she was there for me the next time, after I got out of psych."

"You feel you owe her."

"I do."

On the sidewalk, a heavy woman in a ratty, blue parka shuffled by, pushing a one-legged woman in a wheelchair. They cackled about something and passed a cigarette back and forth. The bigger woman butted out the cig just before they entered the shelter.

In an alley across the street, a teenage drug dealer wearing a fur-lined parka sold to a shivering blonde in a baggy blue sweatsuit. The woman wore soiled pink slippers and hopped from foot to foot, doing the jonesing-junkie jig.

"Right out in the open," Karin marvelled. "What happens if the cops come?"

"Fuck all."

"Must've driven you nuts."

"I wasn't in the game long enough to grow cynical." I watched the girl. Skinny and desperate, she was a flailing mess. I recognized her from Geri's funeral. The girl with the damaged face.

"I've seen her before," I said.

After scoring, the girl weaved diagonally across the intersection toward New Ways and trailed another woman in.

Thirty seconds later, she was frogmarched outside by a butch woman built like a truck. Butch shoved the girl onto the sidewalk, then turned and went back inside. The girl whirled and kicked the door several times. Her moan carried across the street as she staggered away.

"Somebody's upset," Karin said.

The girl clutched her gut and wailed before crossing back to the north side of the street. I opened my door and got out.

"What the *hell*, Sloane?"

"I want to see where she goes. C'mon."

After a moment of deliberation, Karin joined me on the street. We began walking in the direction the girl had taken.

A block further, she staggered onto a side street. This stretch of Cordova was low-track hooker stroll; on nearly every corner the silhouettes of bony, miniskirted women leaned into cars, negotiating rates.

We turned onto Heatley and walked in the shadow of rickety fences and decrepit, rotting houses. She was gone. "Let's go back," Karin said.

Then the distinctive wail came again, down an alley to the left.

Side-stepping a puddle of vomit, we followed the sound. A block ahead, a streetlight illuminated her as she staggered across Jackson Street, nearly getting mashed by a passing delivery truck. She moved in a quick, halting fashion, every so often stopping to moan as she smacked her palms against her stomach.

"If I ever express an interest in hard drugs," Karin said, "remind me of this moment."

The girl stepped onto the grass of Oppenheimer Park. A paved path criss-crossed the park, with a small playground and a brick building housing the washrooms. Scattered throughout the park were makeshift shelters made from plywood, tarps, garbage bags, and corrugated tin. Throngs of dealers occupied the two western corners. Drunks slept or slurred on park benches. The girl pulled on the locked washroom door, then yanked down her sweatpants and pink underwear and squatted.

"Jesus!" said Karin. "Is she going to take a shit right there?"

"Heroin makes you constipated," I explained. "You go when you can."

The girl stood upright, then jumped up and down, repeatedly slapping her stomach. A chill ran through me.

A pink puddle splattered between her feet.

"Oh my God!" Karin said. "Something's wrong." She pulled out her phone and dialed 911.

"Tell them we're in Oppenheimer Park," I said.

A small crowd of locals formed. Someone behind me said, "It's Eva."

Karin spoke to the dispatch as I made a move for the girl. She whirled and let out a bowel-loosening scream. Facing away, she bent forward as though trying to look between her legs. I could see what appeared to be the tip of a bloody cone sticking out from her vulva.

I'm not sure which I saw first: the tattoo of the eye/insect symbol on her ass, or the gory crown of a baby's head making its way into this wicked world.

CHAPTER 21

Thursday, October 24

BEFORE HEADING INTO WORK THE NEXT DAY, I checked my face in the rear-view. The swelling on my cheek was down, but the purpling had deepened, and a yellow halo highlighted the damage.

Hillside members regarded my face warily. In their world, a bruised face only resulted from a trip to the cosmetic surgeon. No one seemed to buy the "slipped while running" tale.

Throughout the workday, I felt episodes of faintness, confusion, and tingling in my hands and feet. Racing heartbeat.

The whispers came.

Lookatherfacelookatherfacewhatswrongwithherdidyouhear whathappenedtohersister...

I told myself that it wasn't real, that no one was saying anything, that it was merely pharmacology-induced paranoia.

While putting clients through their paces, I kept stealing looks out the floor-to-ceiling gym windows, across the inlet, past the cranes, to the Downtown Eastside with its streets of desperation and woe.

Across the gym, Karin stretched the toned hamstring of her client. Our eyes met. Her eye bags told me she hadn't slept. Welcome to my world.

At lunch I called St. Paul's Hospital. I inquired about the status of the girl named Eva who had been brought in the previous night, and was informed that they don't give out patient information over the phone.

I sat in the office and sketched the tattoo from the previous night. After several attempts, I had something pretty close.

I pulled up tattoos on Google images, but out of the million online tats, none was a match. I was convinced Eva's tattoo was identical to the one on the neck of the guy in the Olds the day of the funeral. Then I looked up tattoo parlours in the proximity of the Downtown Eastside. There were eight. I printed off the list.

On my way past the front desk, I passed by the ever-smiling Riven, the dreadlocked hippy receptionist.

"Hey, Riv, you're into Wicca and stuff like that, right?"

"Thinking of joining my coven?" she asked.

"Never been much of a joiner." I pulled out my sketch. "What do you make of this eye symbol with the bug thingy in the middle?"

Riven studied the sketch, and giggled. "That's not an *eye*, Sloane." She turned the paper so that the eye became vertical. "That's a pagan yonic symbol. And the thing in the middle represents money. Duh."

"Yeah, just pretend I'm a total moron and tell me what a yonic symbol is."

"The vag-*een*," she said. "Like in the collective sense. So: money and pussy. If a rap song got turned into a symbol, this would make a good one."

After finishing up with my clients, I drove home and changed into my leather jacket, jeans, and motorcycle boots. I tucked my hair under a black knit beanie and put the Enforcer in my bag.

Quaid's Tattoo Studio, in the Sunrise area of Hastings Street, was first on the list. I walked into the studio and checked out the photos of psychedelic peace and Namaste symbols on various parts of people's anatomies. Dave Matthews played from the stereo. The dreadlocked hippy artist came out of the back.

I flashed my badge and showed him the sketch.

He put on bifocals and squinted at it. I watched his eyes.

"Not one of mine," he said. "I've done the symbols individually before, but never like this. Can I ask where you saw it?"

"On a girl's body," I said.

"It looks like a brand," he said. "Pimps bring their girls in here sometimes, looking for me to ink their ownership on 'em, like they used to do to slaves. I won't do it—bad karma, man. Some of the other punks, though"—he shrugged and scratched a pierced nipple through his undershirt—"they don't give a rat's ass. It always comes down to the money, like this tat says."

The next several hours found me touring the tattoo parlours of the Eastside. Most were like salons, run by faux-tough bearded hipster elite wearing their two-hundred-dollar wife-beaters with red skinny jeans. None claimed to have seen the tattoo before, though a few thought it was pretty cool.

Then I entered Railtown Tattoo on Alexander Street. There's a feeling you can get when you've been tracking someone: you walk through a door, a piece of the puzzle slides into place, and you just *know*.

The place was humid and smelled like weed mixed with the sweat of ne'er-do-wells. Rammstein rumbled from the stereo, and the intermittent buzz of a needle came from behind swinging, saloon-style doors. A Jolly Roger flag covered a red light bulb that hung from the ceiling. The cracked leather couches and chairs were patched with duct tape and looked like they had been repossessed from an alley. Stag antlers on the wall served as a coat rack. Tattoo photos on the walls featured gang slogans, smoking guns, White Power lightning bolts, naked women, and Tupac Shakur. The business licence tacked to the wall by the register told me that the place opened about a year-and-a-half ago, and that the owner was Val Diebold.

A tweaker couple stared at me from the far couch. The man's arms and neck were covered with Gothic script and barbed wire. The right half of his girl's head was shaved, and the side of her skull bore a very realistic 3D tattoo of a rat crawling out of a sewer grate, looking like it was about to bite her ear.

"How's it going?" I asked, taking a seat and picking up a copy of *Inked*.

The man coughed and grimaced, showing rotten meth teeth. "Easy-breezy," he said.

I gestured to the woman. "That's some sweet ink. You get that done here?"

"Val's the best in town," she said, speaking out of the corner of her mouth that didn't have the massive herpes sore.

"Why the rat?" I asked.

"It's in memory of our pet, Zito," she said.

"What happened to him?"

"Ate poison."

"I'm sorry."

Twenty minutes later, an overweight woman in a tank top with a bandaged shoulder walked out, her arms done in a mermaid and dolphin motif. A bald bear of a man followed, wearing a black T-shirt, jeans, and shitkickers.

A person who's done any amount of hard time doesn't need a tattoo to advertise it; their eyes direct suspicion toward any new person they meet. Criminals, ex- or current, also possess a special sense when law enforcement types— ex- or current—are in the house.

The inker kept an eye on me as the woman in the tank top paid him. She left, and I stood.

"How's it going?" I asked. "Your name Val?"

He nodded warily, like he expected to be served a court summons.

I flattened the sketch on the glass-topped display counter.

His face was a coiled spring, but then he blinked and gave a poor attempt at a poker face.

"Tattoo found on the right ass cheek of a girl," I said, "who currently resides in the morgue."

"Not one of mine."

"Take a better look, Val."

His eye twitched as he stared at the photo, not so much studying it as buying time to figure out what to say next.

"How much time you got left on parole?" I asked. From the corner of my eye, I saw the tweakers stiffen.

"I got customers."

I gestured toward the back. "Won't take but a minute."

A short hallway with mildewed, brown carpeting connected two ink rooms. Towels were spread out over the padded tables. The tattoo equipment resembled something out of a Third World dental office.

A small room at the back was furnished with a desk, chair, and filing cabinet. A stoned-out blonde sat at the desk, smoking a cigarette and fiddling with her phone. She looked up with a bored expression. Val motioned her out with a jerk of his head. She raised her eyebrows and took her time butting out her cigarette in an ashtray crafted to look like a cross-section of human lung. She rose and walked past us, eyes on her phone. Val entered, and I followed. He shut the door. On his desk was a framed photo of a young girl in pigtails.

"Look," he said, "maybe I did the tat, maybe I didn't. Unless it was my own design, my memory is for shit. You got a badge?"

I flashed it. "Major Crimes. This tattoo has been found on more than one girl, so if you withhold anything ... you know the drill."

With an I-can't-believe-this-shit smile, he stared at the floor and shook his head.

"C'mon, I think your memory's just fine," I said. "Your eyes are clear, and I bet you've kept clean for some time." I gestured to the photo of the girl. "Probably because of her."

He was mute, his jaw working.

"Tough though, isn't it?" I asked. "Staying straight in such a fucked up and debased world? But it's better than the alternative, right? Better than being inside. What's her name?"

"Natalie."

"What if Natalie were eighteen and some asshole brought her in to have a whore symbol inked on her ass?"

He glared at me.

"I bet you'd kill the guy with your bare hands," I said. "He'd deserve it, too. So when was the last time you did this tattoo?"

"Like I said—"

"Was she blonde, thin, maybe eighteen, with a messed-up face?"

Silence.

"I'm guessing it was *girls,* plural. But first you inked it on their man." I pointed to my neck. "Right here."

"Can't remember, I'm telling you."

"What's in the cabinet? You keep files on all your customers. You must have them sign waivers or something."

"They're optional."

"So yonic man pays in cash, no paper trail?"

He fixed me with a hard look.

"Maybe he pays you in pussy," I said.

"I'm running a *business* here."

"So is he. Look, if it comes down to a warrant, we'll shut this place down, and then get very personal with every area of your life. They'll demand to see the books *and* bank accounts. Imagine Railtown Tattoo being no more, and you going back to slinging or whatever it was that put you inside. Meanwhile, Natalie's getting older by the day. All that because you didn't give me a name."

"Pope," he said, under his breath. "I heard one of the girls call him that."

"Big hair, mustache?"

"Yeah."

"Is Pope his street name, or what?"

"He's not big on conversation."

"How many girls have you inked for him?"

"Five."

"Ass cheeks?"

A nod.

"You do many other brandings?"

A stony stare. "I've done six Nike symbols on people. Coca-Cola, too. No Apple yet."

I smiled, and handed him a card with my number on it. "Give me a call, anything else comes to mind."

He gave a small nod as his eyes grew hard. I had gotten something out of him, and he didn't like it. There was also a possibility that as soon as I left he'd reach out to Pope, and I kind of hoped he would.

I was ready now.

"You've been a great help, Val." I didn't take my eyes off him as I backed out the door. "I'll show myself out."

CHAPTER 22

AFTER A QUICK SHOPPING SPREE AT THE VALUE Village thrift store on Hastings Street, I took my bag of clothes and drove into the alley behind the store. Dumping the garments onto the pavement, I kicked them around in the gravel. Then I tossed them back in the Jeep and washed my face in a mud puddle, making sure to get dirty behind the ears. I climbed back in the car, stripped down, and put on my new wardrobe: a grey sweatshirt with a howling wolf on the chest, a faded jean jacket, and baggy, acid-washed jeans. I'd also picked out a white bandana, which I tied around my head. A glance in the rear-view proved it to be a nice compliment to the bruising on my face.

"Oh, you're cute," I muttered.

I parked on the corner of Powell and Dundas. Removing the sneaker from my left foot, I tucked five twenties beneath the insole, then slipped the shoe back on.

A fifteen-minute walk brought me to New Ways. A huddle of three women with deeply weathered faces smoked near the entrance. One had lumberjack shoulders, dark, slicked back hair, and a face that looked like it had been flattened by a shovel. We made eye contact.

I did a quick loop around the building, making sure the silver Audi wasn't in the rear parking lot. At the front entrance the three women turned silent, watching, and puffing their smokes.

The door was locked, and there was a camera above. "You gotta git buzzed in," said the woman to the left of Shovel Face.

I wiped my nose on my sleeve, mumbled thanks, and pressed the buzzer.

A female voice came through the intercom: "Name and file number?" Through the glass, a large woman sat looking at me from the reception desk fifteen feet away.

"Sheila Dobreiski," I said. "I don't have a file. Geri Harp said I could come any time I was in trouble. I'm in trouble."

The woman looked at me for five seconds. The door buzzed and I walked into a bright room that smelled like a hospital waiting area. Tacked to a bulletin board were posters of missing women, safe sex, adoption services, HIV prevention, continuing education, Planned Parenthood, crisis hotlines, and a long list of shelter rules.

The reception desk was on the right side of the room. On the opposite side was a low oak coffee table stacked with magazines and pamphlets, some of which were pro-life. Flanking the table were two Navajo-print couches.

The women outside were still staring at me, which made me wonder if any of them recognized me from my cop days. They all looked like they'd been arrested at one time or another. Live on these streets and sooner or later you're going to end up with a sheet. Usually sooner.

"Thank you," I told the receptionist, who looked up with casual indifference. "It's freezing out there."

In one of the creases of the woman's pink, flowered muumuu, I saw the nametag: Bette. A black hair sprouted from a brown mole on her cheek. "When did you speak to Geri?" she asked.

"Maybe a month ago."

"You know she's passed, right?"

"I heard," I said, "and I'm real sorry. She was a good person."

Bette sighed like someone long-resigned to a steady diet of tragedy. She slid a yellow form across the desk.

"ID," she said.

I pulled out a driver's licence for Sheila Dobreiski, same DOB as me. The photo was seven years old, a leftover from my undercover days. Bette compared my face with the photo. "It's expired," she said.

"Haven't driven in years," I said.

"Beds are full up," she said, "but if you fill out this form—"

"Please, my old man attacked me and stole all my money. I just need a place to stay for the night, even just to get warm for a couple hours."

Bette sighed. "He bopped you a good one."

"It's what he does best."

"Fill out the form and I'll see what I can do." She gestured to the clock on the wall. 7:15 p.m. "Doors close at eight. You leave, you don't get back in. Been in a shelter before?"

"No."

She pointed with her thumb at the rules on the wall. "Read the Ten Commandments and take a seat."

I sat on a couch and ran down the list. No drugs, alcohol, pets, weapons, and residents were subject to searches at any time. No one would be granted access if under the influence of drugs or alcohol. Any infectious diseases had to be reported upon arrival. No harassment, sexual, physical, or verbal.

It was too hot in the room. Sweat prickled all over my body, and my skin crawled. More women trickled through the doors, mostly white, late teens to middle-aged.

At 8:25, a tattooed, buzzed-cut butch came out. Same one who'd ousted Eva the night before. Bette called me over. "Sheila, Mace'll take you to the medical room for a search, and give you the tour."

Mace looked me up and down before settling on my eyes, where she gave me a good long stare, like she was sizing up an opponent in a wrestling match. "No sharps or surprises?"

"Or low blows or head-butts," I added.

Mace's expression was more sneer than smile. "Come along, then." I followed her back down the dimly lit hall, brightened only by photos of young mothers holding chubby babies. Other photos showed smiling, craggy-faced women wearing chef hats. I paused on one of Geri and Darci and maybe a hundred local women posing outside the shelter on a sunny day.

Mace pointed to closed doors as we passed them. "Arts and Crafts, Neo- and Post-Natal, Health and Lifestyle Training, Fitness and Nutrition—"

"There's a gym?"

"Not that it gets used much," she said. "You lift?"

"Cardio, mostly," I answered. "Seems like a good place to work."

"Until I get that multinational CEO job, it'll have to do."

Near the end of the hall, she opened a white door with a red cross in the middle and ushered me in. Exam table, stool, and chair. Plastic baskets of condoms, syringes, and alcohol swabs.

"Empty your pockets and strip down to your underwear," she said.

From my jacket pockets I took out my change purse, a pack of spearmint gum, my ID, the folded-up sketch of the symbol, and placed them on the counter. She patted down my clothes, turning my pockets inside out. She removed the insoles of my shoes and found the cash.

"All I've got in the world," I said.

She put it back. "Don't lose it, then."

I stripped and her eyebrows rose.

"You *do* keep in shape, don'cha?"

"Lately it's been my old man using me for a sparring partner," I said. "Keeps me on the move."

Her eyes twinkled. "You need to pick better partners."

I tried to smile. Mace must've been an ass girl, because that's where her gaze lingered. Pulling my clothes back on, I told Mace I liked the tattoo of a snake entwined around her forearm.

"I was thinking of getting one, to symbolize starting over." I unfolded the sketch on the counter. "Do you think this is me, or maybe it's too overdone?"

The twinkle disappeared. "It's not really you. I'd pick another one. Maybe a pink unicorn."

After the search, we turned and walked down another hall. Through glass walls on either side were two TV/rec rooms. In the one on the left, several dozen women lounged on couches and beanbag chairs watching one of the *Saw* films. Several women breastfed babies. A few teenagers sprawled on the floor. The room to the right differed in that the women were older and were watching *Forrest Gump*. I recognized the woman with the wheelchair from the other night. She was dozing, the stump of her amputated leg twitching up and down.

"TVs get shut off at nine," Mace said. "You earn viewing privileges by working in the kitchen or laundry or applying any skill that might be useful. Other than being a punching bag, you skillful in any way?"

"I guess time will tell."

We passed the door marked OFFICE, where I imagined Geri spending her days. Now Darci. It occurred to me that I could have just asked her for a tour. But then I'd have to explain why. Not only was Darci not ready for the why, I wouldn't be able to get the information I needed via conventional means.

"What days does Geri's daughter work?"

"She keeps her own schedule." She glanced sideways at me. "You know her?"

"Little bit. You get a lot of street-workers through here?"

She chuckled. "Babe, every damn one of us, with the exception of Bette out there, has given her share of blow jobs to support various habits. Stay on these streets long enough, you will too. That's a mathematical certainty."

We climbed a flight of stairs, turned right, and walked down another hall, passing an industrial-sized kitchen heavy on the stainless steel. Several women in baker's garb pulled bread from an oven. My stomach gurgled, reminding me I'd forgotten lunch and dinner. Again.

Mace led me into an empty dining area consisting of six long communal tables. Next to the kitchen, a counter with stainless steel food warmers ran the length of the far wall.

She led me down another hall, past the bedrooms, three on each side, marked: A, B, C, D, E, and F. I asked how many beds to a room.

"Ten bunks makes twenty," she said. "One-twenty total. You're in the overflow."

Mace showed me two spotless, white washrooms, complete with rows of glass-enclosed showers, Dyson hand dryers, and lavender aromatherapy sticks by the sinks. An obese, naked woman with patchy brown hair towelled off. Another woman sang in the shower. "Three minutes max in there!" Mace called out. "Water's a precious resource." To me: "You feel dirty, Sheila?"

"Pardon?"

"Do you need a shower?"

"I'm good. This place is really nice."

"Don't get any ideas about this being a posh hotel to crash at. The idea is that as soon as you're able, you get your shit together and reintegrate back into the world."

"Did you work here when Geri was in charge?"

I saw her stiffen at the question, and I kicked myself for being so unsubtle.

"What's it to you?"

Because no way would she tolerate your Gestapo attitude. "Just curious."

We went through a doorway, ending up in a dark, windowless room. In the gloom, I could make out at least twelve more sleeping bags. From a shelf, Mace handed me a thin sleeping bag, a pillow, and an airline-sized toiletry bag. There was just enough space to walk down the middle of the room. Laboured wheezing came from a few of the wraith-like shapes on the floor. The air reeked of flatulence and human decay.

"Find a spot for your gear," she said.

An electronic chime sounded through the PA system.

"Snack time," she announced. "Don't be trying to bring food back to bed with you. The other rats'll get it."

As I set my bedding down in the far corner, a sliver of a yellow eye peered from beneath the sleeping bag to my right. It was going to be a cozy night.

Back in the dining area, thirty or so women waited in line for cookies, milk, hot chocolate, or tea. A quick scan of the space told me the room would hold at least triple that number.

I asked Mace where the rest of the women were.

She shrugged. "Sleeping. Most of them are lazy as dirt."

No one made eye contact with me as I joined the line. The three smoking women from outside watched me from the corner of the far-left table. Shovel Face said something, and the others brayed.

I grabbed two cookies and poured myself a cup of milk. Aside from a few loners, the women had already formed loose cliques at tables. There was an old group, a teen group, an Indigenous group, and a mom-and-child group. I felt like the new kid in school. I took a seat near the teens. It was the largest group, about twenty girls between the ages of fourteen and eighteen, all in various stages of street hardness. All wore sweaters or hoodies. Pimples and piercings were plentiful.

Two tables over, Mace sat eating a bowl of chips. No one else had chips.

The closest girl to my left was a pixie with short, dyed-black hair that matched her heavily made-up eyes. As she nibbled a cookie, I noticed she still possessed all her teeth and her skin was clear.

"Hey," I said.

"Hey," she mumbled, not looking up.

"Seems like a pretty dope place. How long you been here?"

"Few days."

"I'm Sheila," I said, extending my fist.

Fist-bumping me with her tiny knuckles, she said, "Zoey."

"Couple weeks ago I was partying with a girl, went by the name Eva," I said. "She told me I should come here if shit got bad."

Zoey's expression was blank.

"You know her?" I asked.

She shook her head. Across the table, a girl with blonde cornrows smirked. The other girls ate in silence. Two of them put in earbuds. I might as well have been their mother. But since I already had an audience, I figured I might as well use it.

"Yeah, we were pretty fucked up," I said, "but I remember her old man came by. Pope or sumshit like that. Big fucker."

Cornrows jutted her chin. "Yeah, doesn't he live in, like, Rome?"

The girls tittered. I laughed along. A few of them knew the people I was talking about, but without sliding them a bill or two, no one was going to talk. I couldn't do that here.

Mace had moved and was talking to the smoking women. Some of the others conversed quietly. Most were silent, some reading paperbacks.

Sitting alone at the end of our table, a strikingly beautiful woman shot me a bemused look. She wore a black ball cap twisted sideways over long, brown hair, and her face was tastefully made up. I wondered why she wasn't sitting with us, and then I realized that she was trans.

The chime sounded again. Like automatons, the women rose with their cups and saucers. I followed. As we filed out of the room, we put the dishes in rubber wash bins.

"Hit the washrooms, ladies!" Mace called out. "Lights out in twenty."

The girls from the young table disappeared, and I ended up in the washroom, brushing my teeth beside some of the older ladies. Beside me, one of them rinsed her false teeth in the sink, and for my benefit, hawked a giant lung oyster into the drain, before putting her teeth back in and making a smooching sound at me, breath like a dead dog's ass.

Despite the oppressive heat in the overflow room, many women were covered head to toe. Some snored or listened to music through earbuds. Lots of wet coughs and rattling lungs. My immune system was in for a challenge. Across the room, the screen of a cellphone illuminated a woman's spectral face as she sent a text. Our eyes met as I removed my jacket and folded it beside my pillow. I took off my Nikes and set them at the foot of my blanket, but kept the rest of my clothes on.

After settling in, I turned to the shape under the blanket to my left. "How's the breakfast around here?" I whispered.

She turned away from me and someone else hissed, "*Shut your fuckin' hole.*"

I closed my eyes. Who knew a women's shelter could be so soothing? The fatigue of the past several days was catching up, and I found myself drifting.

You murdered me, whispered Geri into the ear of a shadowy figure.

I will find out. I will find ... I will ...

"*Fuckin' cop,*" someone hissed. My eyes shot open to meet blackness. I pushed myself up and was immediately shoved back down.

"I'm not—" I began, only to be booted in the stomach. Gasping, I breathed in cigarette stink, cheap perfume, and cheaper wine.

I kicked out and my heel slammed into a soft gut, causing one of the smoking ladies to squeal in pain. Two of them held my arms while the third kicked me in the ribs. I craned my neck to the right and bit a wrist. A shriek, and the attacker released her grip. Kicking out again, my right foot caught someone in the side of the head. I tucked and rolled, then sprang to my feet.

The three women scrambled from the room. "Go home, pig-bitch!" one yelled before disappearing down the hall.

The room was suddenly bright, and in charged Mace. "Out!" She made a grab for me, and I deked away from her grasp.

"But they—"

"The ladies complained that you were harassing them," she said. "Get your things and get out."

"You gotta be kidding—"

"Now! Or I call the cops."

I looked around for my jacket and shoes, but, of course, they were gone. A few remaining women in the room stared at me, annoyed. Others snored on, oblivious. Mace smiled and pointed to the door.

CHAPTER 23

FOUR TAXIS WHIZZED BY, NONE RESPONDING to my waving arms. I considered stepping onto the street and forcing one to stop.

"Sweet cheeks," said a smoky voice behind me, "ain't no cab gonna pick up your whack ass."

I turned to see the trans woman from the shelter approaching. She wore a form-fitting velvet coat with black feathers sprouting from the epaulets. She smoked a cigarette, the ember illuminating her high cheekbones, long false lashes and perfectly sculpted brows.

"Bitches jacked my shoes," I said.

"You look cold as shit."

I peeled off my soiled socks and threw them in some bushes.

"I'm Tia," she said.

"Sheila," I said.

"You got cash, Sheila?" She stepped into the street and whistled like a New Yorker. She was close to six feet; a transgender runway model. A cab pulled over.

"Why?"

"'Cause I can take you to the girl you been asking after."

We got in the back seat.

"Balhaven Hotel," Tia said.

"First," I said, "Powell and Dundas."

Tia looked at me.

"My ride," I explained.

"They said you're a cop," Tia said. The cabbie looked at us the in the rear-view mirror.

"Used to be," I said.

"But you went in there all clandestine and shit."

"I just wanted some information."

"Sheila ain't your real name is it? You don't look like a Sheila."

"Sloane," I said. "How about you? Is Tia *your* real name?"

Tia laughed. She was missing her front-left canine tooth. "Baby, I re*made* myself. Whatever was be*fore* was like a bad dream."

A few minutes later, the cab pulled over and I got out. I retrieved my keys from beneath the Jeep, then opened the door and took out a stash of cash I had hidden under the floor mat.

I grabbed a towel from the back seat and wiped down my filthy and numb feet. Then I pulled on a fresh pair of socks and blue-and-silver Asics. I opened the glovebox, and with my back to Tia, slipped the Enforcer beneath my jacket.

Back in the taxi, Tia instructed the driver to take us to the Balhaven. I asked why Tia was going out of her way to help me.

"This ain't charity. You got to pay the piper, and this piper got to get her *pipe* on."

"You leave the shelter tonight, you can't get back in, right?"

"I can get shelter *anywhere*. What I need to do is get loaded like a *freight* train."

"Which room do you sleep in there?"

"Used to be I got my own room. Times have changed."

"How so?"

"Let's just say New Ways has a high turnover rate these days."

I was about to ask her to elaborate, but the cab pulled up to the curb.

The Balhaven Hotel.

When the place first opened a hundred years ago, it really must have been something, back when this strip of Hastings was bustling with commerce and Vancouver was establishing herself as a port city.

The vertical pink and red neon sign outside the building looked like a radioactive seahorse with its tail curling around a clock. Many different kinds of shoes must have walked through the doors in the past century; the Roaring Twenties would have brought in captains of industry and opium lords, the Thirties and Forties likely attracted stevedores and soldiers. In the Fifties the crowd would have been the same, only the soldiers would have turned into clerks and alcoholic car salesmen. Those guys would have been followed in the Sixties and Seventies by beat poets and folk musicians.

Then came the drugs.

Big time.

For over forty years now, the Balhaven, like all the skid row cesspit hotels on that strip of Hastings, has been a piss-stinking flophouse/asylum for hard-core addicts.

Last time I was here was seven years ago, to bust a meth lab on the eighth floor. Nothing seemed to have changed since. As I got out of the taxi I saw a man crouched down, injecting crack or jib or down into a woman's forehead vein, and I realized that I was wrong: things had gotten worse. In the alley beside the hotel, the silhouette of a man could be seen leaning against a dumpster, one hand holding an umbrella while the other guided the back of a woman's head who squatted and bobbed at his crotch. A police car cruised by and I made brief eye contact with the cop, who regarded the miserable tableau with resigned dispassion.

A block further west, five police cars had converged on a cordoned-off crime scene. Two paddy wagons, two ambulances. The cops had a gang of First Nations toughs face down on the sidewalk. One cop slid an evidence bag over a bloody machete. It took two police to hoist a massive man with a green mohawk to his feet and try and get him in the back of the wagon. Mohawk yelled and kicked out, slamming the door shut. Another cop Tased him in the chest and he roared and fell to the pavement. Another group of First Nations men jeered at the police from behind the yellow tape. Beer bottles were lobbed, shattering against the police cars. It set my adrenaline fizzing.

"Never a dull moment," Tia said, extending her hand.

I peeled off a twenty. Tia snatched it between her long, lacquered blue nails and sashayed over to a coterie of hardfaces. One young entrepreneur on a BMX bike couldn't have been older than thirteen. I recognized another as Sham, a white Rasta-boy, a Downtown Eastside lifer, also an inveterate rock slinger. Sham was a petty criminal who was only alive because he was dumb enough to get himself incarcerated every other week, which meant detox and three squares. He grinned when he recognized me; thirty years old and down to a mouth full of purple nubbins.

"Yo, Flame!"

"What's up, Sham?"

"Same-same, you know." He sniffed and twitched. "We miss you down here, Flame. You one of the good ones."

"That warms my heart, Sham," From five feet away, I watched Tia smoke crack from a scorched glass pipe. "Say, you wouldn't happen to have heard of a baller, goes by the name of Pope, would you?"

"Nah, Flame," he said, "you know I'd say if I knew the man."

Sham was too dumb to be an effective liar; he told the truth.

Tia leaned over. "My girl's gonna need some glass. She's in a bad way."

I sighed and handed over a few extra bills.

Sham nodded at my getup. "Don't tell me you been hittin' the pipe?"

"Looking for someone," I said.

"Ohhh, you in the missing person business now, huh?"

"Something like that."

"Cool," he said, snapping his fingers to an imaginary tune. Then he giggled and said, "What's the difference between the Pope and acne?"

I shrugged and looked around. Sham leaned closer, showing cheeks more cratered than the moon. "Acne don't come on an altar boy's face until he's in his teens."

Gales of laughter from the corner boys, while on the next block, the scene was threatening to escalate into a riot, the law having a hell of a time getting the gang corralled into the wagons.

The Balhaven Pub was a dark cave that reeked of a hundred years of cigarettes, spilled beer, and beshatted trousers. Kind of place that made your liver ache just from walking in. At this hour it was mostly empty, except for a few half-dead barflies. The bloated toad bartender eyeballed Tia's ass as we walked by. The ancient jukebox blared "Ring of Fire." Dark and faceless forms slouched in the shadows, clutching glasses of their favourite poison.

We walked through a door at the end of the bar and into a stairwell. "Elevator's a death trap," Tia said, "and it smells like someone crapped out a corpse."

On the twelfth floor, cockroaches congregated on the ceiling like they were planning an invasion. Couples fought behind closed doors. And open doors. A dog barked loudly.

At the end of the hall, Tia knocked on #1218. "Open up, hooker!"

A muffled moan. Tia turned the knob and swung the door open. She flipped on a light switch to no effect. "Eva's been jibbin' it up with all the bulbs again, huh?"

We stepped inside.

The police lights from the street pulsed through the window, creating blue and red strobe patterns on some anime-style sketches tacked to the cracked and stained walls. I stepped into the room. On a mattress in the corner, beneath a jumble of sheets, lay a vague human shape.

Crouching by the mattress, Tia sparked up a lighter. In the flickering light I saw Eva's blonde hair, partially concealing the badly scarred cheek and lip.

Tia shook Eva's shoulder, and the girl rolled away and coughed.

"Eva," Tia said, "somebody wants to meet you."

Eva shrugged off her hand. A row of prescription pill bottles sat on the edge of a sink overflowing with dishes, cups, fast-food containers, condom wrappers, and glass vials. I picked up a one of the pill bottles. Truvada. Others were for PegIntron and Ribavarin. Antivirals for HIV and Hep

C; I recognized them from rooming house busts. The name on the bottles said Eva Carmichael.

Tia picked up a tea light from the floor and lit it.

"Why isn't she in the hospital?" I asked.

"They kept her in overnight, and she busted out this morning."

From her handbag she pulled out a chamois cloth and spread it on the floor beside the bed. After squirting sanitizer on her hands, she took out a clean rig, a spoon, surgical tubing, a Q-tip, and an alcohol swab, and arranged them all neatly on the cloth.

Mixing the meth shards in a spoon with some fluid from a plastic bottle, she cooked it over the candle flame. She tore off a bit of Q-tip fluff, dropped it into the liquefied crank, and filled a needle and syringe. She got ahold of the girl's skinny arm. Eva's wrist and forearm were riddled with track marks and scabs.

"We have to get her help," I said.

"What we *have* to do is find a fresh vein."

"She tried to go to New Ways the other night, and they kicked her out."

"She was high, and so fucked up she didn't *know* she was preggo. Eva used to be real careful, until she got raped and beaten all kinds of bad. Fuckers left her for dead."

"How long ago?"

"Eight months ago, maybe. She'd been trying to leave the life. They did it to send a message to the other girls."

"Who are 'they?'"

"Baby, *they* is as much as you are getting out of me, 'cuz I don't know and I don't *wanna* know." She pulled the blankets aside and snared Eva's foot. The girl's eyelids twitched and she mumbled something. Clutched in her arms was a stuffed penguin.

"How old is she?" I asked.

"Seventeen … eighteen." Locating an unmarred vein atop Eva's left foot, Tia took the syringe, flicked it a couple times, carefully injected the girl, then used an alcohol swab to disinfect the site.

Thirty seconds later, Eva sat up on the mattress. "Who are you and what the fuck are you doing here?" She had a strong prairie drawl; a small-town girl.

"Tell me about Pope, Eva," I said. Sometimes it was best to just surprise people, see how they'd react.

"What the fuck are you talking about? I didn't invite you up here, so *get out!*"

Sometimes not.

"You got his number on your phone? I'd like to have a word."

Tia popped a crystal into a glass pipe. "Girl, you even *talk* like a cop."

"You're a *cop*?" Eva asked, voice small as she clawed a curtain of hair over her damaged face.

"Not anymore," I said. "I'm just trying to find out what happened to my friend Geri Harp."

She stood and nearly collapsed. When I tried to assist her, she swatted my arm away and hissed like a feral cat. She jerked around the room, kicking aside mounds of clothes and junk. Amid the mess, she found a candle shaped like a fat, black Buddha. She set it in the middle of the floor, atop some high-school math texts. Tia leaned over and lit it with her lighter.

The shuddering séance glow revealed multicoloured school binders lined against the wall. Above them were several sketches of a stagecoach plummeting over a cliff and into a flaming pit. The coach was driven by a young woman and trapped inside were two large, ugly men who looked nearly identical. There was a photo of Eva and Geri, smiling as they worked in a garden outside the shelter. Another photo showed Eva around thirteen, a pretty, bright-eyed blonde with cornflower blue eyes. I compared it to the girl now scuttling around the hovel in filthy blue shorts and wife-beater. Her yonic tattoo kept peeking at me. There were traces of dried blood on her inner thighs.

"I saw you at the church the day of the funeral," I said. "I also remember seeing a guy in a car later that day. He has the same tattoo that you do, only his is on his neck. He goes by Pope."

"I ain't saying shit."

"Okay. Tell me about Geri. How did you meet?"

The hardness in Eva's eyes was giving way to tears. She looked around the pigsty with aching shame, as if seeing it for the first time. Using a copy of *Us Weekly* and a T-shirt, she swept some of the glass from the floor.

I rose and helped Eva tidy her space. Lacking a flame-thrower and a Hazmat team, it was an unwinnable war.

"I don't need your help," she said.

"You're welcome." I extended my hand. "I'm Sloane, by the way."

She looked at my hand like it was a weapon. I put it down.

I found a grocery bag and began gathering garbage, pausing when I came across a pile of blood-soaked tissues. Eva snatched them away and shoved them in the bag.

Then she seemed to give up, and plopped down in the corner to smoke a bowl. I asked her if she was still going to school.

She took another hit and stared off into another dimension.

"That'd be a *no*," Tia said.

"Then why keep the books? Why not just toss them?"

"Maybe she wants the tricks to think she's a smart dick-sucker," Tia said, "like they're really helpin' a wayward *girl* get by in this cruel world."

Eva continued her stare-off with a galaxy of dust motes spinning above the Buddha candle.

"*Maybe* it's because she hasn't given up. Maybe she realizes that she's still young enough to change."

"I want," Eva said, "to die with the penguins."

Tia laughed.

"Why?" I asked.

"I did this report in school once," she said, her voice disembodied and flat, "on penguins in Tierra del Fuego—that's in Argentina, as far as you can go without being in Antarctica—anyhow, there are, like, a million penguins there."

"Here we go with the penguins again," Tia said.

Eva ignored her. "There's also this tribe at the end of the world, called the Yaghan, and they came all the way from Asia, like 15,000 years ago, and they travelled all the way from Alaska—it wasn't called Alaska then; they probably just called it Big Snow or something—and then they came all the way down through North America, through Central America, and into South America, until they got to—"

"The land of the penguins," Tia said. She procured a perfectly rolled joint from her bag of tricks and raised her eyebrows at me.

"Weed makes me paranoid," I say. "I'm liable to jump out that window."

Eva didn't like her story being interrupted and her eyes danced with anger before settling on me. "I don't like you just sitting there and watching me. Smoke it or *sayonara*, Sloane."

I took the joint. "Only because my fragile ego can't take getting kicked out of two places in one night."

Using the Buddha candle to light the blunt, I took a tentative hit. Having not smoked weed since high school, it seared my throat and lungs and I coughed for what seemed like forever. It was sweeter than the weed I remembered. By the time I finished coughing it was as though each exhale expelled years of tension from my body and mind, and every inhale filled me with pure white light. A sunrise bloomed in my chest bringing with it a weightless sensation, like I was floating above my body. Then I sank back down and my limbs melted into the mattress. Tia laughed in slow motion, her voice echoing across a chasm. The room was sepia toned and soft gold around the edges. Euphoric warmth pulsed from my chest out and through my limbs. I was sinking into a warm bath. Pure bliss, like every cell in my body was coming. My eyes rolled back, and I closed them. My head nodded, and I tried to fight the drift, but I couldn't, and I didn't want to because I'd never felt this good in my life. I smiled and drifted and nodded. Nodded and drifted. I heard Tia say, "I envy *you*, girl. Dragon can only pop your cherry *once.*"

My eyes flickered and my tongue didn't work right. "Hair-o-wen," I said in a voice that sounded like someone else was speaking.

Tia's laugh was low and sibilant. *Sssss–sssssss–sssssss.*

CHAPTER 24

MY EYELIDS WERE TOO HEAVY TO OPEN FULLY.
The room was a shimmering slit and dazzling in its chaos.
Eva's pulsating blue eyes peered into mine as she took the
joint. "You're going to get in a lot of trouble," she said.

"Where's the baby?" I mumbled. A moment, later I felt
warmth on the left side of my face where she'd slapped me.

I heard her sobbing, sobbing like a little girl, sobbing as
Tia shushed her. "I'm sorry," I said, and then drifted sideways and out a crack in the window and into the starless
night.

When I awoke, my mouth was pasty, but I was light and
heavy in all the right places and I didn't want to move or
screw up my perfect equilibrium. Tribal drums came from
somewhere.

I opened my eyes. Eva sat cross-legged on the floor, back
slumped, head drooped, hair like a curtain over her face. Tia
laughed and said, "You look like Cousin Itt, girl."

Eva gave her the finger.

"How did you get here?" I said, words still coming slow. I pushed myself upright on the bed. Rain pounded the window like a creature trying to break in.

Eva looked up.

Pointing at the photo on the wall, I said, "From there to here. How did it happen?"

"You writing a book?"

"You're from Saskatchewan. I recognize your accent."

"La Ronge, Saskabush," she said, speaking in a druggy monotone and scrunching her face. "My family kicked me out when I was fourteen. They were religious as shit—Seventh-day Adventist go-to-church-on-Saturday freaks. No TV, no makeup, no booze, no fun. I hooked up with this older guy, Mark, who had a motorcycle. He treated me nice. My sucky honour roll brother ratted me to my parents that he saw me smoking a little dope and they tried to get me into rehab, and I said 'fuck it' and left with Mark and came here. Then Mark cleaned out my bank account and left me to go back to his wife, and I didn't even know he was fuckin' married."

"You ever try calling your parents?" I asked.

"My mother hung up on me."

"What about your dad or brother?"

"Fuckin' brainwashed by their cult. They think I'm a devil-worshipper or something. They wrote me off. I got no family."

Eva sparked up the joint and took a hit.

"You were telling me about Tierra del Fuego," I said.

She squinted into the distance again. "Land of Fire. The Yaghan are almost extinct now. The white men drove them off to this remote island. Only a couple of them left, and one's this ancient shaman."

"The shaman does *magic*," Tia said. Eva glared at her.

"Go on," Tia said, "Sloane looks like she's really digging your fairy tale."

"I don't care who believes me," she said. "This shaman has been proven to cure people."

"Then why'd he let his people die off?" Tia asked. "Some kinda asshole shaman, you ask *me*."

"White people killed off his tribe because they were threatened by their powers, and once people are dead, that's it. He can't bring them back, but he can cure diseases and shit."

"Buddy-boy shaman is going to cure Eva," Tia said, "and she's going to come back a virgin, all pure and whole again."

"It's *true*," Eva said. "I got a B+ on my report and every-thing. You believe me, Sloane, right?"

"I'd like to," I said, then asked how the penguins and the shaman were connected.

"The Yaghan believe that penguins are sacred messengers of the gods. If the shaman doesn't help me, I'll tell him I'm going to go die on the rocks with the penguins."

"Play on the motherfucker's guilt," Tia said. "Send me a postcard when you get there."

They finished the H-joint, and Tia produced another and held it out to me.

"Guest of honour hits first," she said.

Just before I took another hit, I asked Tia how she got this stuff past Mace into the shelter.

She arched a knowing eyebrow as I smoked. I held it in and passed it to Eva. I exhaled, and this time there was hardly any coughing. It was almost, but not quite, as good as the first round. Warmth cascaded through my body as I went from winter to spring to summer in ten seconds. I nodded a few times but didn't go to sleep, though I did dream: Geri and I in her car, drinking and popping pills and laughing; Eva giving birth, the baby plopping down a toilet; Eva flushing and being yanked down into it by the umbilical cord; Dogger fucking me from behind, my face morphing to Geri's, to Darci's, to Naz's, and back to mine; Kai Abacon splashing acid in Eva's screaming face while Pope stood in the background, holding a gun and using it to make the sign of the cross.

When I blinked and opened my eyes, sunlight slashed into the room, so bright we had to cover our eyes.

Across the street, in one of the top floor windows of the St. Regis Hotel, someone had erected a large gold foil cross. It blazed in the sunrise.

Eva took a giant toke, and in a trembling voice said, "It's a sign."

"We should go to *church*," Tia said. "Bathe in holy water, take the communion."

"Visit the Pope," I suggested.

Eva's face went catatonic.

"Okay," I said. "Maybe Pope will come to us. How about a dealer named Kai Abacon?"

Not a flicker.

As the sun rose higher and the objects in the room became sharp and hard, I caught a glimpse of myself in a shard of broken mirror on the floor. Two hits of down, and already I looked vacant-eyed and rough enough to belong here. Tia was looking haggard and her teeth looked yellow in the sunlight. Eva had gone silent and still, and when she began speaking, I held my breath so as not to miss a word.

"First time I saw Geri was on my corner," she said. "I was just about to get in a trick's ride when she came up and scared the shit out of him with a baseball bat. She said that if I went with her, I'd get dinner and a clean bed. I went with her and she did exactly what she promised. Got checked out by a doctor. I was healthy then. She said I needed to finish school and got me enrolled in a program."

She shook her head. "But I was back hustlin' the next day. I remember it was hot as shit out and I'm hummin' this stank-balled grandpa in a little Toyota with no A/C, and all of a sudden the door opens and Geri hauls me out and calls the cops on the dude. Shit was *dope*." She reached for a blue binder marked ENGLISH and removed some photos from the inside flap. I sat cross-legged beside her.

Eva was smiling and healthy in every shot, with other women from New Ways, none of whom I recognized from my earlier stay. Most of the photos were taken at the shelter, and were of Eva working, studying in the library, hair in a ponytail, hope and confidence in her eyes, on track to a better life.

"Look how pretty I was back then," she said.

"You still are," I said. "You know, there are surgeons who could—"

"You saw the pills up there, right?"

I nodded.

"You know what they're for?"

"Yes."

"You got plenty of *those* pills left," Tia said, then shook a small empty baggie. "But this medicine is fresh out." She stood and held her hand out in my direction. "You got any more money?"

I gave her my last twenty and she told us she'd be right back. "Bullshit," Eva said. "Never trust a junkie."

Tia turned and blew a kiss before closing the door.

"You can't give up hope," I said. "As long as you're still alive—"

"Easy for *you* to say. After this, you get to go back to your cushy home and keep collecting your paycheques."

"Life can get tricky for me, too. I've got some pills in my bathroom I'd rather not have there."

"Don't give up your day job to become a motivational coach," she said. "You suck at it."

I gently touched her face. "Who did this to you?"

She pulled her head away.

"Did you go to Geri for help?"

"I let her down too many times," she said. "You wouldn't believe all the chances she gave me."

"I would, actually."

"Yeah, right."

"My sister killed her children and her husband and then herself. I could have prevented it. I have to live with that every day for the rest of my life, but I do live with it, because I believe there's something better out there. Waiting."

Eva crawled across the floor and rooted around under her mattress, coming out with a crumpled paper bag. "I'm sorry about your sister," she said, "but if Geri couldn't help me in the end, how are you going to?"

She dumped out a vial of white powder into a spoon and prepared to cook it up.

I coaxed her hand away. She looked up at me with large, confused eyes.

"I know New Ways won't let you in because of this," I said. "But you *have* to get out of this place. You stay here, you're going to die." She pulled her arm away, sparked up the lighter, and engaged in her ritual of demise. Picking the shard of a mirror from the floor, she held it with one hand, and with the other, injected a vein in her neck. Seconds later, she slumped forward, the needle dangling from her neck. A trickle of blood ran down the syringe and dripped onto her bare foot.

"Jesus Christ! Eva!"

I carefully extracted the sharp, laid her on the mattress, and checked her pulse. She opened her eyes and mumbled, "Y'know that story I told you about the penguins and the shaman and the report?"

"Yeah."

"I *did* do the report, and I *did* get a B+, but it was all bullshit. I made it all up."

I looked at her. "You also drew those sketches on the wall. It means you've got talent, Eva. Everyone lies sometimes."

"Do you think our lies can ever become true?"

"What *happened* to you, Eva?"

"The Carriage," she mumbled. "Evil came in and took everything away. The brothers beat me, gave me the bug . . ."

"What brothers? Is Pope one of them?"

But she was out.

I positioned her on her side, ensuring that her airways were open, then took the rest of her drugs and dumped them out the window. The sun sent steam ghosting off the wet streets, bringing with it an oily, dirty smell.

I closed my eyes and breathed in the cold air, and thought of penguins and a shaman on a rock at the bottom of the world. I wanted to believe in a story like that. When I opened my eyes, first thing I saw was a familiar, white Nissan NX parked half a block down and across the street. The glare off the windshield made it impossible to see if anyone was in the driver's seat.

A loud, angry bang on the door—like someone kicked it—made me jump and whirl.

Bangbangbang.

"Open up!" a gruff voice barked.

I drew the Enforcer, flicked it on, and moved to the side of the door.

The knob twisted and the door opened. Through the gap near the hinges I could just make out a black tracksuit and a black knit skullcap.

When he stepped into the room, I put the Enforcer to his neck and pulled the trigger.

It *could've* been Kai, if Kai were pear-shaped, middle-aged, and white.

The guy spluttered and farted and did a three second Funky Chicken dance. He dropped a bouquet of red roses from one hand and a McDonald's bag from the other.

He fell face-forward on the Buddha candle, simultaneously extinguishing the flame and knocking himself out.

I looked at the Enforcer with admiration.

A new stench told me that the newcomer had kacked his track pants.

Tia stood in the doorway, mouth agape and wrinkling her nose. She took off her Jackie O-style sunglasses. "Girl, what'd you *do?* That was Eva's best customer. Without Gary, she wouldn't even have *this* place."

From my pocket, I pulled out two cards with my number written on them. I gave one to Tia and set the other by Eva's mattress.

I walked toward the door. "Thanks for the party. And tell Gary I'm sorry. I thought he was someone else."

Back on the street, the clock on the Balhaven sign read 10:30 a.m. The Nissan was gone.

"HEROIN?" Wayne said, looking in my eyes. "Are you fucking kidding me?"

"I thought it was weed. At first, anyhow."

We were in his 4Runner on Powell, parked behind my Jeep. Forty minutes earlier, I had gotten in, started the engine, and promptly nodded off. I don't recommend trying to drive on smack.

I told him about my botched undercover job at New Ways, then meeting Tia, who brought me to Eva and how it ended with me zapping a john.

"So let me get this straight," he said. "You spent all your money just to go get junked-up with a couple hookers. I mean, we've all been in *that* position, but what did you get? Some mumbling claptrap from an addict."

"Eva mentioned something about a 'carriage,' and the 'brothers' who beat and raped her. I think one of them is Pope."

"Who may or may not even exist," he said. "Database showed no one with that name or nickname. Your intel originated from an ink-jockey ex-con. Even *if* this guy exists, what's the connection to Geri's death?"

I pointed to my face. "*That's* the connection. I also saw Kai's car down the street from the Balhaven."

"You see him? You get a plate?"

"It was his car."

"You were on *heroin*, for Chrissake. C'mon, Sloane."

A man appeared outside Wayne's window. Medium-height with nondescript features, slicked back hair, and a neatly clipped mustache. Wayne rolled down the window and held out his palm to me. "Keys," he said. "Say hi to Frank the Turban. He's going to drive your car home for you."

"Hi," I said.

"My pleasure," Frank said in an Eastern European accent. He took the keys and walked to my Jeep.

"Why do you call him Frank the Turban?" I asked.

"That guy may not look like much, but that's the point. He can be anybody. We were on a job together in Surrey, and to blend in, fucking guy shows up with a brown face, beard, and a goddamn turban. The kicker is that he spoke Punjabi better than the locals."

"Sounds very PC," I said. "And now you've got him driving for you?"

A shrug. "Bills don't stop coming just because times are tough. Speaking of which, *you're* paying him, by the way."

Once I was back in my car and Frank was behind the wheel, he adjusted the seat and mirrors. "Buckle up, please."

I did. Frank's driving was so smooth I went to sleep immediately and woke up outside my place. I reached under the passenger floor mat and extracted the emergency twenty I kept there. He waved me off and handed me my keys.

"How are you going to get home?" I asked.

"Public transit is excellent in this city," he said, opening his door. "Take care now."

CHAPTER 25

Saturday, October 26

THE FOLLOWING DAY STARTED OUT BRIGHT and clear, but by late afternoon, dark grey clouds rolled in off the ocean and brought with them a premature night and its accompanying chill. I parked on the dirt road with the rushing Capilano River to my right and the hum of vehicles on the bridge above. A minute later, the silver Audi pulled up behind me. Darci and I got out of our vehicles and hugged.

Her eyes registered shock when she saw my face. "What happened?"

"I got attacked."

"*What?* Where?"

"Outside my house. I got home late and was a little drunk. He hit me as I was going in."

"*Who* hit you?"

"Some random guy, I guess."

"Some freak just attacked you out of the blue? What did he want? He didn't—"

I shook my head. "Just assault and robbery."

"'*Just assault and robbery?!*' Sloane, that's fucking nuts! What did he steal?"

"My keys and phone, and the cash you gave me earlier that day."

"Coward piece of *shit*," she said.

I laughed.

"How can you laugh? This is really serious, Sloane. I wouldn't be able to sleep at night if that happened to me. What did the cops say?"

"I didn't call them." When she opened her mouth to speak, I cut her off. "I know the drill, trust me. They come, they take a statement—"

"And send more patrols to your area so maybe the same thing doesn't happen to other women." She frowned at me. "You sure you didn't report it because you were ashamed it happened to you?"

No, more like because it was a targeted attack and therefore part of the case I'm building.

"I deal with battered women all the time, and many feel it's somehow *their* fault that some asshole beat them."

"I know," I said. "You're right." Attempting to steer her off the topic, I pulled out a BioLite headlamp, fitted the strap around her skull, and flicked on the beam. I was already wearing mine, and when I hit the switch she squinted and turned away from the sudden glare.

"I feel like we're about to go down and work in the mines," she joked.

We jogged north on the service road. Down a cliff to our right rushed the river. White puffs of our breath hung in front of our faces. We turned off the road and into the thick of the forest, our feet skimming over rocks and roots of the Cap-Pacific Trail. Darci coughed a few times and stumbled here and there, but quickly found her stride. Soon we were like gliding shadows, guided only by our instincts and bob-bing beams of light.

We came to a steep downhill segment, tricky enough to navigate during the day. I called back for her to be careful. Using long strides, I bounded from rock to rock, landing on the balls of my feet, picking up greater speed to the point it felt like I was flying. No brakes. A fallen hemlock blocked the bottom of the trail. Without stopping, I quickly scram-bled over and jumped to the other side. I looked back.

Darci laughed. "I hope you don't expect me to do any of that ninja shit."

I assisted her over the trunk. "Do you ever wipe out doing this?" she asked.

"I go down, I get up. Repeat as necessary."

"Until you *don't* get up," she said. I looked over. The light on her forehead cast her face in a ghoulish shadow. "I'd be really sad if anything happened to you."

"Nothing's going to happen to me, Darce. I promise."

"After Mom died it's like I've got death on the brain. I keep thinking of how fragile life is and all the shitty ways a person can go: cancer—like Rosie, our housekeeper has—car crashes, getting decapitated by ISIS, dumped into a bar-rel full of acid by a cartel, or bashing in our own damn brains on a frigging trail in the dark."

Or murder made to look like suicide, I thought. We climbed to the top of a steep service road with a view of the Cleveland Dam. The water cresting the dam was white in the moon-light, falling and crashing to a frothy roar five hundred feet below.

Darci held the rail and stared down the concrete drop. "People jump from here," she said. "God, I wonder if when, the moment the step into space, they think, 'this was a fuck-ing terrible idea.'"

"Speaking of terrible ideas, I went out with Andy Peretti the other night, the night I got attacked."

A sharp glance. "Dogger? Why?"

"Morbid curiosity, I suppose."

"Did my mom tell you about their affair?"

"No, but I suspected. How long did it go on?"

"At least a couple years. She was nuts for him."

"Do you think your father knew?"

She snorted. "You kidding? Dad's so dense that the only way he'd know if he was getting shafted would be if it appeared on a profit and loss statement. His ignorance pissed me off nearly as much as her infidelity. I did protect him in the end, by deleting some incriminating evidence from her phone. The truth is often overrated."

I thought of Henry Bourain, the pregnancy and possible other child.

"Was that your mother's first affair?"

"I doubt it, but who knows? My mother lived a duplicitous life. I mean, you were one of her best friends, and you didn't know about it."

"How did you find out?"

"Oh, this is a doozy," she said. "It was last summer and I was driving past the entrance of Hillside when I saw Dogger's Porsche leaving. Mom was in the passenger side, running her hand through his hair, looking over at him with her eyes all lovey-dovey. I'd never seen her look at my dad that way.

"I turned around and followed them, up to Lions Bay, to a secluded beach where we used to go as a family." She shook her head and gave a choked laugh. "So I walk down the path to the beach and stand behind some trees, where I get to see my mom naked on a beach, giving a blow job to Dogger, who I had a major crush on."

"That must've put the kibosh on the crush."

A sideways glance. "Not really. Later on I slept with him, too."

I was at a loss, although the tension between her and Dogger at the funeral now made sense.

"Don't worry," she said. "Our thing was over as soon as it started. Despite certain charms, I discovered the guy's nothing but a sex addict and coke-fiend."

"Not to mention dangerous." *Now's the time. Tell her.*

"Sloane, I came by something today and I trust you, so, um … what're you doing for dinner tonight? I've got some amazing wine that I picked up from the house: my mom's favourite."

"I don't know," I said, even as I salivated at the thought. "I've led a very debauched existence lately."

"Was that before or after you tried to score a bed at New Ways, then got yourself in a scrap and ended up getting turfed?"

My mouth fell open.

"Cameras," she explained. "My mom ingrained in me that whenever an *incident* takes place at the shelter—which is like, *every three hours*—I have to check the camera footage and fill out a report. I'm sure they do that at Hillside. It's for liability, but it also reveals the chronic troublemakers." She slapped me on the shoulder. "And *you*, Sheila Dobrieski, are a troublemaker."

CHAPTER 26

"NICE PAD," DARCI SAID. SHE LOOKED AROUND my condo. "A little stark, but I like it—aside from the, uh ... trashed couches. Did that happen during the attack?"

"More or less."

She shook her head. "Do you really think it was random? It seems so malicious. Did you make any enemies when you were a cop?"

"I haven't been a cop for over five years. Long time to hold a grudge."

"Maybe someone you arrested just got out of prison."

"Anything's possible, I guess."

"How long have you lived here?"

"I lived here with my ex for a couple years," I said, flicking on the gas fireplace. "He's married now, kid on the way."

She held up a bottle of pinot grigio. "You need some liquid salve for a wound of that magnitude."

She handed me the wine, walked into the kitchen and set down several bags of Chinese takeout.

I poured two doses of pinot and handed one to Darci.

Darci took a sip. "The thing I don't get is why you were at New Ways in the first place, with fake ID and a story about your man beating you."

"This is going to sound kind of dumb," I said, "but my friend Karin and I, we concoct these childish bets—usually over too many cocktails. We were talking about life on the street, and she bet me that I couldn't last the night in a homeless shelter."

"Guess she won. But you should've called me first, let me in on your little game, 'cause it's actually kind of cool. First thing I would have told you is not to go in and play Twenty Questions. Most of those ladies have been behind bars; earning trust takes time. I've been there half my life, and some of them still don't like me. Probably they never will, because I'm not my mom. I don't have her nice gene, and I always have my bullshit meter turned on."

We sat at the table and ate our Kung Pao chicken and pork fried rice. Darci poured more wine and we got talking about the Downtown Eastside.

"With the gentrification this city's undergone since the Olympics," she said, "there's been a lot of pressure to get the girls off the corners, so on the surface, things *appear* better. But it's an illusion. Prostitution has simply gone online. But in the long run, it's safer for the girls because they're not climbing into some murderer's car to be taken to a pig farm."

"I still see a lot of women on the street," I said.

"A tragic fact is that most of the hard-core addicts will be out there until they die."

We lapsed into a brief silence before Darci told me how much she loved the painting behind me.

"My sister did that."

"She had a lot of talent. You must miss her a lot."

"I miss what could have been," I said. "We weren't close at the end. I could've tried a lot more. I fucked up bad, actually."

She clinked her glass against mine. We drank.

"To fucking up bad," she said.

Maybe it was the blow to the head the other night, but my eyes lost focus for a second, and in that moment, I could swear it was a younger Geri sitting across from me. I blinked several times and she became Darci again.

"At times, I think I'm going crazy," she said. "Sometimes I just start crying, other times I laugh, and other times I'm so numb I feel dead."

"That's the worst," I said. "To feel nothing."

"The parallels in our lives are kind of spooky. You losing your sister. Me with my mom. I mean, they're different, but the same somehow. Sorry, I'm babbling."

"No, I get it."

Something scraped on the living-room window, and I looked over, hoping it was Eclipse pawing at the glass. But it was only a scraggly branch from the Japanese maple outside.

I asked Darci when she started with Dogger.

"Oh, God. I was hoping you'd forget."

"Sorry. We can talk about something else."

"No, it's fine. That's why we've got wine." She laughed. "It was a quick fling, a regrettable summer fuckfest."

"So it was all about the sex?"

"Oscar Wilde said that 'Everything in the world is about sex, except sex. Sex is about power.'"

"Did you do it to get back at your mom?"

She shook her head and drank more wine. "He seduced and manipulated me in a moment of weakness, plain and simple. He's a predator. It's what he does."

"Did your mother find out?"

"Not a chance. I would have known. She walked around with her heart impaled on her sleeve."

"Do you think he manipulated her, too?"

Darci paused, frowning as though in deliberation. Then she leaned toward the floor, reached into her handbag, and handed me a folded piece of paper.

She watched my face as I unfolded the paper. It was a copy of a legal document and it took me a few seconds to identify it as a codicil from Geri's will, stating that on October 8 of this year, Andrew Peretti was added as a beneficiary of the estate of Geri Harp, to the tune of four million dollars.

I sat back, gobsmacked. "Holy shit."

"I found that among my mom's files earlier today."

"What does your dad think about this?"

"I don't think he knows yet. Or if he does, he's not saying anything. My mom and dad shared an insurance policy, but their finances were completely separate. My mom came from money; my dad didn't, and he was always too proud to use a cent of his wife's money to sully his aggressively self-made image. He would probably assume that her money would go to New Ways."

She pushed her plate aside. I wasn't hungry anymore either. I studied the document.

"When does the money get disbursed?" I asked.

"Her files were a serious mess," she said. "I couldn't find anything else, and when I contacted her lawyer about it, he cited attorney-client privilege."

"No doubt. Even so, a last-minute change like that followed by a death has to raise some eyebrows and slow down probate. I wonder if Dogger knows he's set to be a millionaire."

"He sure acted suspicious as fuck the day of the funeral."

"That he did."

Four million dollars.

As solid a motive as they come.

It was time.

"We *need* to go to the police with this, Darci. I spoke to your mother a few days before her death, and I do *not* think she wanted to kill herself. I believe Dogger had something to do with it. At the time of her death, he wasn't in Seattle like he said. He was hiding in a seedy motel across town."

I could see the wheels turning behind her eyes. She looked almost scared as to what this could mean.

"I found out some other things about him," I went on. "A while back he was arrested for the sexual assault of a tennis player named Yvette Cherlenko. She was later pressured to drop the charges, but I talked to her and she told me that Dogger drugged her. I also know about the fentanyl mixed with your mother's wine the day she died."

"It wasn't the first time my mother mixed drugs. My dad told me she'd struggled with substances since before I was born."

I held up the paper. "I still think we should make a statement to the police."

"This said by the woman who was attacked the other night and doesn't call the cops. Sorry to call you a hypocrite, but you're a hypocrite, Sloane."

She took the paper back and set it down. "This *does* piss me off, that creep getting his venereal hands in our pockets, but that was the way my mom was. I'm surprised she didn't give him *more*."

"We can't be silent about this, Darci. We need to honour your mother."

"If you really want to honour her, you won't go to the police with this. I don't care anymore if they were fucking, or if Dogger manipulated himself into her will or whatever. I just need for all this to be over so I can go on with my life. If this came out and made the news, I don't think I could take it. And despite all her failings, my mother was a good person; she doesn't deserve to have her name trampled in shit. I showed you this in confidence because you're my friend. You *are* my friend, right?"

"Of course I'm your friend, Darci."

She gave me a tight hug.

"The police may be involved at a later date," she said, "but for now we need discretion. Dogger will be dealt with, trust me."

As we got into the second bottle of wine, the conversation shifted to her father. She said he was returning from China tomorrow morning, where he'd been working non-stop setting up three new factories.

"I've been to China a few times," she said, "and it's gross watching my dad grease political wheels over there for the opportunity to exploit thousands of workers. He still has it in his head that I'm going to take over his *empire* one day, even though I've told him I don't want any part of manufacturing a bunch of cheap shit that no one needs."

"What do *you* want to do?"

"I've got some ideas. They involve making it on my own, in my own way."

"Sounds a little like how you described your father earlier."

"Flip sides of the same coin, I suppose." She paused. "But what's it like for you being around rich people all the time? The *one percent*? I mean, our family has some bucks, but there are some at the club who are sickeningly wealthy. Billionaires. Private jets. Ultra-yachts. Mansions around the globe."

I shrugged. "Money's not my engine. How much is enough, anyhow?"

"Once you start playing the game, there's no such thing as too much. And then, too much is never enough. The addiction of greed."

"I heard somewhere that to achieve happiness in life, you've got to find the things you love to do, and then make sure you do them a lot."

"Unless those things get you killed. Speaking of, I'm too drunk to drive. Can I crash here tonight?"

"Sure."

"You won't beat me up and steal my shoes in retaliation for the shelter fiasco?"

"I'm really embarrassed by that."

"Don't worry about it. Makes for a great story. I tried to get your kicks back, but they're already on the Hastings sidewalk flea market."

I finished my wine. "It is what it is."

"I hope you have more vino."

"A client gave me a bottle of Jameson for my birthday," I said. "Shall we partake?"

"Enthusiastically."

I started to get up, but Darci motioned me to stay.

"I gotta pee anyhow." She stood, grimacing. "Jesus, my *legs*! I'm not going to be able to walk tomorrow."

"Whiskey is phenomenally restorative. Cupboard above the fridge."

As soon as the bathroom door closed, I snatched the paper and sprinted down the hall to the office, quickly flicking on the printer/scanner and making a copy. The toilet flushed. I stashed the copy in the desk and sped back down the hall, setting the paper in the same spot. I sat back down just as the bathroom door opened.

Darci returned with the whiskey and two tumblers. Over the next few hours, she pried me open about my relationship with Sam. I talked about the meds I was supposed to be taking and how shitty they made me feel. We talked openly about drugs and I found that she had been introduced to coke and ecstasy by Dogger, but that she didn't use anymore. The Hastings horror show proved an effective deterrent.

"Being Miss Fitness, you've probably never even smoked pot," she said.

"I'll have you know that just yesterday I chased the dragon."

She laughed like it was the most hilarious thing she'd heard all day. Then she suddenly grew silent as she leaned close, looked me in the eye, and asked to see the letter.

My jaw slackened.

"The note your sister left. Did you keep it?"

"I gave it to my mother."

"But you remember what it said."

"Yeah."

"Sorry, if you don't want to talk about it—"

"She left it sitting on the bedside table, under a bottle of Stoli. The scribbling was so bad at first I thought Charlie had written it. But it was from Steph, wrecked out of her gourd and telling us all how awful we made her feel over the years, like she was a burden. She blamed my mother for making her take all the pills that fucked up her life. She blamed me for being a shitty sister and ignoring her after I became a cop. She called us 'hateful human beings.' She also said the reason she had 'taken' her kids was because she wanted to keep them safe forever and didn't want us 'fouling their pure souls.'" I sighed and took a slug of whiskey. "How's *that* for a bedtime story?"

CHAPTER 27

Sunday, October 27

I FOUND DOGGER EATING BREAKFAST AT A COR-
ner table of the club lounge. When I slid into the seat across
from him, he hastily wiped scrambled egg from his lips.

"You look surprised to see me," I said. "I thought maybe
you were in hiding. You know, after the other night."

He looked around. "I've just been busy lately, and you
seemed mad at me in the end."

"You *did* kind of suddenly ditch me. I thought we were
having a good time. But I guess you figured you'd have a
better time with whoever it was you were sexting."

"Look, we're not dating, Sloane, so don't get all—"

"Get over yourself, fella. It's not like I care. You know,
you seem kinda edgy today."

"Too much coffee."

I eyed the redness around his nostrils. *Yeah, that's it.*

The waitress came, and I ordered coffee.

I looked out the window at the misty Burrard Inlet and the Lions Gate Bridge that connected the North Shore with the city. "Nice view. You get some sweet perks, huh?"

"Not bad." He seemed to lack the enthusiasm of a man who knows he's about to be rich. Maybe was he just playing it cool; business as usual until the big payday.

The waitress brought me coffee. "Peon contractor that I am, technically I'm not even supposed to be up here. But what the hell." I sipped the coffee. "Tastes better than the swill in the staff room."

"You'll need about a gallon of coffee," he said. "I can smell the whiskey from here."

"Tied one on with Darci last night. Girl can drink."

He seemed suddenly interested in the freighters on the inlet. "How's she doin'?"

"Pretty good," I said, "all things considered."

"What happened to your face?"

I watched his face. "Fell down running."

"No whiskey involved?"

"Maybe a little."

"You need to be more careful."

The Lounge began to fill with power-breakfasting suits and cliques of tiny-nosed Bambis in yoga pants. A few of them glanced Dogger's way and he smiled in return.

Under the table, I nudged his foot with mine. "You *do* do well around here, don't you?"

He raised an eyebrow and crunched a strip of bacon. "I make no apologies. My life is exactly the way I want it to be."

"Same. I don't earn as much as you, but the client perks are good: concert tickets, bottles of wine. For *you*,"—I continued with the under-table footsie game—"being that you go the extra mile for your clients, your benefits package must be *huge*."

"Some generous people around." The toe of his tennis shoe slid up my inner calf to my knee.

An imposing presence loomed over our table. We looked up to see Grady Harp, wearing a sharp, grey suit with an ice-blue striped tie that matched his eyes.

Dogger's foot hit the floor with a soft thud.

"Andy," Grady said.

Dogger rose partway from his seat and shook his hand. "How you holding up, Grady?"

"Long flight last night, so I'm a little ragged. Other than that, taking things day by day." He turned to me, regarded my bruised face. "Sloane, I talked to Darci this morning and she told me about the attack."

From the corner of my eye, I saw Dogger cock his head: *attack?*

"Right outside your door," he said. "Sometimes I think this city's going to hell."

"I'm all right."

Now it was Dogger's turn to study me.

"I also wanted to thank you for helping Darci," Grady said. "She's never had many close friends, and she really looks up to you."

"She's a great woman, Grady. She's going to be okay."

"I hope so." He turned back to Dogger. "Let's book some lessons soon."

"You bet," he said.

Grady excused himself and walked back to a table of suits across the lounge.

Dogger's face was flushed. I leaned closer. "Guess you got away with it."

"With *what?*"

"Fucking that man's wife."

His eyes flashed with anger as he glanced over to make sure Grady hadn't heard. "Why are you here?"

"Because I started something,"—I raised my foot and pressed it into his crotch—"and I'm not done yet."

His eyes took on a predatory glint. "My car or yours?"

I dropped my foot back to the floor. "Uh-uh," I said, stealing a strip of his bacon and munching it. "You're going to have to do better than *that*, Dogger."

I walked away, a smile spreading across my face.

Parked on 3rd and Lonsdale, I watched Dogger's condo while I called Wayne. "Guess what?"

"You're now injecting meth into your eyeballs," he deadpanned.

"I have a copy of a codicil to Geri Harp's will that states that Dogger was added as a beneficiary only two days before her death."

"So what? If she was nuts for the guy and planning to check out—"

"Four million dollars."

Silence.

"Exactly. You've seen the note. She was *seriously* pissed off at him. You think she'd make him rich if she felt that betrayed?"

"The note doesn't name names," he said. "Where did you get the codicil?"

"Darci showed it to me and I made a copy."

"She just *let* you do that?"

"Not exactly."

"Hide it somewhere," he said. "Not at your home or in your car."

I spotted Naz Farooz exiting Dogger's condo building via the lobby doors. She slipped on her sunglasses as she walked toward her red Miata.

"Gotta go, Wayne," I said, ending the call.

I got out of my Jeep and strolled across 3rd, then headed west, past the strip of hair salons, a Korean BBQ, sushi joints, and new condos. I hung south and then turned east onto 2nd. Here the apartments were older, some three-floor walk-ups that would soon be demolished to make room for something shinier while the current pensioners and single mothers got shuttled off to shittier areas of town. Half the apartment buildings had vacancy signs, but none appeared to have a clear view of Dogger's building.

Except one: a slummy-looking welfare complex with missing shingles, a weedy, trash-strewn lawn, overgrown hedges, and a lopsided, hand-scrawled VACANCY sign by the sidewalk.

From the entrance, I glanced north; between several other buildings, I could see the top half of Dogger's building. I buzzed the manager, and he came down; a bearded, pot-bellied man with a gimme cap and a drinker's nose. I asked him if the suite was north-facing.

"South-east," he said. "I do got a north-facing, but it needs some work. They had a drug lab in there, so the wiring is a mess."

"What floor?"

"Third, but it's not ready—"

"Can I see it?"

During the interminable wait for the elevator, I told him I was from Vancouver Island and that my mother was in the palliative care floor of nearby Lions Gate Hospital. I said I just needed something for the month. He informed me that the rent was eight hundred a month and that there was usually a lease, but—

"I'll pay cash," I said. "Plus an extra fifty for no lease."

"That works, but I'll need access to the suite to work on it over the month."

"That *won't* work."

"A hundred extra."

"Deal."

Except it really wasn't. To be fair, the manager had warned me the place needed work. Serious work, as it turned out. The studio unit had exposed wiring hanging from the walls and ceiling. Half the beige carpet had been stripped away, and the other half was stained beyond repair. The tiny kitchen boasted an avocado-green fridge with spores growing inside. A chemical pong permeated the place and mouse turds in the cupboards provided finishing charm.

But all that could be overlooked, because the balcony window showed a clear view of the top three floors of Dogger's building. A block away, but with a good telephoto—

"On a clear day," the slumlord said, "you get a lovely view of the mountains."

"Perfect."

I returned to work for three afternoon clients, then picked up the equipment from Wayne. I arrived outside Naz's apartment building at 6:15. Checking her file, I found where she worked and looked up the number for Rav's Salon in Gastown. Training my Nikons on the dark window of her apartment, I called and asked the receptionist who was working this evening.

"That would be Joanna, Naz, and Luke."

"Does Naz have anything available, in, say, an hour?"

"I could fit you in at seven-thirty."

"Perfect."

"Your name?"

"Sheila."

A pizza delivery guy walked up to the lobby doors outside her apartment building. I hopped out and followed him in. In addition to my fitness attire, I wore a navy knit cap with my BioLite headlamp like I'd been out for a run. I jogged up the stairs to the eighth floor and pulled on latex gloves as I listened outside Naz's door.

Using my tools, I was inside her dark apartment in less than ten seconds. I flicked on my headlamp and went straight to the bedroom.

I stuck a voice-activated microphone under her bedside table. The device was slightly larger than a postage stamp and only four millimetres thick. As I flicked on the tiny "on" button, in my head I heard Wayne's voice: *Eight hundred bucks a pop if you lose them.*

I went into the living room and found a coffee table with a cast iron stand. The second recorder blended in perfectly with the underside.

On my way out, I grabbed a Stella Artois from the fridge and a chunk of dark chocolate from the freezer. I was down several pounds and needed the calories.

CHAPTER 28

NAZ RAN HER HANDS THROUGH MY HAIR AS I
sat in an orange Lucite swivel chair in Rav's, enjoying my
beer buzz. Up close, Naz was striking: wide-set eyes, blush-
accented cheekbones, and plump lips painted glossy pink.
She wore a blue, form-fitting V-neck top with a scooping
décolletage and booty-hugging jeans. In the corner of her
mirror was a photo of her and Ghorbani.

"I love your hair," she said. "You're so lucky to be a
redhead."

"Tougher to blend in a crowd," I said.

"What kind of style were you thinking?"

"Naz," I said, like we were old friends, "I'm giving you
artistic licence to do whatever your heart desires. Surprise
me."

She rubbed her hands together with glee. "I love it."

For the next forty-five minutes, we made small talk. She
asked me what I did and I responded that I was kind of in
between jobs at the moment, but I wanted a hairstyle that
would make an impression.

I commented on the rock on her finger and inquired how long she'd been married.

"I'm engaged," she said, somewhat flatly.

"To the hunk in the photo?"

"Yeah."

"How long you two been together?"

"Since high school," she said. "Seems like forever."

"Wow," I said. "High-school sweethearts. That's like, *mythical* in this day and age."

She focused on my hair. "I guess."

"If you can stand living with someone for all those years, I guess it's kind of like being married already."

"We don't live together."

"Really?"

"My mother is retarded strict. Old-school Persian."

"Good thing your fiancé is Persian. She doesn't sound like she'd approve of a white boy."

Naz stiffened slightly.

"What's your guy do?" I asked.

"He's a cop."

"Cool," I replied. "He must have some *great* stories. All the murders and twisted stuff he must see."

It was clear she preferred not to discuss her relationship with Cyrus Ghorbani, so I stopped asking questions and let Naz do her thing. The amount of hair she hacked off made me nervous though. The end product was a funky bob style with the nape of my neck shaved, the hair layered overtop.

When she was finished, she held a mirror behind my head. "Brand new me," I said.

"Your hair is a little brittle. I'm going to rub some Moroccan Oil in it."

"Sure."

As she massaged the oil through my scalp and into my hair, I inquired how business was.

"Lots of competition out there. I could be busier."

After she removed the cape from my shoulders, I handed her the copy of the codicil. She looked confused.

"What is it?"

"Just read it."

I watched her in the mirror as she unfolded the paper. Ten seconds later, her eyes narrowed and she chewed her lower lip.

"Kind of explains some things, doesn't it?" I said. "Like why your boy-on-the-sly has been living in Bizarro World the past few weeks, hiding out in skeezy motels, et cetera."

"What. The. Fuck?" she mumbled. "Where the hell did you get this—and why are you showing it to me?"

"Call me congenial," I said. "You can keep it, by the way. I just did you a solid, so kindly refrain from mentioning where you got it. Oh, and another thing. A few years ago Dogger drugged and raped a tennis player named Yvette Cherlenko."

Naz seemed dazed.

I picked up the Moroccan Oil. "Can I take this?"

She stared at the dollar figure on the piece of paper. "Uh, sure ... so this amount here ... this means ..."

"That Dogger's going to be rich," I said. "How much do I owe you for the new hairdo?"

"Don't worry about it," she said, distractedly.

"Thanks, Naz. I'll see you around."

When I was halfway to the door, she called out, "Who's Geri Harp?"

"A woman who died recently. Ask your fiancé about her *before* you ask your lover."

Dogger and I stood shoulder-to-shoulder on his balcony, looking down over LoLo and its revolving red, neon Q. The SeaBus chugged across the inlet toward the downtown lights.

"Sweet view," I said.

He looked directly at me from two inches away. "I agree."

I sipped my vodka gimlet. "Ohhhh, man, like that's not the thousandth time you've used that line."

"It's true," he said. "That hairstyle rocks, by the way. It really suits you."

I laughed louder than I meant to.

He studied me. "You're pretty forward, huh? Practically giving me a foot job in the club this morning."

"A girl wants what a girl wants."

He laughed and finished his drink.

I gave him a sidelong glance. "How long were you with Geri?"

"I don't really know what you want me to say. She's gone, and that's going to fuck with my head for a long time."

"Did you love her?"

"I cared very much for her," he said. "Call it whatever you want."

"What about Darci? Did you 'care for her' too?"

He looked at me, mouth partway open, like he was about to say something but thought better of it. "What did she tell you?"

I tossed back the rest of my drink and clinked the ice cubes in my glass. "That you're a bad, bad boy."

"You got a streak in you, too. I can see it in your eyes."

"Is that right?"

Before I could recoil, he landed a cobra-quick kiss. We looked at each other for a moment and then he came at me again. His kiss was hungry, bordering on aggressive, and his tongue slipped between my lips. I was ambivalent over whether I wanted to screw him or light him up with a million volts from the Enforcer, which was in my bag on a deck chair an arm's-reach away.

Our tongues frolicked for a minute before we came up for air. His hands went to my ass. Undoing the button-fly of his jeans, my fingers slid down to his hardness. No underwear. He moaned into my mouth. With my other hand, I reached around and yanked his jeans down. I laughed as he stumbled around the balcony, jeans tangled around his calves. Grabbing my bag and his empty glass, I skipped into the kitchen. With my back still turned, I set the bag on the counter and from a side pocket pulled a tiny vial and dumped 9 mg of crushed Lunesta into his glass, topping it off with a healthy pour of Smirnoff. I swirled the glass just as he came up behind me, his teeth nipping my earlobe. His hand reached into a nearby ice bucket and then down the back of my skirt. An ice cube entered the crack of my ass.

"Mother*fucker!*" I jumped, and the ice slipped further down. Dogger was now pantless, and for a narcissist with perverted morals, he still had a lot to be proud of. He chuckled, his gold-flecked eyes enhanced by laugh lines. He kissed me hard, then reached under my skirt and into my underwear. I gasped in shock-pain-pleasure as he rubbed me with the melting cube.

He pulled out the cube and sucked on it before slipping it into my mouth. He took it back and went down on me as I leaned back against the stainless-steel fridge. With the combination of ice and the heat from his lips and tongue, it was over in less than a minute. I came so hard I nearly knocked the bag with the Enforcer to the floor.

Dogger came up for air, his cock pressing into my hip. He picked up his glass and drained it. I grabbed my bag in one hand and his collar in the other and led him into the bedroom. A king-size, four-poster bed dominated the room. Red candles glowed on attached shelves on either side of the bed. Black leather manacles were attached to all four posts of the bed. I felt my heart rate rise as adrenaline coursed through my body.

I set the bag by the bed. "Nice ambiance," I said.

We knelt on the bed facing each other. I peeled off his shirt, admiring his lean torso, but was unable to suppress laughter at the snarling dog tattoo on his right shoulder.

"Like you never made a mistake when you were eighteen," he said, sliding my sweater up and kissing my stomach. The sweater came off. A snap of his fingers and my red bra sailed over his shoulder. His lips went to my nipples.

A shaft of light from the hallway sliced the bed in two. Suddenly he picked me up and slammed me hard onto the bed, knocking my wind out. My bag was already out of reach. He laughed and tried to jump on me, but I whipped up my legs, scissoring my thighs around his neck. Squeezing and using a hard torque, I flipped him down and sideways. He managed to use his tongue again, making me release my thigh-clamp. He got the upper hand and pinned me, but he was breathing hard. Then he blinked several times as though trying to focus his eyes. He shook his head, and I imagined he felt pretty foggy all of a sudden.

I felt his muscles relax and I used that second to pull him close and roll. Now I was on top.

"Not tired, are you?" I asked.

Flicking a glance south, he asked, "I *look* tired to you?"

I trailed my tongue down his neck, past his chest, past his six-pack and navel.

"I'm out of practice," I said.

He closed his eyes. "Just like riding a bike," he mumbled.

"You're clean, right? I don't want to get a warty throat down the road."

"Jeez, what a *buzzkill*," he slurred.

I laughed. He gave a tired chuckle. Several minutes later, I was either boring him or the drugs were doing their job, because he was softly snoring. It had been a whopper of a dose, but I figured Dogger looked like a guy who could use a good night's rest.

Snapping my fingers in front of his face to make sure he wasn't faking, I climbed off and grabbed two micro-recorders from my bag. I walked naked back into the living room and affixed one beneath the end table next to his tan leather couch. As I stood up, I noticed the shelves on either side of his entertainment unit lined with DVDs. At least five hundred films, alphabetically arranged by lead actress's names. Brigitte Bardot, Halle Berry, Grace Kelly, Kim Novak, Aishwarya Rai, Margot Robbie, Sharon Stone—to name but a few. Dogger, the film connoisseur.

Back in the bedroom, Dogger was still snoring. Crouching by the left bedside shelf, I reached underneath and felt around for a good spot. My fingers touched something rect-angular that was taped there. Using one of the candles, I got on my knees for a better look.

Fuck me.

It was another hidden recording device, flashing a tiny green light.

I stood and froze, looking down at the naked man in bed as I tried to make sense of this.

"Andy," I said quietly.

"*Zzzzhzhh-hhzzzzz...*"

"Dogger!"

"*Zzzzggghhhhh-hhhhzzzz...*"

Moving to the opposite side of the bed, I kept my eyes on him as I groped beneath the shelf. No devices there, so I stuck mine in the corner, next to the wall, and flicked it on. While crouched, I noticed the manacles again, the leather looking well-worn. I imagined all the women who'd been restrained on this bed: Yvette Cherlenko. Geri. Naz. Maybe Darci. Who knows, if I hadn't drugged the bastard, maybe I'd be spread-eagled on these sheets at that very moment.

I slid open a drawer under the bedside shelf. In the gloom I saw steel winking at me. More handcuffs. A closer look revealed a riding crop, various vibrators, butt plugs, anal beads, blindfolds, a red-roped noose, a straight razor, a mirror with coke residue, several cut straws, a box of Viagra, and a copy of *365 Days of Kink*.

Something else in the drawer caught my eye. I lifted out an unlabelled pill bottle half-full of oblong, pale green tablets. I recognized them from busts back in my cop days: Rohypnol. I looked back at Dogger with disgust, but I couldn't help but see the irony in the current situation. I'm surprised he hadn't tried the drug on *me*, but then I remembered that roofies contain a blue core that dissolves and shows up in clear drinks—such as vodka gimlets.

I stole the roofies and closed the drawer.

Grabbing my bag, along with my bra and sweater from the bedroom floor, I went and fetched my skirt and underwear from the kitchen. I dressed quickly and tiptoed down the hall toward the door. I slipped into my jacket and bent to put on my boots.

"Where *you* goin'?"

I whirled. Dogger yawned as he leaned dopily against his bedroom doorjamb. "Sorry I was so lame there. Guess the partying caught up with me."

"Don't worry about it."

He walked naked toward me, still at half-mast. He smiled, but his eyes were dull as he wrapped his hands around my neck and gave a squeeze. As he kissed me, my mind flashed to the night of my assault. Hand inside bag, I wrapped my fingers around the Enforcer.

"Come back to bed," he said. "I'll make it worth your while."

I pulled free and opened the door. "Early day tomorrow."

"Fucking *tease*."

I stepped out and closed the door, heart hammering in my head so hard I felt dizzy.

CHAPTER 29

Monday, October 28

2:12 A.M. LIKE OLD TIMES, ME SITTING ON A milk crate, wearing headphones attached to a multiport receiver. A tripod held a Nikon camera and bazooka-sized telephoto lens, both of which I'd rented earlier that day. I was in the safe house on East 2nd, looking north through the window. I could see the top of Dogger's head as he played *Call of Duty*. At one point he paused the game to make a call. How he was even conscious defied comprehension.

> Dogger: (yawn) Hey, bud, I'm super tired. You around? (pause) Cool, yeah, the usual. (pause) How long? 'Kay, adios, amigo.

After another twenty minutes of guns, grenades, and screams, the TV was paused again and Dogger rose to answer the door. It was Kai. Dogger gave him a complicated homeboy shake/slap/knuckle thing, and Kai looked like he wanted to punch his face. Dogger ushered him in.

I took photos.

Dogger: S'up, bro? I haven't seen (unintelligible)
out there making an honest living or what?
Kai: Just taking some time off. My mom's sick.
D: Yeah, I heard about that. I'm real sorry, dude.
Listen, you want a beer or something?
K: Pass.
D: I forgot you don't drink. Hey, you want to play
some *Call of Duty*?
K: That stuff promotes violence.
D: (laughs) You're a real trip, man.

Kai left, and the video game resumed.

I plugged into Naz's bedroom. All I could hear was snoring. I shifted over to the living-room mic. Silence.

The devices were voice-activated, so when I rewound them and played back I didn't have to filter through dead air.

According to the digital time on the receiver, Ghorbani arrived at Naz's at 8:24 p.m. and started banging about and humming. Naz had come home at 9:21 and he immediately accused her of being the messiest woman in the world. This ignited an epic bickerfest that lasted forty minutes and ended with them fucking loudly for three and a half minutes. Ghorbani's climax sounded like the culmination of a four-hundred-pound bench press. I flicked over an hour of banal conversation, pausing every few minutes into the recording. Most of their banter had to do with him bitching about work and her justifying her spending.

They watched Jimmy Kimmel. I was about to fast-forward when I heard Naz say something. I played it back, but her words were drowned out by Jimmy singing a song with Matt Damon.

Someone paused the TV.

Naz: —just something this girl at work was talking (unintelligible) she knew this woman who died recently. Geri Harp, I think her name was.
Ghorbani: Yeah, she was found in her Audi behind Hillside Country Club.
N: How did she die?
G: Booze and pills. I guess life's too tough when you're rich.
N: What does the husband do?
G: Who gives a shit? Probably one of those pricks who makes more money while he's taking a dump than I do in an entire year.
N: C'mon, C. You've got the sergeant's exam (unintelligible)
G: They've filled their brown quota this year. They're looking for more women and Chinese. We're gonna end up with a bunch of pygmies running the force.
N: Show me the pictures, baby.
G: What pictures?
N: The ones you have on your computer, of the Geri Harp crime scene. I'm curious. Curious like a kitty.
G: You're a sick kitty. And it wasn't a crime scene.

Kimmel was unmuted and audience applause muffled the conversation, though Naz's whining was unmistakable. Kissing sounds. The television went silent again.

G: All right, get my laptop from my bag.

The television changed to men droning about
hockey trades. Murmurs between Naz and
Ghorbani.

Fifteen minutes passed and the television got
muted again.

G: Happy now?
N: Indescribably, baby.

At 4:42 a.m. I checked the time on my phone and saw a
voicemail from earlier; some lady from my building had
found my cat and had him in suite 409. I yanked off the
headphones and raced home.

I bounded up to the fourth floor and knocked on the
door. An elderly woman answered, wearing a nightie and
bifocals.

"Sorry," I said, "I know it's late, but you have my cat?"

The woman frowned. "What's his name?"

"Eclipse. Where'd you find him?"

"Under my car in the parking lot." A skinny black cat
with white paws slunk past the woman's veiny ankles. My
heart sank. "Here's the little rascal," she said.

"That's not Eclipse."

"Well, don't you want him?"

"I want Eclipse."

"Are you all right, dear?"

"Yes, of course. I'm sorry I bothered you."

Back downstairs, I sat on the edge of the tub for thirty
seconds and decided I could try to drink myself to sleep or
go for a run.

Instead, I went into the woods with a flashlight and
hunted for Eclipse until dawn.

CHAPTER 30

THE GUY AT HERTZ RECOGNIZED ME. "LET ME guess. You want the most boring car on the lot again?"

"A van this time."

From the Salvation Army I picked up a cheap double mattress, a twenty-four-inch Sony TV, several sets of sheets, a microwave, a small wooden kitchen table, and two chairs.

From London Drugs I picked up sanitizing wipes, antibiotic cream, bandages, soap, shampoo, toothpaste, a toothbrush, dental floss, toilet paper, tampons, paper plates, plastic cutlery, and a giant Toblerone bar.

At Save-On-Foods I loaded up with apples, bananas, Honey Nut Cheerios, milk, waffles, butter, maple syrup, bread, cheese, sandwich meat, mayo, mustard, ketchup, tater tots, six frozen burritos, and three frozen pizzas.

I picked up a cheap cellphone from 7-Eleven and loaded it with minutes. From the Liquor Mart I got three bottles of Kiwi Sauv Blanc and an equal number of Tempranillos. I'd already obtained the Ativan and Lunesta from home earlier.

By 9:30 I'd transported all the stuff to the safe house.
Getting the mattress in was a bear, but at the time I could've
single-handedly moved a grand piano. A vegetarian pizza
was in the oven and half a bottle of wine warmed my gut
and mellowed my mind. I was in the midst of sweeping up
mouse turds and dust bunnies when I looked out the window and saw Dogger's lights come on. I dropped the broom,
killed the lights, put on the headphones, and picked up the
telephoto lens. Who did I see?

Naz, oh, Naz.

Capering around the living room wearing a little black
dress, arms full of shopping bags. She dropped the bags on
the couch and Dogger stood behind, appraising her derrière.

Dogger: Been shopping, Naz? What, did Cyrus the
Virus pay down your credit cards again?
Naz: Even better. (picking up a takeout bag) I
picked up Tacofino.
D: What's the catch? Why are you so nice to me all
of a sudden after busting my balls—
N: (pressing a finger to his lips) Last night I was
alone and got to thinking about how much you
mean to me. You know that, right?
D: I know.
N: But you don't love me, do you?
D: We've been through this before. You're with
Virus. You're getting fucking married to the guy.
We both know the score, so let's be real.
N: I'm sorry. I was thinking about you and I got
you some stuff. It was stupid. I'll take it all back.
D: What'd you get?

N: For starters… (opening a Victoria's Secret box)
let me put this on—and then I'll give you your
presents. Eat a taco, baby.

Three minutes later, Dogger sat on the sofa, scarfing
tacos and swigging beer. Lights dimmed, then Naz vamped
into the room wearing a lace teddy, white G-string, and high
heels. Dogger nearly dropped his taco on the floor along
with his tongue.

Naz treated him to a lap dance, whereby he smacked her
ass a number of times. He even bit it at one point, resulting
in a pleasurable shriek and a hard slap on the face, which he
seemed to like. At the end of the song, she produced a baggie of blow and they both did several rails on his coffee table.
I snapped photos throughout.

Naz sat on Dogger's lap and took out a green cashmere
sweater from one bag, sunglasses from another. Designer
jeans. A bottle of Patrón.

By way of thanks, he tried to fuck her on the couch. She
shoved him back, procured a black sash and tied it around
his eyes. From another box she took out a silver choke chain,
slipped it around his neck, and pulled him into the bedroom,
giving a few sharp yanks along the way.

I heard Darci's voice in my head. *Everything in the world
is about sex, except sex. Sex is about power.*

Switching to the other mic, I heard kissing, a smack, a
harder smack, Dogger's laughter.

N: You like that (unintelligible) wanna see if you
enjoy getting it as much as you like giving it. You
like it, you twisted little deviant?
D: Yeah!

N: Do you love me?

D: (unintelligible choking sounds)

N: How about now?

D: (unintelligible choking sounds)

N: Hell, you're not even hard, boy! Maybe you need
to see some pictures to get off. Here's one.

D: (unintelligible choking sounds)

N: Speak English, you turd! Is something the
matter with your throat? Here's another one;
it's one of my favourites. Oh my, are you having
trouble breathing? Let me help.

D: Wha—

N: Why are you such a selfish bastard, Dogger?
You know I've been struggling. Were you even
going to throw me a bone? Open your eyes and
read this shit.

(sounds of paper rustling)

D: Holy fuck! Naz, where'd you get this? Cyrus?
Why would he—

N: A little birdie gave it to me. It doesn't matter.
Only thing that does is the when and how much.
We're going to be rich, baby.

(muffled sounds of a struggle. Naz gave a short yelp
of pain from Naz)

D: Listen to me! I had no fucking idea—

N: Yeah, right. You have something to do with that
woman's death?

D: No! Fuck no! Why would you say that?

N: Because the day after she died you were acting
all furtive and shit, hiding out at that skanky motel.

D: She was pissed at me and trying to track me
down.

N: Why?

D: (unintelligible) dunno. She thought I said
something. Shit got fucked up.
N: You looked pretty guilty for a guy who had
nothing to do with her death.
D: Apparently I was the last person she called
before she died. She kept on saying 'Where are
you? You told me you'd be here. You promised.'
N: Did you tell her?
D: Sure, I told her I'd be there, just to get her off
my back. But you know me; I never follow through.
If I knew she was going to do that, I would have—
N: Then we wouldn't be getting rich, Dogger.
D: Shut the fuck up, Naz!
(hard slap)
N: You shut the fuck up! Cyrus knows about you,
you know: the rape charge—
D: Those were dropped.
N: But these won't be. See this envelope? There's
another copy of this will inside. This could end up
on Cyrus's (unintelligible) about my fiancé is that
he's got ambition. What's your ambition, Dogger?
D: (unintelligible)
N: Get rich or go to jail. What's it gonna be?
D: How much, Naz?
N: Half seems fair.
D: And where are you going to say you got two
million dollars?
N: You just worry about yourself.

CHAPTER 31

Tuesday, October 29

THE ROOM IN THE BALHAVEN WAS ICE-COLD and Eva was motionless on the mattress. She had wet herself and her skin was grey-yellow. I feared she was dead, but when I checked her pulse, it was weak and arrhythmic. She seemed even thinner than before, which made me wonder if she'd lost her meal ticket thanks to me juicing up her john the other morning.

I packed some of her cleaner clothes in a duffle, along with her schoolbooks and photos. Her antivirals went into a Ziploc. I looked at a childhood photo of a grinning Eva, then at the broken-faced girl in the middle of a festering drug lair. I took a photo of her with my phone, and vowed that someone would fucking well pay.

Eva slept fitfully on the ride back to North Vancouver, her head against the window. Looking over, I saw Steph in her final days, face wan and scabby, hair a tangled mess. "You're going to be okay, Eva."

In the safe house, I ran a warm bath. When I peeled off Eva's clothes, my heart sank. Her hipbones looked ready to pierce the skin, but her belly was pouchy and the nipples on her slightly swollen breasts were crusted with milk—sad remnants of a tragic pregnancy. The surface of her skin was mottled with small bruises of varying shades, some from injection sites, some the by-product of careless living, some inflicted by God knew who.

I washed her hair and scrubbed her body. I drained the tub, dried her off, and disinfected the open sores with antibiotic cream and bandaged them. Her head slumped onto my shoulder as I lifted her into bed. I checked her pulse again: a staccato forty-eight beats per minute. Right now the heroin was causing her to feel no pain, but that was going to change.

I called my clients and told them I had to take the rest of the week off. Some were clearly displeased, such as Ashleigh Belmont. I informed her I was staying with a sick friend.

"I'm sorry to hear that, Sloane. But you've cancelled on me several times now. You're a great trainer, but I've got that wedding coming up. I need someone reliable."

"I'll be happy to recommend someone," I said.

"Where am I?" Eva said, sitting up in bed and blinking her eyes in confusion. She looked at me, then at her surroundings.

"North Van," I said. "I had to get you out of that place, Eva. You weren't going to make it."

Her eyes filled with panic as her hands pulled at the sheets. "Where's my shit?"

"I got you food, and brought your pills. There's a TV. If you need anything—"

"My *shit*," she said, "what did you do with it?"

"It's gone."

She jumped out of bed, looking like she might attack me. Then she swooned and nearly collapsed.

"Three days." I guided her back down. "The worst will be over by then. After that, I promise I'll get you shelter and treatment."

She scratched her arms. "I never *asked* for your help!"

"Three days, Eva. You've got food, TV—"

"I'm going to get real sick. I don't wanna get sick!"

"How long have you been using heavy?"

"Nine months."

"It won't be that bad," I lied. "I've got some stuff that will help take the edge off."

"Forget it. I gotta go back. You had no right, you fucking pig."

"That's fine. How about some soup? Minestrone?"

She flopped down and pulled the covers over her head.

9:42 p.m.

> Ghorbani: It's out of control, Naz. You told me
> you'd get a handle on it before we got married. You
> keep going like this (unintelligible)
> Naz: Baby, I got it under control, I'm telling you.
> I've got a solid financial plan.

I looked up to see Eva standing beside me while I sat at my surveillance post. I removed the headset.

"What're you doing?" she asked.

"Gathering information."

"For what?"

"To find out the truth."

Eva took the headset from me and put it on. She listened, looked confused, then removed the headset and handed it back.

"Who are they?" she whispered, as if they were in the next room.

"Nazreen Farooz and Cyrus Ghorbani. They're engaged. She's a hairdresser and he's a cop."

She gestured to Dogger's building. "They live up there?"

"No, but that's where her *boyfriend* lives. Guy by the name of Andy Peretti, who was *also* Geri Harp's lover."

"No way. How do you know?"

"Because I'm the one who found her. She was my friend, and I believe someone went to great lengths to make her death look self-inflicted."

Her teeth chattered. "You think someone killed her?"

Taking the blanket from my lap, I stood and wrapped it around her shoulders. She sat on a chair beside me.

"I do," I said, "but I need evidence. Look, I don't expect you to give a rat's ass about me, but this is all about doing right by Geri."

"Can I have one of those pills now?"

"Let's have something to eat first."

Eva managed to get half a bowl of soup down. I made her take her meds along with a 3 mg Lunesta to help her sleep.

By three a.m. Eva's fever had set in. By four, the sheets were drenched and the air in the apartment had turned toxic. All her fluid faucets were cranked high; her nose dripped and her eyes ran. She shivered and sobbed and complained that her back and legs were killing her. Good thing her fingernails were short because the way she clawed her skin, she'd have been down to the bone. I got her into a fresh T-shirt every few hours and we were into the third set of sheets by daybreak. I tried to get some broth into her, only to have her puke it into a bucket by the bed. I gave her an Ativan and she sipped some water. Her lips dried and cracked, and her eyes had a haunted, faraway look. Moans seemed to issue from somewhere deep in her churning guts as she curled into a fetal position, her spine wracked with spasms. Her fingers clawed at the sheets as she slithered around in bed, her body twisting like she was possessed by a demon.

Next day was more of the same. To muffle Eva's moans from the neighbours, I turned the TV on loud and watched *Seinfeld* reruns. At one point I got up and tacked photos of Dogger and Kai to the wall opposite the bed. On an index card I wrote **POPE** and tacked it beside the photos. Below it went a card that read **THE BROTHERS**. Higher on the wall, I tacked a black-and-white photo of Geri's smiling face. To Geri's right and slightly lower, I put up another card: **OTHER CHILD?**

Over George Costanza's kvetching on TV, I heard a rumble from Eva's stomach. She rolled onto the floor. "Bathroom," she moaned. I helped her up, but diarrhea had already streamed down both legs. As I cleaned her up, she wrapped her arms around me and sobbed into my shoulder. *"I had a baby in me and I didn't even know. He's dead and I'm going to hell. I'm in hell now."*

Eva spent the next hour crying herself dry. I gave her another Lunesta and she went down for another four hours.

"Just give me a taste," she groaned, waking up. "Just a little taste. Otherwise I'll die."

"I won't let you die," I said. I gave her an Ativan and she rested a little easier. I snuck into the fridge and poured a coffee mug full of wine.

Mundane is the nature of the stakeout. Dogger hadn't been home in over twenty-four hours. For all I knew, he could be on another motel bender. I needed to get a GPS on his Porsche, but Eva couldn't be left alone. Most of the day was spent holding the puke bucket and dragging her into the bathroom.

By ten p.m. I'd killed a bottle of wine and Eva's fever had broken, but she was now ice cold. I wrapped her in three blankets. Still wracked with stomach pains, she transitioned to dry heaves.

The next day, I awoke fully clothed on the bed beside Eva. Outside was dismal grey. Rain pattered on the window. Eva ground her teeth and clenched and unclenched her fists in her sleep.

Darci called, asking what I was up to and if I was free for a run this afternoon.

"I'd love to, Darce," I said, "but I'm tied up for the next couple of days."

"With what?"

"Just helping out a sick friend. I'll be back on track soon, I promise."

"I hope so, 'cause I'm getting a muffin-top. Since I've stopped smoking, I've eaten nothing but crap."

Eva rolled out of bed with a groan and stumbled to the bathroom.

"That your friend?" Darci asked.

"Yeah, sorry, but I've got to run. I'll call you soon, okay?"

"Okay … oh, and Sloane?"

"Yeah?"

"It really helped me, talking to you the other night. And thanks for your discretion."

CHAPTER 32

LATER THAT DAY, LUCIDITY BEGAN SLOWLY creeping into Eva's eyes. She became embarrassed for me to be in the bathroom with her, insisting she could shit on her own. I took this as a positive.

I nuked a pepperoni pizza for lunch and we ate it off paper plates and watched *Interstellar*.

After wolfing down two slices, Eva asked: "Was that Darci Harp on the phone earlier?"

I nodded and turned down the volume on the TV. "We've gotten to be friends after her mother died. Do you know her well?"

"Not super well, but she's pretty dope. She had some people come in to New Ways to help us dress and do our hair and look more professional. Thanks for not telling her it's me you're taking care of. I'd be so embarrassed."

"You have another chance, Eva. You can go back to New Ways clean and sober."

"I think I need to get away from there."

"The shelter?"

"The whole Downtown Eastside. Once you're in, it's like you're trapped in a shadow world. It's poisonous. Evil."

"Ever think about going home? Maybe things are different now."

"That would be even worse. Instead of putting a needle in my arm, I'd put a bullet in my head. I am *never* going back there."

"I could talk to Darci. I'm sure she's got connections to other shelters, maybe outside the city."

She shook her head.

"You're so young, Eva. You finish high school, get on track like you were before, there's no telling what could happen."

"I'm sick though."

"The drugs that are available now—you take them and build up your immune system—you can live a normal life."

"*Normal*," she said. "What's that?"

"Honestly, I have no fucking idea." We both laughed.

"Thank you for doing this for me," she said.

I pointed to the wall. "Help me fill in some blanks."

She looked up at the names and photos. "You're wasting your time if you did all this to get me to be a rat or some shit."

"You seemed really agitated last time I brought up Pope. At the hotel you mentioned something about 'the brothers,' and 'a carriage.' I know you're scared, but no one's going to hurt you. I'll protect you."

Eva picked up the remote and turned the volume back up. Matthew McConaughey was yelling into a dust storm. I went to the kitchen and drank from my secret wine stash.

Wednesday, November 6

Eva's drug sick was winding down, but she was still squirrely, snappish, and fidgety. On the positive side, she had consumed a lot of food and had put on some weight. Her skin had lost its jaundiced tinge and she began spending a great deal of time soaking in the bath.

I took her with me on a grocery run. She wore baggy, red sweats and a black beanie pulled low over sunglasses. I was dressed in similar fashion, minus the sunglasses. We looked like a couple of druggy chicks. Eva asked me to buy her smokes, and I made a face.

"Either you buy them or I'll have to blow the clerk for them." After laughing at my expression, she said, "Dude! Chill out. Besides, don't think I haven't noticed you killing all those bottles of wine."

"Fine."

She asked for a pack of Camels. As the clerk handed them over, I happened to glance to the side. "Shit."

Sam. Standing at the nearest checkout aisle, looking at magazines. He had a phenomenal haircut and his face was handsomer than I remembered. His dewy-skinned wife stood in front of him, putting groceries on the conveyor belt. Even pregnant she was an easy ten, especially standing near a couple of bag ladies.

I abruptly turned away.

"What?" Eva said.

"*Sloane?*" Sam said.

Shitfuckpiss.

I turned back and feigned surprise. "Oh, hey. Sam. I was wondering when we'd run into each other. Guess it was bound to be someplace you'd least expect it."

"Yeah." He looked curiously at Eva. His wife turned and smiled with unreal teeth. "Sloane, this is Graziela. Graziela, Sloane."

Graziela's smile grew as she leaned over the magazine stand to shake my hand. "I've heard a lot about you."

I'll bet.

Detecting Eva's nervousness, I said, "This is my friend, Eva."

"S'up?" Eva said. Even through her sunglasses I could see her staring at Graziela's pregnant belly.

"What're you doing in the neighbourhood?" I asked Sam. "I thought you lived in Coal Harbour."

"House shopping. Graziela's due next month, so ... well ... things going good?"

"Very, very excellent. Still doing the training thing ... you know, same same."

The cashier saved us from awkward hell by starting to ring their groceries through.

"Well," Sam said, "good seeing you. Take care."

I forced a smile. "You too."

As we walked away, it felt like my heart was drowning in acid.

"Your ex, huh?" Eva asked.

"Yup."

"Good-looking."

"Yup."

"His woman is hot."

"Uh-huh."

"You really want a drink right now, huh?"

I said nothing as we moved to a self-checkout.

"Yup," Eva answered for me. "Can I have some wine?"

"I need it all. Be happy with your cancer darts."

"Some role model."

Next morning I woke Eva and told her I had to go into work for a few hours, but that I'd be back for lunch.

She opened her eyes. "Okay, Mom."

"I'm not that old," I said. "We'll go out for brunch when I get back. Any requests?"

"A burger." She rolled over and curled up with a pillow. "With bacon," she added.

I smiled and put the cellphone on the floor beside her. "My number's in the speed dial."

At work, clients asked me how my friend was doing. "The worst is over," I said, like it was just a bad flu. "Everything's back on track."

On a morning break, I went to an online directory and looked up the name Carmichael in La Ronge, Saskatchewan. I found two numbers, one for an Edwin, another for a Peter. Edwin sounded like a grandfather, so I called Peter. On the fifth ring, a woman answered.

"Hello," I said. "Are you related to Eva Carmichael?"

After a long pause, "Who's asking?"

"A friend."

"Is she dead or in jail?"

"She's doing well, actually. Getting clean. Are you her mother?"

"I gave birth to that girl, yes," she said.

"I just wanted to let you know how your daughter's doing, and I thought maybe you and your family might like to come out and see her sometime. She could really use some support. I heard you had a falling out, but—"

"We gave that girl everything. She had every chance a child could, and she turned her back on us. That, I could forgive. But when she turned her back on God and stole from the church to buy *drugs* ... that, I will never forgive. She made a mockery of us in the eyes of our people."

"I believe she's sorry. I also believe she needs to know her mother and father love her."

Another laugh. "That's a two-way street, *friend*."

"Your daughter is eighteen, Mrs. Carmichael, and she almost died. But she didn't, and she's here and—"

"Well, I don't have anything to say to her—"

"No, I don't mean she's here this second, I mean she's *alive* and she needs your help, and I think you should do the Christian thing and rise above your differences—"

"You have a lot of gall lecturing me. Like Eva, you probably know nothing about what it means to live a Christian life. Do you even believe in God?"

Oh, Jesus.

"Mrs. Carmichael, may I speak with your husband, please? Or your son?"

"My husband is working, and my son is married and lives in Saskatoon. They're raising a child. You might want to let Eva know, just to show her how different her life could have been if she hadn't rejected us."

"Mrs. Carmichael?"

"What?"

"I think you're a cunt and you and your family probably deserved every nasty thing Eva ever did to you."

"You're going to burn in hell!"

"You first. Bye, now."

I ended the call and turned to see Karin standing in the doorway of the office, wide-eyed and carrying a coffee in each hand. She handed me one. "I'm not sure I even want to know who you were talking to, but it's nice of you to make an appearance. Must be tough living a double life."

"Remember the girl we saw giving birth that night?"

"I'm trying to forget."

"I have her."

"What do you mean, you *have* her?"

"I found her again, and I've got her in a safe house. She's getting clean."

"That's nice of you, Sloane, but *why?*"

"She was going to die. Plus, she has information I need."

"This is still about Geri?"

"I'm getting closer, but I still need to find out more."

"This kind of sounds like something you should be letting the police deal with."

"Soon enough."

"*Soon* you won't have any clients left, the way they're jumping ship. I know your only real expenses are wine and sneakers, but still."

"Geri's the whole reason I'm even working here at all, so for now, finding out what happened is my priority. Clients come and go."

She gave a dubious look. "Still on your meds, right?"

"Yes, mom." I smiled, remembering Eva had said that to me earlier.

Two clients later, my phone buzzed in my pocket. After directing the woman into a glute stretch, I checked the text. From Eva:

WNT 2 HTL 2 PIK UP MY STUFFY DN'T WORRY ILL B GOOD ☺ –E

Shit.

"I'm sorry," I told my client, "but I have to go. It's an emergency."

I parked on Columbia Street, around the corner from the Balhaven. As I walked around the corner onto Hastings, I saw the crowd. A fire truck and an ambulance blocked the westbound lanes. Three police cars were rolled up on the sidewalk. Pushing my way through until I got to the police tape, I saw the stuffed penguin, covered in blood.

I ducked under the tape just as the paramedics sheeted up Eva's splattered body. Intestines flung outward from a blown stomach cavity. A female cop pushed me back. Another cop looked up. "Jumping is getting contagious around here," he said. Inside me something began to shriek, drowning out everything else. Faces whirled together into one vile mass as the cop led me away.

I turned and looked back at the lump under the sheet. It wasn't real. She was still in bed. I blinked, and Geri's dead eyes stared into mine. "*You* did this," she said.

Opening my eyes, the first thing they settled on was a tall man with black hair and a mustache standing in the crowd on the other side. Yonic tattoo on his neck.

Pope.

We made eye contact, and he smiled.

Pulling free of the cop, I ran back toward the scene and ducked under the tape. Pope turned and melted into the crowd. Two cops restrained me, pulled me back. "That's the guy who killed her! Get *off* me!"

"Calm down or get arrested," the female cop said.

I stopped struggling, but the moment they relaxed their grip, I broke free and sprinted into the crowd. Making it to the other side, I looked down the street and into the nearest alley.

Pope had vanished.

A commotion behind me, and the female cop yelled, "*Stop!*"

I ran down the alley, dodging dumpster divers and addicts.

Moments later, I was back in my Jeep. The rear-view showed cops emerging from the alley, looking to see which way I went.

I pounded the wheel and screamed.

CHAPTER 33

Friday, November 8

LYING DOWN WITH A BOTTLE OF WINE, I WAS cried out and numb. The bed smelled like Eva. Four hours earlier, she was here, breathing, healing. Why did she have to go back? If she had just waited ...

I guzzled the wine, staring up at the cracked, cottage-cheese ceiling. My phone vibrated on the table that held the camera equipment, along with the eavesdropping gear. If Eva had wanted to score, she could've ripped me off.

She didn't want to score.

The girl just wanted her fucking stuffed penguin.

I turned my head and stared at the photos and names on the wall. Through my blurred vision, something stood out. I pushed to my feet, staggered to the wall.

Near the bottom of the card marked POPE was a small sketch of an old-fashioned, horse-drawn, canopied carriage.

Pulling out my Mac, I Googled CARRIAGE VANCOUVER and got links to a thrift store of the same name, and horse-drawn carriage rides through Stanley Park.

What were you trying to tell me, Eva?

Saturday, November 9
"She's fucking dead, Wayne."

"You're drunk," he said. "*Who's* dead, by the way?"

I pushed past him, into his basement suite off Commercial Drive.

"Eva Carmichael. She had information on what happened to Geri. It has to do with that guy, Pope. I saw him today, after he pushed Eva off the roof of the Balhaven."

He took the mickey of Jameson's from my hand. "Did you *drive* here?"

"I took her in and now she's on a slab, too." The room spun and I ran to his kitchen sink and puked.

"Jesus, Donovan," he said behind me. "When was the last time you slept?"

The bedroom door opened and a little boy's face peered out. "What's going on, Daddy?"

"Nothing, Theo. This is Sloane, who can't tell time, apparently, because it's two-thirty in the morning."

"Is she sick?"

I forced a smile. "Hi, Theo. Sorry, Wayne. I'll get going."

"No way," he said. "Theo, grab your coat."

Wayne drove, Theo slept in the back, and I rambled. I told him about the safe house and how I'd bugged Naz's and Dogger's places, and approached Naz with a copy of the will. His eyebrows raised when I told him that Naz confronted Dogger about it.

"And you don't think he knew about the will beforehand?" he asked.

"I didn't see his face, and he *was* being strangled at the time, but his surprise seemed genuine. Naz wants half, and she threatened to tip Cyrus off if she doesn't get it."

"Why do I get the feeling I'm never going to see those mics again?"

"I also chased Pope today," I said. "I got a good look at him before he disappeared. Can you gain access to the police facial recognition database?"

He pulled up in front of my building. "Here's what you do. I know you won't do it, but I'm going to tell you anyway. First thing tomorrow, you walk into the cop shop. You tell them you were attacked last week but were too traumatized to make a report. You tell them you tried to help this Eva girl, who you believe was tossed off the Balhaven. Tell them you saw the guy who attacked you in the crowd. Don't say you chased him and don't say any of the other shit. Just give a detailed description and—"

"I also need a GPS iTrail to track Dogger. He drives like a maniac."

"Look, you're spinning your fucking wheels on a bullshit case!" Realizing his son was in the back seat, he lowered his voice to a hiss. "You've managed to find some bad people— good for you—but at best there's only a tenuous link to Geri Harp, and the more I think about it, the clearer it is that the only person to kill her is her*self*."

"No, she didn't." I pulled some bills from my pocket and handed them over. "GPS, please. Here's a deposit. Take Theo and do something fun."

He sighed and flipped open the glovebox.

I lifted the mickey from his pocket and unscrewed the cap. Wayne snatched it back and handed me the GPS.

"You gotta download the app on your phone," he said.

"How long before I'm authorized to carry a gun?"

"Never."

An hour later, I was back at the safe house, where over the wire I listened to Dogger snore. I stared at Eva's things beside the mattress. Books she would never read, photos she would never grow nostalgic over, clothes she would never again wear. I dressed in black running garb and hit the streets.

Two minutes later, I was stretching my hamstrings outside Dogger's parking garage when the gate opened. A silver Lexus pulled out, and I slipped in. There was a camera at the entrance, but not near his blue Porsche.

Crouching by his car, I pretended to tie my shoelace, and popped the tracker underneath the rear bumper. As I walked back up the ramp, I noticed a tickle in my throat, but I was building too much momentum to get sick. Sick was for other people.

I returned to the safe house, drank coffee, and listened in on Dogger's mic. His bedroom light flipped on at 8:30, and through the telephoto I watched him walk bare-chested into the living room, brushing his teeth as he stepped up to the window to check out his view. I gave a little wave.

At 9:13, Naz arrived wearing sweaty yoga clothes. Immediately she leapt on her lover and was carried into the bedroom. Over the next six minutes I could've sworn I was listening to a pack of yipping coyotes, but no, those were just the sounds Naz made in bed.

Post-coital conversation:

Naz: I need an advance on my share.
Dogger: For the love of fuck. We don't even—
N: Just a couple thousand. That's nothing compared to (unintelligible)
D: (unintelligible)
N: Take an advance on your credit card.
D: What if I say no?

N: Cyrus will have your nuts in a vice.

D: If I go down, I'll tell him about us.

N: He'll kill you.

D: He'll kill you, too.

N: Not if I tell him you drugged me (unintelligible)

D: I thought you loved me, Naz.

N: I do love you, baby. But that doesn't keep the creditors from threatening to garnish my wages.

D: I told you not to buy all that shit.

N: (unintelligible) you bastards expect me to look beautiful at all times, but do you ever once buy me something nice to wear? You expect me to get my clothes at fucking Walmart? Cheap-ass Dogger, motherfucker! Three thousand.

D: Not gonna happen. (unintelligible) fuckingfuck!

N: I'll rip 'em off, Dogger, I swear I will. You have no idea what I'm capable of, so don't ever think for a second you can fuck me over. Now get your pants on and let's go; the bank's gonna open in a few minutes.

As I turned off the highway toward Hillside, my phone buzzed. A number I didn't recognize.

"Hello," I said.

"*Sloane?*" whispered a familiar, smoky voice.

"Tia. What is it?"

"I know where he is. Pope."

"Did you go to the police?"

"I got a warrant out on me for some *bull*shit."

I pulled over and got out a pad and pen. "What do you have?"

"It's not safe for me to talk right now. Let's meet. Then I gotta get out of town, so bring money, enough to get me on a bus."

CHAPTER 34

Sunday, November 10

FOGHORNS MOANED ON THE INLET AS I STEPPED onto the frosty gravel pathway of the tiny park that overlooked the train tracks and shipyards. Three empty park benches up ahead. I checked my watch. 7:01.

A chain-link fence separated the park from the steep, brambly embankment leading down to the train tracks below. A car alarm began whooping somewhere behind me. At the end of the path, stairs descended to a partially covered train trestle. Freight trains hissed and clanked fifteen feet below.

It began to rain. Through the mist on the far side of the trestle, a glow from a cigarette ember illuminated distinctive feather epaulets. I started down the stairs. A sign beside the trestle warned against trespassers, over which someone had spray-painted FUCK THE PO-LICE. At the other end, to Tia's right, two flights of stairs led down to Commissioner Street. Drawing near, I could see that Tia was shaking badly, barely able to raise the cigarette to her lips.

"Tia." As I came closer, I saw she wasn't wearing a hat or wig; her hair had been shaved to the skull. She looked up with a badly beaten face: a gash on the bridge of her nose, one eye swollen shut, the other not far behind.

"*Tia*, what the hell—"

I started toward her and then stopped. Moving up the stairs to the right I could make out the black pompadour, leather jacket, and silenced pistol. Tia glanced over her shoulder at me as she walked down toward Pope. "Eva told you before," she said, "never trust a junkie."

In my periphery, another shadow climbed from the brambles, through a gap in the railing, and onto the trellis. He wore some sort of mask and carried a small object in his hand.

Tia was halfway down the first flight of stairs, only a few feet from Pope. I ran after her, leapt off the top step and grabbed each side rail. The momentum propelled my legs up and I slammed my feet between Tia's shoulder blades. Her head snapped back as her body punched forward. Pope grunted as she smashed into him, knocking him backward several steps. He shoved Tia aside and smoothed back his hair, light from the street lamp glinting off his teeth and eyes.

The Enforcer was in my right hand. Pope saw it and smiled, raising his gun the moment he arrived on the trestle.

"Sad thing is," he said, voice a deep bass, "you had so many chances. It didn't have to come to this."

"Come to what, *Pope?* Killing me? Like you did Eva?"

His lupine smile made his eyes smaller and more vicious. "Don't know who you're talking about."

A quick sideways glance told me the other man was behind me. The guy was around my height and smelled of cologne. I considered jumping and flicked a look over the railing. The grey Olds was parked on the weedy berm of

Commissioner Street, its trunk open and lined with black plastic.

My mental circuits jammed as panic jolted through me.

"People know about you," I said. "I've got evidence. If something happens to me—"

"We're pretty thorough. But I do appreciate your concern."

I looked down at the moving trains and wondered if I'd make it or still get shot in the back. From the corner of my eye, I saw a hand reach for my shoulder. I whirled, buried the Enforcer in the armpit of a trim man wearing a translucent, plastic mask, and blasted him with two million volts. His body tightened and convulsed, and when I released the trigger, he crumpled, a canister of pepper spray clattering to the trestle.

I spun back to Pope in time to see his boot coming up. Turning sideways to evade the full force of the kick, I got ahold of his leg and zapped him in the groin. He bellowed like a bull elephant. I kept my hold on his leg to keep him off-balance. We were too close for him to shoot, and I zapped his balls again, juicing him up for three seconds. He gnashed his teeth, saliva splashing my face. His gun dropped with a clatter, landing near the other guy, who was on all fours.

Pope roared, convulsed, and bucked me off. We both stumbled back, catching ourselves on opposite sides of the railing. "Not nice, Sloane," he said. The gun was five feet from me, twice that for Pope. He saw my eyes go to it and smiled again. "On three," he said. "One, two—"

I dove, grabbing the pistol just as Pope tackled me from the side, pinning me to the railing. The silenced barrel inched toward my face as he twisted my gun hand back on me. The hand that held the Enforcer was crushed between our locked torsos. When the barrel was pointed at my left ear, he said, "Let's try that again. One, two—"

I pulled the trigger of the Enforcer, frying us both. A shot rang out and I felt a searing at the top of my ear and wet heat running down my cheek. The bullet zinged off an iron beam overhead. More bullets sang as they met steel, hot casings bouncing off my face. The empty gun continued to click by my ear. Muscle spasms kept my finger on the trigger, and my body firmly in Pope's death-clutch. His face vibrated before me.

My finger slipped from the trigger, cutting the current. Pope pulled back, gun back in hand again. His breath came hard and raspy as he reached into his jacket for another magazine.

I leapt forward, stabbing the Enforcer into the middle of the yonic tattoo, twisting the prongs until skin ripped and blood jumped out. Fumbling for the trigger, I hit the flashlight function by mistake, and Pope's skull appeared to illuminate from within.

Finding the trigger, I zapped his carotid and a crackling sound came from his mouth.

His partner grabbed me from behind, pulling me down. Pope advanced, still fumbling with his pistol. A hissing sound made me squeeze my eyes tight as fire ants stormed into my nose and lungs. I coughed and rolled, blindly kicking him away.

I rose to my feet, eyes still shut. My burning lungs refused air as I grabbed the railing for support.

Through smudged vision, I saw Pope leaning back against the railing, spitting blood as he slammed the magazine into the pistol.

Sirens in the distance.

And a low rumble from the opposite direction.

Footsteps clanged down the stairs as his partner split.

Pope looked up, tears and snot streaming down his face. He raised the gun, and I smashed him in the throat with the butt of the Enforcer, then on his wrist. The gun fell to the tracks below. I zapped him in the heart and held it there as skeins of blood spurted from his nostrils. When I released the trigger, his body went slack, his spine arched over the railing. I dug the prongs of the weapon into his neck wound.

"Who do you work for?"

He coughed out a chuckle as he opened his eyes.

I zapped him, holding the trigger down, pushing him back further.

"Why did you kill Eva? Who ordered it?"

His eyes were withering black pools of hate.

"Why did they have to die?"

"Same reason you will," he rasped. "Because you're too stupid to get it: money always wins."

I looked down to Commissioner Street, where the Olds peeled away from the berm. My vision was too blurry to make the plate.

Through sheets of rain, police lights came from the west. The rumbling grew louder.

In one final burst of strength, he shoved me off. This action resulted in his long torso bending backward over the rail and his feet lifting off the walkway. I grabbed for his legs, but he was too heavy.

Pope did a complete backflip, gonging his head off the corner of the top of a stopped freight train, and landing partly on the tracks—

—where an eastbound locomotive sliced off both legs mid-thigh.

Screaming train brakes drowned out the sirens. I flung the Enforcer into the brambles, where it crashed five feet to the right of a *No Trespassing* sign and disappeared into a thicket. Bounding down the stairs, I ran to Pope, grabbed his jacket and pulled him away from the tracks. Arterial blood fountained rhythmically from the stumps, turning the mud puddles red.

"*Pope!*" I screamed. "*What is the Carriage?*"

Footsteps ran toward us and a flashlight shone in Pope's eyes just in time to see the life flicker out.

CHAPTER 35

POPE'S BULLET HAD ONLY NICKED THE TOP OF my ear. When I told the ER doctor about persistent ringing, he diagnosed it as a ruptured eardrum and informed me there could be lasting damage. The truth about silenced guns is that they aren't that silent. My upper chest sported angry, red scorch marks from the volts I took, and the pepper spray left my throat and lungs feeling sandblasted.

"How did these burns occur?" the doctor asked.

"Stun gun," I said.

"I'll get you something for the pain."

No more fucking pills. "Not necessary," I said.

A cop named Pierce drove me to the Cambie station to take my statement. He had an athletic build and a white-blond buzz cut. I kept my head down and made eye contact with no one as he led me to one of the interview rooms, where he offered me water. I gulped it down and he got me more.

"Had you ever seen either of the men before tonight?" Pierce asked.

"Never," I said. "What was his name—the one who died?"

"Chance Epop."

"How do you spell that?"

"E-P-O-P."

Epop. Pope. Jesus Christ.

"Did Mr. Epop have a record?" I asked.

He looked at me strangely. "Yeah. No arrests the past couple years, though. You got lucky tonight, Sloane." His chin tilted toward my bandaged left ear. "A half-inch more, and ..."

I nodded.

"That stun gun you said the second man had—you were able to turn it around on them—*how?*"

"Dirty tricks."

"Uh-huh. So you say this Tia just contacted you out of the blue saying she had information?"

"She was there the first time I met Eva—the girl I was helping."

After giving Pierce my version of the truth, I was distracted by something through the glass window to my left. It was Steve Bolger, the coroner, eyeballing me. His hammy knuckles rapped on the glass.

"Oh, God," I mumbled.

Bolger opened the door. "Seeing a lot of you these days, Donovan. What's up with you and the bodies? You'll do anything to get back in here, huh?"

Pierce's look got stranger as he slid the statement across the table for me to sign.

"Speaking of," I said to Bolger, "did you do the autopsy on Eva Carmichael?"

Pierce rose. As they passed each other, Bolger gave him a *tell-you-over-a-beer-later* smirk. Pierce left.

"What if I did?" Bolger asked.

"Because Chance Epop threw her off the roof of the Balhaven. Eva didn't commit suicide. I had been helping her. She was clean. You didn't find any drugs in her system, I bet."

"No, but we *did* find a suicide note in her room. Said she couldn't take it anymore. Lotta roof divers down there." He gave me a hard look. "Lotta *mental illness*. People going off their *meds*."

"Was the letter printed off a computer or handwritten?"

"Drop it."

"I'd like to see it."

"In your fucking *dreams*, Donovan. Parents are coming in from Saskatchewan tomorrow to deal with the remains. What's all this to you?"

"Like I said, I was helping her."

"Like you were helping Geri Harp last month. Like you helped your sister? If you really want to keep people alive, maybe the solution is to stop helping them. Just sayin'."

The whining in my ear grew and I shook my head to clear it. I glanced up to see Bolger staring at me with disgust. It was a just a good thing I'd ditched the Enforcer, or I would have shoved it up his fat ass.

A uniform dropped me back at my Jeep. After he drove away, I opened up the rear, took out a BioLite and strapped it around my head. I also pulled a pair of running gloves onto my still-shaking hands. I retraced the same steps down to the trestle as the previous evening. Less than six hours ago, Pope had bled out on the tracks below, and as far as police were concerned, it was one less scumbag ex-con off the streets. No yellow crime scene tape, no chalk outline of a body minus the legs. They would have shut down the tracks for a minimal amount of time, just enough to take photos, cart away the corpse, and conduct a cursory search of the area. If my body had ended up there instead of Pope's, the train schedules might have been thrown off for slightly longer. Of course, the point was moot, for if Pope and his buddy had succeeded, I would have wound up in the trunk of the Olds, to be buried somewhere or dumped in the ocean. Or worse.

I shuddered, in part from the thought, in part from the cold, and in part due to my own carelessness. I had walked straight into a trap that surely would have been fatal had it not been for the Enforcer.

I found the *No Trespassing* sign and climbed over the railing into the brambles. After fifteen minutes of inching my way through and trying not to get ripped alive by thorns, I had my trusty zapper back. Due to prolonged usage the previous night, its battery was dead.

Back in the Jeep, I keyed the ignition and sat there a long time, replaying the scene over and over. After all this, the only thing I had was Pope's real name. He wasn't at the top of the food chain; merely muscle for a larger organization. I still had no link between him and Geri.

I pulled out my phone and called Wayne. "Who died now, Donovan?"

"Pope," I said.

CHAPTER 36

Monday, November 11

BACK AT THE SAFE HOUSE, I MAXED THE thermostats and took a steaming shower to scrub off Pope's blood. Wrapped in a towel, I walked back into the living room with a Sharpie and wrote the name **CHANCE EPOP** above **POPE.** I paused. Then, with a tiny sliver of satisfaction, I put an X through both names.

1:49 a.m. All was dark and quiet at Dogger's. Naz's mic picked up only snoring. The GPS app on my phone showed Dogger's car still at Hillside.

Wayne spotted me in a rear booth of Smile Café. He sat, took in my face and bandaged ear, and shook his head. He opened his mouth, and I raised a hand.

"If I were a guy, it would barely be an issue. So drop it. What do you got?"

He sighed and slid a file across the table. I opened it. Chance Epop. Mug shot and prints. DOB 02/08/85. Three pages of arrests, heavy on assaults and weapons charges. Meth dealing. Extortion. All in Québec and Ontario. Appeared Epop got his crooked gene from his father, who was shot dead in a Montréal bank heist in '88. Just like the cop told me last night, Epop's record had been incongruously clean for nearly two years. No record of him being arrested in Vancouver.

"Here's an interesting thing I learned," he said. "Epop and Tim Womack both did time in Warkworth in Ontario five years ago. Their stretches overlapped by about a year, enough time to become BFFs."

The waitress came to take our order. After she had left, Wayne said, "Now flip to the back page, under 'known associates.'"

I did. Beneath a long list of bad boys from Québec, a Bonnie Tremblay was listed as his long-term girlfriend. In 2012, the two of them were pinched for a home invasion/drug rip where they each did a year.

Wayne did a drum roll on the table, then slid me Bonnie Ellen Tremblay's file. When I opened it to the mug shot, it was like seeing a ghost.

A ghost of a young, pale, hard-eyed Geri Harp.

Or Darci, for that matter.

The woman in the car the day of the funeral.

DOB: 30/08/90 — Montréal.

Adopted when she was six weeks old, birth parents unknown.

I looked up at Wayne, and he nodded.

"The other daughter," I said.

"Fuckin' A."

I scanned the file. Bonnie's sheet wasn't as long as her boyfriend's, but she shared his penchant for violent, drug-related crimes. Like her man, she apparently found the light two years ago. Just like Kai and Tim Womack, it appeared they'd cleaned up their acts at exactly the same time.

I never was one for coincidences, especially when it came to career criminals.

A printout from the motor vehicle department showed two vehicles registered in her name: a 1978 Oldsmobile Cutlass and a 1982 Winnebago.

"A Winnebago?" I said. "Were Bonnie and Pope planning a road trip?"

"I don't know, but it also says in there she cut up a girl's face pretty bad over a drug dispute. Imagine what she could do to the woman who killed her man."

"Didn't Womack also have an RV registered in his name?"

"Lot of white trash do. Handy for cooking meth."

I stood. "Let's go find out."

"Sit the fuck down, Skinny Minnie," Wayne said, just as the waitress brought our eggs, hash browns, bacon, and toast. I wasn't hungry.

He slathered strawberry jam on his toast. "If you don't be a good girl and clean your plate, I'm cutting you out of the information train—hey, you okay? What's with the look?"

"Bit of a headache," I said.

He reached into his jacket pocket. "I never leave home without Tylenol."

I waved him off. "I'm fine."

Brunch over, we hopped in my Jeep and drove out to Renfrew and 22nd, last known address of Bonnie Tremblay, which comprised the left half of a pink stucco duplex. The temperature hovered around freezing, and snow was falling but not enough to stick. I cut down the alley behind the duplex. No Olds. No Winnebago. We parked down the street with a view of the front of the duplex. Wayne told me to stay put as he walked up to the front door and knocked. I held my breath, thinking of Pope's gun and the list of weapons offenses on Bonnie's sheet. Wayne knocked again.

The door on the other side of the duplex opened, and a gangly, middle-aged man stuck his head out. Wayne engaged the man for a minute before walking back to the car.

Wayne climbed back in the car and blew on his hands. "She cleared out in the middle of the night. Woke the neighbour up due to the ruckus she was making. When he looked out, he said she was crying and seemed real flustered. Cops came by an hour ago."

"Think they'll be on the lookout for the vehicles?"

"Only if you told them about the Olds last night. Did you?"

"They didn't ask."

"You know, they just might be able catch some of these people. Bonnie may have been driving the car last night. That would make her an accessory."

"Of all people, Bolger had to make an appearance while I was being interviewed. Had I told them then, I would have been laughed out of the station; they're all convinced I'm nuts."

"Yeah, I get that, but last night was attempted *murder*. That means people go to jail. Meaning members of the tattoo squad aren't floating around looking to finish the job." He snapped his fingers in my face. "Wake up, space case. Jesus."

I blinked and focused my eyes. "When she cleared out, which vehicle did she take?"

"The Olds. Neighbour said he's never once seen a Winnebago around. Maybe she parks it somewhere else."

"We need to find those rides."

"Big city," he said. "If she's even still in it."

"She's somewhere. Can you use your source to send out a BOLO?"

"Impossible. That would require *serious* authorization, *and* justification." He tapped the files sitting between us. "I've been calling in a lot of favours just to get you *this*. Maybe you shouldn't have burned all your bridges when you quit the cops."

I started the Jeep. "The Downtown Eastside is where we need to focus. We canvass the locals. Do a grid search for RVs."

"Uh-uh. You need sleep, and I've got some jobs that actually pay. Promise me you'll go home and rest. And take your goddamn meds."

Back at the safe house, I stared at the wall of names until the room tilted sideways and I had to lie down. I blinked and saw Geri's dead face. Then a speed-reel of faces: Eva, Pope, Bonnie, Dogger, Naz, Grady, Darci, Ghorbani, even Mace and my attackers from New Ways.

I sat up, stayed completely still for a full minute. Then I rose, walked to the wall and tacked a blank card above all the others. On it, based on a gut feeling, I wrote, NEW WAYS WOMEN'S SHELTER?

Four clients and a spin class in the afternoon. Driving into the club, I didn't see the blue Porsche anywhere. I set the iPhone tracker on pinpoint and my heart skipped a beat. It showed the car to be parked on the service road where I'd found Geri.

Parking by the tennis bubble, I checked the app as I jogged down the grassy slope by the courts. Circling behind the groundskeeper's shed, I emerged onto the gravel road with the clearing up ahead. No Porsche.

I walked closer, guided by the pulsing red dot on the screen.

It led me to the light post where the camera was located—where the GPS iTrail was stuck to the post, along with the two microphones.

Back in my car, my heart beat double time. How the hell did he find the GPS so quickly? And who was the other party listening in on his bedroom? Maybe Dogger himself, but I doubted it.

My mind raced in ten different directions. There was an odd buzzing sound, which I first thought was my ear, but then I realized it was coming from the Mac in my shoulder bag. I flipped it open. The buzzing became creepy electronic laughter. My screensaver was of Machu Picchu, but the pixels were quivering, going berserk, and imploding. I clicked on the internet icon, but nothing happened. It looked like hundreds of tiny electronic worms were devouring the screen. Nothing would open. In the lower-left corner, a laughing monkey appeared, pointing at me.

Then the laptop died.

CHAPTER 37

MY HANDS SHOOK AS I WALKED INTO WORK. MY head spun and the buzzing in my ear grew, putting the world even more off-kilter. I sucked it up the best I could and trained a client, who kept stealing glances at my bandaged ear, not buying my story of an infected piercing.

Just before four, I was at the water fountain, when Floyd, Hillside's chief of security approached me and informed me that Mr. Ross, the CEO, wanted to speak with me.

"Right now?"

He wrung his hands. "Right now. I'll walk with you."

I knew what it was about: the day I had joined Dogger in the Club Lounge. Being a contractor, it was a no-no. I'd be written up.

Passing by the admin desks, some of the girls gave me funny looks, others seemed to avoid eye contact.

Let's get this over with, I thought, as Floyd rapped twice on Ross's door. The door opened and there was Cyrus Ghorbani, in uniform. The office was standing room only.

Grady Harp glared at me, flanked by another suit, and an attractive female cop, while in the background, Mr. Ross sat grimly behind his desk. My heart entered my throat and my ear roared.

I considered bolting, but Ghorbani was already closing the door. I noted the laptop on Ross's desk. On the screen, I saw the frozen image of myself by Geri's Audi the day she died. They had my computer files. With a skull full of hornets, I could only make out the odd word from Ghorbani's mouth as he read me my rights.

Ross followed with, "Your contract is terminated immediately."

"I was trying to help," *If you'd just let me explain,* I thought, *you will all understand.* But the words wouldn't come.

"Give me a break," Grady said. "You weaseled your way into my daughter's life under the guise of *helping* her. She told me how you tried to sneak into New Ways under false pretenses."

The suit tried to intervene, but Grady shooed him off.

"I tried to help her," I said.

He tapped a button on the laptop and played the footage from the day I found her. It felt like I was leaving my body as we watched the scene of me performing CPR, then stealing the note before the cops came.

"Where is it?" Grady asked.

"Gone."

"Why?"

"I wanted to save you and Darci pain. I destroyed it."

Grady stepped toward me. The suit held him back. "There'll be a search warrant," he said.

I turned to Ghorbani, who looked slightly amused by all this. "Why you?"

His eyes hardened.

"Why *you?*" I asked again. "Of all the cops in West Vancouver, why are *you* here? You were the first on the scene the day I called it in, and now you're here *again*."

His eyes flicked over to his partner. Her nameplate read: IVANOVITCH. His expressions said, *don't worry, I'm not going to engage this whack job.*

"I'm going to be sick." I turned, opened the door and whirled from the room. Ghorbani yelled and reached for me, but he wasn't built for speed. I made it past the offices and into the women's washroom, where I locked the door and made retching sounds. I pulled out my iPhone and fired Wayne a text:

COMPUTER HACKED ARRESTED AT WORK GRADY HERE WITH LAWYER

I flushed the toilet and ran the faucet. Ghorbani hammered on the door. Hopping up on the toilet seat, I reached up and pushed the rectangular ceiling tile up, slid my phone in there and closed it up again.

The moment I left the washroom, cuffs were slapped on my wrists. Floyd stood nearby, nervously holding my jacket and bag, which he'd retrieved from the Personal Training office. Ivanovitch took my belongings.

En route to the station, I asked Ghorbani if he'd ever heard of a guy named Andy "Dogger" Peretti.

"Should I?"

"He was the last person Geri Harp called before she died. The Hillside tennis pro who was screwing her. And get this: she wrote him into her will to the tune of four million dollars."

Ghorbani was silent; in the mirror, his eyes alternated from the road to back at me. I nearly mentioned Naz, but elected to hold onto that card for now.

"The new codicil to her will was added just days before her death. I'm certain he had something to do with it."

Ghorbani pulled into the alley behind the police station and parked. As they pulled me from the back seat, I looked into his eyes. "Just do me a favour and remember the name *Andrew Peretti*, because you're going to come across it in the near future, I promise you."

I paced my holding cell for just over two hours before the door opened and a different cop escorted me to an interview room, where Wayne's lawyer waited. Ben Tierney was a bald fireplug, around fifty, wearing thick glasses on a thin, silver chain around his neck and a grey suit that was too tight in the shoulders.

After the cop left the room, I shook the lawyer's hand and we sat at the table. In front of him was a file with my name on it. "Capson's filled me in on the situation." Tierney's voice was gilded with a Maritime lilt. "Anything else I need to know?"

I shook my head.

"Good. Here's the thing, Sloane. You've made Grady Harp a very pissed-off man. He's the kind of guy who hires the top lawyers in town to annihilate people for sport. I managed to appeal to a tiny sliver of sensitivity in the man by filling him in on your mental health history. There's also the fact that you and his late wife were friends. Even so, he did file a restraining order. Under no circumstances are you to contact any member of the Harp family. You are not to come within a hundred metres of the Harps or their properties.

This includes New Ways Women's Shelter." Tierney leaned in and made eye contact. "Do you understand this, Sloane?"

"Yes."

"Police will be searching your home, along with your work locker, your car, and any storage units or safety deposit boxes you may have in your name. Is there anything else they might find that would incriminate you?"

I shook my head, and he pushed some papers at me to sign.

From a payphone down the street, I called Karin, who was in hysterics. In my periphery, I saw a black muzzle emerging from a window of a grey sedan, but when I whirled around it was a station wagon with a Canucks pennant attached to the window frame.

"Karin," I said, "calm down. I'll explain later. Just listen … I need you to go into the washroom by the admin office. Stand on the toilet and push up the ceiling panel nearest the left corner. My phone is in there. You got a pen? Here's where I am."

After jogging a circuitous route back to the safe house to make sure I didn't have a tail, I found Naz's microphones still operational. She was exercising to the sounds of a P90X workout, and making similar vocalizations to when she and Dogger had sex. An hour passed. Then, through the window, down on the street, I saw Karin's Kia pull up. She got out, eyeing the building with disdain. She buzzed up, and a minute later, I opened the door. She gave me a hug, then looked around the room wearing a mask of incomprehension.

"If your mother saw this," she said, "you'd be back in psych so fucking fast."

"They made me. Kai Abacon hacked my computer and the files got to Grady Harp."

Her eyes went to the unmade bed in the corner, the surveillance equipment by the window, then up to the photos and names on the wall. "You *live* here now?"

"It's just temporary, but thank God I got it, because this is where I've been keeping the files and evidence."

Silent, Karin handed me back my phone. "I've already called your mother," she said. "I won't tell her about *this*, but she's coming to see you."

Something burst inside me. Everything was suddenly steeped in red. "Thanks for bringing me my phone, Karin. You can leave now."

"I can't stand to see what you're doing to yourself."

"What are you *talking* about? This has nothing to do with me. This is—"

"You just lost your job, Sloane, and you were led out from the club in cuffs."

"And I'm sure that will provide great fodder for the gossip mill at Hillside for the next week. Same way Geri's death did. I can't expect you or anyone up there to understand."

"Understand *what*, exactly?"

"Oh, I don't know ... a good friend of mine was killed and it's a set up, and no one but me gives a shit."

"Why did the police arrest you?"

"I just told you what happened."

"You need to get out of here, Sloane. Please, come with me."

"And do *what?* Go with you and do *what?* Go home and take my meds and watch fucking Netflix?"

"Something like that, yeah. It would be preferable to whatever this is."

"Let's say it was *you* I found dead in the car that day. Everyone—"

"It wasn't me, so—"

"—wants to sweep it under the rug, call it suicide, except I know different, and I don't expect cooperation, but maybe I'd like just a little bit of time to prove that my friend did not *kill herself.* Why the fuck is that too much to ask, Karin?"

"I don't think that's what it is anymore. You're obsessed. And your friend is *gone.* You don't care about anything else and you're not taking care of yourself—"

"You're not listening to me! I'm *doing* something here. I'm in the middle of cracking open a big fucking evil."

Tears welled in her eyes. I nearly slapped her.

"They tossed her off the roof," I said, pacing around the room as Karin stood statue-still and regarded me like I was a bomb counting down to zero. "She was getting better and they murdered her because they knew she was talking to me. Then they tried to kill me but they can't, because I'm *meant* to do this."

"You need help, Sloane."

"You need to get the fuck out of here."

I turned and went to the window and put on the headphones. In the reflection of the glass I watched Karin stand there for a full minute before she turned and walked out the door. A few moments later, I watched her walk out to her car and get in without looking back.

A tiny voice in my head told me to run after her and apologize, tell her that everything would be all right, she'd see.

I killed the fucking voice.

Karin drove away.

On my phone were eleven messages. Most from confused clients who'd heard what happened. Two from my mother, which I erased without listening to.

And Darci.

"I'm really sorry, Sloane. I don't understand ... I don't know what your issue is. I thought we were friends, but I'm hurt that you took my mother's letter and lied to me. For what it's worth, I really enjoyed our time together, and you did *help me when I needed you, so thank you—and goodbye."*

I listened to the message over and over until the words meant nothing and I was wholly numb. My phone began buzzing. Wayne.

I dropped the phone on the floor.

I had failed.

It was over.

CHAPTER 38

FLASHES. LIKE IMAGES FROM A HALF-remembered dream. 3rd Street. Lonsdale. Snow. Cold. Enforcer in hand. Bright lights. Honking horns. Highway. Moon and stars, shadows and movement. If I stopped moving, I would die. Hillside cameras. Woods. Hissing trees. Kissing dead Geri. Sea to Sky Highway. Black mountains. Numbness. Lions Bay. Geri blowing Dogger. Darci watching. Eva's body tumbling over the cliff. Eva's dead baby, hung from its own umbilical cord. The icy wind chimed with the laughter of an unknown woman. Severed legs twitched by the train tracks.

At the Britannia Beach sign, I laughed and ran and ran and fell into a black pit of beautiful nothingness.

"JESUS Christ, what have you done?"

Wayne's blurry face, as he lifted me into the back seat of his Pathfinder.

"How?" I croaked.

He held up the Enforcer, unscrewed the back, and showed me the GPS chip. "Someone's gotta keep an eye on you, kid."

Black.

* * *

I woke up in bed—my own bed, not in a psych ward, thank God. Snowflakes fell outside the window. The clock said 3:47 p.m., and I could smell my mother's Nivea hand cream. My meds sat on the bedside table, along with a glass of water and packets of electrolytes.

I heard her humming in the kitchen, a Fleetwood Mac song I didn't know the title of. My head pounded and my sinuses were packed with jagged stones. My throat felt shredded when I tried to swallow, and every muscle ached and throbbed so bad that if had one of Tia's H-bombers, I would've sparked up pronto.

I sat up and groaned. I was wearing pink pyjamas. I never wore pyjamas. I tried to stand, but my shins shrieked and I fell back onto the bed.

"Wouldn't surprise me if you had stress fractures on your shins," said Dawn Donovan from the doorway. She wore an orange cashmere cardigan and jeans and looked at me with worry-lined eyes. "Thank God Wayne found you when he did. You ran nearly thirty miles with no water. You could've easily died."

She sat on the bed beside me. Her red hair was streaked with silver, and her lean face provided an accurate prediction of my cosmetic future.

"The police came while you were sleeping," she said. "I spent the last three hours cleaning up after them. I don't understand what this is about."

I looked out the window, trying to make sense of anything. I could feel the haze of Ativan or lithium in my brain and had a vague flashback of being made to take a pill and drink some water prior to passing out.

Everyone drugs everyonedrugseveryonedrugseveryone.

Drugs, anyone?

"I want you to come to the Island with me for a while, Sloane, so we can figure out the next step."

"No."

"I am *not* losing another daughter," she said. "I'll do what I have to do, even if it means having you committed again. Karin supports me on this, by the way."

"Yeah, well, Karin—"

"Is someone to whom you owe an apology. You're lucky to have friends who care so much about you. Now, I made an appointment with a new therapist in Victoria—"

"I'm not going to the Island, Mom. This is my home. I am *not* suicidal. And I'm not delusional. Something big is going on. Ask Wayne."

My mother put on her disappointed-parent face, the same one she has used to deal with me since I was four. "I'm staying until I'm convinced you're stabilized," she said. "I'll bring you a cup of French onion soup."

"Not hungry," I said.

"You look like a concentration camp survivor."

"Maybe I'll load up on SSRIs and turn into a big fatty. See how everyone likes me then."

"Must everything be so extreme with you? You've been underweight since you were a teenager. You could easily stand to gain ten pounds. Unlike your cat. Where *is* Eclipse, by the way?"

"He ran away."

"Likely due to your constant fat shaming."

"Yeah, he was sensitive about that."

My mother tsk-tsked, then turned and left the room humming. It was a contented hum. A sick daughter gave her a purpose in life.

Days melted into weeks. I popped pills, ate, watched TV, and slept, spending the entire time in my pyjamas. I gained five pounds the first week. Karin came to visit every day. I apologized, and she just nodded and told me she loved and accepted me, despite everything. "Hillside isn't the same with you gone," she said. "What are you going to do now?"

I shrugged and stared into space. I truly had no idea. That's the thing about the pills: nothing much matters. Oh, you're going to lose both tits and half your face? Them's the breaks. Nuclear holocaust? Oh, well, I guess I won't have to worry about doing my taxes this year. The world takes on a bland Pablum-like flavour. I didn't even want a drink anymore.

Wayne came over for dinner one night, clean-shaven, wearing a blue blazer over a white Oxford, looking like a JW fresh from handing out church pamphlets. My mother made lasagna and garlic bread. She clearly thought he was the cat's ass, and he knew how to charm the old gal. "Now I know where your daughter gets her striking looks," he said upon arrival. I'd never seen my mother blush before.

It was a dry reserve. Milk for Wayne, water for me. When my mother left the room to get dessert, Wayne leaned in and told me he'd snagged the microphones from Naz's place.

"Quite the program you had going at the surveillance pad. I popped in for a look-see. Serious camera you got over there."

Motioning for him to keep his voice down, I whispered that the camera was a rental and I hadn't gotten around to returning it yet. My mother came back with plates of key lime pie and whipped cream.

Wayne rubbed his hands together. "Ms. Donovan, you *do* know the way to this man's heart."

"Call me Dawn," she said.

I made a surreptitious gagging motion behind her back.

My mother kept at me to go out to the Island, and get away from the big, evil city. She even offered to pay my bills while I was away. I was worried that given the right amount of medication, I'd agree to anything. It was getting harder and harder to say no to her.

As far as work went, I wasn't worried. I'd figure out something. I could always do freelance training, or open a dog-walking business, sell ice cream from a van, or turn back-alley tricks. Or just keep sleeping, because it actually felt pretty good to escape into a dreamless void. Steph might have been on to something.

After another ten days, my mother seemed satisfied with my level of zombification, because one day I woke up at noon to see her bags by the door. "I've got to go back to work," she said. "Karin's going to be reporting to me. Daily. This is your last chance, by the way."

Over the next week I slept and dragged myself around the condo. My legs had mostly healed, but I had no desire to run or even venture outside. The ringing in my ear had lessened but still returned from time to time.

Karin came over to play nursemaid and make sure I took my meds. She avoided talking about Hillside, but I wouldn't have cared if she had. Reality seemed distant. We played Cards Against Humanity and watched Netflix. Each night

I fell asleep midway through a show and awoke sometime in the middle of the night with a blanket over me.

One snowy day, a buzzer woke me from an afternoon nap. A UPS deliveryman handed me a package from Minneapolis. Confused, I signed for it, took it inside, and tore it open.

I didn't remember ordering the placebo lithium and Celexa, but I'm glad I did. I drank a large mug of coffee along with two Pre-Workout Energizers to gain some lucidity. Then I counted out the real pills and replaced them with an equal number of the fakes.

I turned on the fireplace and wrapped myself in a blanket and flipped channels. Being out of the loop, I watched the news. A stabbing on Kingsway last night, more traffic woes, City Hall talking about increasing bike lanes. It made me dozy. I was drifting when I heard a familiar voice. My eyes snapped open.

On television, Darci Harp was being interviewed in front of New Ways Shelter. She wore a blue jacket with white pinstripes, and matching skirt. Her hair was auburn and swept back, and her blue eyes were as arresting as ever behind chunky, black glasses.

"It's often said a place should be judged by how it treats its most vulnerable. If that's true, then this city is a failure. For decades now, the Downtown Eastside has been a drug war zone. Our politicians have promised change, but statistically there are twice as many people experiencing homelessness today as there were five years ago. And overdose deaths and violence against women are at an all-time high.

"My goal as director of New Ways Women's Shelter is to carry on with my mother's dream of getting our city's most vulnerable women off the street. To keep them off the street, they need more than a roof over their heads. They need skills that will help them reintegrate into society.

"Gentrification combined with a sharp spike in the cost of living has meant that there are more women on the street than ever. A lot of them are teens, some scarcely more than children. We *need* the public's help to expand our services to the most vulnerable in our community. I implore you to donate—even just a few dollars, whatever you can afford. Your money will directly impact not only these women—these grandmothers, mothers, daughters, and grandchildren—it will help this city actually deserve the title of 'most livable.' It will become more livable for *everyone.*"

The girl was good enough to run for office.

The camera pulled back to show her surrounded by a sea of women: young and old, teens, and teens holding babies. To Darci's immediate right stood Mace and on the left were Shovel Face and the other two smoking women who attacked me at the shelter, showing jagged-toothed smiles for the camera. They looked like a retinue of skid row bodyguards flanking their queen.

I recalled what Darci had told me about reviewing camera footage inside New Ways the night I went undercover. She would have known *exactly* who assaulted me, and rather than reprimand my attackers, it appeared they had been promoted.

A sick feeling began to gnaw at my gut, and it continued as the news crew took the cameras inside the shelter, showing it packed with women. Every seat in the dining area was occupied. The library was full of studious, apparently back-on-track women: pregnant women in neonatal classes; Mace smiling in the background, passing out baby dolls to the teenage mothers-to-be so they could practice changing diapers.

I turned off the TV and stared out the window, watching the snowflakes flutter down. My mind began steering in a different direction, and as a new picture began to emerge, I felt even sicker.

CHAPTER 39

Friday, December 6

WAYNE SAT ON A LAWN CHAIR IN THE SAFE
house, drinking a Pabst, his expression sphinxlike. Earlier,
to enhance the mood, I'd strung some blue Christmas lights
around the railing of the balcony and put up a small, lopsided tree in the corner.

I stood in front of the window, where Dogger's building
was barely visible through the heavy snowfall. "I saw her on
TV trying to rake in donations, as she practically stood arm-
in-arm with the women who attacked me in New Ways. I
think she's turned the shelter into a front. She put on a big
act for the news crew, but when I was there the place was less
than half full, and it felt like a prison. They get the women
in so they're registered, and then kick them out on some
trumped-up charge. Tia hinted that there was a 'high turnover rate.' Being that the entire Downtown Eastside creates
a syndrome of victimization, who are the women going to
complain to? They're just trying to survive day-to-day."

Wayne remained silent.

"Yeah, I know. You probably agree with my mother that I need to be committed."

He shook his head. "I wasn't going to tell you this, but while you were convalescing. I took on a missing teen case. Sixteen-year-old girl, runaway from out in the Fraser Valley, substance problem, ended up hooking."

"Yeah?"

"I spent some time on the skids, and after a couple days got a bead on her. But before I could locate her, she ended up dead. Nose-dive off the Astoria. Typed suicide note left behind. If I'd found her only a few hours earlier, that kid would still be alive." He took a gulp of beer and made a face. "That fucking burns me up, let me tell you."

The hairs on my arms stood on end. "This girl—she have a yonic tattoo?"

"I don't know. But I do know she spent some time at New Ways Shelter."

"We need to talk to any employees who were fired after Geri's death."

He gave me a hard look. "You up to this, Slim?"

"What—you thought I was going to give up?"

"So we need to build a solid case the cops *cannot* ignore. Cracking this thing could give the business a serious boost. Frankly, I'm sick of living like a schmuck."

"My name has to be kept out of this. I'll be arrested the minute the cops think I have anything to do with it."

"You had nothing to do with the missing girl case. We'll start there and keep you deep in the background."

"We need to get back inside New Ways."

"I know just the guy."

The lithium was still puttering around in my system, so I ended up falling asleep in what was once Eva's bed, waking at midnight in a dopey stupor. I pulled on my jacket and was about to go home, when I looked up to Dogger's condo and saw a flicker of movement. I walked to the window and raised the telephoto to my eye—

—and nearly dropped it on the floor.

Darci was naked on the couch, breasts heaving as she rode Dogger. It shouldn't have surprised me, but it did. I pulled myself together and snapped photos. "You lying bitch," I muttered.

They finished, and Darci rose and walked toward the bathroom, laughing and smiling over her shoulder. Dogger lounged back, a dumb but contented smile on his face.

I went to the wall and tacked a fresh index card above all the others. On it I wrote: DARCI.

Then I phoned Wayne, who wasn't happy to have been woken up, but he listened intently when I told him what I just saw.

"I thought she hated the guy," he said.

"Apparently not. We need to assume everything she ever told me is bullshit."

CHAPTER 40

Saturday, December 7

THE FOLLOWING MORNING ARRIVED BRIGHT and sunny, a glare coming off the fresh snow on the sides of Cordova Street. Wayne and I wore sunglasses as we sat in his Pathfinder a block down from New Ways. The rear passenger door opened and an old man climbed in, setting crutches on the seat beside him.

"Francesco, you old dago sonofabitch," Wayne said.

It was Frank. Had I not been wise to his getup, I'd never have recognized him from the last time. He had a neatly clipped silver mustache and appeared thirty years older. He wore a grey-checkered suit with elbow patches, bow tie, and a black fedora.

"My name," he said, affecting a strong Italian accent, "is Francesco Marzocco. And my wife—God rest her beautiful soul—she die in a car crash just down the street."

Wayne grinned and slipped a pen microphone in the breast pocket of Frank's suit jacket and handed him glasses that had a micro-camera built into the frame.

"Love the Italian," Wayne said. "Genius. Frank used to be a voice-over actor in Poland."

We watched Frank get out with his crutches and hobble down Cordova toward New Ways. Wayne turned up the volume on the receiver and set it on the dash.

"Why Italian?" I asked.

"People can't resist an old, broken-hearted Italian guy. British or French, people think they're assholes; won't even crack the door."

Frank buzzed at the New Ways' door.

Bette: This is a women's shelter, sir.
Frank: (emotional) I know, signora, it's my wife. You
see, she die in a car crash (turned and gestured up
the street with his crutch) and one of your workers
was the only witness of the accident.
B: What was her name, sir?
F: I can't remember. My head got hurt. All's I
know is she said she worked here—or used to work
here.
B: How long ago was that?
F: Two months ago.
B: Come in, sir. I'll run down some names for you,
see if any sound familiar.

"Fucking guy deserves an Oscar," Wayne said.

Five minutes later, Frank crutched back to us, opened the door, and climbed in. From the glasses-cam, Wayne downloaded a photo of an employee/volunteer list onto his laptop. He emailed it to me and I pulled it up on my iPhone.

"Any of these names look familiar?" he asked.

I quickly scanned down the list of about twenty names. "Nope. You take the top half, I'll take the rest."

Leaning back over the seat, I grabbed the pen recorder from Frank's pocket, and gave him a kiss on the cheek. I hopped out of the Pathfinder and walked down the block to my Jeep, got in and started calling.

The first three phone numbers were out of service, no great surprise given that many of the volunteers at the shelter were semi-transient. The fourth call was answered by a man who advised me to go and hump a tree. The woman who picked up at number five was so whacked out on something, her gibberish didn't appear to be in any known language. The sixth call merely rang forever. By the seventh, my hope was faltering, then a woman answered the phone.

"Is this Sally Mopper?" I asked.

"Who wants to know?"

"My name is Sandra Donnelly. I'm a journalist, and I'm doing a piece on recent layoffs at New Ways Women's Shelter. I was wondering if I might have a few moments of your time, Ms. Mopper."

A smoker's laugh. "You're wanting to talk to my mother. And her name isn't Mopper, it's Markell. They only called her that because she used to mop the floors at the shelter."

"Do you know where I might find her?"

"She lives with me now, but she's mostly blind."

"Do you mind if I come by for a quick chat?"

"I heard some reporters pay their sources. Do you?"

"Money's a little tight in the paper business these days, but I'll see what I can do."

An ancient woman watched me through the living-room window as I climbed the snowy cement steps and rang the bell. I smiled, but she stared back with cataract-ridden eyes.

The daughter, Jan Markell, ushered me in. She had a greying mullet and wore a yellow polo shirt and Lee jeans.

Some sort of religious program was on television—a sweaty, moon-faced preacher pleading for funds. A log blazed in the fireplace in the overheated living room, which contained a red-tinselled Christmas tree, branches drooping with candy canes and foil-wrapped Santas. The walls were lined with dusty aloe vera plants and cacti, and stacks of old *Reader's Digests* sat on the table beside an overflowing ashtray.

Jan grabbed the remote and muted the television. "Mom, this is the reporter I was telling you about." She turned to me. "What did you say your name was again?"

"Sandra Donnelly. Thank you for taking the time." I started to take off my shoes, but Jan frowned and shook her head. In a low voice she said, "That scratch you talked about?"

I handed her a ten and she frowned again.

"Don't upset her," she said. "She was crushed when they canned her."

"They canned everybody!" the old lady said. "Bunch of jerks."

I pulled up a chair next to her and sat down. "Who exactly do you mean, Mrs. Markell?"

She squinted at me. "Everyone. Every damn person there now."

"Can you be more specific? Was it before or after Geri Harp's death that you were let go?"

"Darn near *right* after," she said. "They cleaned house. Made up a bunch of garbage about how staff were stealing, or smuggling in booze and dope."

"Who are *they*? Are you referring to Darci Harp?"

"After knowing us all those years," she said, shaking her head. "We practically saw that kid grow up. But do you think she had the guts to tell me herself? Hell no, she had that big butch do the canning."

"What reason did they give for letting you go, Mrs. Markell?"

"Somebody said they saw me drinking in the mop closet, but that was a lie. I've been sober twelve years. It was *Geri* that helped keep me that way. She even got an AA meeting up and running at the shelter, God bless her soul."

Jan stood in the hall, a lit cigarette in her hand. "Mom, tell her about what you heard."

Sally took her time, tugging her left earlobe. "I had just finished cleaning the washroom that's attached to the office. I was about to open the door when I heard Geri crying in there. I was gonna knock and ask if she was okay, but then I heard another voice and I recognized it was Darci. They were talking softly at first, so I couldn't hear who was saying what. Then Geri started to yell and cry. She kept saying, 'How could you? How could you hurt me like this?' Then Darci told her she shouldn't have gone snooping through her phone. Geri shot back that she knew about all the money, and asked where it was coming from."

"How did Darci respond?"

"She didn't. A door slammed, and someone ran down the hall. At first I thought it was Darci, but I found out later it was Geri. Heard Bette say something about how she left there crying. She never came back, and a few days later, she was dead."

"Do you remember what day of the week this happened?"

"It was the Tuesday," Sally said. "I always cleaned the office washroom on Tuesdays and Saturdays. My eyes were bad, but I was thorough—I never missed an inch."

"Sally, do you remember a girl named Eva Carmichael? She spent some time at New Ways."

"She was one of the pretty ones, wasn't she?"

"Yes. Do you remember her?"

"The pretty ones never lasted long," she said. "They all ended up getting poached."

"Does the name Chance Epop mean anything to you? He also went by the name Pope."

"Men were never allowed in the shelter."

"How about a woman called Bonnie Tremblay?"

She squinted and blinked. "She never stayed at New Ways, I know that."

"But you know her."

"I didn't *know* her," she said, "but I remember her, all right. It was maybe two years ago, just after the shelter expanded and before my eyes went south. I was cleaning the lobby when this crazy chicky came in, loaded like you wouldn't believe, wanting to see Geri, but Geri wasn't there. She said her name was Bonnie and that she wasn't leaving until Geri came back. Darci came out and talked to her and took her into the office. They were in there a long time."

"Did it seem like they knew each other?"

"No, it was more like the first time they met. You putting this in the newspaper?"

"Right now I'm just gathering information. Did Bonnie get her chance to meet Geri?"

"Not that day, but she did come back to see her, maybe a month or so later," she said, "and Geri was a wreck after. She left for the day, I think."

"Apart from the day Geri and Darci argued, how would you describe their relationship?"

"I kind of felt sorry for that girl. She spent so many years trying to impress her mother at the shelter. She started helping there when she was in grade school, when New Ways was little more than a soup kitchen. When she got older, I 'member she wanted to change the way some things were done, make things run smoother. But every change she'd try to make, Geri would come down on her. I always thought she was a little hard on her, to tell the truth. I assumed that was what they were fighting over that day, that Darci had changed something and her mom had had enough. Maybe that's why Darci did what she did and fired everyone. I forgive her for what she did; it's got to be torture to lose your mother that way."

Back outside, I called Wayne. "So two years ago, Bonnie and Pope trek to the West Coast. Bonnie walks into New Ways looking to reconnect with her mother, probably to hit her up for cash. Only, she runs into Darci instead. Darci sees an opportunity. It's around that time that all these upstanding citizens go straight: Pope, Kai, Tim Womack. Darci puts together a crew. Later on, Bonnie returns to introduce herself to Geri, who likely has no idea that her daughters already knew each other. Everything's ducky for a time, until Geri gets wise and calls Darci out. She finds something in the office and they have a big blow-up. A couple of days later, Geri's dead."

"They're turning out young girls from the shelter."

"Like Eva. Sally Mopper said the pretty ones all get poached."

"An underage prostitution ring is big-time—and big money, depending how many girls they have."

"Sally also said that Geri called Darci out about the money. Maybe she found out Darci was laundering cash through the shelter."

"Would explain Darci's plea for public donations," he said. "Good way to rinse a bunch of dirty money."

"True. There's also the thing about what Geri saw on Darci's phone. That's what really made her lose it."

"Maybe she found out her daughter was screwing Dogger. That might have upset her a touch."

I thought about the note Geri had left. *To those who killed me. You murdered me before I wrote this. I should hate you both.*

CHAPTER 41

THAT NIGHT, KARIN CAME OVER TO MAKE ME take my placebo pills. We ordered pizza and watched a Netflix comedy. I pretended to doze off near the end. On her way out, Karin draped a blanket over me and turned out the lights. "Love you, Karin," I murmured.

"Better not be the meds talking," she said.

The moment she was out the door, I hopped up.

Twenty minutes later, I was at the safe house, watching Dogger's place. There he was, shirtless, drinking beer and doing lines of coke while installing a state-of-the-art entertainment system. Stud muffin was pre-spending.

I put on the headset and listened in on Naz's place. I got dead air and rewound it to a conversation earlier that day.

> Ghorbani: What's with all this new shit? How
> much did these sunglasses cost? Louis Vuitton?
> Jesus Christ!
> Naz: Don't worry about it, baby. I got it under
> control.

G: Who's Andrew Peretti?

(pause)

N: Andrew Perelli? I don't know any Andrew whosit. Oh, wait, maybe I cut his hair. There's an Andy (unintelligible)

G: Why would you have a copy of a will in which he's a beneficiary?

N: What are you talking about?

G: I glanced at your Visa statement when you were in the shower, to, you know, see how much debt you were bringing me. I came across an interesting piece of paper. Looks like this guy stands to gain four million bucks.

N: Oh, if it's who I think it is, he's a real spaz. Musta fallen out of his pocket when he sat down in my chair last week. I've been meaning to phone him back—

G: Why don't you phone him back right now?

N: I don't have his number.

G: I'll just call the station and have them find it.

N: C'mon, baby, don't be silly. We're going to be late for the movie.

(a door clicked open)

G: Is this why you wanted to know so much about Geri Harp's death?

(the door closed)

I pulled off the headset. Something nagged at me. I poured myself a cup of wine, then took the copy of the codicil and sat cross-legged in front of the coffee table. Geri's signature was at the bottom, and I had already verified it against other copies of her signature. The typing of *Andrew*

Peretti appeared a shade darker than the rest of the words on the page, and when I held it up to the light, it looked like something different had been typed there prior. The paper around the name had a slightly different hue.

I called Wayne. "Donovan, you better not be drunk again."

"The will is fake, Wayne. I don't think Dogger's getting a big payday after all. Darci just used it to dupe me." Flicking another glance toward Dogger's condo, I almost felt bad for the dumb bastard.

Sunday, December 8

Billi, Wayne's lanky, South Asian forger pal answered the door. When he saw me, his eyes went wide behind his bifocals.

"Nice to finally meet you, Sandra Donnelly," Billi said in a clipped British accent as he shook my hand. He gave me a brief but blatant once-over in the manner of a nerd whose only exposure to women is through the world of online porn.

We followed him downstairs, to an office that resembled a photo lab. One wall featured a black cloth backdrop behind a stool. A camera sat on a tripod facing it. On a long desk down the right side of the room stood a laminating press and three computers, the screen on one showing a passport photo of a guy who looked a little like Kim Jong-un. Billi killed the screen, and handed me a new laptop. "Beefed-up firewalls. Impenetrable to all but the best hackers. Even so, don't use any of your existing email accounts on it, and don't shop or do any banking. Fifteen hundred."

"You charged me twice that for mine," Wayne said.

"Get good-looking and lose the dick and I'll give you a deal, too."

I gave Billi a wad of bills, which he methodically counted and tucked into his pocket. "Now let's see the other item," he said.

I handed over my copy of the codicil. He sat down at the desk and examined it under a magnifying glass that had a purple UV light attached.

Billi mumbled something about "amateur hour." We leaned in over the forger's shoulders as he took out a bottle of clear solution and used an even tinier brush to coat Dogger's name.

He flicked a glance up at me. "You never saw the original?"

"She said she printed it off a computer."

"What someone *did* was simply print off this Peretti fellow's name, cut it out and paste it over the existing name. See this shadowing here? The papers were different thicknesses. You can even make out several letters from the original document. I've seen ten-year-olds make better copies."

Billi motioned me closer. "There is a double 'n' in what appears to be the first name. *And* that's *definitely* a 'y' at the end of the surname."

Wayne and I glanced at each other. "Bonnie Tremblay," I said.

Back outside, Wayne stopped and turned. "Okay, just so we're clear. Darci gets ahold of the codicil to her mother's will, fudges the names to make Dogger look like the dirty one—purely to throw you off?"

"It almost worked. With his sketchy track record, Dogger being the doer in all this made perfect sense, and it steered the focus away from what Darci was doing at New Ways. It was in her best interests if I kept chasing the Dogger angle, because it would ultimately lead nowhere. Even if I had gone to the cops, all I'd have had was a fake document that would only discredit me further."

Wayne's eyebrows rose as he digested this information. "That bitch is a real treat. She's fucking the guy yet willing to use him as a patsy in her mother's death."

"Same night she showed me the codicil, she quoted Wilde: 'Everything in the world is about sex, except sex. Sex is about power.'"

"I like that. May use it sometime."

"Getting back to the codicil, the *real* one—"

"Keeping in mind we've never seen the real one, only what your devious friend chose to let you see."

"Right. But let's suppose that Bonnie is the true recipient of the four million. Darci obviously knows this, because she's got access to her mother's files."

"Maybe the two sisters conspired to expedite their mother's death. Go halfsies on the loot."

I shook my head. "Darci was born rich, has been around wealth her entire life. No, I think she wants to be self-made. It wasn't so much that she wanted to profit from her mother's death, as that if Geri stayed alive she would have blown the whistle on her enterprise."

He nodded. "What's our next move?"

"I think we should get to know Kai a little better. His mother's really sick, and my money says she doesn't know what her son does in his spare time. We can leverage that against him."

"I like it," Wayne said.

CHAPTER 42

Monday, December 9

WITH ANOTHER HIT OF FRESH SNOW, FOLLOWED by rain overnight and subzero temperatures, the roads were treacherous and clogged with pre-holiday traffic.

Communicating with high-frequency walkie-talkies and using dashboard-mounted GPS to monitor our respective vehicles, Wayne, Frank, and I managed to put a reasonably successful tail on Kai. *Reasonably,* because Kai never seemed to take the same route twice, and often pulled over at a moment's notice, forcing one of us to drive past. I was in my Jeep, Wayne in his Pathfinder, and Frank in a navy Honda Accent. I wore a long, brown wig under a knit cap, and sunglasses. Armed with cameras, two of us would follow behind and take turns looping around on side streets, so someone was always in front of him. It was like a circuitous game of vehicular leapfrog. Frank was especially good at predicting Kai's next move, and he and Wayne made wagers along the way.

Frank: Five bucks says he'll turn left on Cambie.

Wayne: Cambie's a parking lot this time of day. No way he's that stupid, but I'll gladly take your money, Frankie.

Me: He turned left on Cambie,

W: Shit!

F: That's forty-five dollars you owe me, Wayne, in addition to back pay.

W: Yeah, yeah.

Me: You give degenerate gamblers a bad name, Wayne. I'm cutting him off, Frank. No more bets.

Kai looped back downtown and pulled up to the TD Bank on Burrard. A suit got into the Nissan, and Kai circled the block, dropping the man near where he had picked him up.

We trailed him as he made four more downtown deliveries.

Me: He just turned into the parking garage on Dunsmuir.

W: More than one exit?

Me: I don't think so.

W: May be another delivery, but Frank, get on foot and cover the rear pedestrian exit. I'll cover the other.

F: Roger that.

Me: What do I do?

W: Stay in your car. He knows what you look like, but Frank and I are ghosts.

Ninety seconds later, Frank announced that he had a visual—that Kai was on foot, heading west toward the Burrard SkyTrain station. A minute later, he hopped on the

SkyTrain's Millennium Line, and Wayne informed me that Frank did likewise.

> W: I missed it, but I'll grab the next one. In case it's a double-back and we lose him, drive into the garage, get a visual on his car, and wait.

The next two hours found me parked in the corner of the third floor of the garage, with a view of the Nissan five rows over. I was out of walkie-talkie range. At 2:34 p.m. I got a call from Wayne's cell, saying that Frank followed Kai off the SkyTrain at King George, where he hoofed it six blocks, went into a Tim Hortons, and came out a minute later with another man who was carrying a gym bag. I asked what he looked like.

"Middle-aged, medium height and build, ball cap," he said. "Frank says the guy moved like a pro. Smooth. Problem is, they hopped into a cab and he lost them. Too far away to get photos."

Tuesday, December 10
Next morning, the streets were slick, sidewalks were piled with dirty snow, and the pale, yellow smudge in the sky gave no hope of warmth. In separate vehicles we shadowed Kai from his home on 41st and St. Catherine to Forest Lawn Cemetery in Burnaby, where he parked and walked through the gates and down a path between rows of headstones.

> Wayne: Is this where Geri is buried?
> Me: It is.

I raised the camera. Through the telephoto lens, I watched Kai take a seat on a bench, pull his feet up into a cross-legged position and place his hands palms-up on his knees, thumbs and index fingers touching.

W: Fuck's he doing?
F: Looks like meditating.
W: Filipinos are Catholic. Catholics don't meditate. Donovan, is that bench near Geri's plot?
Me: Dunno. I don't do cemeteries.
F: I saw a show on Buddhism, and they said that some Buddhists meditate among the dead.
W: So you're saying this drug-dealing little shit is a Buddhist? Give me a break.
Me: It is weird.
W: Whole fucking thing is weird. Frank, we're too exposed here; let's wait on the next block. Donovan, you got cover?
Me: Yeah.
W: Radio us when he's on the move.

6:12 p.m. Kai rolled up to the Joyce Street SkyTrain station. Wayne radioed for Frank (dressed like a construction worker) to get ready to move. But Kai kept the engine running, and a moment later a nondescript man hopped in the passenger side. It happened so fast I didn't even have time to ID the face or get a photo. All I saw was that he wore a black ball cap and carried a dark gym bag.

We followed them to West Broadway, where Ball Cap jumped out, minus the bag, and into a waiting cab. This time I got a shot of his face, swarthy and intense.

Me: Frank, you get a visual on Ball Cap?
F: Same guy K met in Surrey.

My mind flashed to the night on the trestle, of the shadow materializing from the brambles.

Kai pulled a U-turn and drove right past me, going the opposite direction.

F: I got him.

I circled the block and three minutes later spotted the Nissan again. Kai parked near the corner of Broadway and Main. I pulled over, half a block back. He got out carrying the gym bag and dropped coins in the meter.

W: He's headed for the bus on the other side of the street.

I watched in amazement as Frank appeared on the scene *before* Kai, and actually helped an old lady onto the bus. Kai seemed lost in his thoughts and had no idea.

Ten minutes later, Frank sent a text informing that Kai had dropped the bag in a locker at the Pacific Central bus terminal.

10:12 p.m. Back at the safe house, I watched through the tele-photo as Dogger and Darci sipped wine, ate popcorn, and watched television, just like any normal couple.

I'd brought my printer to the suite and used it to print the day's photos. Beside Kai's photo, I put up one of Ball Cap getting out of Kai's car. I also printed and pinned up one of Dogger and Darci in flagrante delicto.

At 11:34 they turned off the lights and went to bed. I called Wayne and told him where Darci was spending the night.

"I'm on her tomorrow," he said. "Frank's in court testifying on an insurance fraud case, so you're on your own with Kai tomorrow. Can you handle it without getting busted?"

"Have I made any mistakes thus far?"

Wayne brayed like a donkey and hung up.

CHAPTER 43

Wednesday, December 11

JUST BEFORE NOON THE NEXT DAY, KAI PULLED into the parking lot of the long-term care wing of Vancouver General Hospital. He got out, carrying a bouquet of flowers. From down the block and across the street, I watched him walk into the hospital.

Ten minutes later, the door opened again and Kai led his frail and ailing mother out to his car. He opened the door for her and helped her get settled.

Drug dealer.

Hacker.

Suspected murderer.

Buddhist.

Devoted son.

Kai was a regular Renaissance man.

Mother and son went to Cucina Manila, a bustling Filipino restaurant on Joyce. From across the street I watched them enter, where she was greeted with hugs and smiles from the staff and patrons.

At 2:46 p.m., en route back to the hospital, the Nissan veered abruptly to the roadside. I pulled over at a bus stop. The passenger door opened and Rosie vomited onto the sidewalk. I could see the blood from half a block away.

Back at the hospital, Kai parked at the entrance, went in, and came out with a wheelchair and a nurse in tow. They got Rosie from the car and into the building. As Kai returned to the Nissan, he appeared to be fighting tears.

4:22 p.m. Kai parked near Main and Terminal and entered the century-old Pacific Central Station. Grand and majestic, the brick-and-granite structure made the crumbling flophouse hotels and decaying bars to the immediate north look like rotten teeth ready to fall out. To the immediate south sat a Starbucks and an A&W, brightly lit, but bland and soulless, like vultures hovering during a war of attrition.

Two minutes later, Kai exited the terminal wearing a black backpack. Rather than head for his car, he jogged across Main and hopped on a southbound bus seconds before it pulled out. I pulled into traffic, slowly trailing the bus. Three stops later, Kai hopped out and crossed the street diagonally, then stepped onto another bus heading north. He was either paranoid by nature, or he realized he had a tail and was fucking with me. Short of pulling a U-turn on a busy street, there was no way I could follow him without being obvious. I let him go.

Two hours later, I had just wrapped up an early evening run in the Stanley Park trails when Wayne called to tell me he just spotted Kai.

I frowned. "I thought you were on Darci."

"I am. Followed her into Glowbal. Few minutes ago, he came in with a backpack."

"Probably the same one I saw him pick up from the bus station earlier. Looks like these guys are doing locker drops around the city. When I was on the job, we'd see dealers do this with stashes of dope or money. That way, if they got busted, they wouldn't have the stuff on them, and could go back for it when they feel safe."

"Or when they need to pass it up the chain of command. Check your phone; I just sent you a little movie."

I put Wayne on speaker as I checked the video. It was of Kai and Darci, shot from about thirty feet away, as they cozied up in a restaurant booth. With his sad eyes and green polo shirt, Kai could almost pass for cute. Darci put a comforting arm around him.

"Wow," I said.

"The way Kai keeps flashing the puppy dog eyes, I believe our boy's in love. It would also appear that Darci's stringing more than one guy along. Must take after her mother."

"Hey, watch it."

"Okay, I'm laying odds that Darci's going to walk out of here with that pack. I'll find out where it goes next. Someone should be on Kai, too. How soon can you be here?"

"Fifteen."

"Good. The cute couple is just about to share a dessert. If they start spoon-feeding each other, I may just puke. Oh, when you get here, let's swap cars so you don't get made."

Ninety minutes later, I was in the Pathfinder, parked down the block from a Muay Thai gym on Kingsway. Through the steamed-up windows, I could make out Kai working a heavy bag. Kid was wicked with his knee and elbow strikes.

Wayne called to tell me he tailed Darci to the law office of Simon Sardos.

"Why does that name sound familiar?"

"Probably because he's defended half the moneyed thugs in town, and because he's the guy you go to if you want to rinse your dirty money. He takes it offshore, or runs it through charities, some real, some dubious. If they're washing cash with him, it's got to be significant."

"Photos?"

"Not of her meeting with Sardos personally, but certainly of her entering with that backpack and leaving empty-handed."

I watched Kai exit the kickboxing studio, and walk toward his car, a towel around his neck.

"If we got our hands on one of those bags," I said, "it would certainly shake up their game."

"Gotta admit, I'm curious," he said.

"Kai's on the move," I said.

"Stay on him. Good chance there'll be another delivery tonight. Frank and I'll join you in about an hour."

10:48 p.m. McDonald's, Alderbridge Way, Richmond. I was still in Wayne's Pathfinder in the corner of a karaoke bar parking lot across the street. Wayne was in my Jeep on the other side of McDick's, and Frank was posted around the corner.

Through the window, I watched Kai walk in and take a window booth seat across from Ball Cap, who was busy devouring a Big Mac and a large fries. Ball Cap offered him some fries, and Kai shook his head.

W: I just received the file based on the photos
we took of this guy. We're looking at Joe Garza,
another bad boy from Québec. He and Pope did a
string of drug rips ten years ago.
Me: He was the one with Pope that night. I'm sure
of it.

Five minutes later, the two of them left McDonald's, Kai carrying another backpack.

They got in Kai's car and we followed it to the Cambie SkyTrain station, where they both hopped out. Kai carried the bag, and they walked in separate directions—Garza toward the bus stop across the street, Kai toward the station.

W: That line stops near the bus station. We're gonna assume that's where the next drop will be. Donovan, you head there. Frank, we're hoofing.

A minute passed.

W: I missed it.
F: Me, too.

I cut over to Main and hung north, zigzagging through light traffic. I parked on Terminal and jogged toward the bus terminal's south entrance, where I leaned against a post and watched the SkyTrain platform. Kai was easy to spot, threading through a crowd of teens heading down the stairs.

I wore a black and red knit cap over a long, brown wig, black glasses, and fake eyebrow and nose rings. As I entered the building, a mirror to the right reflected an image my own mother wouldn't recognize. I waited in a slow-moving ticket line with a clear view of the storage locker area twenty feet to the right.

Thirty seconds later, Kai entered, not even glancing at the security guard by the door. He strode to the lockers, opened one, stuffed the backpack inside, locked it, and walked toward the station's north exit.

The security guard was busy chatting up a cleaning lady when I left the lineup and strolled past him, making sure I was facing away from the ceiling-mounted camera. No one seemed to care when I pulled out my tools and squatted in front of locker 72B.

Ninety seconds later, as I sat back on a bench with my legs crossed, Wayne walked right past.

Across the mezzanine, Frank, in his old-fart getup—silver hair, pants hiked to his tits—raised his eyebrows as he made me in the same instant I made him.

A short whistle from me made Wayne look over. I held up the backpack. "Guess drinks are on me."

"Nearly fifty grand," Wayne said. He sipped his beer. "Lotta green to be moving every couple days."

Cash-filled backpack stowed beneath our table, the three of us sat in a back booth of Funky's on Hastings. Yet another bar sliding inexorably toward gentrification, it still had cheap beer, sticky floors, last-stand barflies, and washrooms that would gag a maggot.

"Our little sting is gonna unsettle them a little," I said. Frank and I clinked our beer glasses together.

Wayne narrowed his eyes and looked around the room. "We just stole the earnings of killers."

"Technically, *I* stole it."

"Don't forget our boy's a hacker," he said. "He could tap into the security footage and make you."

"My back was to the camera."

"He'd figure it out. From now on, I want you staying at the safe house only. No one else knows about that place, right?"

"Karin knows, but she thinks I gave it up. She's been *supervising* my recovery, so we have dinner at the condo most nights."

"Start going out for dinner. When those goons realize the money's gone, they're gonna come looking hard, and camera footage or not, you're going to be suspect number one."

CHAPTER 44

Thursday, December 12

JUST PAST NOON THE NEXT DAY, I WAS PARKED down the street from VGH. Kai had been inside for a half-hour. A silver Audi cruised past, and I saw Darci's profile, just before she pulled into the lot and took the spot next to Kai's Nissan.

"Hello, friend," I muttered as she walked inside. Wayne would've ordered me to drive away, but he was at soccer with his kid, and Frank was casing the bus station.

Ten minutes later, Darci reappeared, holding the door for Kai, who pushed his wheelchair-bound mother down the ramp. Together, they got Rosie in the passenger seat of the Audi. Kai sat in the back while Darci drove.

I followed them to a grocer where they stopped to buy a poinsettia. I called Wayne. "I think they're heading to the cemetery. Darci's with them."

"I can be there in twenty," he replied. "Hang back. You get made, this is all for nothing."

I went to Forest Lawn anyway. Through the telephoto a block away, I watched Darci hold Rosie's hand as Kai pushed her wheelchair up the path of the tombstone-studded knoll.

Several hundred yards in, they turned left and continued for another fifty, stopping before what I assumed was Geri's resting place. Darci set the poinsettia down, and brushed snow off the top of the headstone. Rosie buried her face in her hands as Kai stared glumly into the distance, one hand on his mother's shoulder. Darci swiped away tears.

They stayed like this for five minutes, holding hands and talking. Rosie appeared to doze off, and Kai and Darci walked over to a nearby bench. She kissed his cheek.

Scattered about the cemetery were a dozen other people paying their respects. A hundred yards to the right of Darci and Kai, I picked out Wayne, wearing a fisherman's hat, sunglasses, and blue windbreaker. He set a bouquet atop of a headstone, which I knew camouflaged a small parabolic dish.

He pulled out his phone, and ten seconds later, I got the text:

I know you're here dummy so at least put on your ears and tune to #4

I switched on the Bluetooth headset and turned the dial. At first, all I heard was wind and static, but very faintly I could make out voices. I turned up the volume.

Kai: —she might not make it till Christmas. She wants to be at home when she goes. (unintelligible) don't know what to do.
Darci: We'll get her round-the-clock nurses (unintelligible) here for you. The same way you helped me when I needed you.

K: But you're leaving. Can't you wait?
D: I have to go set stuff up. You can come as
soon as you're able, then we can have a fresh
(unintelligible)

An elderly couple strolled in front of Wayne, creating
interference and garbling words.

Wayne turned and walked away, a moment before Kai
and Darci returned to Rosie and began rolling her in my
direction. As I drove away, I radioed Wayne.

"Darci's skipping," I said.

W: Frank's on her. I'll take Kai. You're at Pacific
Central.

Dinnertime found me eating Subway in my Jeep near the
bus station. Wayne had been on Kai all afternoon, who was
at home with his mother and the new nurse.

Frank was on Darci. His GPS showed that he followed
her from New Ways to Simon Sardos's law office around
three, where she spent forty-five minutes, before heading
to the TD Bank on Burrard. From there, she went to her
Alexander Street condo, where she'd been ever since.

My walkie-talkie crackled.

Frank: That Dogger guy drive a blue Porsche?
Me: Yeah.
F: He pulled up a few minutes ago. Darci just came
down and put a suitcase in the back. Looks like
they're taking a vacation.

Suddenly I spotted a familiar face climbing from the back of a cab near the terminal entrance: Kai, walking with his head down, tense.

Me: Wayne, where the hell are you?
W: Up the street from Kai's.
Me: He's here.
W: What the fuck? Forty-five minutes ago he poked his head out to pay for a pizza.
Me: He must've gone out the back. He's inside the station now.
W: Well then, things are about to get interesting.

Two minutes later, Kai stormed back outside. For a young, fit guy with meditative tendencies he appeared on the verge of a coronary. I ducked down as he looked all around, then hurried to a payphone by the entrance.

Me: Kai looks pissed. He's on a payphone now.
W: Boy's gonna have some 'splaining to do to his girlfriend. Wonder if that's who he's calling.

Kai talked for just over a minute, holding his forehead with his free hand. He slammed the phone back in its cradle and ran off in the direction of the SkyTrain station.

At 6:18, Frank radioed, saying that Darci and Dogger were wheeling their suitcases through international departures at YVR.

I considered this for several seconds, then told Wayne to remain outside Kai's place.

W: We thinking the same thing?
Me: Yeah. It's time to flip the kid.

CHAPTER 45

KAI RETURNED HOME TO FIND WAYNE AND I sipping green tea with his mother in their living room.

I rose to shake his hand. "Hello Kai, you remember me? Sandra Donnelly. We met and spoke briefly about you being a possible candidate for the Courage to Change Award this year."

Kai's normally brown face paled a few shades.

With a broad grin, Wayne extended his mitt, too. "Congratulations on making the shortlist, pal. Your mother's been telling us how proud she is of you. We were just about to list off your recent accomplishments, although we do prefer to save the surprise for awards day."

Gesturing to the photos of a young, serious-faced Kai on the mantle above the red brick fireplace, I said to Rosie, "I would love it if you could lend me a few photos for a possible article."

She coughed into a tissue. "I would be so happy to."

I felt a little rotten to see her beaming, as though if she were to die that moment, it would be with tremendous grace, knowing that God had granted her a miracle.

"Kai," I said, "we've taken up a great deal of your mother's time, so what do you say we go out and grab a coffee and have a little Q&A. Oh, and bring your laptop. I'm curious to see those computer skills I've heard so much about."

Down the street, Wayne quickly frisked Kai before we climbed into the Pathfinder and drove to a road that dead ended at a ravine. Sitting in the back with Kai, I opened his bag and removed a MacBook Air, his anti-surveillance device, several stacks of hundred-dollar bills (Canadian and US), a passport, a Glock 9mm, a butterfly knife, and a copy of the *Tao Te Ching*. In a side pocket I found a brochure for a Buddhist yoga retreat in Costa Rica. I passed the computer and weapons to Wayne.

"Does she know you lost the money?" I asked.

Silence.

"Who'd you call from the payphone?"

Not a blink.

"How long's Darci been stringing you along?"

A stone would have shown more emotion.

"How long have you been in love with her?"

Catatonia.

"Kid would make a hell of a poker player," Wayne said. He plugged a flash drive into his truck stereo: the recording of the cemetery conversation.

Kai: But you're leaving. Can't you wait?
Darci: I have to go set stuff up. You can come as soon as you're able, then we can have a fresh—

Wayne clicked off the stereo and I pulled out the 8 x 10s I'd printed off of Darci and Dogger's couch coitus. I flicked on the vehicle's dome light and flipped through the photos for Kai's benefit. He watched the photos out of the corner of his eye.

"They're in the air right now," I said. "Drinking cocktails, holding hands, laughing—"

"Probably fucking in the lavatory," Wayne added. "You ever screw in a plane crapper, kid? It's a tight squeeze, but you're small, so you could make it work. Probably thinking it should be *you* up there ... I mean, that's what she *promised* you, right? After taking all those risks? The drugs, the hookers, the money drops? Quite the life, and you're not even twenty yet. But you seem like a reasonably smart thug, what with the hacking and ability to count large sums. What I *don't* get is why you're living out here like a shmuck, driving a shitty car, while your *girlfriend* is flying business class with"—he finger-stabbed the photo of Darci riding Dogger—"*this* asshole. I mean, where's the fairness? Looks to me like you're being used, son."

"You didn't know they were together, did you?" I asked.

Silent rage simmered in his dark eyes. "What do you want?"

"What do *you* want, Kai?" I asked. "Because I know what you *don't* want, and that's for your mother to know you had anything to do with Geri Harp's death."

Kai's nostrils flared. "No comment."

I chucked him under the chin with the Enforcer.

He clenched his teeth. "I got nothing to say to you. Not *here*. No doubt you've got this ride wired."

I handed him his bug sweeper. "Knock yourself out."

Kai paused for thirty seconds, then flicked the device on and slowly swept it around the interior. When he leaned over the seats to run it over the centre console and dash, he brushed up against Wayne, who smacked his arm away.

"How do I know *you're* not wired?" Kai asked.

"Fuck yourself, that's how."

"Just let him, Wayne," I said.

Wayne's eyes glared in the rear-view as he let Kai wave his device over his torso. When Kai did the same to me, the wand's LED bar glowed green. I pulled the microphone pen from my pocket. He took it, examined it, clicked it off, and gave it back. "Switch off your phones," he said.

Wayne powered off his phone and slapped it on the dash. "This better pan out, kid, or I swear to God, I'm gonna fuck your life up beyond repair."

"Can't get much worse."

"That's the thing about lives," I said. "There's always worse. But being a Buddhist, maybe you're just waiting for the next one to come around."

"Maybe in your next life you'll be a dung beetle," Wayne said. "Destined to nose turds up a hill. Fitting karma."

Kai looked at me. "Your pal is a fucking ignoramus."

"He's just a little prejudiced because he married a Filipina who turned out to be a gold digger, who then discovered he didn't have any gold."

"Hey," Wayne said, "remember whose side *you're* on."

"Now me personally," I said, "I'm a wee bit pissed that you hacked my computer and leaked the video footage, which led to my termination from a pretty good gig."

"She told me you were a crazy stalker."

I set the sex photos on his lap. "Oh, I forgot. Everything you did was out of love."

"You can keep those," Wayne said. "We made copies."

"Tell us about your fentanyl that killed Geri Harp," I said.

He shook his head. "I would never—"

"Never do *what?*" I said. "Never conspire with the girl you love to murder her mother, because Geri got wise and threatened to shut down your operation?"

"And you think *you're* going to shut this down? They'll kill you without even blinking. They'll kill me. Anyone who gets in the way is game."

"Who would do the killing?" I asked.

Kai's eyelid twitched.

"You're saying that after this"—I pulled out the photos Wayne took of him and Darci cuddling at the restaurant—"your girl, your one-and-only, who you had done so much for, would just have you *slicked*?"

"She wouldn't, but the others—they'll do anything. Look, I just take the money from A to B and keep everyone in line."

"Like the night you treated Womack to a hot coffee facial?" I asked.

"He had been skimming. Zero-tolerance policy for that."

"What about your dealing? How does that fit in?"

"My own thing."

"When Darci asked you to get fentanyl, what did you think it was for?" I asked.

He shook his head. "She was dead set against that shit. I said I'd get rid of my remaining supply—there wasn't much left—but she took it, said she'd take it to the pharmacy and dispose of it properly."

"And *somehow* it ended up in her mother's water bottle." Wayne said.

"Darci had the stuff in her bag. She figured her mom must have been snooping and found it."

"You keep telling yourself that."

"Geri was like a second mother to me. I would never do anything to hurt her."

"Not intentionally, maybe," I said. "I want you to think back, Kai. Geri died on a Thursday."

"Yeah, I know."

"Two days prior—on Tuesday—a witness reported over-hearing Geri and Darci having a fight at New Ways. It involved something Geri saw on Darci's phone."

Kai's eyes narrowed.

"What?" I asked.

"Darci would never leave her phone out."

"Unless she left it there on purpose," Wayne said, "knowing her mother would see it."

"What day did Darci take the fentanyl off you?" I asked.

Kai stared straight ahead. "Wednesday."

"You're sure?"

"Yes. It was a day before Geri died."

"So," I said. "Tuesday, mom and daughter fight. Wednesday, daughter scores fentanyl from you. Thursday, mom is dead. How do you like that timeline?"

Kai's face tightened.

"Darci *claimed* her mother stole the drugs from her bag, but that doesn't work, because after they scrapped on Tuesday, Geri never *returned* to New Ways and didn't have any contact with Darci. The fentanyl was put into Geri's water bottle, probably while it was in her convertible. It was mid-October, but the weather had been nice all week, so she would've had the top down. Easy access."

Silence.

"Okay, let that one marinate for a bit," I said. "Where's Bonnie Tremblay?"

"I don't know. I barely see her at all."

"Because you collect off Joe Garza," I said. "The delivery boy."

"We have rules. See each other as little as possible and only when necessary. It's not like we go for beers after work."

Wayne handed Kai his laptop. "My blood sugar's dropping, kid. Puts me in a nasty mood. Now show us something concrete, or I'm going to head back and tell Rosie everything. Then you can see how you like meditating over *her* grave."

"I want to know exactly what Geri found out," I said. "Let's start with texts and emails. Darci's, Geri's, Dogger's too."

I handed Kai his Mac and flipped up the screen for him.

"They're probably deleted," Kai said.

"Yeah," Wayne said, "but to a whiz like yourself, they're never *really* gone, are they? Clickety-click through cyberspace and *voi*-fucking-*là*."

"How computer savvy is Darci?" I asked.

Kai mumbled something as he typed rapid strings of letters and numbers onto a strange-looking grey screen.

"Say again?"

"I showed her how to install spyware on any personal device."

"So she had full access to her mother's computer and phone," I said. "Along with the audio from the bugs planted at Dogger's place. Pretty sick girl, wanting to eavesdrop on her mother's sex life, so that she could manipulate her every step of the way."

Kai didn't reply. I told him I wanted to see the content of Darci's phone first.

"You won't find anything."

"Why not?"

"Because I scrubbed it. I can't get it back. There are people who can, but they're out there taking down governments."

"But you know what was on that phone?"

"I respected her privacy."

"You're full of shit," Wayne said.

"Did you scrub Geri's phone, too?" I asked.

"No."

"Whatever's on there," I said, "I want it."

"Get to work," Wayne said. "And if I suspect even a funky keystroke from you, your mom's sleep is going to get interrupted right quick."

I handed Kai a USB drive as I made eye contact. "He'll do it, too."

He plugged the drive into the laptop.

I looked at the pamphlet. "What's the deal with Costa Rica?"

He paused. "Supposed to be our safe place, in case shit went bad."

"She timed it well," Wayne said, "because shit is *indeed* going bad."

"*Where* in Costa Rica? Under what name?" I asked.

"She thought it best if I didn't know till the last minute."

"No doubt," Wayne said. "Wonder if she was planning on changing the sheets before you got there."

CHAPTER 46

Friday, December 13

I POURED MORE WHISKEY INTO MY GLASS. Sitting on the floor of the safe house, I had my laptop and notebook in front of me as I constructed a timeline of emails and texts in the days preceding Geri's death. On Tuesday morning (prior to her fight with Darci) she had sent and received over fifty texts, mainly back and forth correspondence with New Ways' workers and volunteers, as well as contractors who had been scheduled to begin work on a kitchen expansion. There were no messages to or from Darci or Dogger, but that didn't surprise me. Darci and Kai had covered those tracks well.

I looked at the amber liquid in the glass. Hard liquor is almost always a mistake for me, a sign that things have gotten bad. I drank it anyway, liking the numbness that was quickly overtaking my muscles and brain.

Next, I opened up Geri's email. She had two accounts, Gmail and Hotmail. In both accounts, messages in the inboxes only went back several days before her death. Most of the messages again related to day-to-day operations at New Ways. Nothing to or from Darci. Dogger wasn't even in her contact list. It had the feel of being too clean, freshly sanitized of all but the most banal messages. The telling thing was that even though Geri didn't return to New Ways following the fight with Darci, even in the hours up until her death she continued to answer work related emails from employees and various subcontractors. Each of those messages was professional, concise, and perfectly punctuated.

The final email of Geri's life was sent roughly two hours before I found her body. It was to her dentist, confirming a time for a cleaning the following Monday. For some reason, that upset me and I felt hot tears slide down my face. Outside it was snowing again, fat flakes taking their time falling to earth. Through my bleary vision, I could barely make out Dogger's apartment building. His suite was dark. He was gone. To Costa Rica with Darci, who had escaped, having gotten away with killing her mother.

I looked around this pathetic hovel and felt the futility of it all: the photos on the wall, the bed Eva had slept in, the whiskey bottle, and my distorted reflection in the window in front of me.

Closing my eyes, I imagined myself sitting in my Jeep, drinking and taking pills, until I too drifted away. Grabbing the bottle of Jameson, I drank blindly from it, seeking the answer of oblivion, thinking about how good it felt to slip away, to not have to play this sad game anymore and pretend like anything mattered—not of my future, or righting the murder of my friend and seeing justice done.

Then I thought of the dentist appointment.

My friend confirmed a fucking dentist appointment two hours before she died.

Because she had no real intention of dying that day.

I opened my eyes, set down the bottle, and forced my eyes back on the screen. I had read all the texts and emails and was about to go over them again, when I saw the tiny photo icon in the corner. I clicked on it and the first photo I saw was dated 10/08/19.

The day Geri and Darci fought.

It was a blurred photo of a text message on the screen of another phone.

Me or her, Dogger. You said yourself the only reason you haven't broken it off with my mom is that you feel sorry for her. Time to man up and make a choice.

I sat back, imagining my friend's heart breaking as she read that. Darci had left her phone out, knowing her mother would see that message, knowing that it would goad her into action.

My glass was empty, so I poured more. Then I leaned back against the wall and looked at the cache of stored photos from Geri's phone. Most were of other women in the shelter, smiling warmly into the camera as they baked, worked the garden, mended clothes. Geri had captured moments of joy. There were also photos of herself with Darci, taken in better times, in and out of the shelter. There were also some of her and Grady, but not many, and when they were posing together, I could see the distance in their eyes. I came across a photo of Geri and I hugging and laughing and grinning just after we'd run a charity 10K. She'd had a cramp and we'd run the final kilometre with her arm over my shoulder. I remember she had cursed me the entire time for making her do the race. I could still hear her cussing me out. When I began to laugh, I could hear her laugh with me. I closed my eyes and the laptop slipped to the floor, and I began to cry.

When I woke up on the floor, my phone read 4:32 a.m. and there was a text from Frank, an hour prior: **located suspects vehicle franklin n salisbury come asap**

Parking near Dundas and Templeton, I got out and walked west through the early morning fog. I wore black running tights and a matching hoodie, and could feel the weight of Kai's Glock in the nylon fanny pack around my waist.

I padded down the alley of the warehouse district between Pandora and Franklin. Frigid, briny air pushed in from the nearby shipyards. A few construction cranes jutted into the sky, bedecked with red and blue Christmas lights. Through the fog, I made out the boxy silhouette of an RV on the next block. Creeping forward with my back to the warehouse, I unzipped the fanny pack, pulling out the Glock with my right hand and a GPS iTrail with the other. Gulls screeched above, and from the east came the sounds of beeping and industrial clatter of the graveyard shift.

I texted Frank: **I'M HERE WHERE R U?**

Frank: **just around the corner. ill find you.**

I approached the rear of the burnt orange-and-white Winnebago. The rear curtain was open a crack, purple light shining out. Moving closer, I extended the gun down and in front, stopping a few feet away.

Illuminated by the light, the sun-bleached design depicted a horse-drawn carriage. Identical to what Eva sketched beside Pope's name.

The Carriage.

Standing on tiptoe, I peeked through the fogged-up window—to see the large, flabby, white ass of a bald, middle-aged man, grunting and pumping away at a young, drugged-out girl, who stared up at the ceiling and gave the odd lifeless moan.

The girl was Zoey, the pixie from the shelter.

The man rammed harder, raising his large, bald head.

I gasped.

It was the coroner, Steve Bolger.

It took all my restraint not to rip open the door and pistol-whip him, but that wouldn't get me closer to the rest of them.

I stepped back and clicked the GPS beneath the rear bumper, then retreated back into the shadows. In the Carriage, Bolger gave a protracted climactic bellow, which meant that I heard the revving car engine the same moment I felt a metal bumper slam into my left leg. My body flew up and my head hit the windshield, rockets exploding behind my eyes. Then nothing.

CHAPTER 47

A BLUR OF RED AND WHITE. A GHOSTLY SMIL-
ing face. White tracers zipping by in the background. It took
me a few moments to realize that the red was my blood and
the white was a towel, and as features sharpened, there was
Geri Harp smiling at me as she wiped my face. A cigarette
dangled from her lips.

I moved my legs and my left thigh shrieked in pain.

"Finally you get what you come for," Geri said, in a husky,
Québecois-accented voice.

I blinked and squinted against the dim interior of a car's
back seat. My hands were lashed behind my back and tape
covered my mouth. Joe Garza drove, wearing a black knit
cap. I could see his eyes in the rear-view, dark and impassive.
I realized I was in the Cutlass and the woman beside me was
Bonnie Tremblay, brunette, with giant diamonds in her ears.
Her nose had once been broken and a central incisor was
chipped. She pulled back to appraise my face. "Best I could
do and you still look like shit, but … they won't be picky,
will they, Joseph?"

In the rear-view, Garza cocked an eyebrow. "Looks just fine to me."

I looked around. We were driving up bumpy, narrow switchbacks. Snow-covered trees. I was dizzy, and my hands and feet were numb.

"Ever since you killed my love," she said. "I've been waiting for this. She promised me I could have you." She raised Kai's Glock and pushed it to my forehead.

"I am *not* cleaning Ginger's brains out of the upholstery," Garza said. "Seriously, Bon, stick to the plan."

Bonnie set the Glock on the seat and ran her fingers down my face, to my neck and chest. She felt something, stopped, and pulled the microphone pen from the inside pocket of my jacket. She examined it and clicked on the nib.

"Your leg looks a little funkadelic, Sloaney." She stroked the business end of the pen down my left thigh and jabbed it against the spot where I'd been hit. Pain jolted through me, and I banged the back of my head against the passenger window.

Bonnie stuck the pen back in my pocket and wrenched the tape from my mouth. "You look like you have something to say."

"Was it ... worth it?"

"Was *what* worth it?"

"Killing your mother for money."

Bonnie leaned closer, showing microdot pupils. "I didn't have nothing to do with that. Best believe I'd cop to it if I did. That bitch left me to rot when I was a baby."

"And now Darci's gone, too. You know she's left the country, right?"

Bonnie paused and her eyes narrowed.

Garza glanced back. "She's fucking with you, Bon."

My comment had shaken Bonnie, giving me a temporary surge of power, which pushed back some of the pain.

"Two years ago you walked into New Ways to find your mother, maybe hit her up for some cash. Instead you met Darci. She saw you as an opportunity. She had access to the girls. You had the street experience. She proposed running girls out of the Carriage, and you jumped."

"You think you're so fucking smart, eh? But it's not single, it's *plural*. As in *four*. Soon I'll have my own."

"Like a franchise."

"Yeah," she said, proudly, "like Subway."

"How did you not get caught till now?"

"We didn't get caught. *You* got caught. We don't get caught because we have a solid customer base. We even got *cops*."

"Shut up, Bon," Garza said.

Bonnie flicked her hand dismissively at her partner. "Our clients call, we pick them up, take their phones, make sure they're clean, then take them to the Carriage. We never deal with anyone we don't trust, and we check identities. We know all the areas the cops don't patrol, and we always got someone on lookout for any suspicious characters."

"Quite the system," I said.

Bonnie rolled down her window, letting in a blast of freezing air. She threw out her butt and procured a glass pipe. "Three hundred bucks an hour. If they want kink or whatever, it is more. So three hundred, times eighteen hours a day. What's that?"

Bonnie inserted a crystal into the end of the pipe and sparked up, her lungs taking a big suck of meth.

"Never been great at math," I said.

"Fifty-four hundred," she said, exhaling chemical fumes in my face, "per *day*. Six days a week and we're up over thirty-two big. Times four: that's over a hundred twenty a month. Per Carriage. And you thought you were going to just come along and shut our shit down, maybe rescue some little junkie ho-bag along the way?"

"What's your end?" I asked. "And Joe's here?"

"*Bon,*" warned Garza.

"Takes three people to run a Carriage," she said. "Each gets ten percent. Now we only got two."

"Not going to get a replacement for Pope?"

"My love can't be *replaced*. You know, he told me about you. Your sad home, living alone with the cat. Someone like you can't understand what it's like to love someone so bad you'd do anything for them. So bad you'd give up your life for them. Kill for them."

"Guess not. What happened to my cat?"

"My man is dead, and you're worried about a fucking *cat?*"

Garza half-turned and handed Bonnie a needle and syringe. "Enough of this," he said.

"Bonnie, listen to me," I said, "there are others who know what you've done. You kill me, you're not going to get away. At least Darci was smart enough to get out of the country. You think you can hide from a murder charge? I don't care how much mon—"

She squeezed my cheeks with her hand, puckered my lips and gave me a long kiss. "Baby, there won't be any charge, because there's not going to be enough of you to identify. What you don't understand is: I *have* to do this. Because someone like you will always come back to fuck my shit up, and believe me, my goal *is* to live in peace. I make my apologies to God later."

She used her teeth to pull the cap off the needle. I pulled back, but she jammed it in my neck, pressed the plunger, and cement filled my veins. As the darkness closed in, she made a call.

A voice said, "Yeah?"

"Send the word," she said. "It's done."

CHAPTER 48

THE CURTAINS. THE BLURRED IMAGE OF THE Carriage.

I was *inside* the Carriage.

Voices outside. Hard laughter.

The smell of gasoline.

I was on the bed, stripped to my underwear. Arms bound behind my back. Ankles bound, twisted up behind me and attached to my wrist binds. Tape over my mouth. Through a crack in the curtain, wan light filtered into the room. Falling snowflakes. Trees. I had promised my mother I'd make it out for Christmas.

Twisting my head, I saw that the bedroom was partially curtained off from the toilet and cab by velvety, black drapes. I could see part of the driver's seat. Slumped over the steering wheel was ponytailed Tim Womack, his blood and brains blown all over the inside of the windshield, the outside of which was covered with snow. I stared at him for a long time, then forced my eyes away.

The bed took up the bulk of the space: red satin sheets, black pillows. Above the bed, a shelf held tubes of lube, a jar of condoms, vibrators, dildos, sanitizer wipes. Above the shelf was a television and DVD player. On the grey shag carpet of the floor I spotted the microphone pen near my shoes and bunched-up clothes. By the door stood two large, red, plastic gasoline containers.

The driver's door opened. Garza hopped up on the running board, ignoring Womack's body. A series of thumps came from somewhere. I moaned, but Garza ignored me as he used a screwdriver to pry the VIN number off the dash, then jumped back out and slammed the door.

I thrashed and screamed, but couldn't get any leverage from this position.

The side door opened. Two large, homely men shambled in, wearing ski caps and heavy winter coats. They had jaundiced, narrow-set eyes and dumb grins.

Twins.

The brothers.

They shook off snow and removed their hats and coats and hung them by the door. One was slightly taller and uglier.

Ugly said, "Whoa, where'd they find you, honey?"

Other Brother gave a gap-toothed smile as he raised his eyebrows. "She looks a little scared. You scared, baby? What'd you do to piss them off so bad, huh?"

They took off their boots and sweatpants and underwear and left their white T-shirts on. Ugly was already hard and his brother was stroking himself to catch up. In the other hand, he held up a phone and took several photos. "We take some before shots," he explained. "And then some after."

The bed creaked and dipped as they climbed on. Ugly carefully peeled the tape from my mouth, then leaned down and stuck his tongue between my lips. I jerked my head back and head-butted him on the bridge of his nose, splitting it. He smiled, then punched me in the ribs so hard all the air left my body. It felt like my lungs had been flattened. "You're a hot little tamale," he said. "Little past your expiry date, but you'll do just fine for one more kick at the can."

They flipped me on my stomach and cut me loose as I continued to gasp, a little air seeping into my lungs. I struggled, but they were too heavy. My underwear was ripped down past my knees and one of them forced my legs apart and stabbed himself into me. I screamed as they pulled me up on all fours. The other one moved in front. As the other one moved in front, I slipped in and out of blackness.

A streaming montage of faces: Geri ... Steph ... Eva ... Darci ... Karin ... my mother ... my funeral ... all for nothing ... all for nothing ...

A surge of rage. Not like this. Not like this. I chomped, tore, ripped with my teeth. He screamed, and metallic blood filled my mouth and I spat him out. The brother at the rear froze mid-thrust. I whirled away from him, hand fumbling on the floor. My fingers closed on the pen, and he grabbed me by the hips. As he flipped me to face him, I brought the pen up and into his eye. Optic fluid jetted out. He screamed. Blood twizzled down his cheek. I pushed the pen further, through his eye and into his brain. He convulsed and flailed and babbled. The other brother clutched to staunch the blood pouring from his crotch. Half his mangled penis sat on the pillow. He looked up with confused rage and then made a grab for me, but he was weak from sudden shock and blood loss, and I slipped by him.

Leaning back against the door to pull on my underwear, I saw the other brother on his back, body twitching as the pen quivered in his eye. Grabbing the end, I gave a violent side-to-side, doing as much damage as possible before yanking it out. With my other hand, I snatched up my shoes and one of their coats and jumped out into two feet of snow. My left leg collapsed beneath me, and I fell. The Carriage was parked in the woods, with some sort of white camouflage tarp over top.

In a clearing fifty feet to the right sat a blue minivan. The grey Olds was parked a hundred feet beyond, at the treeline. Keys jangled in the coat pocket. I hobbled to the van and opened the driver's side door and climbed in. As I keyed the ignition, a bellow came from behind, and in the rearview I saw one of my rapists—face bone white and lower body covered in crimson—charge from the Carriage.

The engine turned over. I flicked on the wipers and stomped the gas. The tires spun, and the brother's face was at the window. I locked the door. He hammered the window with his fist. Glass shattered and rained all over me. He grabbed my shoulders just as the wheels caught and the vehicle shot forward.

Across the clearing, Garza stood outside the Olds, aiming a pistol in my direction. I wrenched the wheel hard, right, then left, fishtailing the van. Rapist lost his grip and went tumbling, reddening the snow all around him. A gunshot and then a bullet punched through the windshield, *thunking* into the passenger seat. I veered back and forth, fighting to keep the vehicle heading in the general direction of the road.

Garza was back at the wheel. In slow motion, the grey car began moving left, crossing the clearing to block the road. Closer, closer, closer. Both feet jamming the accelerator, I braced as the Olds crashed into the rear-left panel of the van, knocking me off course. The right bumper clipped a tree and I bounced over a short, snowy embankment. The van bottomed out and the tires spun.

In the rear-view mirror I saw Bonnie, cigarette in mouth, pistol in hand, her head out the passenger window of the Olds. She squinted one eye shut and took aim. I ducked. *Crack-crack.* The rear window burst and one bullet exploded through my headrest, lodging in the windshield an inch above the steering wheel. Circuits crackled and sparked as the other bullet shattered the stereo console.

I punched the gas, making the tires spin and the engine scream. The Cutlass pulled closer. Bonnie climbed out. Still ducking down, I shifted into reverse and jolted the van back ten feet. She jumped to the side and fired, taking out my driver's side mirror. I slammed the van into drive and mashed the pedal. The vehicle lurched, shooting over the embankment and down the other side, ripping through a thicket of alder saplings.

Wrenching the wheel to avoid the larger trees, I drove into a ravine that bottomed out at a shallow creek, barely wide enough for the van to drive down.

Several hundred yards further, the creek converged with a river. The van plunged into three feet of water, sending a freezing spray through the broken window. The engine spluttered and died as the steering wheel locked. I grabbed the clothes and jumped in the back of the van, which contained a red toolkit and a rank animal odour.

After pulling on my runners and the rapist's blue parka, I opened the toolbox, rooted around and grabbed the wood handle of a claw hammer. I tried to open the rear doors, but the pressure from the rushing water was too great. The van created a dam-like effect and the water was rising fast, pouring through the windows.

Using the hammer, I smashed out the rest of the jagged glass from the broken rear window and clambered onto the roof. From there I pulled myself onto a boulder a few feet away. I slid down the other side and scrambled along the riverbank.

My shoes were sopping and my feet were numb as I stumbled down a rocky scree.

A dog barked.

I froze. The dog barked again: a ring tone. I thought it was coming from the jacket, but then, from over to the right came Garza's hushed voice: *"No, she's not in the van. Yeah, yeah, she can't have gone far. I can hear him screaming, Bon, so put the fucker down! What? I'm losing you. Reception is shit, can't hear you."*

Creeping sideways, I peered over some deadfall. Twenty feet away, on the other side of the river, stood Garza, gun in hand as he looked around, his eyes going my way. I spun away, putting my back to a massive, splintered stump.

"Know why there aren't many red-haired creatures in nature, Sloane?" he called out. "Too easy to hunt."

My eyes snapped in every direction. Go back up the scree and I was exposed. Down was almost as bad. To my left, away from the river, rose a twenty-foot cliff, thick with brush. Even with two good—

A shot rang out, shredding the dead wood of the stump just above my head. I hopped down the scree in a crouch. A bullet ricocheted off nearby rocks. The next shot was closer, punching into the trunk of a fir a foot in front of my face. Ten feet further, I arrived at the top of a thirty-foot gorge, whitewater cresting over. Over my shoulder, I saw Garza cautiously boulder-hopping across to my side of the river.

I turned and began climbing backwards down the gorge face using the claw of the hammer as a hook. It wasn't sheer, but one mistake and I was done. On the other hand, if I didn't move fast enough Garza would just lean over the top and pick me off.

My feet found tenuous purchase as I descended. Adrenaline, which had up until now been waging war against shock, violence, and the narcotics in my system, had retreated, leaving me spent.

It seemed like I had been descending forever when my right foot hit rock at the bottom, and my leg gave out. I sprawled backward, losing my left shoe. Hearing a crashing sound at the top of the cliff, I tucked into a hollow beneath a small waterfall at the base of the gorge. I could not see above, and I hoped I was hidden from Garza's view. My sneaker sat ten feet away. He might assume I made it into the nearby forest or maybe back across the river.

A string of falling pebbles rattled past my face. After listening to his curses, I chanced a peek past the outcrop. Garza hugged the rock twenty feet above, moving in a downward diagonal. He had chosen a poor route, and his movements were halting and shaky.

Rolling out into the open, I stood and gauged the weight of the hammer and visualized a perfect parabola ending at Garza's skull.

"Never got a mountaineering badge in Boy Scouts, did you, Joseph?" I called out.

His head twisted, and his foot slipped. He grabbed a stunted cliff-hanging tree to right himself. His other hand pulled the gun from his belt.

Fingers nearly numb from cold, I took rough aim with the hammer. "Drop it," I yelled.

He glanced down. "You'll miss. Then I'll climb down and do what I came here to do."

"Or you could drop the gun, help me get Bonnie and Darci, and get yourself a plea deal. It's Canada, so it's possible you don't do any time at all. You're just not smart enough to get away with this any other way. Drop it and climb down. You can't shoot me from there, and you're a shitty shot anyhow."

Garza paused, and I used the moment to slip my foot back into the shoe.

The gun clattered on the wet rocks near my feet. I picked it up as Garza climbed down, jumping the last few feet. I held the gun on him.

He turned and stepped slowly toward me, head down.

"*Stop!*" Garza was ten feet away and picking up speed, getting ready to charge, when I aimed for the chest and squeezed.

Click.

I dropped the gun and swung the hammer: a glancing blow to his right temple. It knocked him sideways, but he didn't go down. A crack of blood opened at his hairline and red gushed down his face. He gave a confused look, then charged again. I smashed him in the side of his head, so hard the hammer embedded itself three inches into his skull and stayed there.

Garza dropped, and I collapsed a second later.

I crawled over, rifled through his pockets. Found the phone and tried to call 911. No service bars.

In his other pocket, I found my iPhone. No bars.

While boulder-hopping across the river, my vision blurred, melting tree, stone, and water together. Somehow I ended up on the other side of the river, belly-crawling through the snow up the steep embankment. I longed to stop, just close my eyes and drift away, but every time I blinked, there was Darci, goading me from five feet away. *C'mon, Sloane, that all you got for me? All the chase been beat out of you? What would Geri say? Maybe you can ask her in a few minutes, quitter.*

Yeah, I'm just going to rest for a minute, Darce. Close my eyes. But I'll be right back.

C'mon, Sloaney! On your feet, soldier! We got work to do. I'm not going to carry you.

I opened my eyes and looked down on the road from where I lay face down on the hard-packed snowbank. The Cutlass rumbled nearby. Cigarette smoke. Something hard pressed into my cheek. The barrel of the Glock.

CHAPTER 49

"LET'S MOVE, SLOANEY," BONNIE SAID, GOING through my pockets and removing both phones and the pen. Noting the blood on it, she said, "This thing has proven useful, eh?"

I stared at her.

Bonnie threw the pen deep into the woods and I closed my eyes.

"Is he down there?" she asked.

I nodded.

"Dead?"

"Guaranteed."

She gestured with the gun for me to move back down to the river. "Good enough for Joseph, good enough for Sloaney."

"I've got fifty thousand," I said.

"Bullshit."

"We jacked one of Kai's drops the other night, probably *your* money."

She pressed the Glock between my eyes. I smiled. Death was beginning to seem welcome. It would certainly solve all of my current problems.

Not like this.

"Shame to lose out on an easy fifty grand, Bon."

The gun pressed harder into my skin and I imagined my brains fanned over the snow. The way it was coming down, I'd end up a vague, white mound; maybe I wouldn't be found till spring.

"Move it," she said, smacking the side of the gun against my cheek. "Time to join the party. You drive. I'm a little impaired. Wouldn't be responsible."

Bonnie slid into the back seat and motioned me behind the wheel. My vision slipped in and out of focus as I cranked the wheel around a hairpin. I searched for a spot to veer over a cliff, kill us both, but on either side of the narrow wash-board was a six-foot embankment with trees disappearing into the opaque sky.

"Where is this cash?" Bonnie asked.

"Safe house."

Our eyes met in the rear-view and she smiled, tossing her hair back. "I believe you are actually crazy enough to steal money from us."

Back in the clearing I saw one of the rapists, face down in the snow, a gory halo around his skull. I had a horrible sensation of the inevitability of fate. No matter which path you take, you always end up at the same place.

"Straight ahead," she said, pressing the gun to my skull. "There, by the stupid piece of shit."

Bonnie kept her distance behind me as we got out of the car.

"Walk back to the Carriage," she said.

I stared at the body. I felt sick and my knees buckled, but I staggered forward, nearly going down several times. From the corner of my eye, I could see Bonnie five feet behind, the gun trained on me. I wondered how many bullets she had left.

If I could catch her unaware, just for a second—

If I could move that fast—

If—

We were outside the Carriage, its open door creaking back and forth in the wind. A puddle of syrupy blood dripped over the door jamb. I turned. Two Bonnies wavered before me. Two guns. She was speaking, but it sounded like we were underwater. She jerked the pistol in an up-up motion. I pulled myself into the Carriage. First thing I saw was the other brother face up on the bed, shot twice in the head.

A thumping came from somewhere. I paused. Through the window I saw Bonnie lighting a cigarette. I eyed the gas containers. A quick splash out the door and—

Thump-thump-thump.

Coming from the tiny, enclosed toilet between a sink and the driver's area. I stepped over the corpse and opened the door.

The badly beaten body of a small man tumbled out, face covered in blood. Mouth taped, along with his hands and feet. He was barely conscious.

Frank.

I pulled the tape from his mouth. "I'm sorry, Sloane." Looking at the roomful of carnage, he croaked, "They got to me, got my phone."

"Oh, my God, Frank. We gotta get out—"

"You found your friend," Bonnie said behind me. "Monsieur Frank was very brave when the tire iron came out."

"You fucking bitch," I said, turning.

Bonnie stood in the doorway, gun trained on us, sadly shaking her head. "None of this was supposed to go this way, Sloaney. Please don't look at me like that. I am not strong like you. I lose my resolve."

I looked at Frank's bludgeoned knuckles, blood seeping through the skin. His head lolled forward.

My fault.

"My Chance used to give people three seconds, so I'm going to allow you the same. Kneel and turn around."

"The fifty thousand—"

"Sometimes it's not about the money," Bonnie said. "One..."

"Bonnie—"

She leapt forward and pistol-whipped me in the side of the head, knocking me down.

"I am sorry, Sloane," Bonnie said. "Un ... deux ... troi—"
Crack. Crack.
Thump.

CHAPTER 50

Saturday, December 14

I AWOKE SCREAMING AND THRASHING.
Someone held me down. "When you going to start listening
to me, Red?"

My vision cleared enough to make out Wayne's worried
face hovering above. A nurse elbowed him aside, checking
to make sure my IV hadn't slipped out.

"You're in Eagle Ridge Hospital, Sloane," the nurse said.

"Port Moody," Wayne added.

"Antivirals," I blurted. "They had HIV and Hep C."

"You told the ER doctor that when you arrived earlier
today," she said. "We've been super-dosing you since then. A
doctor will be in to examine you now that you're conscious."

"Frank—"

"I just spoke to Frank," Wayne said. "He's going to be
okay. Biggest wound is to his pride."

"Did you shoot her?" I asked.

He looked confused and shook his head. "No. An hour
ago, I got a text saying you were here. I came right away."

"How did I get here?"

"Anonymous drop off," the nurse said. "All you had on you was your phone. The police came earlier. They'll be back later to question you."

"My mother doesn't know?"

"You want me to call her?" Wayne asked.

I shook my head, then asked the nurse when I'd get my blood test results.

"In a few hours. The doctor will tell you more." She left and Wayne asked if I knew where I'd been taken.

"Logging road," I said. "Probably nearby in Anmore or Coquitlam. Wayne, Bolger was in the Carriage with a girl. I saw him just before they ran me down."

"He'd be a perfect blackmail candidate for their organization," he said. "A coroner with a taste for young girls. Wife and kids. Better believe he'd fast-track some autopsies to keep his name and perversions out of the paper."

"So, the cops come back and I say what? That I'm investigating Darci Harp for murdering her mother? As soon as I walk out these doors, they'll bust me for breach of the restraining order."

He nodded. "Without a witness, we've still got no hard evidence linking Darci to any crimes. It just looks like an angry and manipulative lovers' triangle: mother and daughter screwing the same guy. Cops wouldn't touch that stuff.

"And one more piece of shit news: shortly before he got nabbed, Frank had been watching New Ways, and apparently lawyers and accountants of Grady Harp had been going in and out of the place. I think they're out to wipe it clean, in case of a pending audit or investigation. At this stage, with Darci gone, the only way to get anything done would be through forensic accountants to look for money laundering and fraud. That *would* be a cop thing, but our say-so wouldn't exactly get them to jump on a warrant."

"So Grady's in on it?"

"My guess is he's just trying to protect his daughter, and his name." He pulled out his phone. "*Someone* texted me the name of this hospital." He held up his phone so I could see the screen. "Same someone also sent this:"

FELICITY BARNES
HOTEL SANTO TOMAS
SAN JOSE C.R.

"Kai," I said.

Shortly after Wayne left, a female doctor arrived with a rape kit. After the procedure, she also diagnosed me with a concussion and a badly sprained MCL. She asked if I needed anything for the pain. I shook my head. She told me the cops would be there in an hour.

I closed my eyes, preparing to play dumb. I would simply say I couldn't remember—something cops were accustomed to hearing.

A stocky female counsellor came to speak with me, but I said I was too tired and closed my eyes. "Of course," she said. When I opened my eyes, there was a card on the bedside tray.

I thought to split before the cops came, but that only meant they'd show up at my door later with the same questions. Almost on cue, the law strolled in: a man and a woman, middle-aged white guy and a Chinese woman with overly sympathetic eyes. They took my statement, such as it was, and I scribbled my name. "If your memory returns..." More cards on the tray.

Soon as they departed, I pulled out my IV. Lifting the sheets, I winced at the sight of my splinted and bandaged leg.

Hopping over and peeking around the curtain, I found my roommate to be an elderly woman with oxygen tubes up her nose. She blinked at me.

"Hi," I said, "I need to borrow some clothes. I'll pay you back."

The woman wearily pointed to a closet to the right. "Don't worry about it," she rasped. "I heard about your predicament. God bless you."

The cab dropped me back at my Jeep in East Van. On my way out of the hospital, I had kipped a pair of crutches and I used them to hobble over and retrieve the hidden key. I popped the trunk and got my money stash. As I paid the driver, he regarded my maple-leaf cardigan, floral-print sweatpants, and yellow Crocs with some amusement. The hospital bracelet was still on my wrist.

In the Jeep, I plugged in my nearly dead phone and and checked my messages. One was from Karin, checking in and rambling on about a hot date. My mother had left two messages to call her. It was 5:22 p.m. I called my mother back and told her I was doing great and had a job interview lined up that might involve some travel.

Then I called Wayne to ask how much remained of the fifty grand.

Sunday, December 15

Grady Harp exited the fogged-up glass door of Cucina Manila and drove off in his Escalade. I got out, crutched across the street, and entered the restaurant, which was warm and packed with people for Rosie Abacon's wake. A veritable shrine was erected near the kitchen, with a large, smiling photo of Rosie taken when she was a young woman, tanned and lovely on a beach in the Philippines.

The room was abuzz with Tagalog and the air was pungent with aromas as servers continuously brought out platters of Filipino dishes to the buffet table in the centre of the room.

I nearly didn't recognize Kai across the room, dressed in a black suit and nodding politely to a group of middle-aged Filipinas. When we made eye contact, Kai did not seem surprised to see me. He excused himself and came over.

"I'm sorry about your mother, Kai," I said.

"Those lies you told her the other night made her very happy," he said.

"She seemed like a beautiful soul," I said.

He nodded. "Why are you here?"

"To thank you for saving my life."

He blinked once but said nothing.

"Fair enough," I said. "What are your plans now?"

"My mother's gone. It doesn't matter now. Maybe I'll turn myself in."

"I think what you really need is a short vacation," I said. "To give you a fresh perspective."

CHAPTER 51

Tuesday, December 17

THE MALE FLIGHT ATTENDANT GUIDED WAYNE away from the lavatory. "This washroom is for business-class travellers only, sir. You can use the ones at the rear of the plane."

"There's a lineup," Wayne groused, scowling as he and I made brief eye contact. I raised my champagne flute, which only made him scowl more. No contact in airports or hotels, Wayne had decreed last night when we had separately booked our tickets to Costa Rica. Because of my leg, once I'd arrived at YVR, they'd upgraded me to business.

"I'm sorry, sir," the flight attendant said. He ushered Wayne out and pulled the curtains tight, restoring class order.

We arrived in San José at two a.m. I crutched through a sleepy customs lineup to be welcomed by a balmy breeze as I hopped in a cab outside the airport. Economy Class Wayne would be some minutes behind. A half-hour later, following a pit stop at an all-night grocery, I was dropped off at a ramshackle hotel in Barrio Amón, one where cash was king and IDs were not required.

The room had a single bed and a rickety desk and chair in the corner beneath a green-shuttered window. A bare light bulb hung from a wire in the centre of the ceiling, and a tiny fan shoved the humid air back and forth. The entire building smelled of mouldy socks.

I pulled out the bottle of Cacique I bought at the store. No glasses in the room meant I drank from the bottle. It went down like warm rocket fuel and did an efficient job at soothing my raw nerves. I opened the window shutters, letting in a waft of moist, dirty air. A dog barked, a bottle smashed, a man laughed drunkenly, and an orange moon hung low over the rooftops.

Sitting in the chair, I winced from the sutures in my ass. Before the flight, I'd called the hospital to get my blood results. Negative. Three more to go. I gazed out the window and took another slug.

Following a fitful two-hour sleep, I slipped on a white singlet, green camo shorts, and sandals. I added a brown wig, a blue Mariners ball cap, and went down to the lobby for a quick breakfast and coffee, before catching a cab to El Barba Azul, a morning drinker's bar on Castro Madiz.

Three Heineken-swilling Ticos occupied barstools and shouted at the fútball game on the tiny TV above the bar. They didn't look over as I crutched past. In the shadowy rear of the bar, Wayne sat drinking a can of beer and conversing with the skinny, shifty-eyed bartender. Wayne's beard was trimmed to a biker goatee and badass wraparound sunglasses were pushed up on his forehead. Wearing a sleeveless denim shirt, his thick right bicep sported a faded tattoo of a snake entwined around the body of an Asian woman in a bikini. Reminding myself to razz him later, I took a seat opposite him.

The bartender looked at me. I gestured to Wayne's Pilsen. "Cerveza, por favor."

The bartender left, and I asked Wayne if he'd brought enough money.

He placed a folded US hundred beneath his beer can. "According to the bartender," he said, "five grand should be plenty."

"Maybe we should wait till his plane arrives," I said. "This *is* his area of expertise."

Wayne sipped his beer. "Yeah, I'm not as trusting as you."

"Then I can back you."

He motioned to my crutches. "Those make you a liability. You've taken your licks. Get some sun."

My beer arrived, and the bartender scooped the hundred and replaced it with a slip of paper and walked away. I felt a twinge in my gut and took a small sip.

Wayne took out two Nokia cellphones and handed me one. "My number's on speed dial. After this is done, ditch the burner."

Then he finished his beer and stood. "If I'm not dead or in jail," he said, "I'll see you later."

Too antsy to sit idle, I hobbled the nearby streets of the nation's capital, a dozen times nearly getting creamed by trucks and errant scooters. Back at the hostel's tiny washroom, I showered under a tepid trickle. I re-bandaged my leg and went down the street to Poas Bar, where I ate a plate of casados by an open window. Up the block and across the street was a Spanish colonial-style mansion that had been refurbished into what is now the Hotel Santo Tomás.

Lunch over, I wandered over to a courtyard by the Teatro Nacional, where hawkers sold pirated DVDs and knockoff Fendi purses. A parade was in full swing on the next street. The place smelled of fried meat, sweat, and horseshit.

Thousands of people milled about, guys drinking cans of beer and grabbing the bubble butts of their pretty, raven-haired girlfriends. I bought a can of Pilsen and sat by a fountain. Halfway through the beer, I suddenly felt eviscerated.

The lack of sleep, the stress, the lies.

The killings.

The rape.

I finished the beer and looked up—

To see Geri Harp floating through the crowd toward me, wearing a floppy black-and-white sun hat. I stopped breathing. She smiled and waved, coming closer.

It wasn't until a man in a suit ran up from behind me and threw his arms around her that I realized the woman bore only a vague resemblance to Geri.

Geri was in the ground.

But Darci wasn't.

After incurring a mild sunburn, I headed back to the Poas Bar. An hour and two beers later, a taxi pulled up in front of Santo Tomás. Out climbed Dogger and Darci, he in a white linen suit and Panama hat, she in a cream skirt with a blue blouse and matching heels. The concierge assisted them with their many shopping bags.

8:03 p.m. I'd been crutch-pacing the tiny hostel room for over an hour when Wayne phoned. "Meet me," he said.

Fifteen minutes later, I sat down beside him on a bench in Parque Morazán, near the eerily green-lit Templo de la Música where a trio of violinists played "Blue Christmas." On benches and on the grass all around us, young Tico couples necked and drank beer. Every ten seconds firecrackers popped somewhere, and across the park, near the monument to Simón Bolívar, stood two stone-faced guards wielding machine guns.

Wayne's eyes were wild and he was ripe with the stink of stress-sweat. He set a red backpack in my lap. I unzipped the bag partway and saw the cellophane-wrapped, ivory-coloured brick. It smelled harsh and chemical. "How do you know it's real?" I asked.

"'Cause they demanded I sample some," he said. "They must'a thought I was a narc. I practically flew back here. Let's jet, in case those dudes over there have sniffer dogs."

We took a roundabout way back to the now-packed Poas Bar. "Back for more?" the waitress asked me. "You must like it here."

"So much for low-key," Wayne mumbled.

10:14 p.m. Dogger and Darci sailed out of the hotel, looking like two gringos heading out to rip it up at the local clubs. She wore a little white dress that showed off her tan and the pounds she'd shed. Dogger was decked out in a grey fedora, black tank top, and white skinny jeans.

"That pretty hijo de puta's ass is gonna get reamed in jail," Wayne said. "You okay with that, considering the dumb shit didn't actually have anything to do with Geri's murder?"

"Maybe not," I said, "but he's far from innocent."

I pulled out a baggie containing several pills and handed it to Wayne.

"What's this?"

"Roofies. I stole 'em from Dogger. Kinda ironic, huh?"

"I'll say. How'd you get them on the plane?"

"Being that I'm now travelling with what feels like my own personal pharmacy, sometimes random pills end up in the wrong bottles."

"I can see how that might happen."

"Don't mix it into a clear drink; it'll turn blue."

He shrugged and pocketed the pills. "What's one more felony charge?"

After watching Darci and Dogger depart in a taxi, we finished our drinks and did a casual neighbourhood reconnaissance. We avoided the entrance of Santo Tomás, which had a camera above the door. "There's a back service entrance," he said, "but it's got a camera, too. I'll have to go over the wall and past the courtyard. They're staying in room 23. Second floor.

"You're on lookout. Stay at Poas. Have a few drinks, but keep sharp. I'm not coming back after, but I'll call you when I'm done."

Before I could say anything, Wayne turned and cut into the crowd, backpack over his shoulder.

A sweaty, pulse-pounding hour crept by. The bar filled up. Handsome Ticos with cowboy hats and BO flirted with me, but I ignored them and they quickly lost interest.

At 11:18, my phone buzzed. "Hola?" I said.

"Delivered," he said. "It's in her open suitcase. I dosed the vino, too. Funny part is, they already had a pile of blow sitting on a coffee table, straws and all. So I just enhanced the set design a little. Listen, my cab just pulled up. Adiós."

I ordered a shot of Cacique and a Pilsen chaser, then took a seat with a better view of Santo Tomás. My hands shook so badly that on the first sip, I spilled booze on my chest. The Ticos laughed and bought me another round.

3:32 a.m. Darci and Dogger staggered from a cab. He had lost his shirt, and she wore his fedora. Barely able to stand, they nevertheless attempted a drunken tango on the sidewalk, ending with a passionate kiss. Onlookers clapped. So did I.

They went inside, and I phoned the policía. After being on hold for an eternity, I used a clear and slow voice to tell him that there was a major drug score to be made in room 23 of the Hotel Santo Tomás, and that it belonged to a woman going by the name Felicity Barnes, whose real name was Darci Harp. I finished with the words jefe del crimen organizado. Organized crime boss.

I suddenly felt sick, and chewed the inside of my cheek for five minutes before picking up the phone again. After waffling several times, I punched in a number from memory and sent a text:

get out NOW cops are coming.

Several minutes later, Dogger emerged, shirtless and confused. He looked this way and that, before jumping in a taxi. The cab pulled away just as the policía screeched up in front of the hotel. Three cars. Six khaki-clad cops with mustaches and guns, two with assault rifles. Everyone in Poas crowded onto the patio and street.

Five minutes later, the cops exited, dragging a semiconscious and handcuffed Darci Harp down the stairs, a hotel robe draped over her. The cop taking up the rear held the brick of coke.

A few Ticos whistled as the cops pushed her into the back of the first car. As it drove past the bar, I saluted her with my drink. She squinted, struggling for recognition. There was a blip of clarity in her glazed eyes, of raw terror for what was coming.

CHAPTER 52

Wednesday, December 18

IT COST ME $300 USD TO TALK TO A PRISONER in a Costa Rican jail.

They'd given Darci her own cell, a dank, tiny room behind a rusted, yellow, steel door. A bored-looking guard opened a sliding panel in the door that was about face height.

"Cinqo minutos," the guard said. Five minutes.

Darci's voice, loud and scared: "I need to make a phone call. I'm Canadian. I know how a shakedown works. How much money do you want? Cuánto dinero?"

I crutched up to the slot, wearing sunglasses and a black ball cap over a blonde wig. "Sometimes it's not about the dinero," I said.

Darci stood on the other side of the door. I removed my sunglasses and we looked at each other.

Her eyes hardened. "You shouldn't have done that, Sloane," she said quietly.

"You shouldn't have killed your mother, Darce, but here we are."

"And this is your scheme to punish me? Plant drugs and call the cops?"

"There's more than one type of justice in the world. Bonnie and Garza are dead, but you're not getting off that easily."

"My father will get me out in a fucking *day*. When we're through, you're going to end up in a straightjacket being wheeled to electroshock therapy."

I smiled. "You work on that one. Meanwhile, I've got enough evidence back home linking you to murder, prostitution, and money laundering, all centred around New Ways. See, I don't think your dad knows the full extent of what you've done, only that you cooked the books. How far will he pull for you when he knows that you killed his wife?"

Her lips trembled. "You don't—"

"Your own *mother*, Darci," I said. "She suspected something was going on at the shelter and called you out on it. To really push her over the deep end, you also made sure she saw that text from you to Dogger. Then you spiked her water bottle with fentanyl, probably expecting her to drive off the road."

The fire in her eyes replaced the fear. "She undermined me every step of the way, vetoed every decision I made. Nothing I did was ever good enough. I sacrificed my entire teenage life down there, in the kitchen, teaching the girls to read, to fucking brush their teeth. The whole reason I took an interest in accounting at all was because she was so shitty at it. Did I ever get any credit? Any thanks for stepping up, for working long hours, helping her troll the streets for missing junkies she loved more than her own daughter?"

I held up my right hand and rubbed my thumb and index finger together. "World's smallest violin," I said. "You know, not long ago I thought of you as a friend, and you were one of the reasons I pursued this. I thought that by finding the truth, I could ease your pain."

"Bullshit. The only person you did this for is *you*. You did all this because you're a whack job. You think because you got the video from the club and read her letter it's somehow proof she was murdered?"

"A few hours before she died, her final email was to her dentist to confirm an appointment the following week. I don't care *who* you are, you don't do that if you're planning on checking out. That thing with the wine and the pills and the letter was just a cry for help. She wasn't going to kill herself; she expected Dogger to come and save her. Except he didn't show, and because of you, she died in the club junkyard, scared and alone."

She stepped closer to the slot so she could see more than just my face, maybe to see if I held any recording devices.

"It wasn't *really* that she could derail your business, was it?" I said. "I mean, you could set up your Carriage formula elsewhere. And it had nothing to do with Dogger. You *killed her* because you couldn't stand the look of shame on her face the day she found out who you truly are."

I turned to leave.

"You *really* think it's going to go down like this, Sloane?" she asked. "There are cameras outside this jail. My father will have a legal team here in a heartbeat."

"Compared to their neighbours, Costa Rica is a little more progressive in its approach to *narcos,* meaning they don't like 'em much. Possession of a trafficable amount of cocaine in this country is worth eight to ten years. Nowhere near the time you'll do if you face the music for your crimes back home."

"If you think this is some ploy to get me to confess—"

"Here's how this is going to go down. You're going to plead guilty and do your time here. I'm satisfied with that. If you let daddy pull strings and I hear that you arrive back on Canadian soil in anything less than three years, I'll see that you go down for your mother's murder. New Ways will be exposed as a sham and shut down. Hundreds of women will be on the street and your mother's legacy will go up in flames. I don't want that to happen."

"Sloane Donovan and her grandiose delusions," she said. "Spout this nonsense to the cops back home and they'll lock you up for violating your restraining order."

Darci's mouth suddenly went slack. She was no longer looking at me, but at Kai, who had stepped out of the shadows and now stood to my right. It was the first time I had seen her stunned, looking as though a trap door had just opened below her feet and the fall was infinite.

"How come you don't look happy to see me, D?" he said.

"I'll give you two a minute," I said.

CHAPTER 53

Friday, December 20

BACK IN YVR AIRPORT, AN ATTENDANT PUSHED me in a wheelchair, fast-tracking me toward the Canadian customs gate. My phone buzzed in my pocket and I took it out and checked the display. "Hi, Mom," I answered.

"Sloane, where in God's name have you been?"

"I'm fine. I just needed to get away for a few days to clear my head."

"I thought you left because of a job."

"Kind of a business and pleasure thing."

"Sounds vague," she said. "You're still coming for Christmas?"

"As promised." Something to my left distracted me. "Mom, I'm about to go through customs. Call you later."

Four lines over, Andy "Dogger" Peretti was getting hassled by a customs agent. We'd been on the same flight, but I'd been in business, while he'd been holed up in economy.

After clearing customs, I called Frank, asking him to make a lawyerly phone call to Mr. Andrew Peretti, to arrange a meeting for the following day.

Once outside and settled in a taxi, I told the driver to wait. It was mid-afternoon, and a layer of snow had crusted over the city, blinding under a brilliant blue sky.

Twenty-five minutes later, out of the international arrivals doors came Dogger and Naz, kissing as they walked toward the red Miata parked in a handicap stall. Naz crumpled the parking ticket and tossed it to the ground. They hopped in and drove off.

I told the driver he could go. As he pulled out, a black Mustang veered from the short-term parking, Cyrus Ghorbani at the wheel, wearing a leather jacket and black skullcap. He looked less like a cop and more like a hitter for the Persian mafia.

Checking out the taxi operator's registration, I said, "Hamid, this is going to sound cliché, but I need you to follow those cars up ahead: the Miata and the Mustang."

"What if they split?"

"Stick with the Miata."

It was an easy tail. They went straight to Dogger's, pulling into the underground parking. Ghorbani parked on Lonsdale. Since the safe house was paid up until the end of the month, I instructed the driver to take me there.

Home sweet home. Inside, it was freezing. I threw on an extra jacket and cranked the thermostat.

Ignoring a bottle of Jameson that beckoned from a shelf, I reached for the camera. In Dogger's place, Naz was topless and trying on a colourful green-and-red Costa Rican dress. I had seen the same one in a shop display at the San José airport.

Dogger popped the cork on a bottle of champagne and drank from it. Then he grabbed Naz, whirled her in the air, and carried her to the bedroom.

Sadly, Ghorbani wouldn't get this view. If he weren't such a dick, maybe I would've invited him up for the big show.

Hmmmmmm.

Fishing through my handbag, I found his card.

Hobbling back outside, I crutched two blocks south to the nearest payphone, which was outside the entrance of Lonsdale Quay. A Salvation Army Santa jingled and ho-ho-hoed nearby. I plunked in a quarter and punched in a number.

"Ghorbani," he answered.

"The will is a fake," I said. "They only *think* they're getting the money."

"Who the hell is this?"

"Listen, tomorrow morning they're going to leave his place to see a bogus lawyer. Your girl thinks she's in it for half, so I'm assuming she'll want to tag along."

"What the fuck—"

I hung up. For the first time in a long time, I felt hungry. I crutched up the street and around the corner to Burgoo, where the hostess seated me by the fireplace. I ordered beef bourguignon and treated myself to a nice bottle of pinot noir. I sat back and sipped the wine. It was very good. Day had turned to night. I stared out the window, hypnotized by the falling snow that just kept coming and coming.

Saturday, December 21

My eyes snapped open, and for a moment I forgot I was in the safe house. The clock said 9:15. "Shit." I yanked on my shoes. Through the telephoto I saw Dogger and Naz leave his condo. Grabbing the Enforcer from the table, I crutched out to my Jeep. I gunned it up Lonsdale, turned left on 3rd, then hung a right into the alley that ran behind Dogger's building. Fifty feet in, a black Mustang blocked the alley. A shouting brouhaha raged on the other side of the vehicle.

I parked and got out. Leaving the crutch behind, I hopped toward the chaos, Enforcer in my right hand and iPhone in my left. Dogger's Porsche was on the other side of the Mustang, both doors open. Naz jumped up and down between the cars, crying and holding her head. When she found me standing beside her, she stopped and did a shocked double take.

Holding up my phone to film the show, I said, "Almost time for another haircut."

Cyrus had pinned Dogger to the slushy street and was methodically jackhammering his fists into his face. Right, left, right, left, right, left. The snow was splattered with blood. A sparkling white tooth landed in the mud puddle near my foot. I plucked it up, wiped it off, and handed it to Naz, who looked ill.

"How did you guys meet, by the way?" I asked. "You and Dogger?"

Naz sobbed through her words. "He came in for a haircut one day. When he found out I was engaged, he asked me out. I should've turned him down, but he wanted me so bad and he was so hot."

"Not so much anymore," I said.

Naz tentatively moved closer. Ghorbani turned and spat on her red Manolo boots. "You money-grubbing slut, do you know how much I loved you?"

"You're going to kill him!"

Ghorbani clouted Dogger's right ear, splitting it open. "I gave you fucking everything, Naz. I don't care what happens now."

She stepped forward, touching her fiancé's bear-like back. *"Please, stop, baby."* A violent, reflexive fling of his arm sent her sprawling on a nearby snowbank. He rose off Dogger, who managed to roll over and climb to his hands and knees.

Ghorbani kicked him back down. "Going to see some lawyer today, huh? You fucktards *know* there's no money, right? It's all a scam." He finally saw me filming, and in that moment put two and two together. *"You!* Gimme that!"

He lunged for my phone. I deked left and zapped his wrist with two million volts. The force spun him around and onto his knees. He reached under his jacket for his gun. I swung the Enforcer, whacking the back of his head. He dropped the gun and I kicked it away.

Ghorbani rose to his feet, looking completely beaten. I went back to filming. Nodding toward Dogger, who was crawling away down the alley, I said, "Okay, Cyrus, one more shot. You earned it."

"Put your phone away."

I did.

With a running start, the big cop delivered a field-goal-worthy kick between Dogger's legs.

I winced. "Ouch."

He climbed back in his Mustang. I picked up his gun. "If you're nice," I said, "when I come visit you in the station in a few hours, *if* you listen to a story I have to tell, and promise to launch a prelim investigation, I'll return your gun. If not, no gat, *and* that beating will go viral. Bye-bye career, but they're always in need of good security guards at the local mall."

He looked mad enough to punch a hole in the earth's crust, only his hands weren't functional enough to start the ignition, and he dropped his keys.

"You better help your fiancé, Naz," I said.

Ghorbani glared at her. "You coming with *me*, or the eunuch over there?"

Naz sniffled and looked ruefully toward Dogger, who lay in the fetal position, moaning and clutching at his bruised nuts. Her face flashed with anger at the thought of losing all the money that never was. She walked to the car, and Ghorbani slid awkwardly into the passenger seat. I stepped back as the Mustang sprayed slush. The muscle car did a doughnut, digging deep furrows in a neighbour's lawn, before fishtailing out of the alley.

I hopped over to Dogger. "Hurts, I'll bet."

He looked up at me in confused, broken-toothed, ripped-ear agony.

"That makes *twice* I've saved your ass these past few days," I said.

"I didn't deserve any of this," he moaned.

"Doubtful," I said.

CHAPTER 54

Sunday, December 27

"EIGHT YEARS, DOWN TO FOUR ON A GUILTY plea," Wayne said. From a corner booth in Funky's, we raised our pints. "Best daddy's money could buy. But even with bribes, it's hard time in a Third World women's prison."

"What about the others?" I asked. "Bonnie said there were four Carriages."

"She may have been lying. I cross-referenced the rest of the associates on both Pope's and Garza's sheets, and they're all either dead or in prison back east. But who cares? All the known suspects are where they need to be, and we even got paid, though we can't exactly claim it come tax time."

"Didn't quite get you the press you wanted."

He shrugged. "Whatever. It's over."

Our attention was diverted as two teenage girls wobbled into the bar. One wore a black halter top, tight red pleather pants and red heels. The other wore a neon pink fishnet body stocking over a pink bra and underwear. The two teens began making friends with some of the solo male drinkers.

Fishnet propositioned a sixtysomething man with a yellow walrus mustache and an overcoat. They spoke for several moments and he stood. They walked past. Even with makeup, the girl looked no older than fifteen. Behind us, the bar door opened as they departed into the stark afternoon light. The door swung shut, once again leaving us in the shadows of the bar. The city was changing along with the rest of the world, but some sad facts of existence were too ancient to ever disappear.

"It's not quite over," I said.

"Nice chunk of real estate for a coroner," Wayne commented from the driver's seat. We were parked on Morven Drive in West Vancouver, near Collingwood Private School. Half a block away, two police cars and a white tech-crime van blocked the driveway of a dark-wood-panelled rancher half-hidden behind stately, snow-covered hedges. Wayne added, "Wonder if Bolger was getting a taste of the Carriage profits?"

"I think his wife comes from money," I said.

"Wonder if she's gonna stand by her pederast?" he said.

"The shit he already had on his computer," said Kai from the back seat, "was way sicker than anything I was going to plant. He had photos of kids, like *little* kids, taken at parks and pools. Plus recordings of him with some of the girls. Made me want to puke."

"This from a guy who until recently made his living off the avails of prostituting those same girls," Wayne said.

"Hey, ignoramus," Kai said, "I never personally made a nickel off that. Plus, I was ready to do my bid until you talked me out of it. Probably because if they dug deeper, *you'd* be sitting in a cell beside me for helping yourself to the ill-gotten money."

"He makes a solid point," Frank said. He sat beside Kai in the back, his arm in a sling. The bruising on his face was faint, but still visible.

"I suppose I *could've* donated it back to New Ways," Wayne said. "But, nah, Grady's dumped so much of his money into legitimizing the place that the ladies there are likely staying in posher digs than mine."

"There's talk of an annex with with two hundred new beds and a full medical clinic," I said. "Lot of women off the street."

"Papers said he pumped in eight *million*," Wayne said. "Round-the-clock counsellors and nurses, part-time teaching staff. Smart move. If he'd just shut the place down, the books would have been examined, revealing discrepancies. Now, not only does this make him look like a grieving hero, out to do right by his late wife, but it's enough dough to drown any financial fudgery."

A CTV News van cruised past and parked across the street from the rancher. The circus had begun. "Right on time," I said.

"Donovan," Wayne said, "remind me to never get on your bad side."

A Global News van arrived and parked near their competition.

We watched as the reporters and news crews hopped out and began setting up cameras near the police cars. A few middle-aged neighbours stepped onto the street to see what the commotion was about.

Ten minutes later, the front door of the house opened and out walked two officers. Cyrus Ghorbani followed, looking like a barrel-chested vanquisher as he escorted a handcuffed and flummoxed Steve Bolger, whose normally florid complexion now matched his white dress shirt, which hung untucked over his jeans. Bolger's downcast eyes blinked dumbly at the reporters and cameramen already in attack mode. I got a flash of him grunting and pumping Zoey in the Carriage.

Bolger ignored the reporters' questions but didn't turn away from the cameras. I couldn't tell if he saw his neighbours standing down the street, but they certainly saw him being guided into the back seat of the cruiser. His face was set in the grim resignation of a man who knows that while his life may not technically be over, things are going to get a whole lot worse before they ever got better. *If* they ever got any better.

Big *if.*

As the police car drove past, I made eye contact with Ghorbani, who arched an eyebrow in acknowledgment. I only wished Bolger had seen me.

Wayne clapped his hands. "Time to celebrate?"

CHAPTER 55

Tuesday, December 31

I DIDN'T DO CEMETERIES.

But I was going to start with this one.

That's what I told myself as I drove into Forest Lawn. I parked in the far corner of the lot and took a few deep breaths in an attempt to quell the panic inside.

I picked up the bouquet of white lilies from the passenger seat, along with Geri's note and a Bic lighter. Ashes to ashes. I sat for a moment, deliberating, imagining my friend sitting beside me. Would she have approved of what I'd done, the justice I thought I'd accomplished in Costa Rica? The more I considered Geri, the more I realized she was of different stock than people like Darci and me. She was emotionally—and financially—giving on a large scale, while at the same time inwardly needy. Like a jilted schoolgirl whose feelings had been crushed.

Her form of payback was an attempt to instill guilt in her daughter and her lover, distribute some of her pain to them.

It backfired in both cases, and in the end she paid the ultimate price.

Maybe it had to do with me sitting in the cemetery parking lot, but for a moment I pictured Geri gazing down on this tragic aftermath. Having witnessed the kindness in her eyes many times over, I believe she was one of those who could eventually forgive her own daughter for murdering her. For all I knew, my friend may well be up there, watching, hating me for my part in the whole thing.

Right or wrong, Geri, I did what I had to do.

Least that's what I told myself.

I climbed out of the car and limped down the path between the headstones. Stepping over the crest, I thought back to the woodland runs with Darci. The laughter. The easy camaraderie. The sharing of secrets and the telling of lies. Something I couldn't shake was that only a short time ago, I'd been convinced of a friendship that was in some strange and ineffable way, a continuation of what her mother and I had.

I stopped.

Standing twenty feet away, by Geri's headstone, was Grady Harp. He looked thinner than I remembered, cheeks hollow and face lined. I turned to go, then looked at the letter in my hand.

It occurred to me that I hardly knew him at all, this austere figure standing on the sidelines. I wondered how culpable he felt in all this. He had always seemed cold, but I couldn't believe he was stupid or naïve enough not to have noticed any of his wife's indiscretions. His icy veneer might have been a shield erected over the years to combat the pain of being a cuckold.

I ended up standing by Grady's side.

We both stared silently down at the headstone. He had set down a large bouquet.

Love Lies Here
Geraldine Annette Harp
June 7/1965

———

October 10/2019

He didn't look at me. "One phone call and you're arrested."

I handed him Geri's letter. "Lot of that going around."

He looked down at it for a long time, then opened it and read it. Finally, he exhaled through his nose, his tiny nod of confirmation nearly imperceptible. His eyes remained unchanged. He'd known.

"I'm very sorry." I set the lilies down and walked away.

I hired movers to take all the furnishings from the safe house back to the Sally Ann. I dropped the keys to the landlord and returned the camera equipment to the store. It was dark when I got home. Sounds of revelry came from other condos. Tinkling glasses and laughter. It had taken all the willpower I had not to stop for a bottle.

Blocking all thoughts, I went inside, slapped on a knee brace and wrapped a tensor bandage over my thigh. I geared up: knit cap, headlamp, gloves, trail shoes.

A feeble jog led me up Roche Point Drive and across the Parkway. Even though my lungs wanted to push, my leg demanded I go easy. Fog rose through the trees of the Old Buck. My phone buzzed.

I slowed to a walk and checked it. Wayne.

"Hey," I said, more winded than I ought to have been.

"Where you at, Donovan?"

"Out getting some fresh air."

"How'd the test results go?"

"So far so good. More to come."

"You're gonna be okay," he said. "Listen, I've been getting some calls lately, for cases. I'm thinking with the leftover money, I'd get some office space, and—"

"That's a good idea, Wayne."

"I was also thinking that if you might make a good front man, er … front woman—you know what I'm talking about. You do your training under me and get your licence."

"Who says I want the job?"

He laughed. "Way you keep losing jobs, you can't afford not to. Even if you can't take orders for shit, this stuff's in your blood and you know it. Just promise you'll think about it."

"I will."

"Now don't run too far, 'cause tonight I'm going to be too drunk to come save you."

No danger of that. My leg had reached its limit. Tottering back down the trail, my thoughts were of a hot bath and bed. Karin had invited me out, but I was beyond beat.

I stripped and ran the water in the tub and looked at my skinny body in the mirror. As I opened up the medicine cabinet, I was about to take out the bottle of lithium when I remembered the pills were fake.

Scratch-scratch—scratch—scratch

At first I thought it was the Japanese maple outside. Then it happened again, and it sounded like someone trying to pick the lock on the sliding glass door.

I threw on my robe and grabbed the Enforcer off the kitchen counter. I flicked off the lights and peered around the corner.

Scratch-scratch—

I nearly fainted when I saw, on the other side of the glass, the silhouette of Eclipse, pawing to be let in. Rushing over, I opened the door and scooped him up in my arms. He was soaked, all matted fur and bones, half his normal weight. A chunk was missing from his left ear.

Eclipse meowed in confusion as I held him close and kissed the top of his head. "I thought you were dead, buddy," I said. "What happened to you?"

With an indignant meow, he broke away, leapt down, and shook out his coat before sauntering toward his food bowl like it was just another day.

ACKNOWLEDGEMENTS

MOST FIRST NOVELS ARE A LONG TIME IN THE making, and this one is no exception. Over the years, the manuscript endured title changes and innumerable drafts, and during that time, it was foisted upon many friends. To those kind souls, you know who you are, and I offer you my thanks—and my apologies. Sloane Donovan may have arrived more or less fully formed, but the book (and its author) had a long way to go.

Somewhere amid those early drafts, I was fortunate to attend a crime writing class taught by the legendary William Deverell. Bill told me my work had potential, but also advised me to go back to the beginning, draw up an outline, and essentially start over. Not exactly what I wanted to hear, but had I not followed his advice, I wouldn't be writing this to thank him now.

At a Crime Writers of Canada event, I met R.M. Greenaway, author of the BC Blues series, who encouraged me to submit the manuscript for the prestigious Arthur Ellis Awards. I did, it was nominated, and when I flew to Toronto for the ceremony, I met Judy Toews (of Stella Mosconi fame), who was up for the same award. Neither of us won, but it felt great to be establishing friendships within the Canadian crime writing community. Everyone I met was so incredibly warm and welcoming that it was difficult to imagine that we were all creators of murder and mayhem. Rachel and Judy have both offered guidance and bolstered my confidence at a time when I was getting pounded by seemingly ceaseless waves of rejection.

Vancouver's Noir at the Bar is a great way to hobnob with crime authors and hear them read their latest works. It was during those events that I was able to meet and collect advice and inspiration from local greats such as Sam Wiebe, Dietrich Kalteis, and Robin Spano. Not only do they write first-rate crime fiction, they're also cool people to hang out with.

Now, finally seeing this novel in print brings with it an immense sense of gratitude. I have to give an especially loud and exuberant shout out to my amigo and fellow crime-writing badass, A.J. Devlin, who energetically championed this book, and who opened the door to the fine folks at NeWest Press. That phone call from Matt Bowes, General Manager, in May of 2020, was truly the high point in a very challenging year. Matt has been phenomenal to work with at every stage of the editing process and has provided invaluable insight into strengthening the manuscript in subtle yet significant ways that simply eluded this writer. Big thanks also to Claire Kelly, Marketing and Production Coordinator, for her guidance and skill in delivering a fine-looking book into the world. And thanks to Michel Vrana for the killer cover and overall design.

I'd be remiss if I didn't mention my good friend, Sylvia Leong, avant-garde fantasy author, who was kind and patient enough to slog through numerous drafts, offering feedback and never hesitating to tell me what she *really* thought. Thanks also to Liezle Moreland, for her artistic skill in sketching the yonic tattoo design worn by Pope and Eva. Thanks to Tamea Burd for the wonderful author photos. I also offer gratitude to Jen Wickson, Anjulie Latta, Tony Leong, Nicole Rigler, Daniela Sosa, and Craig Watson.

This book would not be what it is without the sharp eyes and honest tongue of the beautiful Wendy Laverty, who also happens to be the love of my life. She accompanies me on research trips to the kinds to places that fall somewhat short of romantic. ("So honey, *that's* what a maximum-security prison looks like. What kind of guns do you think the guards have up in those towers?") Her unflagging enthusiasm, sense of adventure, and expertise in all things related to grammar and punctuation are this writer's dream.

J.T. SIEMENS grew up in Vernon, BC, and moved to Vancouver to pursue a career as a personal trainer. A long-standing love of books and movies led him to study screenwriting and creative writing, and he has been published in *Mystery Weekly*, *Down in the Dirt*, *CC&D*, and *Vancouver Magazine*.